I, Hogarth

I, Hogarth

Michael Dean

Overlook Duckworth
New York • London

This edition first published in paperback in
the United States and the United Kingdom in 2014 by
Overlook Duckworth, Peter Mayer Publishers, Inc.

NEW YORK
141 Wooster Street
New York, NY 10012
www.overlookpress.com
For bulk and special sales, please contact sales@overlookny.com,
or write to the above address.

LONDON
30 Calvin Street
London E1 6NW
info@duckworth-publishers.co.uk
www.ducknet.co.uk

Cataloging-in-Publication Data is available
from the Library of Congress
A catalogue record for this book is available
from the British Library

ISBN 978-1-4683-0822-8 (US)
ISBN 978-0-7156-4751-6 (UK)
Typeset by Ray Davies
Manufactured in the United States of America

1 3 5 7 9 10 8 6 4 2

Contents

For my late parents, Anne and Joe Dean

Cast of Characters

Listed here under the part in which they first appear

PART I

William Hogarth – *painter and engraver*
Richard Hogarth – *William's father*
Anne Hogarth (née Gibbons) – *William's mother*
Anne and Mary Hogarth – *William's sisters*

John Dalton – *painter*

Lavinia Fenton – *actress, later Duchess of Bolton*
Edmund Curll – *bookseller-publisher*

John Huggins – *prison-keeper (governor) of the Fleet Prison*
Anthony (Moses) da Costa – *banker and financier*
Kate – *a bawd at da Costa's house*

PART II

Ellis Gamble – *silver engraver*

Felix Pellett (Frenchy) – *apprentice to Ellis Gamble*
Stephen Fowler (Birdcatcher) – *apprentice to Ellis Gamble*

Sir James Thornhill – *Hogarth's patron, later his father-in-law*
John Thornhill – *friend of Hogarth, Sir James's son*
Jane Thornhill – *Hogarth's wife, Sir James's daughter*
Lady Judith Thornhill – *Sir James Thornhill's wife*
Fanny – *Jane Thornhill's maid*
Sarah Young – *assistant to Hogarth's sisters, later the Hogarths' housemaid*

Mother Douglas – *keeper of a bawdy house*

Francis Hayman – *painter, later Old Slaughter group*

PART III

Trump – *a pug dog*

Theosophus Taylor – *apothecary*

George Lambert – *painter, Old Slaughter group*
Jack Laguerre – *painter, Old Slaughter group*
Thomas Hudson – *painter, Old Slaughter group*
Hubert Gravelot – *engraver, Old Slaughter group*
Louis-François Roubiliac – *sculptor, Old Slaughter group*

Henry Tompion – *butler at the Hogarths' Leicester Fields house*
George Wells – *footman at the Hogarths' Leicester Fields house*
Charles Mahon – *second footman at the Hogarths' Leicester Fields house*
Mrs Parsons – *cook at the Hogarths' Leicester Fields house*

William Huggins – *lawyer, son of John Huggins*

Sir Archibald Grant – *parliamentarian*
James Edward Oglethorpe – *parliamentarian*

Thomas Coram – *sea captain and trader, started the Foundling Hospital*
Jonathan Tyers – *developer of Vauxhall Gardens*
Henry Fielding – *novelist*
Daniel Graham – *apothecary*
Daniel Lock – *governor of the Foundling Hospital,
founder of the Lock Hospital*
John Wilkes – *governor of the Foundling Hospital,
later editor of* The North Briton

PART IV

Sir Richard Grosvenor – *wealthy aristocrat*
Sir Joshua Reynolds – *painter*
Charles Churchill – *poet, later deputy editor of* The North Briton

Si vis me flere, dolendum est primum ipsi tibi
Horace, *Ars Poetica*

If you want to move me to tears, you must
first feel grief yourself

Part I

The Finger of God
1697–1714

1

I WAS BORN beside a printer's owned by a certain Mr Downinge of Bartholomew Close, East Spitalfields. As I was born, the stink of ink filled my nostrils. The clank of prints as they were made assailed my ears the very instant I barged my way out of my mother.

My fate was sealed, then, even as the midwife grasped me by the ankle with a cry of 'Gotcha! You slippery boy!' I was born to make images, prints and paintings. William Hogarth, Serjeant Painter at the court of George II, phiz-monger to the high and mighty. At your service, out I came.

I was born, then, but I was not yet finished, not yet complete. What my father called 'The Finger of God' had not yet been laid upon my head. That happened some seven years later.

It was November. I am sure of that because my two sisters were born in that month: Anne was born on the same day of the month as me, and then came Mary. So our rooms were November-dark by the time of our meal at three o'clock.

Two bars at the window made the sign of the cross over us Hogarths as we ate. That cross of bars was the first image I trained my memory to keep. It was soon to form the backdrop to my father's prison cell. Many years later I even placed it in a gleam of light on a globe of the world in my portrait of my friend Thomas Coram: the portrait that was to be my masterpiece.

After gnawing my shank of Essex mutton clean of meat, placing the bone carefully on the trencher, I took my leave: 'Excuse me, pater. Thank you for the meal, mama.' And away I sped.

Bartholomew Close was the shape of a bulging bib on a baby, with narrow alleys north and south for drawstrings. I ran out of the Close through a paved alley to the south, my little shoes slapping on the loose cobbles of Duck Lane. Even as I turned from there into the first waving curve of Little Britain, past the first dingy clutch of printers and bookshops, the smog was descending, swirling under the eaves which leaned towards each other above me, nearly touching overhead. The air smelled acrid with burning coal.

I was heading for St Botolph Churchyard, to play tip-cat with my friends over the remains of my grandfather – my mother's father, John Gibbons. As I ran, a wind blew up. At first I took no notice. Wind and rain were nothing new that year; we had experienced little else for nearly two weeks.

But the wind grew fiercer, now thick with black dust. It carried the lowing and bleating of the Smithfield Market cattle and sheep. I imagined them protesting as the soot flecks hit them, black on white and black on brown.

I feared for my calamanco shirt, so skilfully stitched by mama from a piece of her oldest nightgown. My second shirt was still drying. I would be confined to our rooms if anything happened to this one. Mama was slow to anger, but when it came it was terrible. It was she, and never father, who slapped my sisters and me when there was cause.

I placed my arm across my chest as I ran to ward off the dust; not a sensible act, really, because the wind was coming from behind me. The gale, for a gale it now was, was growing fiercer.

Little Britain was a wide street with two bold curves in an 'S' shape. I was walking along the second of the curves, opposite one of the fine houses which mixed in with more humble homes and shops.

The raging wind was frightening me. As I hesitated, a roaring gust lifted me half off my feet, then tumbled me along at a forward-leaning trot. I saved myself from falling only by clutching at the grand railings of the house I was passing. Surely my friends would never keep to our planned meeting at St Botolph through this?

I turned to face the storm. Cruel little pricks of stone scattered into my face, making me cry aloud. Suddenly my face was wet, then my hair, then my chest, my poor shirt soaked tight to me; within seconds my breeches drenched through to my drawers. I threw myself forwards, battling the gale; our room, shortly before so gladly abandoned, was now a vividly pictured sanctuary.

I saw the crowd in Little Britain not, as I would normally have done, as subjects of great fascination, but as buffers against the wind and rain, which may with luck save me. Now all those in the crowd were moving fast with jerking limbs for fear of being lifted and tossed through the air.

There was a woman, a hawker of apples I believe, just about to abandon her produce as wind and rain whipped her mantua around her, showing her comely, firm curves. Her eyes widened at me, for a second seeking help, then, as she registered my tender years, unmistakeably offering help herself, with a waving arm which was itself lifted by the wind.

Chapter 1

It was a gesture of goodness I have never forgotten, and far from being the last I have received from women. But she was facing me and in a blinking she was driven past at a run. I heard her scream, but I have no idea where she finished when the wind and rain had had its way with her.

Varlets were running in the street, grasping at anything, including each other, which might slow their hurtling along. Many were screaming and shouting, a cacophony of terror.

'It is the end of the world,' bellowed one fellow known to me by sight, a baker.

'God's wrath! God's wrath is come upon us,' moaned another, a chimney-sweep, his black clothes stained with blood down one sleeve.

An old fellow lay himself down, clutching at the cobbles with his hands, to let the storm pass over him. Others made their way backwards or sideways like crabs, the better to progress.

'We have sinned! We have sinned!'

London was Sodom under good Queen Anne; overweening, overmighty, bloated with riches. We had forgotten God and this was His retribution. It was borne on the wind, lashed into us all by the rain.

Half a tree blew past me, lifted in the air by the wind so it seemed to run like a man. The lowing of cattle from the market grew louder, as if they, too, were trumpeting the end of the world. The street was becoming slippery with mud.

As I battled my way back into the curve of Little Britain and had the straight in sight, I gave a growl of triumph through clenched teeth, pushing into the wind with my left shoulder as prow, right hand on my privy parts, thanking the Lord for my small stature and chunky physique.

My bleary gaze perceived a sedan chair just going over, tilting milord onto the muddy street way, Mechlin-laced cuffs and all, with his periwig in the grub with the piss and the dead dogs, while the no-doubt thankful chairmen, front and back, dropped the gilded poles and legged it as best they could into the storm.

Some sheep running loose overtook me.

To the right, I saw a dead cow belly-up outside a chandler's shop, which had its iron bar up across its front. The poor beast may well have met its end before these gusts from hell blew up, for all I knew, but I had no recollection of it from the walk the other way.

Lamps from the grander houses were crashing to the ground, so a novel hazard was broken glass, piling up with the tile shards and rubbish from the roofs of houses. Some tiles stuck upright in the mud like miniature gravestones.

The crowd around me appealed for mercy with their eyes, as far as they could open them. Some opened their mouths, but we were mute to each other in the howl of the wind. Still, I knew, as they knew, that it was the crowd which was saving its constituent members, by breaking the gale.

I had battled my way back to Duck Lane. I let loose a growl of triumph. Here, there was a glut of small businesses from pawnbrokers to barbers to printers and back again, with their street signs swinging wildly, bashing into each other and one and then another coming smashing down into the narrow street.

Between here and the warren of foetid alleys, the dingy courts and the lanes too narrow for two men to walk abreast which surrounded Bartholomew Close were some of the oldest streets in London: Cloth Fair, Barley Mow Passage, Rising Sun Court, Half Moon Court, Kinghorn Street.

Scorched but spared by the Great Fire, the whole stinking lot had also been preserved from Sir Christopher Wren, who had a grand design to rebuild them but had not been permitted to for lack of public money. The wind and rain, however, seemed bent on offering the good architect a second chance, as the old wood and wattle of these decaying buildings shook like the teeth in a nodding dowager.

I heard the crack first, just as Bartholomew Passage – the alley that led into Bartholomew Close – assumed an impossible angle, a thing of wild diagonals and steep bending rhomboids. Then it grew dark above me as a clockmaker's came down on me, sign first then the establishment itself. There was a sharp pain in the front of my head. I was aware of sticky blood in my nose. I felt hard cobbles against my back and the stench of freshly churned mud in my nostrils, and then nothing.

Nothing, that is, until strong hands reached under my armpits some time later. Hands that I knew even then, semi-conscious and seven years old, represented my salvation and my destiny. They were the hands of our neighbour John Dalton. And John Dalton was a painter.

My destiny was lifting my mud-bespattered, bloodied body out of the gutter.

2

I DO NOT KNOW for how long I was unconscious, nor when John Dalton finally got me home. It was like death, as I have always imagined it. It gave me an awareness of the finality of things unusual, I believe, in one so young. It made me tenacious in my haste to accomplish whatever task I set myself, all too aware, even then, of fighting against time.

I awoke to a state of groaning half-being in my own bed, dressed in a nightgown, ragingly thirsty, with the devil's own pain in my head and a smile on my face.

'Hello, little man! I thought we'd lost you!'

My smile widened. This hurt me quite a lot, but I had no control over it. I smiled whenever my father spoke, or even as he cleared his throat in languid preparation to speak, as he tended to do. I smiled at the sight of him, at the thought of him. I believe my smile would even come at the smell of him, or at the trace of any evidence of him, like the touch of one of the books he wrote.

A diffident, though lengthy, clearing of the throat, accompanied no doubt by a stroking of the paternal chin. I can't be sure of that; I had my eyes shut.

'Um … Little man? Can you … er … hear me?'

I tried to stop smiling, as it hurt so much, but the effort of stopping smiling amused me and made me smile more.

'Hello, pater,' I said. 'Yes, I can hear you. I am sorry I have worried you and mama.'

Speaking drove agonising pains through my head, so I stopped, noticing as I did so that my forehead was covered by a linen cloth soaked in water of cloves. The bed was pitching and yawing as if I were at sea. I drifted into a half-sleep, aware that the storm was still raging outside, wind lashing rain against our poor tiny window. It was to rage all night.

'*Aeris impulsum*,' pater was saying, to the room in general. 'That's what Aristotle called the wind.'

'Never mind Aristotle,' snapped mama. 'Tear me some fresh strips of cloth. And tear them straight, for heaven's sake.'

I awoke next time to the sound of baby Anne bawling. Pater took her from her crib and rocked her in his arms, which soon soothed her. My bed was still afloat on its own wild sea. Little Mary held a bowl of scented water in which mama dabbed a cloth, then mopped my wounded brow. It hurt like the torments of hell and I shrieked at her to stop it.

'William!' she cried angrily. 'I am trying to help you!'

Then she told me to say the Lord's Prayer. Thinking I was about to meet my maker, I burst into tears, which caused the wound on my forehead to bleed afresh.

'Shan't!' I shouted at mama, regardless of the pain it caused me.

'Stubborn boy!' she shouted back, angrily flapping the succouring cloth at me, splashing the baby with clove-water.

'Will I live?' I asked pater.

'Of course you will,' snapped mama, in reply.

'It is thought,' said pater, with his customary care, as if cherishing each word, 'that the cause of storms is the influence of the sun upon vaporous matter, which ...'

'Make fast the door downstairs, Richard. This storm may be a curse on Christian folk but it is a blessing to thieves.'

'... which being dilated are obliged to possess themselves of more space than ...'

I fear I fell asleep again at that point.

We continued in this manner until morning, none of the Hogarth family sleeping; the storm, if anything, increasing in its ferocity. I awoke, for the first of many times, from feeble sleep to hear pater's soft voice.

'I shall fetch him something soothing for that wound.'

'Richard! You know very well we do not have the money for an apothecary.'

'Mr Reynolds sells it.'

Mr Reynolds kept the toy shop, a magnificent emporium, an Aladdin's cave of wonders. Mama was still refusing her consent when pater, without another word, trod softly to the door and left the room. I smiled defiance at mama.

'Stubborn boy!'

Pater was gone for what seemed to me a long time, but mama was not concerned. When he finally returned, he had an earthenware pot in his hand.

'How is it, outside?' said mama.

'Great destruction, sad to say. Whole houses down, or sometimes just the tops. Many chimneys down. The streets calf-deep in debris.'

'Everywhere?'

'Strange to say, not. Some places on the lee side have escaped untouched.'

'And people abroad?' For the first time a flicker of fear crossed mama's flat face.

'A few. Only a few.'

She looked relieved. 'We are not the only ones left then.'

'No, no …'

She nodded to herself. 'I feared we may be another Noah family. The only ones left on God's earth.'

Pater smiled. 'Or like Deucalion after Zeus's flood. No, no. All will be well, and all will be well. And every good thing will be well.'

'Oh, will it, now?'

Pater grimaced comically as he took the wax paper off the top of the small earthenware pot. I laughed and held his hand tight. The salve for my wound turned out to be a thick brown ointment which stank and put me in mind of animal dung.

Papa squeezed my hand, then gently said, 'I say, little chap, nothing wrong with your little grip is there? Tight as a vice. Odysseus clung to the ram's belly no tighter than you!'

'Oh, Richard! For heaven's sake …'

Mama tried to seize the pot of balm, but pater merely smiled, gently turned aside, slowly disengaged my grip and applied the balm himself, tenderly, with two fingers.

'I say, little chap, that's quite a groove you've got there. On your poor little forehead. A valley, a veritable chasm, indeed. William … my little Bill, say you are all right because … to be frank with you, little chap, I don't think I could bear it if …'

My eyes filled with tears. 'I am well, pater, aside from pain in the head. I am myself, as ever was!'

'Oh, Billy Boy, my little chap. Thank God … Oh, thank God for it!'

Pater began to weep. Mama sent him from the room, on the excuse of coddling baby Anne. Even then, I do believe, as early as that, with caked blood still new on my groove, I began to wonder at the meaning of what papa called 'The Finger of God' laid on my forehead.

Did 'The Finger of God' make me special?

3

IN THE EVENINGS, pater worked in our room at his hack jobs. One of these was correcting the Latin in books, before they were published.

'I am cleaning the Augean Stable of error, little chap!' he would cry to me, as his pen swooped on some error or infelicity in conjugation or declension.

I can recall the title of one of these books, it was *Opera Posthuma*. If you ever see this book, please remember that its immaculate Latin is entirely due to my pater, and to none other. And remember him please, remember him for it, for he was a good man and the purest soul I was ever to meet in my life.

Only late at night did my pater turn to his latest *magnum opus* as he always called it. This was sometimes a textbook for schools, sometimes a play. I would sneak from my bed while my little sisters slept, to watch him write.

With a half-smile of fulfilment playing round his face, the quill resting elegantly in a languid hand, he scratched his head under his wig, just behind the right ear, as he wrote: whether to ease the head lice or for greater inspiration I never knew. But I hear him to this day:

'This is the one that will make our fortune, little chap!'

Mama sometimes sat opposite him as he worked, mending and patching our clothes or doing the household accounts with a tally-stick. She flicked sly glances at him over her sewing, sometimes muttering to herself: 'Looking for gold in the mines of Peru.'

I never understood this expression, though I suspected that Peru was devoid of gold mines.

When I was older, papa used to take me with him to book shops, printers and coffee houses, looking for publishers for his latest gold from the mines of Peru. Overton, the print seller, was at The White Horse. Wyat sold at The Golden Lion, St Paul's Churchyard; Charles Ackers at St John's Close. Another I remember especially was one called Bowles, who I was to have dealings with myself, some years later.

We would trudge round Paternoster Row, Ave Maria Lane, Warwick Lane, listening to the same refusals, most of them cordial. Everyone knew Richard Hogarth, everyone liked him; nobody gave what he said much credence.

A visit to a coffee house stays in my mind, Fenton's in Charing Cross. Pater, as ever, had his manuscript with him, in a sprawling pile on the table. I was draining a sludgy bowl of coffee like the lower reaches of the Thames, happy to be part of pater's schemes. I, like he, scoured the tables for printers and booksellers, though with only a hazy idea of how I would recognise them.

We were approached by a handsome woman and a child. The woman was buxom. Something about her made me take her for a bawd at first sight, young though I was. The child was waif thin, exquisitely pretty, although her nose was running. She was about seven or eight, I thought.

I glanced at pater, whose face had stiffened, one hand protectively on his manuscript. I had always taken him for a moral man, and so it proved. But, to my horror, the bawd offered not herself but the child.

'Come sir, this pretty girl would like to make your closer acquaintance. Say hello to the man, Lavinia.'

Lavinia sniffled and said hello.

'Please go away, madam,' pater said. 'We have matters to discuss here.'

The bawd laughed. I noticed her heaving bosom, under a red apron. 'Town matters or country matters?' laughed the bawd.

'Madam, please desist with this.' Pater sounded miserable rather than angry.

'Perhaps the young man,' persisted the bawd, meaning me. 'What do you think, young sir? She will make a man of you for a guinea.'

I said nothing, though secretly I would rather have had the bawd than the girl.

Pater, however, stood, one hand still on his manuscript, as near to anger as I believe he would ever reach. 'Madam! That girl should be with her mother!'

The bawd put her hands on her hips and laughed fit to split her stays. 'She *is* with her mother, sir. That she is.' And with that the bawd, seeing there was no sale to be had with us, swept off to another table, the daughter in her wake. Though as she walked off the daughter gave me the sweetest smile, shrugging her shoulders slightly, a gesture I was to remember clearly the next time I saw her. I found her fascinating.

Pater's mood was quite spoiled. We left Fenton's without even finishing our coffee, spending the rest of the afternoon visiting printers and booksellers, with pater failing to interest any of them in his manuscript.

'One should not undertake selling in a sour mood,' pater muttered, as we trudged round Crag's Court and then Scotland Yard and then White Hall, from one establishment to the next, being shown the door pretty smartly at every one.

But by that evening he was fully restored to his usual sunny humour, perhaps even more so than usual, as if his optimism and joy at life had even been boosted by that day's adversity.

Pater and I were supping coffee at Tom King's Coffee House, a ramshackle shed just about holding itself up in a corner of Covent Garden. It was well after midnight; I was struggling to stay awake.

I had started to bridle when pater called me 'little chap', especially in public, so, sensitive as ever to the feelings of others, he had elevated me to 'old chap'. I was, after all, old enough to be sitting in the midst of this company of bucks and their bawds, even having some idea why the couples kept leaving the premises together. And so it was as 'old chap' that I accepted a second bowl of stygian coffee from Moll King herself, having made the first one last over an hour, as had pater.

'I've changed tactics, old chap.'

I nodded with sagacious interest, though pater had explained this point several times already.

'The plays are … problematic. I am perhaps ahead of my time. So I intend to make my name with the pedagogic works first. Not only *Disputationes*. There's my *Compendium of Geography*, my *Thesaurium* for use with no teacher – radical stuff, that. Then, when the printers and booksellers know me, I get copies of the play printed, *then* approach a theatre manager with a whole set. The theatre manager can mount the play within a week, the next day if he likes. You see, old chap?'

'Mmm,' I gave the appearance of wisdom, sipping at my coffee, trying to stay awake.

'Meanwhile, there's good old *Disputationes Grammaticales*.'

He smacked the manuscript of the grammar book with the flat of his hand, as it sat on the table. I was reminded of a rake smacking the rump of a bawd or a courtesan. I was plagued by such thoughts of late, some considerably more vivid, raw and rude than that.

'I'm going to get the good old *Disputationes* into the church schools. It will last a generation. We're all going to be very, very rich, old chap; you'd better start getting used to that fact.'

'I wouldn't say that to mama, if I were you.'

Mama was fond of saying he would have us all in Beech Lane. It was years before I learned that this was a workhouse.

'Eh? What? My my, you are growing up, aren't you?'

'I'm thirteen, papa.'

'Are you? Good lord!'

At that point the auction finally started. A reedy voice from the front of the coffee house started bawling out wares, while simultaneously an urchin distributed copies of a bookseller's catalogue. Pater opened the catalogue, a glazed, dreamy look spreading on his face. I understood that his tactic was to wait for the auction to finish, and then beard the bookseller, face to face.

Meanwhile, as the reedy voice piped on, I glanced at the frontispiece. The catalogue, it seemed, was that of a printer and bookseller – one Edmund Curll. His emblem was a partridge in full plume, drawn sideways on, with neat hatching round the feet to give depth. Well done, but I could do as well, if not better. His emporium was out at Temple Bar. We had not yet traipsed so far, father and I, in our badgering of booksellers as they went about their business. So this Curll was unknown to me.

But not for long. Oh, no, not for long. My father was turning the pages of *Bibliotheca Selecta*, as the catalogue was called, clearly imagining his own works proudly taking their place within it. He whistled to himself.

'Close on nine hundred works, here. Just think of that, old chap. Bladen's translation of Caesar's *Commentaries*. That's good … that's very good. Sound man, Bladen. I'd be keeping good company.'

'Mmm.'

Father turned the pages of the catalogue faster. '*The Devout Christian's Companion*, Archbishop Tillotson. Well, that should sell. Sell by the wheelbarrow-load, I shouldn't wonder. Or at least by the congregation-load. That's what you want, you see, old chap, a captive audience. Some sort of group of people of the same mind. Preferably a large group.'

The auction was nearly over; the urchin was passing among the tables collecting up the catalogues. Father slipped a silver penny in his grubby hand.

Chapter 3

'Please tell your master, Mister Curll, that Richard Hogarth wishes to discuss a business matter with him, if he would be so good as to join us at this table.'

Nothing happened. I wondered if father had wasted his silver penny, but after a goodly while, a slight wisp of a fellow with inky fingers and a brown doublet that had seen better days introduced himself as Edmund Curll. My father introduced himself then said 'And I am proud to say that this fine chap here is my son.'

Curll gave no reaction to that, but joined us at the table, his shoulders askew, his squint so pronounced he seemed to be looking out at the Covent Garden whores rather than at us.

My first impression was that he was one of those hilarious creatures who had grown to be like his name; his body curlled, his gaze curlled, his demeanour curlled – Curll was anything but straight. But he proceeded to business quickly enough.

'What have you got for me, then?' He looked down at the manuscript, his mandibles circling beneath the squint like a praying mantis about to devour a frog.

My father launched into a breathless and somewhat rambling account of the work he was trying to sell: how he divided words into syllables to aid the learning of them, how he tried to bring joy to learning by the playing of games, how he always had an element of study without the teacher. Curll, head down over the manuscript, nodded in agreement. My father nodded at his nodding. We all nodded.

Father was still talking. I willed him to be silent, to give Curll a chance to assimilate the material in front of him. But I understood, too, that father had spoken to dozens, perhaps scores, of booksellers who had not given him the time of day. By considering the manuscript, or at least giving the appearance of so doing, Curll had undammed torrents of frustration from my poor artistic father's being.

'This is very good.' Curll patted the manuscript much as father often did, perhaps more gently. 'I'd be pleased to take this on for you, Mr Hogarth. Then we'll see about any other work you may have.'

There were tears in father's eyes. My eyes, too, were moist. I took father's hand and squeezed it.

'I … This is a splendid moment for me, Mr Curll. A moment looked forward to, no, more, longed for, I may say, all my life. It is the culmination of much hard work. My dear son William knows …'

Curll was pulling a tangle of yellowing documents from inside his old-fashioned doublet (I wondered if it were second-hand – Curll himself did not cut much of a figure, but the original owner, if there was one, must have been even smaller).

'Standard letter,' the bookseller announced briskly. 'Same for everybody: prince or pauper, bishop or thief. Although come to think of it we ought to pay the thieves more, or at least the ordinaries who write their life stories. You wouldn't believe how many copies we're selling of that sort of thing, once the thief has gone to Tyburn.'

My father and I laughed politely. Curll's urchin had appeared like a genie from a bottle and Curll sent him for pen and ink. These artefacts arrived so quickly that the urchin must have fetched them from the table at the front of the coffee house, from which Curll had conducted the auction.

Father had started to read the standard letter.

'Three guineas, Mr Hogarth. That's for the first one thousand copies of your book. And one further guinea for reprinting. Would you like the money now?' A teasing smile, wavy naturally, was curling round Curll's lips.

'Oh. Well … If that's …'

Curll fished for the coins in a leather purse tied with a thong round his waist. 'Best bit of Spanish gold for you there, Mr Hogarth, on the production of your fair signature, sir.'

My father smiled and signed, the coins were handed over. Father left them on the table, as if afraid they might vanish if he did not constantly watch them.

'I would usually baptise our agreement with you, Mr Hogarth, but on this occasion I have to rush to another meeting. However, it's been a pleasure and there will be many other times, I'm sure.'

Curll stood, bent into a question mark, and pumped father's hand. 'A pleasure,' he repeated. 'And young Mr William Hogarth, too.' Curll attempted a look in my direction, which was about as accurate as a Frenchie broadside at one of our great ships. And then he was gone.

Father slowly picked up the coins, even then not putting them away, merely smiling at them in his hand. Tom King, the coffee house owner, was beaming at him, having witnessed the transaction.

'Do you want a glass of gin, Mr Hogarth?' he said. He spoke like a real gent, as if his mouth were full of fruit. 'Have it as my guest, on me and Moll,' he went on. 'And young William's surely old enough to join you, now?'

'Why thank you, Tom!' My father was crying.

I was pleased, naturally I was. More than pleased. I was thrilled for my dear father. Delighted. But I did wonder why he did not have a copy of whatever it was he had signed.

4

FATHER SUCCUMBED to a delirious euphoria, redolent of far-away places and exotic, elevated people. He paced our dingy set of rooms on the second floor of the house in Bartholomew Close in a reverie of imagined success, living who knows what dreams of the author-life in who knows what locations. Sometimes his lips moved as the conversations in his mind nearly broke into the real world.

And as for me, the darling son and heir, he broke into Curll's three guineas to buy me drawing materials and paid for lessons for me with our neighbour, John Dalton, the painter. Some things were also bought for my little sisters, but I no longer remember what they were. Toys, no doubt. Pater enjoyed going to the huge and glorious toy emporiums. (*Emporia!* I can hear the gentle correction from the grave – my apologies, pater.)

At any rate, Curll's three guineas did not disturb the trudge of our lives at Bartholomew Close for very long, before they were almost gone. Then, at some point, it occurred to my father to wonder what had happened to the copies of his masterpiece, presented to Curll at Tom King's Coffee House. There was no sign of them, but my father, a heady optimist if ever there was one, was not too concerned.

'I'm sure Mr Curll's terribly busy, old chap. A successful man like him … Don't like to bother him.'

It was me who pressed him to visit Curll to enquire how matters stood. We set off to Curll's premises in Temple Bar, the proud author and son, merely paying a courtesy visit to the publisher, no thought of complaint. In such a spirit I imagine country squires visit the palaces of the local magnate to discuss fishing rights, or some such.

Temple Bar was just off Fleet Street, a stiffish walk from Spitalfields. But papa eased the way with his usual running commentary on the throng as we made our way through it, or a digression on something he had read, or a digression from the digression about some musing on life, such as whether character was a product of the emotion or the mind.

Chapter 4

This particular perambulation is marked on my memory, no doubt forever, partly because of what happened when we got there, partly because we stopped to watch the masons putting the finishing touches to St Paul's Cathedral. Sir Christopher Wren's masterpiece, especially the curve of the dome, has long formed my ideal of pleasing symmetry and beauty, and on that day I imbibed it, nourished by it, given life by it, as if by my mother's breast.

We finally reached Curll's establishment. It was a large bookshop, with prints, woodcuts and engravings in the window as well as books. I was much struck by a woodcut by Albert Duerer of a woman with a naughty smile. He had caught much of the woman's life, let alone her character, in her face. It was an admirable work.

I felt father's usual bonhomie, borne of the energy of the artist, desert him as we entered Curll's workplace. He was pale, father was, his slightly prominent nose pointier, his narrow lips tight as he looked round the courtroom of his dreams.

An assistant was dispatched to fetch Curll, who duly appeared from the print works behind the bookshop, wiping his inky hands with a rag. He stood due north of us, his squinty gaze somewhere to the south-east.

'Ah, Mr Hogarth. What have you been up to? I was just about to contact you.'

I smile wryly as I recall these words of Curll's, to write them, from the vantage of passed time. I was about to learn, at the age of thirteen in the year 1710, that it is the fate of the artist to be patronised, as well as cheated, by those of lesser talents than he.

For make no mistake, my dear father was an artist, in his inner being, just as much as Albert Duerer or Raphael or Milton or Fielding, come to that. But he was the saddest form of artist, one who never found his metier, so expression of his artistic soul remained trapped within him.

'Ah!' said my father, in innocent relief. He was beside himself with nerves before this fellow not fit to lick his boots. 'About to contact me? About the copies no doubt ...'

'In a manner of speaking, yes,' said the Curll churl glibly, wiping one inky hand round his face. 'The next thing to discuss is the transportation.'

'The transportation? Of ... er ...?'

'The transportation of the copies, Mr Hogarth. To the schools which will buy them. They won't, sad to say, get there of their own accord.' Curll chuckled merrily at this witticism.

'Where are the copies, then?' said father, sounding stupid in his desperation to stop his dream coming crashing down around him. I believe he even looked round Curll's bookshop, peered through the open door through to the printworks, even up at the ceiling.

Curll gave a dry, mirthless chuckle, like paper tearing. 'We can't make the copies until we've arranged the transport, can we now, Mr Hogarth? Otherwise the copies would be here, where there isn't room for them. You've brought the six guineas, I take it?'

My father's face crumpled. 'What ... the what?'

'Six guineas, Mr Hogarth. For the transportation of books to the schools. And that's throughout the country, even as far as Edinburgh. It's in your agreement.'

'I didn't ... I haven't got it ... the agreement ... six guineas? The agreement doesn't say six guineas. Does it? I'm sure it doesn't. I've read it. Where is it?'

'Calm yourself, Mr Hogarth. Calm yourself. The author undertakes to pay any transportation costs. No figure is mentioned. It's right at the end of the agreement. Do you want me to go and fetch it?'

'Oh, I've no doubt you're right, Mr Curll.' The first traces of bitterness were entering father's voice. 'But six guineas is three guineas more than *you* paid *me*. Is it not?'

'Initially, yes. But don't forget, Mr Hogarth, that under the terms of the agreement, after the initial printing, you earn another guinea every time more copies are demanded and printed.'

'But six guineas ...? I should take my manuscript back, then.' Pater's eyes were moist, his voice unconvincing.

'I'm afraid you've already sold me the manuscript, Mr Hogarth. For the very fair sum of three guineas. The manuscript, sir, is mine.'

'All that work. I spent years ... It took me ... years.'

'No doubt it did, Mr Hogarth. And a very scholarly work it is, too.'

As my poor dear father was being destroyed before my eyes, my mind was racing. I perceived instantly that the nub of the matter was to get the manuscript into print.

I pulled father by the arm and whispered in his ear. 'I'm sure Mr Curll could be persuaded to initiate printing for four guineas,' I said.

Curll shot me a sharp look. 'A wise head on young shoulders you have there, Mr Hogarth junior. Can't do it for four, though. Five guineas. Five guineas might be a possibility. I say *might*, mind.'

'We would not be able to achieve that, sir,' I said, before my father could agree to it. 'It's impossible. Come, four gives you a guinea profit on the original transaction and you can recover more as we go along.'

Curll gave me a look I have come to recognise over the years – grudging respect won from initial contempt. He would take a guinea profit, a handful of copies would be printed and there the matter would end. The city of Edinburgh would no more see copies of father's book than Mr Curll would see heaven on Judgement Day.

'The deal is done, at four guineas,' said Curll abruptly, turning on his heel to go back to his printing.

I now needed to get father home to see how much of Curll's coffee house money, as we had come to call the initial three guineas, we had left; as we now had to find four to have any hope even of recovering father's manuscript.

Back in our rooms, my mother's reaction was even worse than I had feared. She had always been sharp-tongued, with more than a touch of the shrew about her, but no sooner had I explained the ins and outs than she flew at my father, beating him on the breast with her fists.

'You fool! You bloody fool! Oh, why did I marry such a gull? My father told me to have nothing to do with a simple country bumpkin. Would that I had listened to him.' (This recalled father's lodging with mother's family when he first arrived in London from Westmoreland. He had won the hand of the eldest daughter of his landlord, as mama then was.)

My little sisters were screaming, comprehending, naturally, only the anger and the sad coming apart of our family, not the issue of it.

'How much of Curll's three guineas do we have left?' I said to mother, as much to calm her as anything.

She went to the kitchen to find out. 'Just under half a guinea,' she said, coming back into our living room, sounding calmer.

'Then we need to find three and three-quarter guineas,' I said.

'Why?' mother said. 'Suppose we don't? Suppose we just keep Curll's money? What's to stop us?'

'The booksellers all act together,' father said. 'They control prices and work. If Curll is not paid what he takes to be his due, he will blacken my name with the others. They keep lists. All writing work will stop; you can take my word on that.'

We moved from Bartholomew Close to a smaller place in St John Street. It was so close to the Smithfield Market we could hear the lowing of the cattle day and night. If you shut your eyes, you could imagine yourself surrounded by fields; open them, peer through a grimy square of window, and you saw a tumble of wood and lathe houses leaning towards each other in a foetid alleyway.

I remember the changes in our board the most keenly. Beef, indeed meat of any sort, became a distant memory. Even fish was beyond our means, save for the occasional Yarmouth herring. We kept life and limb together with broths of peas and beans, bulked out with carefully measured cuts of bread and cheese.

To add to our woes, that winter was a cruel one, with biting winds which ripped through our thin clothes and snow so high and wet it made leaving the house like wading calf-high through an icy river. Some ragamuffins made a snow house in the distillers' courtyard, I recall, which stood for months and was so commodious a group of ten could stand around in it in comfort.

My young sisters seemed to have no future or prospects; the drudgery of servitude hung over them, coming very soon. But as for me, I could dimly discern a future course; I continued to struggle through the snow to John Dalton's studio in Duck Lane, where he taught me the rudiments of line and plane and copying.

I do not believe he was paid for his work with me, for as I have described, there was now nothing to pay him with. He was a Nonconformist, like father, and that may have been the reason for his charity towards my family.

He would set me a copying task, usually part of a plaster statue of Diana or Flora or Zeus, then resume his own work. At the end, I would show him what I had accomplished. He silently and patiently corrected my line by guiding my hand with his own. There was little encouragement, but little blame either. I visited him twice a week, on Monday and Wednesday, towards midday when what little light there was in our quarter during the winter was at its best.

My father's frame was always lean, but about this time he appeared gaunt, almost skeletal. His dealings with my mother became fractious; the love in their voices slowly fading from impatience, blame and occasional spite all brought on by the grinding blight of poverty.

His dealings with my sisters, which formerly could be summarised as cordiality tinged with indifference, were now marked by a new anger, with storms bursting from him at intervals. He smacked little Anne occasionally when she cried, and Mary, too. He withdrew a little, even from me. I was more often 'William', less often 'old chap'.

Mother had stomach pains to contend with these days, and hardly ate at all. She enlisted my help in trying to get father to complete the scraps of hack work which still came in. Neither mother nor I could follow the details of his work, but it was clear that he neglected it every time a fresh idea or scheme came upon him, so jobs were more and more often taken away from him and given to other hacks to finish.

His latest scheme was a reform of the alphabet, involving the removal of the letters F, G, H, K, Q, W, X, Y and Z. In support of this scheme, he not only wrote letters, which was expensive, but tramped the streets proselytising to printers and booksellers, including the egregious Curll.

At mother's insistence I went with him. I believe she did not trust him to act rationally in his dealings, or perhaps even to return home. Curll received us cordially enough, even offering refreshment – food and drink we were sorely in need of. But needless to say there was no progress on any front in our dealings with him.

Mother and I had a long discussion, deciding in the end that we should at least try to recover all the money owed to father by the booksellers, for they were slow in paying and often did not pay at all unless continually nagged to. At mother's insistence, I set off for the booksellers without father.

Armed with the names of booksellers and the places where they could be found in my head, I resolved to ask for 'payment for Richard Hogarth for work already done, if you please.' The booksellers, as I recall, were Richard Smith, John Pemberton, Jakob Le Blon and Francis Gosling. I made a plan in my head of my route, starting with the most distant and ending with the nearest.

I found John Pemberton at the Golden Buck in Fleet Street. He told me that monies due to father would be paid 'any day now'. This was not to be the last time I was to hear this refrain. Francis Gosling had premises at The Flying Horse in Grub Street. He gave me a sixpence. Richard Smith, who plied his trade in Drury Lane, said he was only days from bankruptcy. He asked me for a loan of money, no doubt with satirical intent. Jakob Le Blon promised payment to Richard Hogarth as soon as his colour printing process brought him the profits which he expected of it.

At the end of the day I gave Francis Gosling's sixpence to mother, who kissed me on the top of the head. As she did so we heard an ominous thundering of boots on the stairs. It was a tipstaff flanked by two burly fellows in leather jerkins. The curled cur of a bookseller, Curll, had played the outraged creditor, mobilising other creditors into the bargain. Mother and I knew nothing of this, until the tipstaff told us.

They took father off to prison, telling him roughly he was now a debtor. Mother left my little sisters with the woman next door, so we could go with him.

5

WE WERE taken by cart to the debtor's prison at The Fleet. We floated in a bubble of silence through the Belphegor's concert of noise that echoed and bounced off the houses of east London. The tight-packed throng itself parted ahead of us, closing behind us, already exiling us from worthy citizens not in debt.

We reached the vast stone walls garlanded with lichen and mould, and in through the iron gates we went. Disembarking from the cart, we crossed the Press Yard, where offenders who refused to plead were crushed to death with due ceremony. In better days, how father would have loved to explain the Latin for the punishment – *peine forte et dure*.

Even out here, the stench was making my stomach rise to my throat. It was said that no chairman would take a customer who had so much as visited the Fleet, as the stink soaked the clothes and lingered in any trapped air.

The tipstaff led the way down stone stairs to dungeons beneath the pavement, the two roughs in leather jerkins bringing up the rear. Here we all stopped, while my mother and father were bidden to look through a grille in the dungeon door. I could just see through it myself, standing on tiptoe, peering between them. The grinning tipstaff encouraged my viewing.

There were upwards of twenty wretches in the cell, ankle deep in foetid water. Opposite me, one fellow had his hands trapped in stocks built against the stone wall. The top plank of the stocks had the improving motto 'Better to Work than to Stand Thus' carved into it. A shirker then, this poor fellow. And indeed all those around him were beating hemp with wooden mallets. One plank behind an old fellow working there was carved with yet another motto: 'The Wages of Idleness'.

Outside the door, my father was white in the face but composed. I thought him brave. I felt a surge of love for him, laced with defiance on his behalf.

'Am I to be among them?' father asked the tipstaff.

He spoke in hope. There was something about the official's manner which indicated the cell was being offered only as a spectacle.

25

'That's up to you, sir,' said the tipstaff. 'Follow me.'

With relief, we were led away, back across the Press Yard to quarters off a dingy alley. This was a spunging house, rooms within the prison precinct which, while not exactly salubrious, were not so much worse than what we had just left and called our own. The other prisoners in this spunging house, ten or so men and two or three women, looked up when we came in, then ignored us.

My spirits rose a little, as they always tend to do, until an under-keeper produced fetters and shackled father to the wall. Only then did I notice that two of the other prisoners were also chained. The others were free.

At that moment a short, square figure in a worn broadcloth coat and grubby cravat stumped in through the open door. This strutting personage introduced himself as Mister Huggins, the keeper, or, as he called himself, the governor of the prison. Speaking in the fluting tones of one who would like to be a gentleman, but was not, Huggins demanded a garnish of £1 6s 8d for the fetters, meaning, I supposed, for their removal.

'You shall have it by the end of the day, sir,' mother said. 'Please release my husband.'

'That is not how the system works, madam,' said this Huggins. 'Action follows on the payment of cash. My men will give you the tariff for food here, and for bedding, too. I look forward to our further acquaintance.'

And with that he strutted out again.

'Your footing here is a six shilling bowl of punch, madam,' intoned the tipstaff, who had the name of Corbett, with obvious boredom at the repetition of his litany. 'A shilling a day for food and bedding, thereafter.'

A dreadful scream broke in on us from outside, as if to tell us what tortures awaited father if we did not pay. I caught sight of his face, mute, frozen pleading, his shoulders already slumped from the shackles.

Touching me on the arm to bid me follow, mother turned on her heel and left, neither of us looking at father, as much for his sake as our own.

'What are we going to do?' I said to mother, as soon as we were outside again.

Mother was seized by a coughing fit, answering me in a breathless voice when she had finished. 'Get the money,' she said. 'We need the garnish now, today, or they will only spunge more from us. We can have him moved from the spunging house to better quarters when they have the first monies.'

I nodded, relieved she knew what to do. 'You mean a money-lender?'

'Yes. There's no other way.'

'A Jew?' I said.

'Yes,' mother said. 'I know one. He is a good fellow. Many in Spitalfields trust him.'

Mother led me to Great Montagu Court, one of the passageways off Little Britain, near where we used to live. Here, surrounded by tumbledown shacks, was a flat-fronted brick house of the better sort.

'Moses da Costa lives here,' mother murmured to me.

She boldly rang the bell, explaining our business to a maid who answered. The maid wordlessly led us along a passageway to a wondrous, richly appointed parlour. There was yellow silk wallpaper with an embossed pattern picked out in red, plush green velvet draperies, a coffee table and a dressing table hung with a patterned, fringed cloth.

I recognised the paintings on the wall from my bible studies with father: Jonah outside Nineveh, and David and Uzzah dancing before the ark. I had never before seen such beauty, such luxury, such taste.

But all this was merely the backdrop. The Jew, all laced at cuff and ruffed at throat, lavendered and sprayed till he smelled like a pharmacy, immaculate from the tip of his powdered wig to the shiny silk buckles on his shoes, was delicately sipping from the smallest coffee cup I have ever seen. I swear I have encountered bigger thimbles.

Oh, there was so much new experience for me in this one chamber of marvels; I had heard of blackamoors – who hasn't? But there, in a corner, was an exquisite miniature man, black as ebony and carrying a copper kettle, ready to replenish, as I supposed, his master's drink. And tied to the table there was a monkey. I wager it was the only monkey in Spitalfields, perhaps in all of London, certainly the only one I had ever seen.

But the most marvellous wonder, for the *tabula rasa* of a boy that I then was, was sitting across from the Jew, to his right. She had a round, sweet face beneath her bonnet, a black patch just right of centre on her forehead, a bow of a mouth, an old gold dress of Spitalfields silk faced with white lace, pretty little red shoes.

But none of that was what stopped my heart; drained my mouth of spit, like I'd just eaten a sour Maidstone apple; widened my eyes to pebbles. The skin of her arms and neck was white but with the depth of cream. As she leaned forwards I saw, for the first time, the most beautiful curves in all nature. Did I see as far as the pink tipped wonder at the centre, on that day? Or did my imagination add it over all the years and the many times I recalled the scene?

While I gawped in helpless thrall, uncomfortably aware of the stiff stirrings in my breeches, my mother was introducing us, then crisply outlining our plight.

'Are we talking of Richard Hogarth, the Latin scholar?' said da Costa, when he had attentively heard mother out.

Mother nodded, pleased at hearing father so described, as was I.

'Madam, your news saddens me greatly. Your husband's scholarship is in different fields to mine. But scholarship is scholarship, madam. Learning is learning, something always to be respected. And Anthony da Costa respects it.'

'I thought your first name was Moses,' I blurted out. 'That's what my mother said.'

I flushed scarlet at my importunate words, pulled from my mouth in my derangement at the beauty and her curves. Mother looked first horrified then angry. At home, there would have been a vigorous slap round the face, even now, when I was bigger and she was weak from illness. The beauty, who still had not been introduced, laughed a tinkling, liquid laugh that was another novelty to add to those of this remarkable day.

'I am known in some quarters as Moses,' said da Costa, sounding far from pleased, 'and in others as Anthony.'

'And in bed as cudgel,' said the beauty. She looked at mother with mock innocence. 'A different weapon to a rapier, somewhat harder and rougher and with a round end.' She laughed a surprisingly deep laugh, staring mother in the eye as, mindful of our errand and our supplicant status, she struggled to control her anger.

Anthony, or Moses, da Costa laughed. As he did so the monkey strained at its leash, tipping the ornate mahogany coffee table over, sending the beauty's empty coffee cup sliding to the hardwood floor, where it broke. da Costa, discomfited, called for his maid to clear up the mess. The beauty laughed and leaned forwards, showing, I was sure deliberately, a renewed glimpse of the most wondrous loveliness life has to offer.

As the maid went about her work, da Costa spoke brusquely, belying the kindness of his words. 'Mrs Hogarth, I suggest the following; borrow enough to release your husband from the spunging house and see him within the Rules, immediately. Ask for rooms at Black and White Court, near Ludgate Hill. I will give you enough to bribe Huggins, to ensure you get them.'

'Thank you, sir …' My mother's voice cracked.

'Oh, no need for thanks. The rooms there are not too bad. Your husband may even venture out from them, though not far.'

'Thank you, I …'

'I will lend you ten guineas, as they will demand a caption fee, if they haven't already …'

'No.'

'Don't give them more than £5 16s 4d. It's standard.'

Mother nodded.

'Good. I can do the ten guineas at six per cent. That's the lowest you'll find anywhere.'

'I know it is. Thank you, sir.'

da Costa waved away the thanks in a talced flurry of laced hand. 'What I can do as well, is extend the repayment period, as far as I dare. I'll make it over two years, payments monthly.'

'That's very generous, sir.'

'I wouldn't get too tearful, my duck,' said the beauty. 'Anthony's got over £7,000 in Bank of England stock alone. Haven't you, Anthony?'

da Costa ignored her. 'Come back tomorrow,' he said to mother, 'and my clerk will have the calculation done for you, so you know exactly how much you have to repay. I'll give you a month's grace before the payments start.'

Even I, a half-schooled boy climbing the stairs to the first landing to manhood, could see that these terms were exceptionally generous.

'You can come back for advice at any time, but I won't lend you more. It would not be fair to you, as you would never be able to pay it back. You need to find a weekly income. Quickly. Can you work?'

'Yes, but I have two small daughters to care for.'

'You may have to give them away, or leave them with relatives for now. Can the boy work?'

I could feel the beauty's eyes on me, as da Costa named me. I was carmine red again.

'Yes sir!' I piped up. 'I can and will work, to help my father.'

da Costa nodded and smiled.

The beauty laughed. 'You can come back here when you've got some money, young man. What's your name?'

'William, madam. William Hogarth.'

'Well, William Hogarth, I'll see you again when you're just a *little* bit bigger.' She wiggled her little finger at me. 'Shall I?'

'Kate, that's enough!' said da Costa, sharply.

The beauty, Kate, ignored him. 'Would you like to see more of me, little willy? When Willy has grown. Although methinks willy is growing, even as we speak.'

She leaned forwards again, just a fraction. I stepped forwards, openly looking at the wondrous orbs, my entire being consumed with desire. Until my mother grabbed me by the ear.

'Ouch!'

To howls of laughter from the beauteous Kate, da Costa waved us away.

As we left, a clerk, who must have been listening at the door, presented mother with ten guineas and a paper to sign. Mother glanced at it and laboriously wrote her initials, propping the paper on a side table.

As the clerk was showing us out of the front door, Kate appeared, hurrying down the passageway. She opened a door to an inner room and pulled a young man out by the hand. This buck gave her a kiss on the mouth, fondled her briefly, then ran past the clerk out of the half-open door. Kate brushed her dress down and returned to da Silva, ignoring the clerk and mother and me.

Outside in the street, mother was clutching the purse in which she had put the money. I was looking round, on guard for cut-purses and thieves, although still in torment from my experiences with Kate.

'We must get back to the prison,' mother said, absently.

'Who was that man?' I asked. 'The one who kissed Kate.'

'Your Kate is a bawd,' mother said, as we hurried out of Great Montagu Court, back to Little Britain. 'She's a strumpet, a common whore. And you just made a fool of yourself, staring at her like that.'

I flushed again. 'I don't care,' I said, though I did. 'Was she ... was she cuckolding Mr da Costa with that other fellow?'

Mother was hurrying along the street. 'Now, what do you think, William, eh? You're as big a fool as your father.'

Oh no, I'm not. I'm not. I'm not. I'm not. Oh no, I'm not.

We made our way back to the prison, where John Huggins took our money with due solemnity. Father was shivering in his shirt in the spunging house, the other prisoners having already stolen his coat. He was released from his fetters, whereupon we were all conveyed by cart to Black and White Court, guarded by two under-keepers.

The quarters in Black and White Court were in the Old Bailey, next door to the Ship Inn. The rooms were tolerable, boasting a table and chairs, two shelves and a straw mattress on the floor.

Father brightened immediately, much his old self, wanting mother and me to stay while he sent out for food. He was so unnaturally bright, with burning eyes, I feared he would order a quart of Rhenish wine, as he often did when joy came over him.

'I shall write here,' he said. 'My mind will be at peace, you see, free from all the distractions I had before.'

'Like feeding your family,' said mother, acidly.

'I have an idea already, for a play. It came upon me even as I was in chains. This one will make our fortune, you wait and see. One develops a feeling, you know, an instinct for these things.'

'I am a fool, for I married a fool,' muttered mother into the air, as she walked out.

I kissed father goodbye then ran after her, fearful, I must admit, of being left behind in such a place.

6

BACK IN our quarters in St John Street, we found my sisters running around, the neighbour charged with their care having grown tired of the task. Mary, the elder by two years, had at least made a good fist of looking after little Anne. My mother had an attack of the stomach cramps, followed by vomiting.

'What are we going to do?' I said, looking mother in the eye. 'I can apply to the silk weaver's in Benjamin Street, or one of the others if you prefer. Let me go now, mother. I shall bring you some money, I promise you.'

'Sit down, William,' she said.

I sat, obediently, at the table. My little sisters, sensing the seriousness of the occasion, ceased their screaming for a while.

Mother sighed then began: 'The girls are too young to go into service. Anyone who took them at that age would want their ruin. And I am too old and sick for work.'

'Mother ...'

'Hear me out, William.' She put her rough hand on mine, on the table. 'You are a good boy, and no mistake. But even the journeymen silk weavers earn only 10s a week, not enough for our needs. And you would have to learn the trade first. So here's a better idea.'

I nodded. 'Patent medicines.'

Mother gasped. I was pleased as Punch with myself.

'You read minds, boy,' mother said, shifting uncomfortably in her seat. She left patches of blood on the chairs sometimes. 'Yes, that was my idea. I can concoct something here. And you have your wits about you. You can go out and sell it.'

I stood and went over to a big sea chest where father kept all his papers. I fished about in the mess, finally producing a yellowing copy of the *Post Man*. It was a January edition, issued at four o'clock.

I found the advertisement I was looking for and read aloud: '*Dr James's Powders for Fevers, the Small Pox, Measles, Pleurisies, Quinsies, Acute Rheumatism ...*'

'What about spending your life in a dream?' said mother. 'Will it cure that? We'll get your father some.'

'... *Epidemical Disorders* ...' I continued sternly, '*as well as for those which are called Hypochondriac and Hysteric.*' I put the newspaper down. 'All we need to know now is what is in this stuff.'

Mother shook her head, mastering herself, returning to her customary sternness. 'No, I've got a better idea. Something easier. We are going to make and sell gripe ointment, for the relief of gripes in babies.'

The idea of peddling some sort of medication, it later transpired, occurred to both mother and me as a result of the day of the storm, when father sent out to Mr Reynolds at the toy emporium for ointment. That very day that was indented in me forever by the groove in my head. And now it was to lead to our salvation.

I was sent to old man Reynolds to enquire if he would let us have some pots on credit. My mission was so successful, I returned clutching as many small earthenware pots as I could carry. My reward was a look of respect from mother, a look I was to earn often in the months to come. Meanwhile, we allotted our roles. Mary declared herself old enough to help mother with the preparation of our nostrum. Little Anne, too, shrieked a readiness to be of use, though she understood little of the matter.

My tasks were to be the gathering of the raw ingredients to prepare the concoction, then the selling of the finished gripe ointment to those who could be persuaded they had a need of it. For the first time, I felt that tingling at the pit of my stomach which heralded the start of a new scheme.

Within the next few days, to save one lot of rent, we left our rooms in St John Street and joined father in his debtor's prison within the Rules. Huggins had raised the rent for the prison room, together with fees to the chaplain, porter, chamberlain and turnkey, to £3 5s 4d, but we still managed to pay without too badly dipping into our loan from Mr da Costa.

We did not have the means for the 5s 6d day pass for father to go beyond the Rules, so he would have to remain within the immediate area. This did not appear to concern him, impatient as he was to start writing. He had already sent word out to booksellers, who visited in a steady stream to buy his books. He was in high spirits, declaring he had no need of books to write his play, the play which would make our fortune.

I set off for the country, for the first time in my life, to gather herbs for the gripe ointment. Until now, much of my life had been circumscribed within a ring around our first home, running round St Botolph Churchyard, Christ's Hospital, St Sepulchre's Church, Smithfield Market, St Bartholomew's Hospital and back to St Botolph – the whole being less than five miles. I had broken the ring only with father, when we saw people on his business, like when we went to visit Edmund Curll.

Now, with the weight of my family's survival on my shoulders, I felt I was breaking the eggshell of my childhood world, stepping out as a man onto new ground. Dangerous new ground, in fact, for the country was where the wild men lived, everyone knew that.

I made my way north past Smithfield Bars and Porter's Block, the sun on my face, warming down through my jerkin. I was carrying an old leather satchel of father's, stamped in fading lettering with his initials: RWH.

I memorised the faces of people as I passed them by. Also their walks: the Cheapside Swing of those with a bit of money – or the pretension to it – the Ludgate Hobble of the cowherds, the sway of the old navy men.

As St John Street gave way to the Islington Road, I saw the first smudges of smoke from the brick kilns making tracery patterns against the pale blue of the sky. The first market gardens appeared in the fields. The crowd of people on the track thinned; more of them were ragged vagabonds. Some glanced at me. It was not worth a blackguard bothering with a boy with a flapping, empty satchel, but even so I learned early to stare every man in the eye, as I do even to this day.

So, this, then, was the country, was it? It was generously larded with cow shit, judging by the smell. Even so, I preferred it to the rank smells of the town and inhaled appreciatively as I saw the first of the dill I was looking for. I went into the fields and plucked it, together with some fennel. Both were plentiful, although I hated bending. Agricultural labour!

Then I had a slice of that luck always associated with the start of ventures. On the lee side of a ramshackle shed, hidden from the path that the thoroughfare had become, there was a wheelbarrow. I tiptoed round the shed, making sure nobody was in it, then I wheeled the wheelbarrow away. I filled it with handfuls of dill and fennel before turning for our new home.

The following day, at our room within the prison Rules, I applied my thoughts to obtaining the gin which was to be the other ingredient of our ointment. Despite my tender years, my dear mother was all for sending me round the stew-pots of St Giles, to one of the myriad gin houses there. Father gave no opinion, being immersed in the writing of his play.

But I remembered our visits to Curll's premises in Temple Bar. Near there, just off Fleet Street, I had noticed a distillery at Bride Lane: the premises, according to the sign, of one Alexander Nightingale.

But it would be a long walk with an open wheelbarrow full of gin. With all the vagabonds, footpads, cut-purses and ruffians abroad in London, I would be robbed, my cargo drunk, before I had gone twenty yards, no doubt of that. I put the problem to John Dalton, my drawing master, at the next of the free lessons he was kindly continuing to give me.

Dalton considered my predicament, hand on chin, elbow bent out, with his customary seriousness. He had the largest Adam's apple I have ever seen on a man.

'Bring the wheelbarrow here,' he said judiciously, swallowing, so the Adam's apple leaped up his throat. 'I will make a cover for it.'

The cover John made was of canvas and wood, cut to fit the wheelbarrow. On it, the artist placed some bricks. 'A *tromped doily* in its way,' he said slowly, in his rich baritone voice. 'The wheelbarrow, you see, appears to be full of bricks. The eye suggests; the mind completes the picture.'

When I appeared at Alexander Nightingale's distillery, no demur was made at selling me as much clear gin as would go in the wheelbarrow. I wheeled it slowly and carefully back to our new home, there triumphantly unveiling my purchase to shrieks of appreciation from my sisters. My mother gave her grim smile. Father, with a cloth over his head, merely appealed for quiet so he could go on composing his play, the play which would make our fortune.

One more ingredient was required. This ointment, mother explained to me, was to be applied to the baby's stomach when the gripes or fits threatened it. We dared not offer a medicine to be ingested, in case we killed babies all over London. A setting agent was therefore needed to turn the liquid of the soon-to-be-flavoured gin into an ointment thick enough to be applied.

'Beef fat,' mother said, speaking wearily, as ever.

'Beef fat. Get your mother some,' father echoed, as he scratched away at his play. He kept shutting his eyes, the better to shut out the world.

The gin was ladled out of the wheelbarrow off into cooking pots, leaving the wheelbarrow free for its journey to Smithfield Market, where I was to search for beef fat. I felt like a character in a fairy story – Jack, say, from 'Jack the Giant Killer' – as I wheeled my way to the slaughterhouse.

Over the familiar lowing of cattle and sheep at the end of their lives, I made my wants known to men who knew my family. The slaughtermen told me I could scrape as much fat off as many carcasses as I wished, with no charge.

My mother now had all the ingredients she needed for the family business. Helped by Mary and even little Anne, she began to fabricate the ointment, coughing all the time. I offered to help but, as soon as a few pots were ready, she told me to get out and sell them.

'How much for?'

'Sixpence the jar.'

I nodded, saying nothing but resolving to sell each jar for half a crown. The more expensive it was, I thought, the more efficacious it will be, at least in the eye of the purchaser, and that is all that matters. I have found this principle to be applied with great success by the foreign painters who from time to time visit our shores. The more they charge for their second-rate works, the more merit is perceived in them.

7

MOTHER, Mary and little Anne produced gripe ointment as fast as I could provide the pots, while father worked at his play, complaining at every noise or distraction, constantly appealing to us not to talk.

As for me, I would emerge from our quarters in Black and White Court every morning with a wheelbarrow full of Mrs Hogarth's Patent Gripe Ointment – a most noble and very safe medicine! My sales perambulation began at Newgate Market, but then I would bend my route to walk down Paternoster Row, standing as a mute dot beneath the wonder of St Paul's, staring up at the highest stone on the cupola, newly laid by the great Sir Christopher Wren in person.

Then on, drawing lines in my mind from the premises of one apothecary to the next, with some toyshops, too. And I was not above bawling my wares, as I trundled them along.

'Gripe ointment! Cures the gripes in young children! Prevents fits! One half-crown pot and your child is past all danger!'

I kept a weather eye out for footpads, who would no doubt delight in robbing me of my wares, as well as the money from them. Just once, I saw a bunch of them up ahead, but resolved to brazen it out.

'Good morrow, gentlemen,' I cried, looking them in the eyes as I trundled my wheelbarrow past them.

'What you got there, little man?' said one of them, a gnarled old fellow.

'Ointment,' said I, without breaking my stride. 'Cure you of your gripes.'

That started all the footpads laughing. They left me in peace, so I learned early the lesson that a droll little fellow who weakens and disarms his enemies by making them laugh comes through all right.

I quickly found the spots where the gentry would wait for a hackney, from the bottom of Ludgate Hill to the Puddle Dock stairs. From here, the lighters put out to the billowing ships moored in the middle of the river. Sometimes, on fine summer days, I followed the curves of the Thames, just for fun, taking sales of my medicine as they came on the stitches lining the river bank.

Father sat at his table in his shabby dressing gown, wig awry, surrounded by books, unsharpened quills and three quires of white paper, far more than he needed. In front of him, screwed up once and opening out of its own will, as if to mock him, was a letter. It said, 'Sir, I have read your play and find it will not do.' It was the fifth such letter he had received. There were five theatres in London.

Mother shrugged, sniffed, coughed and fidgeted while mending his holey hose. She was a mass of tiny movements, forever in motion, forever uncomfortable, forever making me uncomfortable. Why do we love one parent more than the other? I know of nobody who has achieved symmetry, so to speak, in this regard. And often enough there is no rhyme or reason behind love's alighting on one of the two in this way. Whatever mother did on this earth, I would love father more.

Our benefactor, Mr da Costa, paid for an advertisement in the *Daily Courant*, so that purchasers could come to our room in Black and White Court for their medicine. I was amazed at how powerful this advertisement was to prove. A stream of purchasers appeared, leaving us merely to take their money and give them a pot of ointment. How simple! I learned another lesson: that advertisements influence men.

Mr da Costa also told me of a chamber pot maker who could supply us with small pewter pots. Until now, the finding and purchasing of pots had been the biggest problem with our venture.

My father was pacing the tiny confines of our room, animatedly explaining a letter he had written. He spoke in the strange staccato style he had lately adopted, so quickly we could barely follow him.

'My situation, you see, is a microcosm of that of the country,' he flung his arm out at an odd angle, like a drowning orator. 'The country is bowed under a huge national debt, as am I. In both cases undeserved, but that is not the meat of it.'

He stopped in the middle of the room, staring at us wild-eyed.

'Who is your letter addressed to, father?' I asked him.

'Why, to Harley, who else? Robert Harley, the Chancellor of the Exchequer. I am sharing my solutions with him. All the Crown needs to do, you see, is to make and sell its own products to pay off the national debt, as we have done.

For our debt, I have included some details and ideas and assistance of a practical nature. Here ...' he hit the letter, 'I say, for example ...'

'You are ripe for Bedlam,' mother said, matter-of-factly.

I glanced at my sisters. Mary looked worried, little Anne merely curious.

I sighed. 'Why don't you send the letter, father?' I said. 'Here, give it to me. I will give it to the turnkey, to ensure it is sent in good time.'

I did this, and similarly with the next letter to Robert Harley, and the next. Father insisted on reading them all aloud to us, as they grew more and more intemperate. The later letters were in Latin, as he was convinced that people at court were stealing his ideas, but he translated them to us, always pacing the length of our tiny room, the while.

'I would run to you through the window if I could, but I cannot, so I beg for your pity. Ignorant butchers and cobblers are stealing my ideas, but I know you will treat these criminals with the disdain they deserve.'

By now, I was the only one of his possible audience still listening; the women were all busying themselves making the gripe ointment, completely ignoring him.

'Here I am gaoled by perverse misfortune and my soul wastes away under the weight of those twenty-two children, those born to me, those entrusted to me and still living.'

My mother looked up at that, her face an angry mask. Twenty-two? How many of my brothers and sisters had died? I knew some had. There was a Richard. Another Anne. But not that many surely? Did he mean his books were his children?

'Give me the letter, father,' I said. 'I will see it safely on its way, as I have done with the others.'

I went to see Mr da Costa the next day. My head was full of my family's business but my body was rigid, breathing shallow, with dreams of Kate and the hope of seeing her again. There was no trace of her, though, and of course I did not dare ask after her. Business it was then, in Mr da Costa's magnificent parlour.

'We need to lighten your family's load,' he said. 'William, have you ever thought about your own future?'

'You mean an apprenticeship, sir?'

'That is exactly what I mean,' said Moses da Costa, gravely.

'Well, sir, my talent is for drawing. So I could be apprenticed to an engraver, where I could earn some money from the skill.'

'How old are you now?'

'Sixteen, sir.'

'High time, then. I will find you one.'

It was soon arranged that I was to become the apprentice of one Ellis Gamble, engraver. Mr da Costa then found a milliner's shop in the Cloisters in St Bartholomew's, where my sisters were to work before taking it over completely with Mr da Costa's finance, when they were old enough and had learned the trade.

Soon after this plan was put into action, my father faded into nothingness peacefully, still sound of mind, though only just: made tranquil by the securing of his children's future. He died at his table, working on a new play and with an unfinished letter to Robert Harley, Chancellor of the Exchequer, clutched in his fist.

I showed little reaction, outwardly, to the world. But this I knew with full certainty – the storm cut its groove in my head for all to see, but my dear father's death cut a groove in my heart which nobody could see, and which never stopped bleeding.

Part II

From Gamble to Rich
1714–32

1

AN APPRENTICE! I was an ap-PREN-tice! Oh, what a fine fellow I was as I strutted and swaggered my way, shoulders swinging, along the Hay Market and then James Street en route to Blue Cross Street, hard by Leicester Fields. Apprentices started most of the riots in London, and finished the rest. Slit your nose soon as look at you, me! I glared down the length of James Street, hoping for a riot I could join.

No luck yet, but perhaps it was too early in the morning. The bells of the French Church had not yet chimed out five, which was as well because that was the time I was to report for my work. I shifted my box, with its leather handle, from one hand to the other. The box contained my clothes and books, plus some food my sisters packed for me. All my earthly possessions, ready to be transferred to the home of the man to whom I had assigned my life for the next five years. My master, so to speak.

In Blue Cross Street I glanced at the advertisements festooning the walls. A drawing of a bear advertising a nearby beargarden was especially fine; so too a portrait of the boxer James Figg, advertising his famous amphitheatre, where Soho met the Oxford Road.

Ahead of me, there, hung the sign of my master; below a huge winged figure, against a cerulean sky with creamy clouds there was the legend 'Ellis Gamble, Goldsmith. At the sign of the Angel, Blue Cross Street. Makes, buys and sells all sorts of plates, rings and jewels, etc.' The sign was swaying slightly as a breeze blew down the street.

I ducked under the sign and went in. I was breathless and half-tumescent from thoughts of Kate, the bawd at da Costa's, as I heaved my box onto my shoulder, the more to give an impression of manly strength. I announced myself:

'Here I am,' I said. 'William Hogarth. Apprentice.'

I had met Ellis Gamble once before, when I visited Anthony da Costa's establishment to sign papers of indenture, which had been torn in half thereafter, I keeping my half, now tucked away at the bottom of my box, Ellis Gamble taking the other half. The bargain was signed and sealed with a handshake and a glass of sherry.

Even then, at that first meeting, I had called my master 'Stout Gamble' in my head. I don't know why, except that he was moderately stout, though not excessively so. Like many people who mimic others' voices, I was much given to nicknames. Some of these names I never gave voice to, they lived in a silent place in my head. Other names I said aloud, but to the fellow's face, always to his face. I have always prided myself on saying nothing behind a man's back that I would not look him in the eye and say.

Stout Gamble was not more than a dozen years older than me. He greeted me warmly and promptly introduced me to the other two apprentices in his care. I had been looking forward to this moment, as I was by nature a sociable soul, growing itchily restless and gloomy when too much alone.

'This here's Bill,' said Stout Gamble, as I laid the burden of my possessions on the floor, the better to shake hands. 'He's Bill Hogarth. Come to join us.'

I felt a stab of wary fear, puncturing the bubble of my pleasure at meeting them. They were young! Younger than me. That meant they were ahead of me. Ahead of me already and I had only just arrived …

'This here's Stephen,' Stout Gamble continued the introductions: Stephen Fowler, a genial youth with an interestingly large nose and sticking-out red ears. Stephen, soon to be known as Birdcatcher, turned at his desk and smiled at me. 'Hello Bill.' We shook hands.

'And this 'ere's Felix Pellett. 'Ee's French, but we don't 'old that against 'im, do we Felix?'

Felix nodded to me from his desk at the far end of the room. 'You got no choice,' he said, speaking directly to me, ignoring Stout Gamble. 'All the best engravers are French.' He laughed. He had laughter and smile lines round his mouth and grooved in his cheeks, in a handsome, attractive face.

'Will you teach me French, please, Felix?' I said.

Felix looked surprised, his fine face appearing smaller as it creased. He hesitated a second, then said '*Avec plaisir, mon brave.*'

'Does that mean "with pleasure"?'

Felix looked solemn. 'Yes, it does. You are a quick learner, Bill. I'll teach you engraving as well, if you like.'

'Big 'ead!' said Stout Gamble, genially.

Felix stuck his tongue out at him and, to my amazement, put his thumbs to

44

his ears and wiggled his fingers: a gesture I had not seen before. Birdcatcher, the Fowler boy, weighed in with a farting noise, which may possibly have come from a genuine fart.

The other two apprentices were also living at the Gamble establishment, so we would be together night and day.

'Tell 'im the rules, Stephen,' said Stout Gamble, rubbing a hand round his stomach.

'Work from five in the morning till seven at night,' Birdcatcher said. 'No dice, no cards, no football, no mumming and dancing ...'

'What about going to the theatre?' I said, staring Stout Gamble in the eye.

Gamble shrugged. 'Tha's all right. If you got nothing better to do.'

'I like theatre.'

Stout Gamble looked serious. 'We don't have flash dressers here,' he said, with a nod at my mustard-yellow waistcoat. 'And get your 'air cut.'

'Can't afford it.'

A moment's silence. Then ... 'I'll do it for you.' It was Felix Pellett.

'Thanks Felix,' I said, with an air of studied nonchalance, which made everyone laugh.

Amid further hilarity, centring on disrespect for Stout Gamble, which did not seem to worry him greatly, I was shown to my new desk.

I had light coming in from the left, via 5 by 5 panes of mullioned glass, and light came in straight ahead through a plain glass Dutch sash window. A sloping mirror, burnished to perfection, was tied to the top of the sash window by a cord. The other two apprentices were engraving at such a mirror when I came in. On the oak work desk were a range of engraving tools, some of which I recognised and some not, and a vice.

I sat at my new place of work, perfectly content, leaning forwards a little: the better to admire myself in my new sloping mirror. Gamble and the two apprentices burst out laughing at my vanity. I joined in.

'Let's see what you can do, then.' Gamble spoke casually enough, but this was my first piece of work. Felix Pellett and Stephen Fowler were silent, the atmosphere gathering with tension.

The silversmith had already cast the plate, which sat in front of me, beautiful and baleful, reflected in my mirror. The outline of the shield had already been engraved on the silver, as had the ornate rectangle which would carry the motto. I was to subdivide the shield into four quadrants: one line down, one line across.

I remembered my drawing lessons with John Dalton, the painter, and all the gods and goddesses we reproduced, both Roman and Greek. But I also remembered how he always corrected my line afterwards. No correction here; the engraved line would be carved in silver, as fixed as the groove in my head.

I saw my thick, stubby fingers, sausages, not the elegant cords that Felix Pellett had. Even my short, thick, sturdy body was wrong. Oh, I was cast wrong for this! I shut my eyes, drew breath, opened my eyes again and began the downward cut.

'Good boy,' Felix said. He had appeared behind me. 'Just a little harder, that's all.'

Could this new life have been wrong for me? I gritted my teeth and made once-and-for-all cuts, as fixed as God's design for sinners. I felt my father watching me.

'That'll do,' grunted Stout Gamble, as I fell back in my seat, exhausted by the scraping of two lines. 'Not the best I've ever seen, but not the worst either.'

Mediocrity? I would take it then, and with gratitude.

Over the next few weeks, I learned that the very mechanical repetition of the work held the key to competence, if not excellence. For the lifeless griffin of heraldry remained the same when scratched into the handles of a hundred different tankards, salvers, knives, forks and spoons. Copying was merely pouring water out of one vessel into another. So, needs must, I mastered the *griffin per fess argent*; I mastered the *wyvern gulles collared*.

Yes, Felix was still more precise, elegantly so, and Stephen the Birdcatcher faster. But I was not so far behind. I could chase and burnish; I could do the cross-hatch; I could do the double cypher. I had mastered the mechanics of my trade, but I found it a barren and unprofitable study.

Stout Gamble disappeared every day to the tavern or the mughouse: a vote of confidence in its way. We apprentices worked alone. But they were younger than me! I was still haunted by that. Felix and Stephen. They were YOUNGER than me!

And I was falling to earth faster than Icarus; Stout Gamble said I was 'too quick, too rough' with my little, fat fingers. I could not manage the delicate tintos; I could not manage the proper reticulations of scroll foliage. All of this stuff had to be passed to Felix, and when he was busy, to Stephen. This was always to be so. My younger companions were to remain fixed ahead of me. This squat tortoise was never to catch the elegant hares. It was mortifying, let me tell you. Mortifying!

I took refuge in drawing. I drew Mrs Stout Gamble in her Oudenarde attire. I drew laughing griffins and dancing lions. I took revenge on my dead subjects by making them live. My gambadoes on their hind legs made Stephen and Felix laugh.

Laughing Felix showed me an etching by Jacques Callot called *The Temptation of St Anthony*. So much action and detail there, so much GOING ON. It was a wondrous revelation.

I pleaded with Frenchy, as I now called Felix, to show me more works by Callot. He laughed once more and said I must understand that one first. I sulked and snubbed him. He smiled, ruffled my hair and called me 'Beely Boy' in that Frenchie accent of his. He spoke more and more French to me. I could usually understand.

'Buying shares,' announced Stout Gamble in a basso rumble, 'is like playing loo, faro or basset, with the gratifying difference that you cannot lose.'

He peered over my shoulder as I worked, struggling into his coat before going off to a coffee house. 'Let Felix do the motto, Bill. Your letters is shaky. I ain't risking it.'

'I'm good at letters,' I protested.

'Felix is better. Do what I say or I'll clip you round the ear. Take breeding silkworms in Chelsea Park, for example.' Stout Gamble adjusted his wig, then stood with his arms akimbo.

'What? What are you talking about?'

'Can't lose. Take a wheel that goes round forever. Wonderful thing, science. And there's a scheme I'm in, making fresh water from the sea. I'll buy you boys in, if you like. There's an offer for you.'

Felix smiled, his pretty, small features creasing.

'Goldmines in Peru,' I said. 'Goldmines in Peru, all of it.'

'Eh? What's that? Shows how much you know, Billy Boy. Mr Walpole is about to get them for England, them goldmines. He's swopping Gibraltar and Port Mahon for 'em. Hot news that is.'

I put my salver down. 'Oh, you are the very prince of jesters, Mr Gamble.'

'You get on with your work, Bill. Enough of your sauce. What about you?' Gamble was addressing jug-eared Stephen. 'Fancy a wager, boy? Fancy a stake?'

'No money, Mr Gamble,' said the Fowler boy, without breaking off from his engraving.

'No ambition, more like!' Stout Gamble shook his head in mock despair. 'See, there's the difference between you boys and me. England's on a ride to riches and I'm aboard. Richer and richer! No need to work. Work is for donkeys.'

'Thank you very much!' I said. 'Go off to your coffee, Mr Gamble. Us donkeys'll pull your cart for you.'

Felix laughed; Gamble joined in, before giving us an extravagant wave goodbye.

'What we going to do this evening?' I said, as soon as he'd gone.

I counted the minutes till the evening's entertainment as soon as I got up. I pictured it in my head, clear as life, to get me through the engraving drudgery. What I really wanted, that evening, was a whorehouse or a bagnio, as the pressure in my member weighed heavy. But I was still shy with Frenchy and Birdcatcher, though I liked them both, and too afraid to go alone. So I suggested the theatre.

That evening, then, I dressed in my scarlet waistcoat and gold lace hat. No fustian for me, thank you Mr Ellis-Stout Gamble! Arm in arm, we three companions strode to Lincoln's Inn Fields, singing sea shanties as we went, feeling like royalty ourselves on the way to the Theatre Royal. The place was packed, not to mention stinking; a short-arse like me could barely see. A sword fight broke out on the stage before the play even started, with us lustily cheering on the winner.

The play itself, when it finally got started, turned out to be a piece called *The Man's The Master*, which was obvious enough. And very dreary it was, except for some of the singing and dancing, which I always enjoyed. But about ten minutes into the spectacle, I recognised a figure on the stage. She was veiled, she was shrouded, which was a pity as she was clearly full-breasted, and she had hardly spoken. But I knew her; I knew I knew her.

'I shall write that actress a billet,' I shouted in Frenchy's ear, above the din. 'I am acquainted with her.'

Frenchy laughed. 'I think you confuse the desire with the reality,' he shouted back.

While the dreary mumming continued on stage I pulled out a sheet of the paper I always carried for sketching, together with a crayon.

'Madam ...' I wrote. 'Pray cast your mind back to Fenton's Coffee House where, some years ago, I had the pleasure of making your acquaintance when you were but a child, and so was I. You wore, as I recall ...' and then I sketched her yellow brocaded dress with the red roses. 'And very fetching, too. My two companions and I would like to meet you after the entertainment and have a drink with you, to talk over old times.'

Birdcatcher and Frenchy read my billet as I printed out the letters with difficulty in the swaying crowd, with people constantly banging into me. The Fowler boy, who was a little drunk, gave a whoop as I wrote the invitation part of my billet.

'Good for you, Bill,' he said, solemnly. 'And, why not?'

I led the way as we pushed ourselves into a five-shilling box seat we had not paid for. There, I found a footman who was keeping a place for his mistress for the afterpiece and offered him two pennies to take the letter to Miss Lavinia Fenton, who, as luck would have it, was just walking off the stage. The footman got his colleague in the same livery to keep his lady's place, and agreed to run my errand.

'That's the last you see of your *monnai*, Bill,' said Felix-Frenchy, through his grin.

But that showed how much he knew. The footman was back just as Lavinia came onto the stage again. She had returned my billet, but with a scrawl at the bottom saying we should come to the side entrance after the performance.

'See!' I cried in triumph. 'See! I am a person of substance after all!'

Frenchy and Birdcatcher clapped me on the back for my triumph. And Lavinia even remembered me, when we saw her at the actors' entrance.

'You was with your dad, right? You're ... wait a minute ...?'

'William! William Hogarth.'

'Tha's right!'

'And these are my friends, Felix Pellett and Stephen Fowler.'

'Pleased to meet you, I'm sure.' There was a silence. My triumph had rendered Birdcatcher and Frenchy speechless. 'Well, where we going then? This acting lark don't half make me hungry. I could eat a bloody horse, and no mistake.'

'There's a chop house near here,' I said. 'Would you care to ...?'

'Too bloody right I would. Excuse me boys, but you *are* paying, aren't you? I'm just a hireling, you know. We don't earn much.'

'Of course!' I said, so earnestly the other two laughed. 'It is our pleasure, Miss Fenton. *Avec plaisir.*'

'Good accent,' said Frenchy, drily.

'You can cut the "Miss Fenton". It's plain Lavinia to you, William.'

I offered my arm. She took it with an elegant flourish. We skirted the fringe of Lincoln's Inn Fields to Portugal Row, with my companions trotting along behind. I looked up to the heavens, silently beseeching my father to look at me now. OH, JUST LOOK AT ME NOW!

2

M Y VIRGIN state was causing me much anguish. How could I strut the streets – bully-boy apprentice, emergent artist, yellow-waistcoated dandy, fine fellow of London town – when I had not rogered a woman of real flesh and blood? My dreams told me clearly what I had not done: dreams of Kate, now dreams of Lavinia. But the fact remained that I had not done it. This had to change, and it had to change that very night.

London boasted a girl for every wallet. There were places – Catherine Street, Drury Lane, Fleet Street – where the crowds of harlots were thicker than a Spitalfields weavers' riot. I wanted one, just one, and I wanted her for the night; no hoisted-skirts bunter up against the wall for me, thank you very much.

We settled on Lovejoy's bagnio, my companions and I. But first we dined on whole breast of veal at the dear old Bedford Arms. There, over a large glass of porter, and in a spirit of good fellowship, I confessed my unwanted burden to my companions, Stephen Fowler and Felix Pellett.

I regretted it instantly. Frenchy told me that my beauty was only for the connoisseur, while ruffling my hair. I bit his hand, hard, and yelled at him hotly to desist. He licked the blood I had drawn on his hand and stared at me with burning, small black eyes. He looked mad. I memorised his face.

Stephen the Birdcatcher, the most drunk of us, as usual, told the tale of his own first time with a girl. He was of a wealthy family. To hear him tell it, a maid shared his bed in his boyhood, taking his member in her mouth every night, finally sliding it home.

'I was nine years old at the time,' said Stephen, slyly.

'Oh, shut up!' I shouted, ready to walk out on both of them.

Instead, we all left the Bedford Arms, but drunken Stephen turned the wrong way outside. I steered him by the shoulder past Old Hummums Hotel, which also had bawds outside it, to Lovejoy's bagnio in Russell Street.

This was the place Stephen himself recommended, though he now appeared to have no recollection of that. As Stephen and I were going in, Frenchy surprisingly took his leave, with sudden excuses about 'work tomorrow'.

'Come back!' I shouted after him. 'Oh, run off then, you foreign spoilsport!' I picked up a pebble from the street and slung it at Frenchy's departing back, but missed him. 'Come on, Stephen,' I said.

We went in, Stephen and I.

As we entered the bagnio, we were enveloped by a cloud of steam from the baths. We were met in the vestibule by Mother Douglas herself, on the lookout, no doubt, for new flesh among the customers as much as new flesh to add to the stock of ladies.

'Now here's a couple of handsome young blades! A right couple of gallants and no mistake. My girls are truly in luck tonight. What's it to be then, gentlemen? A turn at the baths, a nice rub down with a nice rub up? Or how about some refreshment while you sit and think about it? A glass of champagne perhaps, or punch? Or we have some good Queen of Scots soup on tonight, just made. Warms your pickle against the cold of the night. Tell me what you fancy, young sirs. This is your home from home.'

The Mother waved at the somewhat faded plush couches and chairs where we were invited to disport ourselves. The Fowler boy, sobering, or so it appeared, named two girls from a list, speaking nonchalantly like a connoisseur, or a cunnyseur, as I had heard it called. I glanced admiringly at him. He no longer appeared jug-eared and ruddy-cheeked: less like a teapot altogether, suddenly the *homme du monde* – a phrase I had learned from the departed Frenchy Pellett.

Mother Douglas opened wide her eyes, agog with admiration at the Man Who Knew His Own Will So Well.

'Charlotte Kennedy is no longer with us,' she purred smoothly. 'But you can have Fanny Burton. And there's a new girl, Gertrude Eliot, just up from the country and closed as the day God made her. Just waiting for you.'

For some reason, this last phrase was addressed to me, as she gazed down at me, for she was a good head taller.

'Huh!' I said knowingly, having heard from Stephen of a bawd's deceit with a sponge soaked in pig's blood, which enabled the lass to re-sell her precious seal nightly, and on occasion more often than that.

'Huh!' I repeated, so there was no doubt I saw through the ruse.

'Do you have the ague, sir?' said Mother Douglas, solicitously. 'The soup is very good for a chest cough.'

'Bring me to Fanny Burton, please, good Mother,' I commanded, forcefully. 'And something similar for my companion.'

I pressed my half-guinea into Mother Douglas's practiced hand, whereupon I was led upstairs to a corridor of rooms. I forgot all about Stephen Fowler. Mother Douglas knocked on a door, called out and I was bade enter. In a sparse, darkened room sat Fanny Burton, I assumed, on a bed, legs crossed, wearing only black stockings, red garters and a linen shift.

The door closed behind me.

'Good evening, sir,' said Fanny, waving a stockinged leg in welcome.

Fanny was dark-haired with lustrous dark eyes, but with the alabaster skin more common in redheads, which made a dramatic contrast. She was smaller than Lavinia Fenton, with more compact features, especially her nose and mouth, but otherwise the resemblance was close, which pleased me. I thought of her as fascinating Lavinia, but more easily available.

With a sinuous wriggle of her shoulders, one of her snowy beauties was free of the shift, then the other. Wondrous! Oh, wondrous! Her bubbies were perfect-small, perfect-high-round, like cupping glasses, like peaches made of snow. The lovely bud-nipples were pointing different ways. And around the nipples, lovely rings of salmon pink. What were they? In all the art I had seen, I did not recall these rings of wonder, leading the eye and – oh, bliss! – the hand to the lovely, puckering points.

'My name is William,' I said.

'Is it, now?' she said, her eyes widening at the news. 'Would you like to kiss me, William?'

As we kissed, a final shimmer saw her shift on the floor. I touched her neck, the perfect, round shoulders, so white they had blues buried deep. And then, the greatest long pleasure in any man's life, I touched the orbs of bliss, the firm flesh of delight, first the right and then the left.

'Put this on.'

'What? What! What is it?'

She giggled. 'It's a condom, silly. Gives me a right tickle. Oh, come here! I'll do it.'

She hauled my breeches down, then slipped the furry sheath, like a brown caterpillar, over my agonised member, grown puce with withheld desire. Thus attired, she pushed me home. She was kind and by gentle holds, grips and pushes, caused me to prolong my slow ecstasy. I mounted, I pushed, I thrusted, I came. Exploded.

I was dozing, moments later, when a remarkable scene was played out before me. First, the door burst open and a young fellow in a nightshirt and nightcap charged in, carrying his clothes. As Fanny screamed, he was followed by a woman in her shift and mob cap who was shouting 'Run John, run!'

The man addressed as John made for the window of Fanny's room, as a third party entered, sword drawn. This latest addition to the sudden crowd in our room sported an elegant silver frock-coat, a Spencer wig and boasted large silver buckles covering three quarters of his shoes. I drew the curtains to our bed, muffling Fanny's screams, and hoisted up my breeches as frock-coat caught nightshirt and made to run him through.

The woman in her shift and cap screamed 'No!' and then 'Run, John!' and threw herself on her knees in front of frock-coat, impeding him from running nightshirt through. By then I realised that nightshirt had taken a room at the bagnio to be with the woman, who was no doubt frock-coat's wife.

'Hey!' I shouted. 'Stop all this, leave this room at once!'

But frock-coat and nightshirt were struggling over the sword, with the woman still on her knees between them, her arms round frock-coat's legs. I do not know if she intended thus to hamper frock-coat, but that was the effect of her actions. In the struggle, the sword turned into frock-coat's chest: he groaned, he bled, and he lay there, mortally wounded.

At that moment, the constable and two men of the watch appeared at the door.

Nightshirt picked his pile of clothes from off the floor and thrust them at me. His face was close to mine. He was blonde, with the pasty flesh of dissipation and pale watery-blue eyes, bloodshot and somewhat protuberant.

'I'll collect them tomorrow,' he breathed, with remarkable composure in the circumstances, nodding at the clothes. 'Hide them till then. Where will you be?'

'At Ellis Gamble's, the engraver,' I said. 'It's my place of work.'

'I know it,' he said.

I thrust nightshirt's clothes under the bed covers, provoking a squawk from Fanny. Just as the constable and his men entered the room, nightshirt dived out of the window and the woman on her knees, realising her husband was dead, commenced howling like a banshee.

Chapter 2

The constable was a plump fellow with a lantern and a stave. He waddled to the window, ignoring the howls of the widow, as I supposed, on the floor. Putting down his stave, he held onto his battered felt hat to stop it falling off and peered into darkness through the gale of wind coming through the window.

'After him!' he bellowed, to the two fellows of the watch: lanky, cretinous looking individuals, both of them. And with that, the watch left the room, followed by the plump one at a lumbering trot.

Mother Douglas entered shortly afterwards, not outwardly discomfited. 'That was John Rakesby,' she sighed, nodding at the open window through which the blonde, dissipated and clothesless one lately exited. 'There's always trouble when he comes.'

Fanny emerged from the hinterland of the bed, pleasantly pink, and put her shift back on. 'I think it is best that you leave now, William,' she said. 'The constable will come back, no doubt, for this fine fellow.' She indicated the corpse on the floor, blood staining from red to black on his white silk shirt. 'Come back and see us soon, though, won't you? It will be *such* a pleasure.' She fluttered her eyelashes at me.

I nodded, smiled, gathered John Rakesby's clothes together, kissed Fanny goodbye and walked slowly to the door. Stephen appeared and we left together, after a more than usually memorable night.

3

WE NEVER SAW Stout Gamble at the Gamble home, for the noble Mrs G, calm as a millpond, settled the minimal living needs of we scruffy little band of apprentices. Gamble would first appear at ten in the morning at the emporium which bore his name, freshly minted to spend himself on the demands of the day. There he would find a veritable tick-tock of working activity, which, unbeknown to Stout Gamble, was all of five minutes old: having wound itself up just before we knew he was coming.

He saw me engraving a wyvern, a beast I detest, the more so as it never existed. I have a marked prejudice in favour of forms of life which actually live. The repeated engraving of wyverns was an activity designed to constrict and finally crush the human spirit. It was only Frenchy doing so much of my work that kept my élan up and stopped me running feral, and I shall forever be grateful to him.

Stout Gamble, then, evidently unaware of the regularity and predictability of his plod through life, would hold forth at something past ten in the morning.

'What price work, then?' rumbled Gamble, from his customary place at the doorway, hand in waistcoat, overseeing eyes. '£100 South Sea stock worth £126 at Christmas. And now new dividends at thirty per cent voted. The company is so rich it has taken over the national debt. Anyone who is not a complete fool will be richer than Croesus in a year.'

'Not for me,' I piped up, thankfully dropping my engraving tool. 'I'm putting my money in Puckle's Defence Gun: fires round bullets against Christians and square bullets against the unbelieving Turks.'

Frenchy laughed, staring Gamble in the eye. Stephen snorted, head down at his work.

Gamble gave me a long look, then a volley of rapid blinks.

'That's as may be, Bill,' was Gamble's ponderous summation of the situation.

He gave his belly a final rub, his throat a final clear, then rolled out of his emporium to hoots of laughter before the door had even closed.

'Bugger wyverns,' quoth I, at the shade of my departed employer.

I made an impatient cut at the silver; it was obviously crooked. 'Damn! Oh Lord, it's ruined. Gamble will kick me out.'

'Let me see.' Frenchy came over, stared judiciously at my clumsy groove. 'We can make that line the top line of the scroll. Thicken it a bit. Give it to me. I'll do it.'

I handed the salver over. 'Thanks Felix. You're a life-saver and no mistake.'

'That's all right! I bought you something.'

He had something hidden behind his back. He displayed it, flourishing and waving like a conjuror. It was a well-thumbed book with a black cover.

'Etchings,' he said, 'by Jacques Callot. You must look at all his pictures of the war. There is the movement you always talk about.'

I nodded. 'I'll look at it later,' I said.

'Look at it whenever you like. It's a present, *cherie. Parce que je t'aime.*'

'What?'

'Because you are my friend.'

'Why, thank you, Monsieur Pellett!'

'You are most welcome, Monsieur Hogarth.'

Stephen and I laughed because he pronounced it 'O-Gart', like I was an Irishman.

Felix got on with my work while I pulled out the drawing I had hidden under the desk at Gamble's coming. I no longer drew from life at all, instead training myself to memorise a scene, then sketch the story of it later, as soon as the engraved images of the pestilential beasts of mythology could be put aside.

This particular drawing of mine celebrated the denizens of Button's Coffee House. I was pleased with it; it excited me. Three verticals, pillars if you like: the first, a sober citizen with a fine full-bottom periwig, tricorn hat on the table. The middle, shorter vertical was formed by a little man standing and a bigger one sitting opposite him, so that he had his black-inked back to the viewer. The third pillar was a cadaverous gent who was pulling the little man's shoulder, his sheathed sword emphasising the vertical.

There were two diagonals: sober citizen's staff and the cadaverous man's arm. But here's the rub, the little man facing us was talking, he had his mouth open but we could not quite see what cadaverous was doing with his hand – so our narrative was open, our story to be completed in the imagination of the viewer.

It was a brilliant construct. Brilliant! The world should see that drawing soon, recognise its greatness, seize me and pluck me from the repetitious grooving of bloodless beasts and Latin tags. Come on! Come on!'

Frenchy Pellett came to stand behind me, hands on my shoulders, one hand sliding up to caress my neck. He looked at my drawing.

'Well?' I said. 'Is it not magnificent? Brilliant?'

'Not far off,' he said, his accent thick. 'You are an artist, Bill, no doubt of that.'

At that point the door opened with a ding of the bell. We dashed back to mime working, thinking we had a customer. It was John Rakesby, the dissolute one from Lovejoy's bagnio, fresh from killing a man, come for his clothes, no doubt.

Rakesby had the same aura of apartness I remembered from the hectic events at the bagnio, as if his essence was elsewhere and what remained to us in the room was a pictorial representation. That did not stop him greeting me and then Stephen Fowler cordially enough. Frenchy, of course, he had not met, though Monsieur Pellett was aware of the events at Lovejoy's, as Stephen and I had told the story several times, in our excitement at it all.

'John Rakesby!' I cried. 'This is my good friend and companion, Felix Pellett. Felix – John.'

John and Felix shook hands solemnly, for all the world as if Frenchy was ceding Calais all over again.

Stephen, the while, who was becoming increasingly clown-like, was holding John's waistcoat over his chest. 'Nice stuff,' he murmured, to nobody in particular.

I gathered John's clothing from where it was screwed up in a ball beneath the shelf at my feet. It comprised his drawers, his white silk stockings, buckled shoes, calico shirt, three-cornered hat, wig, blue cloth coat with gold braiding and buttons. I handed the lot over to him, then rescued his waistcoat from Stephen and handed that over, too.

John took it expressionlessly and stuffed it in a linen bag he had presumably brought for the purpose. I noticed that the set of clothes he had on now were every bit as fine as those he was collecting.

'No sign of my sword, I suppose,' he muttered, in that absent manner I was already getting used to.

'Never saw a sword, John,' I said, cheerily.

'Stephen? A sword?'

The Birdcatcher shook his head.

'No sword,' I confirmed. 'Will you stay and take a drink with us, John? We would invite you to a coffee house or a tavern or something, but if we do that one of us must stay here in case a customer comes, or even our esteemed employer, unlikely though that is.'

John laughed good-naturedly. 'I'll happily stay here with you good fellows,' he said, 'and whatever refreshment you can provide. Or indeed none.'

We broke open some bottles of beer and swigged from them, sitting in a circle.

'What happened?' I asked John. 'At the bagnio. That chap, you know, he's …'

'Yes, I know,' said John. Then he paused to gulp beer. 'That was not meant to happen. A jealous husband, I'm afraid.' He shrugged, as if indicating a routine hazard of his profession, like burns on the hand for a baker or drowning for a waterman. 'I have no idea how he found out where we were. Mother Douglas, perhaps. If he paid her more shillings than I do.'

'Yo-ho!' I cried. 'You're a merry one and no mistake.'

'In truth, I am rather sad,' said John, and looked it.

'I steer clear of married women,' said Stephen. 'Too complicated.'

'I wish to marry a girl with a rich father,' I said. 'How about you, Felix?'

Frenchy shrugged. 'No marriage for me,' he said. 'Just beauty. Beauty in art, sometimes in people, but mainly in art.'

'Well said,' I said, for no particular reason. 'Come, come now, we must plan our next expedition. So, where are we going then?'

For theatre it was not too difficult to get up a party, Felix was always among the first to agree, Stephen less enthusiastic. My new friend, John Rakesby, preferred the brothels but would genially agree to other plans when pressed. He was my guide to the girls, with Stephen sometimes joining us at that sport, but Felix never.

Going to see paintings was the most difficult to get companions for: nobody being terribly keen. Felix Pellett continued to teach me about Callot, occasionally joining me on my pilgrimages to St Paul's, though not as often as I wished. John came along now and again, Stephen Fowler never.

At St Paul's, I worshipped the paintings of our great *English* painter, Sir James Thornhill. There, above us, a sequence on the life of St Paul, in the vast upturned eggshell of the cupola.

'Magnificent!' I gasped to John and Felix, my breath leaving my body at the wondrousness of it. 'St Paul before Agrippa. There! Look! Look! You see how he puts a frame between the viewer and the action? You see how the eye is drawn in and back, to that Palladian building in the background?'

John nodded, palely. He did not say much, being usually too exhausted from drink and debauchery to offer a lot in the way of opinion. Felix peered up judiciously, as if this was the first time we had ever been there, which it was not.

'It's not bad,' he said, with a shrug. 'Competent execution, grisaille is always effective, grouping of the figures perhaps too close.'

'Too close ... competent ...?' I squared up to him, my fists clenched, further enraged by his knowing smile. 'How dare you damn our great *English* painter with faint praise?'

There was a pause. Felix gave a faint, thin-lipped smile.

'All right, who do you like, then, Frenchy?'

Felix shrugged in that world-weary way he knew infuriated me. 'Chardin,' he murmured.

'Chardin!' I shouted, so loud my voice echoed round the gallery, back down and along the nave. 'When I compare ... Very well, who is he?'

Felix laughed. 'I will show you some Chardin.'

'Thank you,' I said, humbly.

'And I will show you some etchings of the St Paul grisaille series,' said Felix, solemnly.

'Can you ...?'

'Oh, yes! They are in a book. I can borrow it, at least. We can study the detail together, if you would like that?'

I hugged him. 'You are a prince among men, Pellett the Frenchy. A prince among men.'

John was smiling quietly to himself.

Greenwich was very difficult to organise. To my disappointment, even Felix cried off. But John, when he dropped in, which he did nearly every day now, readily agreed to go. Greenwich, naturally, was important because the wondrous artistic genius Sir James Thornhill was painting the frescoes at Greenwich Hospital.

As we were rowed across the Thames on a Saturday, a choppy ride with the river at swell, John was sick all over his coat collar, down the front of his waistcoat, splashing his cravat and soaking through to his silk shirt. His wig fell off, lying at his feet as he gave the appearance of heaving up every morsel he had ever eaten in his life. As I tried to reach over to him to hold his head, a fresh stream of vomit hit the inside of his upended wig.

The boatman yelled at me to sit down, as my efforts to help John were unbalancing the little bumboat we had hired, because it was cheap. I yelled back at the boatman to hold his salty tongue and know his place. He yelled back to me that he would tip me into the sea if I as much as said another word.

It was at this point, for reasons that were not clear to me, that John told me he was a painter. The information, or confession perhaps, stopped him vomiting, so it was welcome as well as of interest to me. As we tied up, the waterman and I were still trading insults, some of the waterman's being so vivid, although anatomically dubious, that I lodged them for my own future use.

And so on to Greenwich Hospital, which turned out to be the most wondrous experience of my life to that date. Some of it was not finished; Thornhill was still working on it, so we were not allowed in those places. But there, on those walls, the wondrous Sir James Thornhill told the story in pictures of our great country's progress from the sickly mysticism and gloved threat of Catholic power to the glorious Protestant shining light, from William to our present great and glorious King George.

There, as I gazed in wonder, was good Queen Anne and her consort, supported by Hercules. There, our glorious Prince of Wales, in armour. There, if I was not mistaken, was the figure of Justice and there Juno ... And was that man, could it be, was he their creator, half turning to face the viewer, like that?

'Yes, that is the figure of James Thornhill himself, near the list of English naval victories.'

A voice had answered my unspoken question! The voice belonged to John. I must have spoken my question out loud without being aware of it, so deep was my trance before these paintings.

'Have you been here before, John?' I said absently, my eyes never leaving the paintings on the wall, my spirits soaring in a way I knew was lifting me forever.

'Oh yes,' said John, absently wiping his hat on his forearm in a forlorn attempt to clean the vomit from it. 'You see ... the issue for the painter was how real to make his representation without losing the regality and ... hence the grandeur of the subject.'

'What?'

John cleared his throat. 'Well, take the king landing in ... when was it? September 1714.' He flapped his encrusted hat at the representation of our good King George landing after his journey from Hanover. 'It was actually night, so do you paint it as night? Where's the grandeur if you can hardly see anything? Do you paint the king in full kingly regalia, although that would be ridiculous after a long sea journey? Do you paint the other ships, accompanying, guarding, thus emphasising the majesty but cluttering up the background?'

My eyes were wide. I stared up at him. 'John, how do you know all this?'

'Oh ... He used to discuss it with my sister and me. He talked about it all the time.'

'*Who* did?' I seriously wondered if our short sea journey had unhinged his mind.

'My ... Bill, there's something I haven't told you. I use the name John Rakesby in the bagnios because ... well, I get into so much trouble. But my name is really John Thornhill. Sir James Thornhill is my father. Would you like to meet him?'

4

I ALWAYS THOUGHT of my sisters as one person, not two: as Mary-Anne or Anne-Mary, not as Mary and Anne. Mary being two years older than Anne made less and less difference now they were grown women. They looked astonishingly alike, both being big, fleshy women with big jaws – far too big in Mary's case – small ears and eyes, and thin, pinched noses.

I wished them no harm, I even wished them happiness, but I wished they were not there. When they were not an irrelevance, they were a distraction from my efforts to improve my situation. They pulled me back into my past, just by being. All I wanted from my past was my father, not my mother and not them. My father lived on in me, not them. Good or bad, right or wrong, that was how matters stood. What mattered was how things were, not how we would like them to be.

But I went to see them now and again, my sisters. Why? Because I was still looking for Kate, the bawd I saw at da Costa's, who I dreamed of night and day, and my sisters' shop was nearby. My visits to the bawdy houses, bagnios and brothels with John and Stephen had started a fiery itch in me, a place where satiety was brief – satisfaction led only to further and stronger desire. More and more this slakeless thirst was for Kate. I choose bawds who resembled her, I called her name, all to no avail. It was her my nether regions craved.

But as Priapus led me to my sisters' shop, politeness at least determined some civility before I resumed my low quest. I burst open the door, roaring out my greetings as the owner as the shop bell dinged. (I was not the owner, I know that, but without me my sisters would not have found our benefactor, da Costa, so I behaved like the owner and was treated as such.)

My sisters hurried towards me, Mary leaving the stocking of shelves, Anne the attendance on a customer to do so.

'William!'

I was made much of, this was very gratifying. The attention of these two large women was like being pressed between two feather bolsters. Only when I emerged did I take pleasure in the colour of their shop: bolts of cloth, high on shelves where they could be reached only by a ladder, and finished frocks of every hue in the rainbow, some on stands which mimicked the female form. There was a riot of Genoa velvet, paduasoys, tabbies watered and unwatered, mantuas, sarsnets, Perscans and I didn't know what. Oh, the eye, queen of senses, so royally served!

But who was this?

'My name is Sarah Young, sir.'

She dropped the deepest of curtsies, even lowering her eyes to the floor, lowering, indeed, her whole head so far the nape of her neck was visible. She was plain, red in the face but full in her bosom, something that readily excited me, these days.

'We have been able to take on an assistant, William,' said Mary.

'Sarah is our assistant,' added Anne.

My sisters often spoke to me in this Greek chorus manner, with overlapping information, Anne most often adding the redundant elements.

'William Hogarth,' I said loftily, to the heaving employee, ignoring my sisters. 'I am the owner of this establishment.'

There was, as I have said, a degree of artistic licence in that statement. Anne laughed at it; Mary pursed her lips severely.

'You may stand,' I conceded magnanimously, as the wench Sarah was showing no sign of doing so, as a result growing even redder in the face from the exertion of holding her supplicant position. Her bosom really was splendid ... The wench struggled awkwardly to her feet, like a poleaxed pugilist about to leave the ring.

I ignored her, for a while. 'What of our benefactor?' I asked my sisters. 'Is he still satisfied with the arrangements?'

'Mr da Costa's clerk comes monthly to collect the rent and the repayment portion of the loan,' said Mary. 'He confesses himself happy.'

'Content with everything,' added Anne. She laughed. 'We even sold him a Kashmir shawl last time he was here, a present for his wife.'

'He has become a customer,' Mary smiled. 'And with you, William? How are ...?'

'I am already the best man at silver engraving. The best the engraver Gamble has ever had. He said the other day he was lucky to have me.'

I glanced at Sarah Young. Her eyes were still at the floor, like one not daring to look at the sun. Her red-raw hands were twisting each other at the front of her apron, beneath the swelling and heaving bosom. I tore my eyes away and looked at Anne. Should I broach …? I was shy but ploughed on.

'Did the clerk mention …?'

'I asked him, William, as you asked me to.'

'Well?' I did not mean to speak sharply, but did. I was always sharper with Anne, although she was the one, to be honest, who was closer to my heart, as she was more like me than serious Mary.

'William, things have not gone well with her.'

'Oh, get on with it!'

Mary pouted, exacerbating the jut of her chin. 'She lost Mr da Costa's protection, because of her other paramours …'

'She had other men …'

'So what happened?' I yelled. I was consumed with the need to find Kate.

'I'm telling you,' said Mary mildly. 'The clerk said she ended up in a brothel. He *thought* she was rounded up in one of Gonson's raids. But he wasn't sure.'

I tut-tutted. The newspapers were full of Sir John Gonson's attempts to clean up Covent Garden by raiding the brothels and shutting them down. Rumour had it that he was not above trying out the merchandise for himself first, so he knew exactly the nature of the evil he was opposing, which was normally the way with men of morality.

'Oh Kate, Kate. Are you all right?' I muttered, more to myself than to the ladies present. I meant the clap, more than Gonson, though naturally I could hardly have said so out loud.

'May God preserve her,' said Anne, with a sudden access of piety.

'God help her,' contributed Mary.

The poor Sarah Young creature stopped wringing her red-raw hands, and made the sign of the cross over her proud bosom.

I resolved to ask Mother Douglas if she knew of Kate's fate. I did not know her second name and dared not ask Mr da Costa – even with my wits scrambled, I had that much sense left. But the Gonson raid, if that was true, narrowed down the brothels where she might have been from thousands to a handful.

'Very good!' I said, as if listening to a business report the whole time. 'What is through there?' I pointed to a door, knowing very well it was a store room. Upon having this confirmed by my sisters, I announced my intention of speaking to Sarah Young in this room. My sisters looked at each other but did not demur.

'Come with me a moment, if you please,' I commanded Sarah. 'I wish to talk to you.'

Sarah followed me to the store room, which had a key on the outside. Once the door was shut behind us, I confirmed my impression of her complete submissiveness to me by kissing her hard on the lips. She was small of stature fortunately, no taller than I was. Her eyes opened a little in surprise but she responded *con brio*, as they say.

'That was nice, wasn't it?' I said roughly, when our mouths finally unlocked. This total submissiveness, when I had not paid a penny, was most promising.

'Yes, sir. Thank you, sir,' she said.

'Good girl!'

This time, when repeating the performance with the kisses, I allowed myself liberties with the bosom, finally desisting only to lift her skirts and the meagre petticoat beneath. My questing fingers reached their goal; I was in, indeed, up to the knuckle, when there was a knock on the door accompanied by a cry of 'William!'

I sighed, letting her skirts drop. The tiny cupboard now smelled like a Yarmouth bloater. Sarah was dribbling slightly, but her eyes were fixed on me in wide devotion. I intended to test this devotion further.

'What is it?' I shouted, irritably.

'It's supper time,' came the news through the door.

'Time for supper.'

Damn!

5

I WAS DRESSED in my very finest: the yellow waistcoat again, a sword newly polished, buckles for my shoes. I strode along, my feet crunching and slipping on the gravel of Covent Garden's Middle Piazza, brave and quaking, my thrust-out chest the spacious carapace for an ever-shrinking heart.

I rolled to a halt in the middle of the Piazza, where there was a column with a sundial. Round the battered wooden picket fence, the ladies in their straw hats and blue aprons were doing a roaring trade selling flowers, fruit, vegetables, nosegays; there were even some stalls offering samplers, brass rings and suchlike gewgaws. The bustle of selling-life made me smile.

'Hello, Bill!' A leather-faced but still striking old woman with a splendid prow of a nose was calling out to me, showing gappy, yellow teeth. Gertrude, the flower-seller.

'Hello to you, Gertrude!'

An idea! I would buy flowers to present to the Thornhill household, as I introduced myself.

'I am off to see a most important man, Gertrude. So I need some luck. Come, what are the flowers for luck? I'll have some from you.'

Gertrude pushed her straw hat back on her head. 'You don't need luck, Bill. Not you, you handsome charmer.'

'Oy! Keep it believable, my darling!'

Gertrude, hands on hips, roared with laughter. 'Here's what you need.' She pulled at some flowers on the stall. 'Yellow poppies bring success,' she chanted. 'And here's lavender roses.'

'What do they bring?'

Gertrude's rather lovely almond eyes opened wide. 'Why, love at first sight, Bill. Need you ask?'

'I'll take them, Gertrude. Thank you. Both of them. Poppies and roses.'

So I was stood before the mansion, the fine glorious house, which I had seen myriad times yet not seen because I did not know its significance. It was the same as with every face or every street scene if you look but do not see the significance. I shifted my poppies and roses to my left hand so I could ring at the door.

It rang, ding-dong, a footman answered. I realised I had bought too many poppies and roses, making me scarcely visible through a swaying thicket of blooms.

I cleared my throat, panicked, blurted out that I was here for *John* Thornhill. 'He's not at home,' said the footman and closed the door.

I rang at the bell again. Nothing. And again. Nothing. This day was to mark the beginning of my longed-for rise. Was it to end in ignominy, standing in vain on a great man's threshold, half-smothered in self-imposed foliage? Never! I touched my sword in defiance. Then I rang again, hard, ding-dong, on the clapper. *Ding-dong-ding-dong-ding.*

Another footman answered, shorter than the first one, not much taller than me.

'Hey! What's all that noise? Did you ring before?'

'No, I've just got here. Sorry about the noise. The bell kept ringing.'

'What ...?'

'I am here to see Sir James Thornhill. He is expecting me. William Hogarth.'

I walked forwards, giving the liveried flunky no alternative but to give ground and admit me. I was IN. Setting foot in a great house for the first time, and besides this was the house of a revered artist.

'Wait there ...' said the footman. I glared at him, demanding it. 'Please.' He said it grudgingly but he said it. Next time he would say 'sir', I swore it.

But I was summoned quickly. The HOUSE. Ah, the house! I followed the footman through to a drawing room on the first floor. As we entered, a maid thankfully relieved me of my abundance of flowers and foliage, dipping a pretty curtsey and saying she would put them in water.

My mouth was open to greet Sir James with phrases well-oiled from practice in my head. But the drawing room was empty. I took in the ceiling-length, oval window to the left, from which the light was coming, with a claw-legged table pushed against it; a patterned oriental rug on the floor before a Portland fireplace with a high picture fire screen. A fire burned merrily in the grate. Above, on the mantelpiece, were an ornate clock, a candelabrum and a painting, heavily framed, of twins against a celestial white background.

Sir James did not leave me waiting long, entering briskly, arm outstretched.

He could hardly have been less imposing: tubby to the point of blubbery, not much taller than me. His nose was a most interesting artefact: slightly bent with the middle extending down almost onto the bow of his upper lip, the framework left the nostrils no choice but to flare upwards, like a baulked horse.

But he was dressed most elegantly in a green frock-coat with large pockets, hanging to the knee, pulled back to reveal the most beautiful long waistcoat, white satin with metal thread – ten guineas at least, or I'm a Dutchman.

We shook hands. 'It's Bill, isn't it? Bill Hogarth?'

'William, sir.'

'Very well, William.'

The maid carried in the flowers I brought.

'Heavens! What a lot of flowers. Thank you, William. Very good of you.'

'Not at all, sir. I'm very pleased to be here!' I blurted this out with more force than intended, at the same time registering Sir James's burring accent, which at first I thought was northern, like my father's, but later identified as West Country.

'I was looking for John.' Sir James adopted what I took to be a mannerist pose, showing himself to be a man of taste. His right wrist, not his hand, was placed on his hip, with the hand splayed outwards, as if preparing to receive a secret payment in coin from someone approaching from the rear.

Thus posed, he turned unsteadily on small, block-shoed feet, still searching, as if the watched-for John may pop up behind him, in jest. As John did no such thing, Sir James completed the full 360 degrees at the same even speed until he was facing me again. 'He's probably forgotten you were coming,' he said, consolingly.

'No matter, sir.' Pause. 'I was just admiring the room.' I was also hoping for an invitation to sit, which was not forthcoming. Sir James's watery features rippled into a faint smile at the compliment. Silence.

How about the offer of refreshment? A glass of beer? Some cakes? Silence. He began to turn on his axis again but then stopped. Just making himself comfortable, I supposed.

'I was just admiring the painting, sir.' I flapped at the heavily-framed oil over the mantelpiece. 'One of your own, is it not, sir?'

Sir James nodded thoughtfully, not disturbing the watery features this time. 'Yes, *Constellation of Gemini with Caris Minor*. Twins, you see.'

'Masterful, sir!' Actually, I thought the background a bit empty, too much white. But the compliment seemed genuinely to please him.

'Oh, well, thank you.'

'And, um, the embroidery,' I plunged on. I shook an arm at it; it was on the wall. Great big thing, must have been over nine feet long, but narrow. Rows of leaves in gold running down a madder background. I truly did like it; I'd never seen such luxury. 'Very nice, um, embroidery.'

'Do you like it? Yes. It's from Patmos, I believe. Lady Mary Whatsit brought it back from those travels of hers. She's always charging about. Brilliant woman, even if she is as ugly as sin. They say its smallpox. Face like the wall of a day-labourer's privy. Do you know her?'

'Lady Mary er …? Um. Probably not.' Silence. 'I do engravings, at the moment, sir. But I have aspirations to be an artist. A proper …'

'Artist, eh?' Sir James was impelled to half-turn again. For a moment I wondered if he was driven by the sun, or something. 'So where do you stand on the issues of the day, Bill? Hmm. I mean, what styles do you favour?'

I felt myself colouring. 'Oh, English, sir,' I yelled out, truthfully enough. 'Can't stand that foreign muck. Palladio and all, from Italy. And that William Kent, its exponent here. No, sir! Not for me. Far too ornate and curvy. It's not our way.'

Fortunately John had primed me about Sir James's enmity for William Kent, the local champion, so to speak, of the Italian Palladian style. He and Sir James had had a huge falling out over some commission or other, John said.

Sir James gave a watery smile, accompanied by another quarter rotation. For some reason I was longing to sit down. I even nodded at one of the handsome marquetry chairs with serpentine seats, although, mind you, they looked as if nobody had ever sat on them.

'So you want to learn the English style, eh?'

'Yes, sir! It's my dream, sir. And I shall make it come true! I shall, sir!'

I realised that I was clenching my fists and was squaring up to Sir James. I blushed and wondered if I should apologise.

'Well, Bill. I run a painting school, you know. I run a painting school here.'

WHAT! I WOULD KILL HIM! I WOULD … *KILL* HIM! THAT JOHN THORNHILL! THAT BLOODY WASTREL! I WOULD SLOW-ROAST HIM OVER A BLOODY SPIT.

DID HE NOT THINK TO *TELL* ME THAT? DID HE NOT THINK IT WORTHY OF *MENTION*, THIS VITAL PIECE OF INTELLIGENCE THAT COULD HAVE CHANGED MY WHOLE *LIFE*? 'Oh, do you really, sir? I didn't know that. May I …? I'd be very interested to um …'

Chapter 5

'Are you thinking of enrolling?'

'Very much so, sir.' You're my hero. No, don't say that.

'Good. Well. Can you show me something? Some work?'

'Not painting, sir. But I have done some drawings.'

'Good, good.'

'Scenes in coffee houses and the like. Some faces ...'

'Good.'

'And etchings on bronze, sir. Just starting. After the style of ...' I stopped, realising Callot was French.

'Bring them along. Next time you come. Show me. And then we'll get you started in the school.'

'That's wonderful! Thank you so much, sir.'

'Not at all, well ...' Another rotation was beginning.

'I'd better go.'

A young girl bustled in, all petticoats and shoulders. 'Oh, papa, I ... Oh, I'm sorry. You have a guest.' Some charming confusion. 'I'll come back later.'

'Bill was just leaving.'

She looked me in the eye. Grey eyes. Frank, decent and fair. Intelligent brow. Full breasts.

'Oh, did you bring the flowers?'

'Yes! Yes. That was me.'

'They're lovely! It was me that put them in the vase.'

'Well done! I think they were placed in the vase with great taste. And no little élan.'

She laughed. 'Élan, eh? For flower arranging ...?'

'They say taste is innate, you know. I mean, anyone who can arrange flowers like that ...' I stopped, horrified at myself, but Sir James did not seem to have heard, so I finished, '... has, um, *taste*.'

She showed me out, I remember that. I do not remember taking my leave of the great man. I was in mid-air somewhere between my future and heaven.

'Did papa not offer you refreshment?'

'He did not!'

'He just forgets, you know.'

'He is a great painter, he is entitled to forget refreshment.'

She laughed again. I loved it when she laughed. I loved it even more when it was me who had made her laugh. I was swelling like a balloon.

'I shall offer you refreshment then.' She was blushing. Oh, lovely!

'And I shall accept.'

'Tea?'

'Bloody hell. I don't think I've ever tried it. In for a penny, in for a pound.'

'And cake? Have you tried that?'

'Cake? Let me think.' I adopted an exaggerated thinking posture in the classical manner of Socrates. She laughed again. I LOVED this! 'Yes, I have tried cake. And … let me report to you … the experiment was a success. I liked the cake I had. I wish to eat more.'

'And so you shall. So you shall.'

'What is your name, please …?' You delightful girl. No, don't say that.

Eyes downcast, pinking slightly. 'Jane, sir.' She looked up.

'And how old are you, Jane?'

A second of hesitation. 'Fifteen. How old are you?'

'Fourteen. Oh, all right. I'm twenty blah-blah.'

'Twenty blah-blah?'

'Correct. Until my next birthday. Then I'll be twenty blah-blah-blah.'

She laughed until her eyes sparkled with tears. Oh, bliss!

'And you are Bill? Are you not? John's friend?'

'I am NOT! I am NOT Bill! I deny your accu … your impu … to me of the name of Bill! I, young lady, am Guilemus Hogarth. Artist, soon to be. But you can call me William.' Because I was soaringly happy and you had wonderful breasts and I didn't even care, because you were you, and wonderful, and that mattered even more.

It was everything.

Some universes later I soared back to Gamble's emporium, full of tea and cake and so happy I could have exploded. With what little brain I had left, I plotted how to see her again. Gamble was sprawled over a workbench. He said the South Sea scheme had gone belly-up. He had lost all his money. His establishment was to close.

6

W. HOGARTH, ENGRAVER. That was what it said on my shop card. And the date of the start of my business sat proudly on the card, too. 23 April. St George's Day. When else for an English patriot such as me? So the Spitalfields boy now had his own shop, where he was the master, in his own trade. It was near the Black Bull, Long Lane, a few streets north of the place where I first blinked, then bawled and clenched my fists at the world.

So here was my own engraver's press, my own workbench with a plate on a leather cushion to keep it steady, my own ink slab, engraving tools, ground and dabber. My own stove, my own pans stinking of varnish, resin, oil, acid vinegar and ink. My own designs and my own engravings.

It was a tiny room, but *my* room, as the sound of rumbling carts and cries of a boot boy shouting 'Clean your honour's shoes' came loudly through the damask curtains from my sisters' shop, that Anne and Mary insisted on hanging at the windows.

But ... but, but, but ... Young though I was in so many ways, I was still too old to learn the craft of 'graver. I would *never* do it, not with these stubby hands. Not with my mind so quick and the craft so slow. When I drew I wanted to catch the passing moment, quick, quick, quick, not scratch away laboriously like a whore with the clap, easing her itch. And unlike the whore with the clap, one wrong scratch and the whole thing was ruined. That was not me!

There was a noise outside. I could sense that the visitor was a woman before the door moved. My heart constricted and twisted in case it was Jane. Oh, I had so begged and pleaded with her to come to me at this workshop but so far ... so far ...

The door opened. It was not Jane; it was Sarah Young, the assistant from my sisters' shop. She was enclosed in cloak and bonnet, a trickle of transparent snot running down that interesting, useless groove we all carry between nose and mouth.

'Oh, it's you!'

'Don't sound so disappointed.' She threw the cloak and bonnet off, going straight to the heart of the matter. 'I will do whatever pleases you.'

73

That was enough. That was what I required from her. Her ample bosom was heaving. Breathing hard, I thankfully threw the engraving tool at the wall, from whence it clanged to the ground. I pushed a tea chest, kept largely for this purpose, against the door so we could not be disturbed. It contained some of my worldly goods, the chest did, the rest being at my new abode, a room in Long Lane even tinier than the workshop.

I lowered my breeches and drawers and sat back down at my engraving chair, my member springing obligingly to attention as I did so, for Sarah was reaching behind her to unbutton her dress, after which she pulled the front down and wriggled out of her shift. She kneeled, then her practiced mouth took my member, while I reached for her breasts – a duet we managed after a bit of initial fidgeting.

It occurred to me to imagine that it was Jane performing this service upon my person but, horrified, I rejected the thought: losing some stiffness in the process, unfortunately. I would not defile her, Jane, even in my mind. Let me never forget that the Choice of Hercules was between virtue and pleasure. I chose virtue, but nevertheless groaned aloud, as the Young girl gobbled my prick.

She let me slip from her mouth. 'What? What did you say?'

'I wasn't talking to you!'

'Then who ...?'

'Oh, get on with it, woman. I'm losing the ... power.'

She took me back in her mouth and chewed away like a grenadier on a saveloy, until finally I loosed my load in her mouth.

I was dozing, spent, over spoons to be engraved and thus become instruments of torture to me, when my next visitor arrived.

'Felix!'

He was carrying a folder of prints but put them down so we could embrace, which we did, long, hard and enthusiastically, banging each other's backs. Then he kissed me all over my face like the wet foreigner he was.

'*Mon petit choux.*'

'Felix you are saving my sanity, probably my life. Come on, let's get to work. How are you?'

Felix shrugged. Now that he was no longer with Ellis Gamble, Frenchy-Felix was earning his daily crust by engraving copies of paintings for half the painters in London. He had come to help me with engraving, at no charge.

Chapter 6

I took out the rough drawing and the engraving plate. We both sat down at the bench. I was happy. I pushed the tea chest across the door again, so nobody could come in. It occurred to me that the tea chest was my barrier to shut out the world, for both sex and work. But I needed to improve both. The work had to get better and one day the sex had to be with Jane Thornhill. And have some love in it, which it would, with her.

There was silence a moment. My member was on the rise again at the thought of Jane. I grabbed my breeches between my legs and thrust it down. Felix was looking at me.

'Can I help at all?' There was a faint smile, but he looked tense.

I looked him in the eye. 'Not now, we have work to do.'

'But one day? One day …'

'Maybe. One day. Now look.'

I showed him the rough drawing of *The South Sea Bubble (Who'll Ride?)*. We were to engrave it, together. He was to help me.

'There, in the centre of a carnival scene, is the South Sea merry-go-round with all sorts of greedy fools on it. They have all lost their money in the crash. Like Stout Gamble.'

'Yes, good. Strong in the middle, there.'

'I want a symbol on top. What's the symbol for a fool? Jester's cap?'

'Hmm. Why don't you have a goat? Symbol of desire.'

'Good idea. And in the foreground, honesty is broken on the wheel, attended, of course, by a hypocritical clergyman, kneeling in prayer.'

Felix laughed. 'All this is good.'

'But! Come on. But. There's always a bloody but with you. *Mais, mais, mais …*'

A smile from his thin lips. He was handsome enough and smelled good. Could I …? No, only if I really had to. Mind you, it would depend on what he wanted.

He was holding the drawing at arm's length, as he usually did. 'At the moment there is no depth. You need diagonals drawing the eye to the back. All this carnival can stay at the front.'

I nodded. 'So …?'

'This London Fire Monument, move it from the left to the right.'

'Why?'

'It's massive and holds the eye. The viewer looks from left to right. It should be the last thing they see, not the first.'

75

'Yes! Thank you, Felix!'

'What's the inscription? You've just doodled there.'

I thought for a second. 'This monument was erected in memory of the destruction of this city by the South Sea in 1720.'

Felix roared with laughter, hands on hips. 'Oh, that's good. That's very good. Can you engrave the lettering? It will have to be capitals, you know.'

'No, I thought you could do that.'

'And what do I get out of it?' Face all innocent.

'Behave.'

Felix sighed. 'What are you going to have on the left? Diagonal, drawing the eye to the back. Something very much London.'

'Guildhall,' I said firmly, 'possessed by the devil. He butchers Fortune and throws the flesh to the mob.'

'My God! Bill, there has been nothing like this in London. It's tough and raw and brave.'

'Thank you!' I took a mock bow, doffing an imaginary plumed hat. 'And behind the Guildhall, because we need a deeper diagonal, a house where women are selling themselves, to Greed as king.'

'Magnificent! *C'est magnifique ça.*'

'Come on! Let's do it together. This engraver's shop is closed.'

Felix ran a hand over the plate, ready to start. 'Indeed, indeed! You know I will help you, always. Come what may. Yes or no. But … Please, Bill! Please. For me? Just …'

He mimed what he wanted, then kneeled at my feet.

'Oh, all right then.'

For two decades nobody wanted my whang, now the bloody thing was no sooner tucked in, than my drawers were down and it was out again.

'Hey, we could have a "Who'll Ride?" sign on the South Sea merry-go-round,' I said.

But Felix didn't reply, only moaned and groaned in that foreign way of his.

7

THERE WAS nobody around and I was early for my lesson, so I tucked my folio of drawings under my arm and popped into the drawing room. The drawing room at Sir James's place was massy and airy. Despite being one of the smaller rooms on the ground floor, the ceiling was so high and so much light came in the two arched windows that it was like being outdoors.

I had always measured my progress by space, as well as money: the two being naturally closely related. A painter represents priority by space, as well as positioning; life rewards its favoured children by giving them more space.

I pictured the expanse of drawing room as containing cartouche-like squares of the incarcerations of my boyhood, the dingy vault in Bartholomew Close, the damp dark in the Rules of the Fleet Prison. And slowly the squares grew smaller, even faded, though they never entirely disappeared.

The drawing room, naturally, was the epitome of taste; one would have expected no less from the newly appointed Serjeant Painter to the King, as Sir James now was. Yellow walls, of course. Oh, the exquisite taste! A glorious pendant chandelier, of finest Venetian glass. Corniced pillars of salmon pink, just touching a sky of white ceiling with all the delicacy and disdain of a countess drinking tea from a tradesman's china.

The ceiling itself was adorned with allegories by Sir James of the cardinal virtues: temperance, justice, prudence and fortitude. Justice and prudence had a panel to themselves, temperance and fortitude shared. This pleased me, as too precise a symmetry does not create balance, but on the contrary is its enemy, not to mention being a sign of the second-rate.

The furniture was a mix of modern Flemish and older pieces dating from the time of Queen Anne, wavy-legs and suchlike, walnut much in evidence. The upholstered pieces were in an exquisite pale green, with white embossed motifs.

'Mr Hogarth? Sir?' The 'sir' was very much an afterthought, tinged perhaps with irony.

I descended from my reverie, where I was at one with the room, regarding, instead, the speaker. She was a pert young lady whose rank was uncertain to me, as I could not tell it from her attire. (I found out later that the floral patterned silk gown she habitually wore was an old, much altered and reduced one of Jane's.)

'I am Fanny, the maid,' the person supplied.

She was damnably attractive, pert little thing.

'I'm William Hogarth. I am here for ...'

'... Your lesson. Yes, I know.'

'It's not exactly a lesson. I'm not a beginner. I'm an artist in my own right. I ...'

'Miss Jane asks you to return to the drawing room after your lesson. She says she will meet you there.'

My whole being soared, but I hid it from this self-possessed Fanny person. 'Righty-ho.'

Fanny the maid turned on her pretty heel, the epitome of pert self-possession.

I made my way to the door to Sir James's studio, a door I promptly threw wide, before striding in – first entrances establishing the man. And instantly everything was wrong, jarring and out of tune. The scene that met my eyes was one of marbled limbs, torsos and heads, all disconnected, all there to be copied.

I had assumed when I started that Sir James himself would be taking the lessons. But no! They took place under the dead gaze of a cadaverous fellow in black, with a red indoor cap, a spectre by the name of John Vanderbank, a Hollander who had studied under Kneller. A former habitué of debtor's prison, like my father, the Vanderbank fellow's academy was known to me, but not that it was now being held under Sir James's auspices.

I proffered my guinea fee, payable in advance, which was snapped up. I was set to the mindless copying of bits and parts, in what was laughably known as the 'academic style'.

When something was wrong, I had learned, everything was wrong; John Vanderbank, instigator of this brain-and-soul eroding classical copying, was hardly older than I was. And my fellow copiers, once again, as at Stout Gamble's establishment, were younger than me to a man. I was behind in life's race for the second time! My spirits ached worse than my poor tired copying-arm.

However, they rose when we broke from our labours – by then a twisted column copied, as well as a dismembered arm – for my companions, as so often, lifted my mood.

There was George Knapton of the Knapton bookseller family. John Ellys, absurdly young. Samuel Barker, Arthur Pond. And towering over the lot of us, the still-a-boy of Francis Hayman. You could never overlook Hayman. He worked hard, copying furiously, but that did not stop him eating and drinking at the same time – beer and a massive pie, on this occasion.

He was a huge, shambling bear of a man. At the much longed-for break, he regaled us with stories of his apprenticeship to a history painter known to me, one Robert Browne. *See, see! Younger than me and ahead of me. Already with a proper painter's apprenticeship behind him.* But as Francis rolled on with his stories, in his deep Devon burr – a much richer accent than Sir James's West Country overlay – it was impossible not to feel fondness for him.

I asked my new friend Francis Hayman questions in his own Devonshire accent, which, far from offending him, caused him to roar with laughter through mouthfuls of food. Then he coached me in imitating him better.

After the lesson in how to shrink the soul, I would usually, of course, go drinking with Francis and the others. But even better things awaited me. Eventually, I found my way back to the drawing room where I was to meet Jane.

And suddenly there she was! In the same room as me! I was elevated again. I was a new me, an entity made to please and entertain her, a man that was a part of us. I gently took her hands as she lowered to the settee beside me.

She was composed, as always, sometimes a little flushed in the cheek, perhaps, but prettily so. Her earnest grey eyes always sought out my face, penetrating the surface with forceful honesty and innate wisdom. She was serious, but not sombre or sad, though I could make her laugh and delight in doing so. I never thought of any difference in age between us, but if I did, and knew no better, I would have thought her older, not some eleven years younger. She was bigger than me: taller and broader.

'I brought drawings to show you. And some prints. All my latest.'

She smoothed her skirt – one of the many small gestures I had come to love – there, sat next to me, slightly turned towards me on the settle, face in quarter profile. She said nothing, waiting, but she was WITH me, IN THE SAME ROOM, and that made me a different person, one I wanted to be, a better one, a soaring one.

'Shall I ...? Shall I show ...?'

She nodded slightly impatiently, then softened with a smile. 'Yes, of course.'

I had my drawings between stiff covers in a folio. I had agonised for days over the order in which to show them to her. Needless to say, I had not shown them to my copying-master. What would be the point?

My final decision, after all that agonising, was to show the man examining a watch first. I changed my mind at the last second, took a deep breath, and passed her the drawing of the waiter, the beggar and the dog. The passing was a votive offering, she the seer and goddess.

'Here ...' I was croaking, my voice gone, my belly in some fiend's grip. 'What ...?'

'Oh, William, it's marvellous! No, truly!'

'What ... think ...? What do you think is *happening*? What's the *story*? In my drawing?'

She looked closely. 'The beggar's giving something to the waiter, not the other way around. No, wait a minute. The beggar's hand is clasped round something. That could be his cup, couldn't it? And the waiter is about to pour him ... what? ... Coffee from that pot he has in his hand. Is that ...?'

'Yes! Yes!'

'Oh, William. I love that disdain on the waiter's face. He's bent away from the beggar, look. The beggar smells, doesn't he! The waiter's going "Pooh! Pooh!" to himself! I can smell the beggar myself.' She laughed. 'Pooh! Pooh! You smelly beggar! And look at the dog, there, sniffing up the beggar's ...' She stopped and giggled.

'Do you like dogs?'

'I *adore* dogs. Papa won't let me have one. Do you like ...?'

'Oh, yes! Yes! Very much so. I hate it so when people misuse dogs, well, any animals but especially dogs ...' My words were tumbling over each other. So much to say, so little time. So much to do, for that matter. 'We shall have a dog when we are married. Two dogs. Ten dogs. And horses. Which dogs would you like?'

She coloured red. Not a salmon maiden-blush. Robust. 'Any ... Which dogs do you like?'

'Terriers. Or maybe Dutch Pugs. D'you know them?'

'I ...'

'See. Here. In my drawing. How I've got the beggar bent? Do you remember my *Game of Draughts Interrupted*? I had an old man bent in that. I can draw bent old men now. The curve adds interest to the composition.'

'Oh, I do love that dog! That's my favourite. Look how intelligent and alert ... One paw up.' She imitated the dog's paw by crooking her wrist, then laughed.

I wailed. 'Oh, we've got so little time! I haven't even shown you the other one yet. Will you come and see me at my shop?'

'William! You know I can't.'

'Please! Please. We could talk. I won't … Jane, I wouldn't dream of … Just …'

She touched my hand to quieten me. 'Show me the next drawing.'

I breathed deeply to calm myself, then replaced the waiter *et al* between the stiff covers. I pulled out the drawing of the man examining a watch, passed it to her, shutting my eyes. She laughed softly at my performance.

I cleared my throat. 'Now! What do you think is happening here? I have tried to catch the moment in a moving story. What's the story?'

'Well …' She shifted a little on the settle. She was rarely still for long. 'He's a rich man, isn't he? Even though he is pawning his watch. He *is*, isn't he?'

'I should think so, yes.'

'Oh, yes. Look, he's rich. That's a cigar in his hand, isn't it? Or is that his finger?'

'Of course it's not his bloody finger! Jane! You stupid girl! Then he'd have six fingers, wouldn't he? And one outsized. Use your brains, girl, for heaven's sake!'

'William, I think perhaps it's time for me to go.'

'NO! No, no, no, no! Oh, Jane, I'm sorry. I'm an oaf, I'm a boor, I'm a clod.' I clambered off the settle and kneeled at her feet in supplication, taking her hand. 'Jane, read the picture, please. Please. Your William is so, so sorry.'

'Oh, get up! Nincompoop! Silly boy!'

'Yes. Sorry, Jane.' I resumed my place on the settle, only closer than I was before, sliding my arm along the settee-back for the first time ever. She allowed it.

Jane cleared her throat, in what I thought she thought was a businesslike way. She was colouring again, though in a subtly different way, also her voice was lower.

'I take it they are doing business in a coffee house, a bowl of coffee in front of the man as he pawns his watch. The pawnbroker is quite prosperous, isn't he? Good quality broadcloth coat. What's on that paper between them? Votes …?'

'The pawnbroker buys and sells votes. Everything is for sale you see. The national debt. South Sea shares. Walpole himself. There is a price for everything and everybody.'

She sniffed. 'Hmm! The idea's too big for the drawing.'

'Oh, rubbish! Hey, look, you see how I've got the man's hat upside down, on the bench? That's damnably difficult, that is. Do you realise how few artists could do that? I'm not sure that even your father ...' I stopped, sensing I had gone too far. *Bite your tongue, Billy Hogarth. Bite your tongue.* And keep it bit.

She handed back the drawing, yawning. 'I'm tired.'

'Don't be.' I spoke softly. Then ... 'The next step is to sell the engravings. We'll start with the South Sea one ...'

'Where will you sell it?'

'I'll go round the booksellers. Frenchy-Felix has promised to come with me. He's been a good friend. A good help to me.'

'John would help you. He's most fond of you, you know, William.'

I was with John last night. We visited three bagnios, rogering a total of six whores before returning to my shop, exhausted, at four in the morning, where we slept on the floor. John knew about my trysts with his sister, but seemed unconcerned. He would not have been the least use with booksellers. I realised I had spoken this last thought aloud.

'Oh, John wouldn't be any use.'

She was silent. We stayed unspeaking for a while. She was the only person I could be silent with. My arm was getting stiff, so I took it from the back of the settle. I felt I may have upset or offended her but, against all logic, it was at this moment that I took her hand for the first time. She allowed it, looking me seriously in the eye, wide eyed. More silence. And then ...

'William, I know you dislike the copying you do at my father's academy.'

'Yes.'

'William, I have spoken with my father. I told him I have seen your drawings. I praised them.'

'What? Did you ...?' My hand tightened on hers.

'I'm afraid I gave my father the impression that our meeting was more by chance than it in fact was. And also that it only happened the once.'

'Good!'

'But he said you could help him, with his paintings. As his assistant. Should you like to.' She turned on the settle, facing me even more. 'Is that what you would like?'

'I would like nothing more!' I roared out, so fervently she laughed. 'Oh, you are wonderful, Jane. You make gold of the base metal of my life, you know?'

'Oh, William, don't!'

'Why! Why? It's the truth! It's my heart speaking. My lost heart. My heart that belongs to you.'

'I believe you, William.' Her eyes widened; they filled the world. 'But …'

'But! No buts, please. I hate buts. Buts are anathema. Anathema, buts.'

She laughed. 'William, I'm so young.'

I let go her hand, so I could clap mine together. 'I have the solution! Jane, I have it! You must get older. See? You will achieve this by ageing. As for me, I have a plan. Here it is: I shall wait while you get older. I shall talk to you and be with you. Maybe I shall take you in my arms, but I swear before God and man that all that side of it comes a distant second. It is you, Jane, wonderful Jane, you I want.'

She started to cry. I kissed her gently, chastely, on the lips, which she allowed. She took an embroidered handkerchief from her sleeve, dabbing her eyes with it. We held hands again, she smiling. Which was the tableau when her mother came in.

I had seen Lady Judith before, naturally; we had exchanged pleasantries, but no more than that. She was dark, shrewd, smaller than her daughter. She had the mien of a small furry, burrowing animal: a mole, say, or, less benignly, a ferret.

The small beady, dark-eyed gaze was hard on her daughter, ignoring me, as she saw, burrowed, searched beneath the surface of her flesh and blood, reading her like a book or a painting. The reading completed, she turned to me, closing the daughter out, now.

'William Hogarth.'

I had already released Jane's hand, indeed with alacrity. Now I sprang up from the settee like a jack-in-the-box. 'At your service, madam.'

The beady gaze flicked back to Jane, then me, as if she did not wish to encompass us both for fear of compromising Jane. 'My daughter looks happy, Master Hogarth. Let us see if we can keep it that way, shall we?'

'Always, madam.' For a mad moment it occurred to me to propose to Jane, there and then, in front of her mother. It was one of the few occasions in my life when cooler counsels within me have prevailed over those more heated. 'Always,' I repeated.

'Always is a long time, Master Hogarth.' Her eyes flicked round the extensive room, as if cleaning, or rather purging, it with her gaze. Then back to me. 'You are monopolising my family, young William Hogarth. A pupil at my husband's art class, now conversation with my daughter. Last night, I believe, an evening in the company of my son.'

I could feel myself blushing. Surely John hadn't ... HIS MOTHER! He can't have told ... I remembered Sally, one of the whores we had both had, then hastily cleansed my mind.

'A good supper at the Bedford Arms, I believe,' said the Lady Judith Thornhill, drily. 'I'm told they always do a good meal there.'

'Er ... Yes, indeed, ma'am.'

'And now you are to become assistant to my husband? Following the advances you have made ...' she shot Jane a glance, '... in the art class.'

I, too, looked at Jane, not bothering to hide not only my gratitude but my blazing love. Why should I? I was bloody proud of it. It was the best thing about me.

'I ...'

'Be here at ten tomorrow. Oh ...' she stopped a touch theatrically, as if she had just thought of this. Which she hadn't. I'd wager she'd planned every pause and inflection. 'What about your shop? The ... um ... engraving business, isn't it?'

'Yes, ma'am. I'll shut the shop. And I'll shut it permanently the second I can make my living from painting.'

'That is your intention, is it? Your ambition?'

'Very much so, ma'am. I shall be a painter. A successful one.'

'His drawings really are very good, mama,' said Jane gently, pleading.

'I'm sure they are,' said Lady Judith. 'At least ...' she continued hastily to forestall my attempt to pull them out and show them, 'at least my daughter believes they are, and that is good enough for me. Which rather brings us full circle, William, in this little tête-à-tête of ours, does it not? By which I mean that I will follow my daughter's lead in the matter of you, providing she remains happy.'

'I ...'

'Yes, don't say it again. Fanny will see you out.' Fanny the maid appeared magically on cue. 'And don't trust the other household staff. My husband can pay them more than I can, and they know it. Fanny loves me, don't you Fanny?'

Fanny, who I must say was really extremely pretty, smiled and curtsied. 'Yes, ma'am. And I love my Lady Jane even more.'

'Cheeky minx! Ten o'clock tomorrow, then, Master Hogarth. Bring your brushes. Oh, I tell you what. Come at half past nine, then you can spend half an hour with my daughter. If you'd like that?'

I advanced on Lady Judith and took her hand. 'Thank you, ma'am. I won't let you down, not in any respect. You can be certain of that.'

Lady Judith did not withdraw her hand from my grasp, nor her gaze from mine as our eyes locked. 'Do you know, William, I think you may be right about that.'

8

'IT'S £3 for a square yard of ceiling, £1 for a square yard of wall,' Sir James's West Country words rolled forwards precisely, as if afraid they may trip over if they did not watch their step. 'It's not much, but I demand the same as Kent. Always ask for as much as or more than your rivals, William.'

I nodded, taking from all that speech only the implication that one day it would be me, naming my price against my rivals. Who knows? Life can deliver amazing surprises. One minute I was bobbing by skiff to Greenwich with one John Rakesby, the next I bobbed again with Sir James Thornhill, who turned out to be Rakesby's father; Rakesby, meanwhile, turned out not to be Rakesby. With luck like that you should trust to your lucky stars, you Spitalfields Billy, you, young William Hogarth.

Sir James was waving at the huge wall of the Upper Hall of the Royal Naval Hospital. His wave was a little unsteady, even at this early hour he had sunk a few brandies. He disliked beer, he had already confided in me, as the bulk of it pushed his stomach out. He also disliked drinking alone. Being unused to the tipple, my customary swagger had nearly tipped me over twice, and all we had so far done was unpacked the paints and walked up and down.

'I'm glad you are here to assist me, William.'

'I'm glad to be here, sir.'

'It's too much for one man. It really is, especially at my age.'

'Why? How old are you, sir?'

Sir James did not laugh, as I rather tipsily hoped he would, but neither did he take offence.

'Within the sight of fifty, William. And I do believe, within the sight of my maker, too.'

'Oh, surely not, sir!'

Sir James started that strange pirouette he did back at his home. I believed he was dizzy, or perhaps just trying to remain upright. I liked him enormously. Once you got used to him, there was much less difference between him and me than I had expected.

The business we engaged on, over the coming weeks, was a portrait of the king and his family, among gods and angels: Hercules prominent, with St Paul's in the background. The king himself was outlined at the top of five steps, with the deities piling to heaven. Sir James himself began work on the king's face, sending me up a ladder to create a sky and clouds around St Paul's.

I eased on the thin underpainting – off-white usually, or grey, as he showed me – not worrying overmuch, as he assured me, if I went over his line to indicate the dome of St Paul's or the outstretched arm of the topmost angel. I enjoyed it, my work was even, it was well applied. Then, at some time during our work together, I believe quicker than he originally intended, I blocked in a blue-verditer sky and some lead-white impasto for the clouds. My heaven!

Sir James could not see my work as it proceeded, up there in the sky, so I made my own firmament and would show him afterwards, as often as not at the end of the day. BLOCKS OF COLOUR, BLOCKS OF COLOUR, SOLID BLOCKS OF COLOUR. I understood that I was finding myself, up there in Sir James's heaven, though not yet exactly what I was finding nor how I was to use it. I was becoming a painter, I knew that much. And my engraving shop remained thankfully closed, and would do, while I was transported to my Greenwich heaven.

We spoke little, Sir James and I, and never of deeper matters of opinion or the more secret aspects of our lives. In this way, we created a placidity for our days, an ease: even a gentle joy. He was easy company, an emollient being.

To my surprise, he never guided my work, beyond indicating where I should start for the day and what I should represent. So this was Hogarth's sky, Hogarth's clouds, one Hogarth pillar, as against two from Sir James, and even a Hogarth dome of St Paul's.

Sir James had mastered the art of drinking just enough to elevate the perceptions, without tipping into blackness of any sort. I climbed down from above our St Paul's to partake of brandy at regular intervals, with the occasional interpolation of a game pie, leg of mutton or suchlike, brought from the kitchens of Sir James's home in a basket with a chequered linen cover over it.

I was a painter. At least, over those next few weeks, I became one. BLOCKS OF COLOUR, BLOCKS OF COLOUR. It was so simple, almost meaningless, yet it was the key for me as a painter, as it showed the way forward, even if I could not put it into words, or even thoughts, which made sense.

I neglected my engraving at the shop more and more, participating in the copying lessons at Sir James's house only so I might see my Jane. I told Jane about the painting and my love for Jane went into the painting. To me all the angels and goddesses we painted were Jane, even the king's consort.

Sir James told me that this was one Sophia of somewhere or other near Hanover. Nobody knew what she looked like – Sir James assured me, slurring his words, drunk as a lord – so we could make it up. And anyway, the king couldn't stand her. Later on, he told me this Sophia was the king's cousin, so I suggested, half-mischievously, that he make her look like the king.

Sir James took me seriously: neither the first nor the last time my facetious teasing had been thus received. Sophia and George ended up looking like brother and sister. As Sophia was, for some reason, standing a step higher than George, as angels and goddesses crowded in on them, she gave the impression of his older sister. When Sir James was not there I gave her features a tweak, so she looked more like Jane.

Then, out of the blue, so to speak, Sir James said something that made my heart leap. 'I am to be away for a while, William. I have another commission to fulfil, at Headley Park, in Hampshire. Can you paint on alone here for a while?'

'Why, yes, Sir James,' I cried. 'I can paint on here. Then I can come to the country, paint with you there, be your assistant on all your projects.' TOO MUCH, TOO MUCH, HOGARTH.

Sir James smiled. 'Whoa! Not so fast. One thing at a time, my dear William. One thing at a time.'

'Yes, of course. I'm sorry, Sir James …'

'No need to apologise, my dear boy.'

'May I be so bold as to ask who the commission is for in Hamp … in the country?'

'Why? You know people there?'

'Er … Not exactly.'

'You may know the name. He spends most of his time in London, after all. My patron for this particular commission is one John Huggins. Is the name familiar to you?'

Huggins! I could hear his voice in my head. '£1 6s 8d for the fetters.' I could smell his oily skin, his filthy clothes. I could feel his touch on my mother's hand as he took our money, in exchange for not torturing my darling pater further. John Huggins, keeper, governor of the Fleet Prison. 'No, sir. I know no John Huggins; our paths have not crossed.'

'Pity. He's a genial fellow. I'm looking forward to his company.'

9

BUSINESS! I was marching through London, chest out, head back, hell-bent on making my first sale as an artist. The engraving shop was closed. Good King George and the consort Sophia, not to mention angels, goddesses and St Paul's looked down, I imagined, alone and blankly unfinished at Greenwich. And marching by my side, struggling to keep up even though his legs were longer, was Felix Frenchy Pellett: tutor, friend, guide and occasional molly-boy.

The offering which made up my first sale was clutched under my left arm, allowing the right to swing in rhythm with my bantam-cock strut. It was a print of an engraving depicting the collapse of the South Sea scheme.

I needed much less help than I expected from Felix with *South Sea,* a tribute to my ease of learning, not to mention the great progress I was making at the calling which had chosen me. But now I descended from the apex of creation to fight my way into the market place, among the throng of those scrabbling at the base, who I was at this moment merely joining.

I had the route of the print shops we would visit fixed in my head like a pattern of dots on the shape of the streets. We would begin at the outer rim, working inwards. We would begin with the booksellers I knew, the ones who swindled my father, or at least some of them; the egregious, squinting Curll-cur was too much for me to stomach.

Felix, calm, even as happy as his name, paced by my side as we reached Charles Ackers' print shop in St John's Close, north of Smithfield, not far from Clerkenwell Green. The last time I was there, father did the talking. His ghost appeared as I entered.

Charles Ackers, it appeared, was no more; a young cousin, John, looked at my prints. There was a silence.

'Topical,' he intoned at *South Sea.* 'Perhaps a little too topical.'

I started to speak, to make vigorous protest, in fact, but Frenchy-Felix rammed me hard in the ribs with his elbow. I punched him on the arm and glared at him.

If John Ackers noticed us squabbling, he made no comment. 'How much can you contribute to the printing costs?' he said.

'How much …? What …? Contribute …?' I squared up to Ackers, clenching my fists.

'We can perhaps come up with a formula per copy for you, but that would depend on how much you can put in.'

I saw my father's dear face in front of me, in all its haggard suffering after these rabid dogs had eaten his flesh. 'These are *my* prints!' I yelled at him in inconsequential fury. '*My* work … *my* effort … *my* …'

It was going to be 'My talent' but Frenchy-Felix grabbed my arm and hauled me away from the printer, who was backing off in alarm. Felix kept pulling, spinning me round, until I was dragged, apoplectic and still yelling from the print shop, back outside to the street.

'Here, give me the print,' said Felix. 'You don't want to crease it after we've come all this way.'

I let Felix take the print. He checked it for damage, which calmed me.

'They often ask for money towards the printing,' he said. 'As a beginner, you may have to pay. This time at least. But he thinks they will sell, this Ackers, I could see that.'

Against my will, I was pleased by Ackers' good opinion. CRAVEN, HOGARTH, CRAVEN!

We headed south again, so fast in my anger Felix could barely keep up. Next we visited Bowes' in St Paul's Churchyard, right near the Thornhill place, where Curll also had a stall, then Regnier's in Great Newport Street, Hennekin's at the corner of Hemmings Row, and lastly Overton's at the market at the corner of Pall Mall.

More and more I let Felix do the talking. It was the first time, on my own account, that I appeared as supplicant to people with considerably less talent than myself, but it was by no means the last.

It is the fate of the artist to be so cast down by those who have one life, and that a base one, usually; whereas the artist has two, for he inhabits the world of his art, alongside the quotidian world of clay and mud in which we all subsist and work and fornicate and belch and piss.

These people. THESE PEOPLE the artist had to deal with. Regnier wanted to keep the original plate at his shop to prevent extra unauthorised copies, he said, except by him, of course. Hennekin offered me extra money to make more copies, with the ingenious argument that many people would pirate my work, so I may as well be one of them.

We settled on John Bowes as the least worst of this shower of cheats, charlatans, pimps and whores, shaking his stained paw on a deal that put the sale price at a decent 1s a print.

Within days, copies appeared on sale at every one of the printers we visited, some good some bad, but all priced cheaper than my genuine ones. It was with difficulty that Felix restrained me from another perambulation round the print shops, this time armed with a cudgel.

We were in Jane's bedroom, I having been shown there via back-passages by the faithful Fanny-the-maid, as Sir James was away on his travels and the Lady Judith nowhere to be found. My beloved sat at an inlaid mahogany table, watching my exertions at my news, her usually calm grey eyes shining with anticipation, her joy at my joy.

I held her by the shoulders, looking up into her gentle, virtuous, serious face. 'You *are* wonderful, you know.'

'Sometimes, I feel if you left me, I would die.'

I cried a little, but softly, not out of control, more a release like steam escaping. Then we kissed awhile, pressing our lips together, not the way the whores taught me to kiss, with open tongue.

She broke the kiss. 'By the way, mama and I are trying to get father to take you with him to his masonic lodge.'

'Thank you!'

'You need more and better contacts at this time, William. And the masons are the people to provide them. Don't say anything to father though.'

'Of course not!'

'Leave it to us.'

'Jane, you know I love you? You believe I am true? You are more to me than … All the rest is dross, Jane! Dross!'

She stroked my cheek. For the first time, I touched her breast as we kissed. She allowed it.

'Jane, I can wait. If you would rather?'

'No. I am ready, William. If you want to.'

'Will you …?' I waved with both arms.

She understood what I meant, laughing merrily. 'My dear, I'm afraid I can't remove my dress without Fanny's help.'

'Aaahh!' I nodded wisely. The whores, of whom by now I had known many, always started the evening in their shifts. 'Shall I call Fanny?'

She coloured. 'I think not.'

I took both her hands in mine; we stood on either side of the table. 'Let me have a look,' I said.

I walked behind her, to be confronted by a swirl of brocaded silk and chenille in yellow and green, a myriad maze of buttons, ties and lacing, most of it half-hidden by pleats. I could not get near her for the hoops, and was anyway never more conscious of my stubby fingers, as I timidly tried to work the first pearl button I saw, just below her neck. At this rate we should still be there when Sir James returned from Hampshire.

'I am not a military man, my darling, but I think the answer may lie with what soldiers call a frontal assault.'

She was silent, unmoving, I could not see her face as I was round the back. Finally she cleared her throat. 'As you wish.'

I walked round the front, led her to a low settee and lifted her skirt and all her petticoats in one bunch. She sighed, cleared her throat again and laid back on the settee with one leg extended, the other on the ground like one of those Boucher odalisque drawings Frenchy Pellett delighted in showing me.

I lowered my breeches and drawers, spoke endearments into her ear, kissed her, fondled her, as well as I could through the upper part of her dress, then completed the Platonic ideal of unity; staying in place for quite a while, and then with steady motion giving her, I had reason to believe, the pleasure I craved to.

It was my first act of love that had the future in it.

10

JOHN THORNHILL was taking the class today, as he did from time to time, when the lugubrious John Vanderbank was indisposed, or perhaps simply had more pressing matters to attend to. He was a revelation as a painter, John, with extraordinary natural gifts, perhaps more so than me, but no application – even, I suspected, no interest – so he would never amount to anything: for it's all in the energy.

All poor John wanted to do was while away his time in suppering, wagering, then on to the pleasures of Mother Douglas and her ladies. He had few friends, so I was wary of refusing his invitations to join him; also it hardly seemed politic to alienate a Thornhill, but in any case I did not wish to, for I liked him enormously, for all his deep inner sadness. While on the subject of his character, it intrigued me that he so completely lacked his sister's penetrating powers of intellect and analysis.

'So tonight, then?' he was saying.

'Tonight, John,' I replied, 'I shall bring Stephen Fowler and perhaps one or two men from our class.'

He brightened, some of the cloud lifting from his sad, pale face. 'That's good. Thank you.'

We were speaking by the vestibule of the house; I was on my way out, when Sir James appeared from nowhere.

'Ah! I thought I heard your voice, there, Bill.'

At his father's appearance, pale John drifted off like a cloud before the wind.

'Hello, sir! What a pleasant surprise. I didn't know you were back in London.'

'Arrived back yesterday. From Hampshire. Just on my way to court. Try to keep my end up there.'

His face fell to sombre lines. I knew he was losing ground to Kent's Palladian faction, falling out of favour, even considered old-fashioned. It was wrong, wrong, wrong!

'Yes, sir.'

He spoke as if to someone standing immediately behind me, as he customarily did, also executing his half-pirouette. 'I've got an invitation for you, Hogarth.'

HO-garth? Why suddenly Ho ...? But this must be the masons! I adopted a serious mien, as of one worthy of the secrets of a conspiratorial society. 'Yes, sir?'

'I'm going to Newgate Prison ... um ... soon.'

I cleared my throat, as Jane does, and tried to look politely enquiring. 'Er ...'

'To draw the murderess, Sarah Malcolm. Why don't you come along? Keep me company?' His gaze shifted to a point behind my right shoulder. 'Do a drawing yourself? Eh? No, I tell you what. Why don't you do an oil? John thinks highly of your abilities and so do I. About time you got away from these engravings and did some proper painting.'

'I should love to, sir. Thank you. Thank you for the opportunity.'

We were in a hackney carriage on the way to Newgate, the first time I had ever been in one. My portable easel, brushes and oil paints were across my lap, as was a basket of provisions for the murderess Sarah Malcolm.

'I saw your drawing of Jack Sheppard, sir,' I said, to make conversation.

'Oh? Yes? Where did you see that?'

Jane showed it to me. 'It's ... prints of it are everywhere, sir. A fine likeness.' Idiot! You've never seen Jack Sheppard, he knows that. You're burbling, man. I cleared my throat. 'I mean, you can see his life of crime ... in his face. The way you ...'

We arrived at Newgate. It was even nearer to where I was born than The Fleet; cut through Christ's Hospital and you could run there in three minutes from St Botolph Churchyard, where I used to play.

The grimy towers were familiar enough, but I'd never been inside before. However, we were treated like visiting dignitaries, which I suppose is what we were. A turnkey showed us to a cell, where Sarah Malcolm had been sat down alone at a table with a lamp, to be painted: days before she was due to be hanged.

I thankfully put down my painting equipment then handed over the provisions, which, on arrival, I insisted on giving Sarah myself to make sure they reached her intact. In the basket were three bottles of beer, some hard-boiled eggs obtained from Stout Gamble's wife – with whom I was still on cordial terms, visiting from time to time – also some fresh-baked bread and a hunk of meat I bought from one of the stalls in Porridge Island, just off Covent Garden, on the way to Sir James's place.

Sarah Malcolm's eyes opened wide at the extent of my largesse. She stood behind the table and bobbed a curtsey. 'Thank 'ee, sir.'

'You are welcome, Sarah. I would have brought more if I could carry it.'

I looked at her keenly, already wanting to paint the woman, not the murderess. She had wrapped her head in a linen cap with wings, covering her hair, no doubt because it was greasy from prison, but this added rather than detracted from the overall proportion of her face.

Fine features, which would have been finer had they been allowed to sharpen on a duchess: an aquiline nose, redolent of pride; the kind of narrow but shaped mouth often seen on the Irish; a heavily emphasised concave part under the arch of the brow, beneath which there was the gland in the middle of the brain, the place where the soul received the images of the passions (according to Frenchy Pellett's instruction); the eyebrow was sloping up towards the middle of the brow, representing pain and sorrow.

And she had much to be sorrowful about, the poor wretch. I had read of her deeds in the newspapers, even before this commission. After it, I invested 2d at a printer's shop in Henrietta Street, which bought me a second-hand copy of *A full and particular Account of the barbarous Murders of Mrs Lydia Duncomb, with a Narrative of the infamous Actions of Sarah Malcolm, now in Newgate for the said Murders.*

Two old women and their maids, it seemed, found with their throats cut from ear to ear. Sarah Malcolm, formerly a servant to the old gentlewoman, was found guilty of wilful murder for the sake of forty-five guineas and a silver tankard.

I adopted a position to the side of Sarah Malcolm, so she had to turn her face to look at me, keeping her broad shoulders in a line. Her left elbow and right hand were on the oak table, causing me to notice what lovely long fingers she had. I would paint them apart no matter what she did with them.

My concentration on the subject was total; no snake in the spell of an eastern fakir was more at one with a single entity than me. It was only when I set up my little easel that I remembered Sir James, realising I had posed the subject, starting my work as if the Serjeant Painter to the King were not even in the room.

Oh well, too late to worry now. My apology was stillborn. I began my work, starting with a preliminary drawing to establish proportion and shape, before quickly applying white ground and proceeding to paint in blocks of colour. After a while I became aware of Sir James, fidgeting on the edge of my vision, the man was never entirely still, but shut it out from my mind.

After what seemed a few minutes, but was in reality a matter of hours, a turnkey knocked politely on the door to signal the end of our time with Sarah Malcolm. There could be no second visit; Sarah Malcolm was due the one-way cart ride to Tyburn in two days' time. We would, of course, finish our work later at the studio, Sir James and I.

Exhausted, I glanced at his piece, becoming uneasily aware that he had not said a word for a long time. His posing of Sarah was far more conventional than mine. Mind you, that might have been because I stole the most original vantage point in the small room without asking him. I took a deep breath, looking at his work with an air of casualness as he began to pack away his easel.

I suppressed a gasp, I suppressed glee: oh, unworthy glee! BUT MINE WAS BETTER. I knew it as well as I knew my name, William Hogarth, Guilemus Hogarth, Bill Hogarth, Billy Hogarth. This man was my St Luke, my god of painting. BUT MINE WAS ... I should stop it, this was getting dangerous!

Sir James was looking at my work, now resting against the stone wall, preparatory to our departure. 'That's good, William. A good likeness.'

BANAL REMARK. Oh, stop it! 'Thank you, Sir James.'

We bade farewell to Sarah Malcolm. Sir James lapsed into silence as the turnkey walked ahead of us through the winding corridors to the main gate, where we again hailed a hackney carriage. Inside, he suddenly resumed where he had left off before.

'Perhaps you should ... Have you thought of the painter's life? Rather than doing so much engraving?'

'I think of little else, Sir James.'

'Well, I can help you find an outlet for your work.'

'Thank you! Thank you very much, Sir James.'

'No, not at all, my boy. You show talent. And you have made a good impression on my household. John sings your painterly praises quite often. You appear to have made a favourable impression on my wife, too. And she's a good judge of a man, always was.'

'Pleased to hear it, sir.'

'I *think* even my daughter mentioned your name, and perhaps your work. Can't remember now. Have you met Jane?'

'We have exchanged … some … words, I believe.'

Silence. The hackney trundled on. But the release of stopping work was making me garrulous, a trait I would have with me all my life. Besides, Sir James's silence created a nothingness I felt impelled to fill with chatter, another permanent condition with me.

'These places …' I heard myself babble. 'The way they behave in these prisons, the cruelty of it all if you don't pay them their money.'

Sir James looked startled. I charged on. 'I heard the other day of a man, a man of quality at that, unable to pay the governor what he took as his due, placed shackled in a deep dungeon until he drowned in brackish water seeping into the place.'

There was a bell in my head. It was ringing. I knew all this was wrong for me, but still the words came out. Being in a prison again had done this. My long-dead father was sitting next to me in the hackney carriage. 'The things we do to each other, the cruelties we impose on the helpless: prisoners, children, dumb animals of every kind. Why are we such monsters? Why must we be so?'

Sir James next spoke as the hackney slowed in traffic. 'A subject that might interest you as a painter, William, is this committee of the House of Commons that is coming up.'

'Oh! Indeed, sir?'

'Yes. They are enquiring into conditions at the Fleet Prison. I can get you in, if that would be of any interest? Prisons. Interesting, at all?'

'Yes, sir. Yes, indeed, it would be of interest.'

11

HUGGINS! John Huggins, warden of the Fleet, the man who heaped misery on my father when he was in that monster's power, the man who sent my family into the streets to pawn its soul to protect poor father from yet worse. The newspapers were full of the case; Huggins was arraigned before men of the House of Commons. The hearing was in a panelled office in the Fleet, but I would paint him against the dripping stones of a foetid cell.

For Huggins had made mistakes, several of them. He had let the Fleet go to rack and ruin, rather than spend any of his £5,000 patent on repairs, to the extent that parts of the building were falling down. Further, his allowing prisoners to escape to the Indies on payment of a hefty sum had occasioned scandal.

But his biggest mistake of all was to extend his maltreatment from the poor – all as indistinguishable as clay, unless one of them happened to be your father – to the rich, notably (ho ho) Sir William Rich, Bart. Sir William was left manacled and shackled in a place named a strong-room, actually a vault over an open sewer, for refusal to cough up a second payment of 'Baronet's Fee', a tax Huggins had invented, of the sum of £51.

What a joy to see Huggins there on the first day! I ignored him, of course, now I was a famous painter (well, known at least), not a supplicant boy of a helpless prisoner. I was the official recorder for posterity of those just and vital proceedings (well, not actually official, but Sir James had obtained permission for me to be there, from Sir James Oglethorpe, the chairman of the committee).

After self-consciously unpacking my easel, palette, maulstick and paints on the first day, then posing a while beside the same, I sketched the faces of all the committee members, close and large.

Back in my studio I outlined the oil sketch modello, with blank faces, then asked Sir James Oglethorpe if he was interested in a copy of the finished painting. To my joy, he accepted without equivocation, whereupon five of the six others, as is the way of these things, fell into line. Six sales before I'd even put brush to finished canvas!

I promised each of the six their own individualised painting, featuring their own good selves in prominence, thus committing myself to six versions of the painting. Each of them would show the patron to advantage, yet would be a truthful record, not only of the events, but of that man Huggins' deepest nature, caught in a moment of time. If Antonis van Dyck could do it, so could I.

An hour into day one and I was pleased with my preliminary drawing. Half the space was for the action, the other half for the audience, shown as tronies. In the action half: the table at a sharp angle, a victim testifying before the committee, three of the committee in conversation, one standing behind them to give depth and a vertical.

Oglethorpe himself was shown in a Choice of Hercules pose, with the evil Huggins to his right and the poor plaintiff to his left. (Everybody now recognised the Choice of Hercules dilemma from the Earl of Shaftesbury's writings about it. It was flattering to the person who had the dilemma, which was good.)

Over the next two or three days, as the hearing went on, I had to make changes. The committee members did not feel they were prominent enough. I had to drop the audience altogether, the prisoner was on his knees, so we could see the committee members better; more of the committee members had to be shown standing, ditto. The composition was now stilted and too linear, like the early Dutch, but six sales were six sales, and thereafter the engravings should fly off the presses, given the topicality of the subject.

Then I came to a halt in my work, altogether. There, fastidiously taking his place in the audience in a resplendent pale green silk coat and the whitest wig I had ever seen, was Anthony (Moses) da Costa, my benefactor and that of my sisters, now ensconced so cosily in their shop, thanks to him. And where was Kate, his sometime bawd?

KATE, KATE, KATE. *Your face, your bosom*. My arm felt heavy, I could not paint, falling to tinkering with blocks of dirtied lead white for the imaginary stone walls. I started to listen to the proceedings, almost for the first time. The foul Huggins was telling the committee that he sold his patent to the wardenship of the Fleet to his deputy, Thomas Bambridge, so he was not responsible for anything.

The committee were ready for this sleight of hand; the next accuser dated from the time before the sale, so Huggins was in charge at the time. The accuser, the one who appeared in all the versions of the finished painting, was Jacob

Mendes de Sola, a Portuguese Jew. I winced as he detailed his travails at the hands of Huggins.

I waited impatiently – I was always impatient, but even more impatient than usual – for the next break in proceedings. But at that point Anthony da Costa made his way with surprising alacrity, though losing none of his elegance, to Jacob Mendes de Sola; the latter, clearly shaken by his own testimony, was bleeding lightly from the nose. I joined the growing crowd round the two of them. KATE, KATE. *Was it possible I may find you?*

Finally, with the poor bleeding witness sat on a chair with his head back, I approached my benefactor.

'Mr da Costa, sir. How nice to see you again.'

'William! Yes, I heard you were painting the scene. It was even in the *London Journal*, I believe. Splendid to see you doing so well, my boy!'

'Thank you, sir!'

'I was at your sisters' shop only the other day. All is progressing very well there, I'm happy to say. Your sisters did say you visit them rarely?'

'Yes, I ... er ... so little time.'

da Costa favoured me with a shrewd look. 'You feel you are leaving them behind, no doubt. Let me give you some advice, William. Don't. Don't cut yourself off. Your family are like your limbs, my boy. Cut them off and you bleed. Go and see Mary and Anne, that's my advice. This week.'

'Yes, sir. I wanted to ask you. When I was at your house that first time. I was little more than a lad. But there was a ... a woman. Her name was Kate.'

da Costa, until then all solicitous smiles, indeed he even had his arm round me, jumped back as if stung by a bee. 'What? What plan is this? What are you accusing me of?'

'Sir, you mistake my meaning. Nothing ...'

'I know nobody of that name ...'

'Yes, you do. I just want to find her, sir. I ...'

He looked hard at me, his face pale, shocked and afraid. I did not understand what I had done to occasion this, I regretted it, but my need to see Kate overcame even this. 'If you know anything, please tell me.' This emerged from my mouth far more harshly than I intended.

He reeled back, now really afraid. 'I truly do not know. For certain. But I heard she was in the clutches of Charteris, of Colonel Charteris.'

At that he swivelled on his heel and made off, so needful to be rid of my questions that he abandoned, at least temporarily, his friend Jacob Mendes de Sola. I regretted this but I was now pale, too.

This Colonel Charteris, who lived a life of riches in his prosperous house in George Street near Hanover Square, raped any woman who came within his ambit, needful and helpless servant girls of his own establishment and others. He had been brought to the courts many times, but always managed to wriggle free, by fair means or foul. The only brake on his appetites was his falling foul of good old English decency and the need to see fair play. Society had finally judged him guilty on these counts even if the court had not. *Oh Kate, oh my Kate! I had to find you.*

But first I had to show my six paintings of *A Committee of the House of Commons* to Sir James Thornhill, back at his house, as he had arranged the commission for me. I watched while he looked at them, secure in my ability to rouse his approbation, expecting his praise, waiting, truth to tell, for this to be over, so I could try to find my Kate.

Sir James cleared his throat. 'Huggins.'

'What about him?'

'I didn't mean for you to include him in the painting, I thought you were just going to do the committee.'

'Well, he's ...'

Sir James held up an admonitory hand. 'I would never have become Serjeant Painter to the King without Huggins. He knows how to organise these things. And now that I'm losing ground at court, I need him even more.'

'You're not suggesting ...'

'I'm not suggesting anything. But you can't expect me to help you, if you don't help me. In fact, you are damaging me with this painting.'

'But I've done it now,' I wailed.

'Have you delivered any copies?'

'No, not yet.'

'Then it's not too late to change it.'

'How am I going to do that?' I heard myself whine.

'Just change Huggins' face. Make it Bambridge.'

'I've never met Bambridge.'

'What's that got to do with anything?'

Everything. It was Huggins I wanted revenge on, for what he did to my father. Bambridge was after our time.

Sir James was staring right at me, perhaps the first time he had met my gaze. 'There's the door, William. If you won't change the painting, go now and don't come back.'

'I'm sorry, sir. I didn't mean to upset you. I didn't understand. I'll change all the paintings immediately. Bambridge, not Huggins, it will be.'

12

I WAS GETTING somewhere. I was close to obtaining society portraits, through the good offices of Sir James; moreover, even the theatre visits, which sent my spirits soaring, held the promise of painting commissions, too (aside from my portrait of Lavinia Fenton, which I was carrying out without a guaranteed buyer, just for the love of her fascinating being).

With money coming in from the engravings and my first paintings, I sallied forth every night, always for supper, usually to the theatre, now and again to the brothels and bagnios – this last usually with John Thornhill, who was working his way through every whore in the *New Atlantis* guidebook, or so it seemed. I felt my little room in Long Lane was a prison cell; it pained and trapped me to be there too long, to be there alone, at any time, but especially after dark.

I eagerly watched every theatre piece Lavinia was in, often more than once, if it ran for more than one performance. She really was extraordinarily good on the stage: funny and pathetic by turns, giving as good as she got from the audience.

Whenever she was on stage, I hoped there would not be a riot in the theatre, doing my best to quell one if it occurred. If she was not there, I rather enjoyed joining in.

Lately, I had seen Lavinia as Mrs Squeamish in *The Country Wife*, as Lucy in *Tunbridge Wells* and as a country lass in *The Rape of Proserpine*. This last was arranged by the impresario John Rich. I kept nagging Lavinia for an introduction to him; I had had no luck so far, but I was sure it would happen.

Lavinia and I ate supper together at those low places she liked, with bare floorboards and chairs so high I could barely drum my heels on the floor. Sometimes we went for walks, or to side-shows; but, to my pleasure, she too felt compassion for the freaks on show, the midgets, giants, hermaphrodites, Siamese twins and all the rest of it. We refused to laugh at them, indeed gave them money as often as we could.

I brought Jane to these meetings with Lavinia sometimes, arranging her escape from the Thornhill household past the male Thornhills, with her mother's gleeful assistance and that of Fanny, the gigglingly complicit (and very personable) maid.

Jane had even joined me, on occasion, for sittings while I painted Lavinia's portrait. I found Jane's remarkable stillness, which came from her goodness of soul and spirit, soothing to me as I worked. As I told her often, I painted better when she was there.

I asked her opinion at every stage of the work, but by smilingly saying little, sometimes nothing, and so letting me fill the silence with my own chatter and blather, she achieved the revelation of my own opinion to me. It took some little while before I realised that this was the process which was passing between us; I am still convinced she was herself unaware of it.

My painting of Lavinia took place in her tiny room near the Cowpats soap factory. Lavinia talked non-stop during the sittings, my futile attempts to stop or even limit this were at an end; one may as well have tried to stop the lapping of the Thames. The themes of Lavinia's monologues were love (her own) and money (her own and everybody else's): in this she was the epitome of the modern Miss.

I called Jane over to come and stand behind the easel, which she did.

'What do you think?'

Lavinia was shown in her new role as Polly Peachum in *The Beggar's Opera*, opening the next week at Lincoln's Inn Fields, with John Rich the producer. Her blue dress fell fetchingly back over her shoulders before widening to bell shape over her hooped petticoats.

Jane looked at my work so far. 'It's good,' she said, then met my gaze with those honest grey eyes, which went wide and wet as our gazes met.

'Honestly?'

'Among the best you've done, William. If not *the* best.'

'I can't bloody move,' wailed Lavinia. 'Jane, they're making me wear these bloody hoops. I look like the dome on bleedin' St Paul's. I daren't move on the stage, I'll fall over and show everybody me bare arse.'

'So?' I said.

'What yer mean, "so"? They 'aven't bleedin' paid for it, 'ave they? Oh, look. I'm serious. Jane, show me 'ow to move. Please. Please, luv.'

'Yes, certainly.'

'Oh, thanks!'

'Take the dress off, Lavinia. Let me put it on. Then I'll do a demonstration for you.'

'Oh, thank you darlin'. You are a *diamond*, you are. Twenty-four carat gold. Don't let this one go, William.'

'I don't intend to!'

A fiery glance from Jane made my eyes water and stirred my loins. But the two women, with some girlish laughter, quickly fell to helping each other off with their dresses. Jane then donned, from Lavinia, what looked like a bent birdcage – a peculiar construction of oval hoops.

'I ain't never seen anything like these,' Lavinia wailed, as the cage was transferred to Jane, who had removed most of her petticoats, putting the contraption over her shift and one under-petticoat. I reflected, the while, that there were worse vocations than that of painter, but after a quick glance at Lavinia in her shift (breathtaking) I kept my eyes loyally on my beloved, though mainly on the secret parts.

'John Rich found this bloody contraption,' wailed Lavinia, skipping about. ''Ee's weird, 'ee is.'

'He's got a very sharp nose,' I murmured. 'Slightly hooked, too.'

'That's funny!' Lavinia screamed. ''Is cock's exactly the same. No, really, I mean it. Pointy but very bent.' Lavinia demonstrated with a crooked finger. ''Ee 'ad me when we played pantomime. 'Ee was Mr Lun. It was worth it, 'cos he got me my role as Poll Peachum.'

'He must have been to France,' Jane said, putting her dress on over the hoops.

'Why, they got bent cocks there, 'ave they?'

Jane was hooting, laughing again. 'No! At least not as far as I know. Your Mr Rich must have got this contraption in France, though. They are the latest from Paris. They're called criardes. This and small handkerchiefs of Brussels lace are the new fashion.'

'So, 'ow ...?'

'You take very small steps, see, like this.' Jane appeared to glide round the tiny room. 'Then the skirt swings out, keeping its bell-shape.'

Lavinia put both hands to her mouth, which was how she registered surprise onstage.

'Oh, Jane! You look so elegant! No! Look, this is really important. I've got a new beau. Best I've 'ad since ... the last one.'

'Good as that?'

Lavinia stuck her tongue out at me. 'Change back, change back! Jane, quick! I wasn't going to say nothing for fear I'd jinx my luck. But this one could be the making of me.'

The two women were changing back to their original clothes.

'Who is he? King George?'

'No! I don't do Germans. But almost. He's the Duke of Bolton. Now what do you think of that?'

Back in her criardes and dress, Lavinia took a few tiny-toed steps. Like the born actress she was, you had only to show her something the once and she could mimic it.

'That's lovely, Lavinia!' said Jane. 'Graceful!'

Lavinia minced over to her in the new tasteful walk. 'You're a darlin', you are Jane. A real lovely person, you know that?'

The two women embraced.

'You're not so bad yourself.'

'You will come and see me on the first night, won't you?'

I felt a twinge of jealousy, as this was addressed solely to Jane, but banished the unworthy thought. 'Yes, of course we will,' I said. 'Half of London is already talking about it. The word is that John Gay has written something truly revolutionary with his new opera, and Rich ...'

'Oh, bugger John Gay. Bugger John Rich. I'm getting thirty shillings a week and my Charlie is coming to the opening. That's the Duke of Bolton to you peasants. And now, thanks to Jane here, I won't be tripping over and showing me arse. That's all I want. Oh, I'm so happy.'

'I hope he's good to you, Lavinia,' said Jane, firmly as ever.

'Bugger that 'an all. Look, he's not much bigger than Little Will ...' (That was the waiter at Button's Coffee House) '... and he's *ugly*. That's the best of it. Fat little face like a baby's arse. Never go for the handsome ones, except for fun, except for a jiggle. If it's serious, they *have* to be ugly. Then they'll stay, then they'll pay.'

'I'll remember that,' said Jane with mock seriousness.

'Oy, thanks!'

But we were already laughing, all three of us, as Lavinia again tore off her dress and the fashionable French bird-cage and danced round the room in her shift, singing a made-up ditty which ran, 'My Charlie'll stay. My Charlie'll pay.' And then, ''Ere, William. Your sisters 'ave got a dress shop, 'aven't they?'

I looked wary. 'Go on.'

'I need another dress for act III of *Bugger's Opera*. The gaol scene. You couldn't sort of …?'

'I'll have a word with them, with Mary and Anne.'

'I 'aven't got much money. Well, none at the moment.'

'As I said, I'll have a word with them.'

'Thanks William, my darling. I need to look my best to take my Charlie away from 'is wife.'

Thanks to lovely Lavinia, John Rich's commission to paint *The Beggar's Opera* on stage was through. I would be in the newspapers for it, sales of the painting and the prints from the engravings were assured. BUT. I really wanted to do a good job; I REALLY wanted it to be something special.

Armed with folded sheets of the blue paper I now used for the first sketches, with crayons tucked into a leather pouch, I met Jane at our trysting place, on the way to the opening night of *Beggar*.

We met at half past three, where the hackney carriages gathered, at the corner of Covent Garden Piazza. Fanny the maid or sometimes her mother, sometimes both, always accompanied her that far, then we sneaked into a carriage. I always insisted on paying for the carriage; this afternoon I also insisted on paying the entrance to *Beggar* – five shillings for box seats, nothing but the best for my Jane.

She was fetching in green silk with a new French bonnet. As we clip-clopped along – *hey, look at the Smithfield boy now* – I was heady with success, seeing not the path ahead but the heights reached so far, something I later learned not to do.

I leaned towards her. 'Have you and your mother made any progress getting Sir James to invite me to a masonic lodge?'

Firstly, it came out all wrong, far too direct. Secondly, when I leaned towards her she thought I wanted to kiss her, in the secret dark of the carriage, and she started to respond. So I messed that up, and no mistake.

'Not really.' She always spoke calmly, evenly, but the tone was a little frosty.

Gawping out of the carriage window, like a Spitalfields boy unused to the ride, I spoke without thinking, a far from unusual occurrence: 'What? You mean you haven't spoken to him, or he said no? Which?'

'We …'

'I *need* this, Jane. You know that. Yes, I've got portraits and groups for the demi-monde, but the masons can give me an entry into society. And that's where the money is. Come on, Jane! Get your old ma mobilised and set to. Please!'

There was silence in the dark of the carriage. I saw her shoulders move, recognising that she was crying. She even cried with dignity, quietly. *Oh, Hogarth, you unworthy wretch. You greedy poltroon, you low-bred fool.*

'Oh, Jane, I'm so sorry! I spoke ... My heart is good, especially where you are concerned, but I want too much too soon. I know that. It was ever a fault.'

She sniffled, pulling a Brussels lace handkerchief from her sleeve. 'It's all right.'

'No, it's not! I would as soon hurt my own arm, or my leg or my head, as hurt you.' I cuddled her against the sway and jolt of the carriage. 'I am truly sorry. Please forgive me.'

She smiled, then pecked me on the nose, giggling as the peck half missed because the carriage hit something, probably a dead dog or something, and lurched. 'You are forgiven!' she said brightly.

But I was William Hogarth, so I stumbled from one blunder to the next, albeit on a rush that carried forever forwards and upwards. As we cuddled in companionable love, pressing soft, chaste lip-kisses (I still gave tongue only with the whores), I said for some reason, 'We are meeting Frenchy, Francis Hayman and the others in Holbourn Row, then we can all go into Lincoln's Inn Fields together ...'

She stiffened, then pulled away. 'Others? What others?'

'Well ... Felix and his French crowd. Some of the painters. Stephen Fowler.'

'I thought it was to be us, alone.'

'Well, Felix ... He's ... down on his luck at the moment. I just wanted to cheer him up.' SHE IS YOUR VIRTUE. STOP IT. STOP LYING TO HER! 'Look, we can avoid them all if you like, break the arrangement.'

She was horrified. 'William, no! Not once you have given your word. I won't hear of it.'

'I'm a fool! Jane, darling, as you've had so much practice, do you think, just possibly, that you could forgive me just one more time?'

She laughed. Thank God I could always make her laugh. There was another peck on the lips. As we alighted at the place where all the hackney carriages were stopping, at the three-way corner of Yeates Street, Holbourn Row and Lincoln's

Inn Fields, a crowd of eight or ten of my friends, including my old apprentice friends Felix and Stephen, were there to greet us.

The company included most of the up-and-coming painters from Sir James's copying school. Francis Hayman was there, eating, gesticulating, and talking, all at once, with his shirt hanging out over the arse of his breeches, as ever. George Lambert was of the company. John Ellys, George Knapton.

Oh, and there was Jack Laguerre. I think he was one of Felix's French mob, not from the bloody copying class. I couldn't remember if the boys from the copying class knew about me and Jane or not. They did now.

When I had finished the last sitting for her portrait, Lavinia said she would meet us outside the theatre, before the opening. She was at the flood tide of her acting career. To my knowledge, she was already in *The Fortune Hunters* (as Nanny), *The Pilgrim* (Alinda, with her legs showing in a breeches part), and Jaculine in *The Royal Merchant*, as well as giving a richly moving Ophelia. Her opening in *Beggar* that night made that at least six plays in which she took the stage, all going on at once; I suspected there may have been more.

There was, naturally, no sign of her outside the theatre to meet us, as she would forget any arrangement minutes after making it. She was as much a creature of chance and influence as a butterfly in a cross-current, was our Lavinia.

Anyway, the rest of us fought our way through the throng at the theatre door, me holding tight to Jane. At least this warmed us up against the late January frost, though it was our good fortune (and Lavinia's) that it wasn't snowing.

By the time we pushed our way through to the box seats some of our companions were gone, no doubt heading for the cheaper areas in the pit, but there was enough of a crowd in the theatre to warm us – over a thousand, by the look of it: from pit to rafters the place was heaving like a bishop's belly.

The Theatre Royal was one of my favourite places of entertainment in the whole of London, but like the others they kept the place as chill, not to mention dark, as possible for as long as possible to save money. The only candles burning were in the floats at the front, but they at least gave out *some* warmth.

As usual, the place reeked like a dead dog rotting in the devil's privy. The aristocratic faction, on the stage, in the boxes or in the slips, were sniffing Hungary water or violets or buying oranges, some even cutting them with their swords, against the odour. Effete, bloodless fops, the lot of them.

I recognised one of them from the House of Commons committee, a blob of meaningless fat called Bubb Dodington, an individual without purpose who was very rude to me on the two occasions he deigned to speak to me at all.

Instantly forgetting Blub-Blub, I glanced sideways at Jane, steady, as ever, in repose. Her eyes were shining.

'Happy?'

'Mmm. I've never been to a theatre before. This is the naughtiest thing I've ever done. Well ...'

We looked at each other, both bursting out laughing together. No matter how many people were around me, when I was with her all I could see was her eyes. Still, I did notice the place was quieter than usual. They, we, the audience, were all waiting, holding our collective breath. That daring title – *Opera* suggested high Italian (foreign); *Beggar* suggested low English. This was something new.

I wouldn't start my preliminary sketch until Lavinia was on the stage but, even so, I had that tightening in my guts that presaged creation: that winding up of emotions, brains, eyes, like the cogs and wheels of a clock being put into motion.

Francis Hayman was on the other side of me, chattering away with his heavy bonhomie, but everyone and everything except Jane, the theatre play and my coming creation was a dashed-off background of sound and noise.

And then it started!

One of the four doors onto the stage opened. A beggar walked on and addressed the audience. I remember it still, thirty-six years later, as I write this: *'If poverty be a title to poetry, I'm sure nobody can dispute mine. I own myself of the Company of Beggars; and I make one at their weekly festivals at St Giles's.'*

There was a roar of recognition at the mention of St Giles; I joined it lustily: none of your foreign places here, your MIlans, your PADuas, your PARises. I pictured the verminous back-alleys of St Giles: the scrofulous streets, thick with grime, and the filthy Dutch-gin shops, floors coated with sick, which formed every other establishment. St Giles, the Bethlehem of pleasure, profit and dirt. St Giles in an opera! I knew what I was roaring about, too, unlike the fops on the sides of the stage or at the front.

But the scene shifted as the story was told. The scene shifted to Newgate Prison! Newgate Prison, just a few streets down from where I played tip-cat with my friends of the day, while the sound of St Sepulchre's bell tolled every time some poor wretch took the cart to Tyburn to be hanged. Newgate Prison, where

I had painted Sarah Malcolm, and so did Sir James. Newgate, a prison, just like the prison in which I lived my boyhood. Another prison.

There it was, represented in painted boards on the stage: a tableau of moving, speaking pictures. I clutched Jane's hand so hard I did believe the poor darling girl whimpered. Stories! If it was possible to tell stories in tableaux, then why not in paint? And real stories, stories about me, my world, London – not worn out myths from the past, in foreign places nobody knows or cares about.

The audience was hushed, hardly talking; never before had I experienced theatre-watchers so quiet, so dough-like, being shaped by what they were seeing. I was part of the audience but I should soon be a player; I would paint this scene, I would paint this story!

Our Lavinia, by the way, was a peach as the daughter of Peachum the peacher: that is, the betrayer. She entered in an ivory white dress with a yellow sash, on loan from my sisters' shop, her bosom hefted up by her stays, also provided by my sisters, her face pushed forwards to hide her double-chin. All her supporters, myself included, cried 'Hurrah for Lavinia!'

Lavinia, meanwhile, was singing to great effect on the stage. She had an angelic, fluting voice, much suited to the English ballad style. For a while I listened; as ever, I was enthralled, captivated, transported, by matters on the stage. Then I started sketching.

BUT, and now here was the breakthrough for me, THIS time I would include the audience. I tried it with my painting of *The Committee of the House of Commons* when I painted Huggins brought to justice. Huh! But I was unable to bring off the painting of the audience that time.

Now, however! Lavinia was staring at the Duke of Bolton in the audience, just behind the spikes in the front row, as he stared back at her, quite besotted. We were not the only playgoers who knew of the drama between them, so knew what we were witnessing. Half of London knew it. So the audience was as good a play as the play. We were all actors – *totus mundus agit histrionem* – even when we believed ourselves to be spectators.

This was a modern thought. I should be the first with it, in my finished painting. It would make my fame and fortune, enabling me to marry Jane in triumph.

I stood: the better to complete my lines of structure on my blue paper.

'Sit down! Sit down, boy!' They cried behind me.

'Oh, shut up!' I shouted back. 'I am William Hogarth, the artist. And I shall stand, if I so please.'

'William!' Jane touched my sleeve, with ineffable gentleness.

I sat down, but went on sketching.

Painting my *Beggar's Opera* in my little room in Long Lane began well enough. I sang the enchanting ditties from the piece as I laid on colour for the brick inside walls of Newgate. I could remember the words of songs with the same felicity as I could remember scenes, having heard the words only once and having only glimpsed the scene.

Through all the employments of life
Each neighbour abuses his brother.

I roared away to myself as I plastered Newgate prison into life, occasionally wiping my painty hands on my smock or pushing my red cap back from my head, so the scar on my head always showed.

Whore and rogue they call husband and wife:
All professions be-rogue one another.

The swag of the curtains, blocked in black, showed all life was on the stage; the curtains falling until they hovered above the audience; the audience as much on the stage, then, as the players. And in the swag of the curtains, there on high, the stage motto *'Utile et Dulce'* – of use and loveliness.

And, oh, I sang!

But this happy time of blocking colour with sung accompaniment did not last. IT WAS NOT RIGHT! IT WAS NOT RIGHT! Its success was assured (the first night's audience actually numbered over 1,300 – even more than I thought – the piece was the talk of the town: this would sell and sell and sell). BUT IT WAS NOT RIGHT!

I was painting the only scene in the opera in which all five major players were together. (Why, William? Because it was the most difficult?) And of course I had the personages of the audience too:

Bolton, of course, in love with Lavinia as Polly; then Major Paunceford, Sir Robert Fagg, Mr Rich, to whom we all owed the entire production; my friend and Sir James's neighbour, Christopher Cock, the auctioneer; Mr Gay, who actually wrote the piece; Lady Jane Cook, Anthony Henley, Lord Gage, Sir

Conyers D'Arcy, Sir Thomas Robinson of Rokeby, who I had met as an entertainer; all looking as if they were listening and watching; all looking like themselves, to themselves (as important purchasers) and to others (as important purchasers). Not the same thing, those last two, by the way.

And what was wrong? I couldn't do Peachum's hat without unbalancing the whole piece; the personages of the audience were much too caricatured for the overall tone; Lucy's face was stiff (because I did not love Mrs Egleton as I loved Lavinia/Polly, I didn't even like her much) … Oh!

I was suffering agonies. I went to sleep on my mattress on the floor, shivering even under my thick quilt, and it was not right. I woke, teeth chattering, coughing from the chest with the cold, and it was not right. I started again, and it was not right. I started again and again. It was not right.

Worst of all was when I made an irrevocable improvement, then found it was better before. And I could not, *could not*, get it back to what it was. So what was wrong, deep down? I did not know precisely – that, naturally, being the key to putting it right.

This version had not enough of the audience, that version too much. When I was satisfied with the structure of one version, I could not transfer the breathing life I conveyed in an earlier version to the later one in which the structure was right. I stopped awhile and drank cheap gin, but it only made me more miserable. I needed Jane!

Jane still wouldn't come to my room, but I needed her to look at those paintings.

I had to find a way to marry Jane, or die in the attempt. I achieved a modicum of peace, when a painting would not come right, by the only means possible to me: start something else.

13

I HAD AN IDEA for a series of paintings which would tell a story, as *The Beggar's Opera* did in its scenes. Like the opera, it was to be about low life, but with references to high life. It would be a progress, then, about a girl who came to London from the north, as my father did, and was ruined by great men's promises, as my father was, ending her time languishing in gaol, as my father did.

I took a swig of gin from a bottle, then spat it out on the sawdusted floor. That was not the way. I remembered how angry my benefactor, Anthony da Costa, was when I asked about Kate at the Fleet, when I was painting the House of Commons committee. He also said she was in the hands of Colonel Charteris.

Dared I try to find Charteris? *No!* Dared I visit Anthony da Costa, to ask him about Kate?

He had been so good to my family, I dared not risk his wrath, and he would have been right to be angry. I HAD to get out of the studio – or bring Kate in – or my head would burst. I had to find Kate.

I clenched my fists, digging my nails into the flesh of my palms until they bled. Then I went and saw Mother Douglas.

'Kate?' Mother Douglas repeated, disbelievingly. 'Just shut your eyes, then all of them are called Kate. Or just call her Kate, at your moment of bliss, even if she be Nell or Florence.'

'Look, I really deeply need ... I'm looking for one specific ...'

'I know. You said. All right. So what did she look like, this Kate of yours?'

'Dark. Wondrous ...'

'Yeah. Skip the wonders. They can all hoik their orbs with decent stays.'

I sighed. 'Regular features, straight nose, long black hair, deep blue eyes. A kind of spot. Here.' I pointed to my forehead.

'Syphilis?'

'No! At least, I don't think so.'

Mother Douglas shrugged. 'Kate Repton, Katie Keppel, Kate Hackabout, Kath O'Mara ... You look done in, William. Want me to find you a girl who looks like Jane?'

I burst out laughing. 'No! I don't need ...'

'You haven't!' Now Mother Douglas was laughing. 'Oh, you naughty boy! Now, how did you manage that? Does John know?'

'John Rakesby?'

'Oh, William! You're a dear boy and I'm truly fond of you. But play me for a fool and we'll fall out. No, dear, not John Rakesby. John Thornhill from down the road who calls himself Rakesby when he lowers his breeches, not in polite society, and doesn't tell his father, Sir James.'

I shook my head in mock sorrow. 'No, John doesn't know about ... how far it's gone. And he's not to.'

Mother Douglas cleared her throat.

'Oh! Mother!' I sighed and reached for my purse. 'A guinea do you?'

'What? From the painter half of London is talking about. When do we see this *Bugger's Opera* then?'

I laughed. 'Lavinia calls it that, too. Oh, you wicked woman.'

'That's why they pay me. Three guineas, if you please, young Master William.'

I shook my head ruefully. I needed her. For one thing, she sent her tally women to my sisters' shop to buy clothes for her girls who walked Drury Lane and the Strand. 'And that's a final payment, in this matter?' I said.

'Yup!' Mother Douglas held out a practiced hand, brown and hard as a tanner's fist.

I gave her the money and got up to go.

'Stay awhile, William. There's only two or three girls around as early as this, but I'll see you get a good time.'

'Not now, Mother. I'll see you with John *Rakesby* this evening.' And then an idea. A brilliant one. Brilliant ideas started from the stomach, I always found, then worked upwards.

'When coaches come down from the north to London, Mother dear, where do they finish their journey?'

The Bell Inn in Wood Street. I did not have to wait long before the wagon from York arrived. And lo and behold, a young lady actually descended! She was nowhere near as pretty as my Kate, but what were artists for, after all, but to prettify reality here and there?

A clergyman alighted from the wagon, too. And Charteris, the evil rapist? Have him in the picture, too. It was *so* much more powerful to use real people. It would signal poor Kate's fate from the off.

Then what? A series of four pictures? Six? The more you painted, the more you sold Modern moral subjects. After her arrival, a courtesan at the house of a Jew like my benefactor. I could use his interior. Then she would betray him. Downhill, after that. A cheap bawd with a bunter. And in the end? Dead from the pox. Sketch the other pictures in the series later.

I was deeply exhausted. I took a chair back to my studio, then slept the sleep of the righteous, or the sleep of the dead, whichever was deeper.

After that I painted well, finishing the first of four versions of the *Beggar's Opera* painting. In all of them, you could see the stage as far as the side-wings, though not as far forward as the orchestra. I showed Lucy, Macheath and Polly as part of the audience, as well as on the stage. And I showed the audience as part of the play – the married Duke of Bolton's adoration of Lavinia/Polly and her acceptance of it.

The *Beggar's Opera* paintings were the success everyone predicted. They made me rich. All I needed then were contacts in society, so I may continue those group portraits. I'd show them the modello of *Beggar's Opera*, if I could get near enough to them. Jane! Oh, Jane. When was Sir James going to take me along to the masons, eh?

14

A S WINTER turned to spring, I painted and sold even more representations of *The Beggar's Opera*, all of them on commission. Each representation had its own engraving; prints from the engraving compounding its sales and my success. And I was a success, I had not failed in life! Oh, what a relief!

By the time James finally deigned to introduce me to the masons, all London knew of me. My *Beggar's Opera* was everywhere you looked: copied on snuffboxes and fans, praised and attacked in pamphlets and verses, chastised in sermons, celebrated in songs. Two more originals of the scene had been commissioned by London worthies, prominently featuring them in the audience.

So it was a man of substance, no ragged painter with his arse hanging out his breeches, who was presented at the new lodge (mind you, they were all new) at the Hand and Appletree in Little Queen Street, in Holbourn, round the corner from Lincoln's Inn Fields.

There, old James was Lodge Master; presiding over the assemblage slumped in an elegant *fauteuil* dating from the time of some high-numbered French Louis (fifteen? Felix would know) with stuffed back, stuffed seat and stuffed arms, while we all sat, about ten of us, necessarily fidgeting and shifting occasionally on a motley assortment of mismatched but uniformly hard hall chairs.

Still, the company was convivial enough. We drank brandy punch, mainly from the serving ladle, while feeding our faces from food piled high on side tables. There was beef aplenty; I was always happy when there was good English beef, so bloody raw you could still hear it moo. There were churchwarden pipes available – some white, some brown with use – plus a pot of Dutch tobacco, for those who preferred. But as for me, I ate.

And to my further delight, we sang songs around the table.

There was I roaring lustily – drunk, full, belching, farting and red in the face:

The girls of the town are such ladies of pleasure,
They go to the town and stitch at their leisure.
With their black jokes and bellies so white:

Chapter 14

Their cullies they call 'em my dear and my honey,
They let down their breeches and lug out their money
For their coal black joke that will lather like soap …

My eye caught Sir James's as we roared away; no knight and courtier now, but an elderly boy in his cups, singing away, not as well as me because he was flat and out of tune. But he smiled as we roared together, my future father-in-law and I.

I wondered when my initiation would begin, those ceremonies so much mocked in pamphlets and newspapers. How about a drawn sword at the door, then? A ladder in a dark room? No! An all-seeing eye? Isis on an ass? A halter to lead me blindfolded by the neck? *Pish and poh, had I just been invited to bloody supper? I could get supper bloody anywhere. Ye gods, I was drunk!*

I was being hauled to my feet. Was this because I was drunk? No, it was because I was about to become a mason. Two wardens, as they called them, were gripping me by the arms.

Ah, the mysterious ceremony! The initiation! First, I was searched for all metal, in order to remove it. My noble sword was therefore taken and laid across the chair I had newly vacated, while the two wardens took one stubby Hogarthian arm each, extending them to the full, leading me thus to the door, where they folded my arms inwards so we might all exeunt in step. Once outside, my tasteful scarlet waistcoat with the gold trim was also removed, leaving me in silk shirt and breeches. (This was good; I was hot from all that brandy punch.)

Then I was hoodwinked – a thick blindfold placed over my eyes. I was stripped to my drawers. (By whom? I prayed I did not become stiff from all that fiddle-faddling about, down there. I tried thinking of Sir James to avoid arousal: this succeeded.) I was dressed in what I discovered later was a loose-fitting white linen shirt and voluminous white linen trousers, à la Turk. My bare feet were guided into soft slippers, which felt pointed (from the same Turk?).

My left leg was exposed to the knee, my left breast similarly bared to the elements and to any of the company who cared to look. I gasped in surprise, tinged with fear, as what was clearly a noose, reeking of tar, was slipped over my head, leaving its attached rope trailing down my torso.

I was led, still hoodwinked, the few steps to the door, whereupon I was bade to knock three times. This I did, so lustily there was a ripple of laughter. Sir James's voice from inside bade me come in.

119

With one warden pulling at my rope from in front of me, the second warden holding my shoulders for guidance from behind, I shuffled forwards in the Turk's slippers. The irregularity of the situation, perhaps coupled with my helplessness, made me want to piss. I wished I had used one of the pots under the table before my initiation, but naturally I could hardly ask for one now. The pressure on my rope ceased, the warden behind me squeezed my shoulders to stop: I stopped.

'Here is a poor candidate in a state of darkness,' intoned one of my wardens. '*Ma'at-neb-men-aa. Ma'at-ba-aa.*' This was in Sir James's voice.

'What?' SHUT UP, HOGARTH. I loosened my noose.

'Those words in Egyptian mean "Great is the established Master of Freemasonry. Great is the Spirit of Freemasonry." William Hogarth, why do you wish to enter the fellowship of masons as a member of the first order?'

TO GET CONTACTS FOR COMMISSIONS, SAME AS YOU, YOU OLD ROGUE. 'To help others and to help my fellow brothers.'

Jane, who appeared at times to know everything on earth despite her tender years, had primed me on the correct answer (James didn't), though I spoke sincerely enough.

Many masonic lodges had formed joint stock companies to help the needy, thereby doing good work, where others only turned a blind eye. Furthermore, I did believe that a man should help his fellow man, where he could, and if masons wished for conviviality while they did so, so much the better. As for the strange garb, well, there was stranger in molly houses and the Hell-Fire Club. Ditto the mumbo-jumbo, meaning nobody batted an eyelid when the Catholics did it.

'William, you are accepted as a member of the lodge at the Hand and Appletree.'

There was a chaotic roar from the assemblage; my blindfold and the rope were removed. Sir James was still speaking: 'Here is your sign, William.' Sir James gripped his right thumb in his left hand. 'Your password is Boaz, the left-hand pillar in the porchway of Solomon's Temple. Here is your fleece.'

Sir James nodded to one of the wardens, who presented me with a white lambswool fleece. I noticed for the first time that Sir James had one tied round his middle, too, as well as something else which looked like a costermonger's money belt.

There was more of the mumbo-jumbo. The volume of the sacred law was revealed to me, but this turned out to be the Bible. I was shown a square and a compass, mindful of the literal origin of the masons, as stoneworkers.

Flushed and surprisingly tired, I was finally allowed to re-join the company round the table, which I did, after relieving what I could no longer contain in the piss pot in the corner.

Minutes later, there was a tug at my white linen masonic sleeve. A slight chap, unassuming to the point of diffidence in his manner, introduced himself as Richard Child (I later discovered him to be *Sir* Richard Child, Viscount Castle-maine). He murmured that his parents would be celebrating their twenty-fifth anniversary shortly. Would I come to Essex, to paint Lord and Lady Castle-maine, family and friends, against a backdrop of their home, Wanstead House?

Yes, I would. I would indeed.

I HAD ARRIVED. I HAD ARRIVED. I WAS HERE.

When the assembled masons finally disgorged into the street, I was drunk with brandy punch and success. I sang snatches of the refrain we sang earlier, my arm round the portly figure of Sir James, though I dimly sensed this did not please him.

We approached his carriage in the darkness, as the company dispersed. I stopped the good Serjeant Painter, as his postilion was opening the carriage door.

'Sir James, old chap. I ask for the hand of your loverly ... loverly daughter, Jane. I wish her as my wife. There, what do you say to ...?'

Sir James disengaged himself from my clutches. His gaze was white cold in the dark.

'Jane? You hardly know Jane. Have you met her above once?'

'Oh ... more often than you think, sir. More ...'

'So, that's your game, is it?' His pudgy face was suddenly lean with fury. 'Well, you will not see her again, sir. That, I promise you. For you shall not set foot in my house again. And my help too, my friendly patronage which you spurn in this filthy manner, is hereby withdrawn.'

'James ... Sir James, please. You misunderstand. I love ...'

The postilion and a footman in Sir James's livery, perceiving the (one-sided) altercation, came running up. For a second, I believed Sir James was about to set them on me. The postilion was indeed carrying a whip. But Sir James waved them down.

'I am your enemy, sir. From this moment forthwith. I give you notice of that, which is more than you gave me when you abused my hospitality with your ... I can hardly say it ... with your designs on my daughter.'

Sir James turned on his heel. As I tried to follow, his footman pushed me. I stumbled and fell on the cobbles, into a pile of horse shit.

15

GIN WAS QUICKER, so I was drinking gin; less bulk than beer, less money than brandy, easier to find than wine – so I was drinking, knocking back, gin. Even John, scion of the Thornhills, was concerned about how much gin, how fast, not to mention how many brothels and bagnios.

I hated lying, to John or anyone else, it was totally against my nature, it was mean and small and convoluted. But at the beginning, at any rate, I had the idea in my head that John must have been told some story or other about my sudden absence from the copying class he and Vanderbank were taking. His star pupil suddenly gone.

My attempts at fabrication had him cocking his pale head at an extreme angle – eyebrows, the while, sloping up towards the middle.

'Oh, all right then,' I roared at John. We were in a St Giles Geneva-shop, too low even for him: my choice. From the low roof to the sharp tip of the proprietor's nose, the place was covered in grime. 'All right then!' I knocked back another tuppeny gin, banging on the soot-grimed table for more, waiting until the glass was filled. 'Here's the truth of it. I asked your father for his daughter's hand.'

'Jane?'

'Yes, Jane. How many bloody daughters has he got? Too much, eh? His beloved daughter and a Spitalfields boy. Too much for you, too. I'll be bound. You are welcome to leave my company.'

'I had no idea ...'

'Yes, horrifying, isn't it? Your sister so sullied and defiled. Goodbye John. I'm sure you'd like to go now.'

John looked round uneasily, for I was yelling, causing the lascars who packed the dingy hole, some close enough to touch, to look round at us curiously. Swarthy, long-bearded types off the ships, these lascars were, filling the dingy room with pungent, thick smoke from their clay pipes.

'Jane always speaks most highly of you,' said John with unusual firmness, but speaking quietly. 'Both to me and in company, but ...'

'BUT! But, but, but. But, but, but, but. I know what the bloody but is, John, so bugger off.'

An Englishman swaggered up to us, dressed up in white silk stockings, a Brussels lace handkerchief in his sleeve. I was interested in the gait people adopted, mimicking it sometimes, as I did their voices. I liked to catch it in paint, if I could. Anyway, this worthy affected what they called a Ludgate Hill hobble. As he passed, he gave a wavy-dribbly smile, saying something I took to be 'sister'. I leaped up, hand on sword hilt, blocking his way.

'What say you there, good friend? Hmm!'

The lascars were looking at us curiously. I let go my sword hilt to push the pretentious promenader in the chest; he was considerably taller than me, but that was nothing new.

'Leave it, William!' John stood. 'I am Viscount Thornhill,' said John to the promenader. 'My friend is intoxicated with the gin, but means no harm. Here, sir, a tot on me.' John proffered a shilling.

The promenader waved away the offer, swaying on his way to the soot-black counter from where gin was dispensed.

'William, we are leaving,' said the newly-firm John. 'I wish for some cunny, while we both still can, preferably without a dose of the pox to follow. So none of your St Giles punks, thank you all the same. We'll find a chair somewhere, to take us to the Folie.'

'Wha's …?'

'It's a brothel afloat, moored opposite Somerset House. You must do it to the rise and fall of the tide, William. It will be the making of you.'

'Oh, very well.' I stopped as John was walking me to the door. 'Afloat, eh? Seems a sound idea! And your sister? Me and your … You don't mind?'

'No, not in the least.'

I tried visiting the Thornhill residence; a footman threw me out. I tried twice more with the same result. The fourth time, Lady Judith saw me coming from an upstairs window and waylaid me on the threshold.

She held me by the arm, as if escape was my intention, before being characteristically blunt: 'You must give it up, William. All thoughts of Jane. I have tried, my dear boy. Believe me, I have tried.' She sighed. 'I tried because I like you, I believe in you and I cherished hopes for you and Jane.'

'Thank you.'

'But once he is driven to stubbornness, there is no more stubborn man than Sir James. He will not budge on this.'

'I ...'

'William, nobody knows him better than I do. And if I cannot move him ...'

'And Jane? How ...?'

I fought back tears, then let them go. I loved Lady Judith, more, if truth be told, than I loved my own mother. My poor powers of dissembling were even poorer with her.

Lady Judith shrugged, a masculine gesture only she could bring off. 'Jane is sad, naturally. But she is young. There is another suitor and ...'

Her eyes were down, looking at the ground. A bolt of hot hope shot through my misery. Another suitor? Oh, no! Lady Judith, you were lying to me.

I was working intently on my *Harlot's Progress*: a new type of painting. I was also completely changing the way I worked. Until then, I had always prided myself on my memory for the line, scorning the preliminary sketch-drawing as leading to copying. But now I resolved to make sketches properly, to take my time.

So there were six good sketches, or rather many variants of six good sketches, as the base for six paintings, telling an exciting story; just as Sir James told the story of St Paul in his works in St Paul's Cathedral.

Mine would be a new story, though: the story of Kate, given the heroine name Moll Hackabout (MH for short) for the purposes of the tale. Kate, newly arrived in London on the York wagon, fell, became the mistress of a Jew, then a Drury Lane harlot, fell even from there to debtor's prison in Bridewell, then died of the pox at just twenty-three, leaving behind her a beloved son. That was my tale.

I kept the door securely locked while working on *Harlot*; I wanted no other world intruding on mine. So I ignored the knock when it came; it was certainly not the first, nor would be the last. But then I caught a glimpse of a figure at the window. A brown linen dress ... It couldn't be!

I unbolted and unlocked the door impatiently, more thumbs than fingers, finally achieving it. I stepped into Long Lane, away from the world in my head. A roar of street clamour hit me like foetid air.

'Fanny!'

The pert creature looked delighted to see me, pouting demurely. 'Mr William, sir!'

A letter for me! She must have had a letter for me from … I was so certain of it I held out my hand for this missive I had imagined, which had suddenly turned my world on its head by becoming the most important thing in it. *Give me the* …

'Hello, William. Will you not invite me in?'

Her voice was as calm and steady as her grey eyes, as if our meeting (oh, would that it were!) were some routine of every day. SHE WAS HERE! SHE WAS HERE! HERE, BEFORE ME! STANDING BEFORE ME! OH, I SWEAR BEFORE GOD AND ALL HIS ANGELS I HAD NEVER BEEN HAPPIER. I COULDN'T TAKE IT. I COULDN'T TAKE LIFE WITHOUT YOU, I KNOW I COULDN'T.

'Yes, of course. Come in.'

She had a hood up round her face, which she lowered as she entered my room, my studio, I mean. She looked round, examining the small space, the tools, the paintings, coolly, with a crisp, fresh curiosity. It appeared incredible, unnatural, that she had never been here before.

'It's smaller than I thought it would be.'

BUGGER SMALL. BUGGER LARGE. IT HAD JUST BECOME PARADISE BECAUSE YOU WERE IN IT. 'Yes.'

'Aren't you going to ask me to sit down?' Her eyes were twinkling now. She knew the effect she was having on me.

'Oh, Jane! Jane! I came. I came to your house. They wouldn't let me in. They wouldn't let me see you.' I started to cry.

'Mmm. I know. Mama told me.'

'Your mother … Your mother said …' I staunched the sobs, with an effort.

'Yuh, I know. I know what she said. She is a wonderful woman in many ways, certainly very clever. But she is not the oracle at Delphi. Do you not possess any chairs?'

'Chairs? Yes. Um …'

I pulled a chair from under the workbench. She perched on it. I paced up and down in the confined space, wiping my painty hands on my mucky breeches.

'You were painting? I disturbed you?'

I paused in pacing, staring at her. 'Yes, you disturbed me. Don't ever do it again.'

She laughed wholeheartedly. MY JANE. 'Oh, Jane. Oh, I am so pleased to see you.'

'Mmm. Me too.' She glanced outside the window, where we could see Fanny, keeping watch.

I paced to her chair, standing over her, and shyly took both her hands in my painterly ones. I kissed her ineffably, gently on the cheek, then brushed her lips with mine. 'Oh, I love you, Jane. I love you so much!'

'Yes, I love you, too. That's why I'm here. *Harlot*'s coming along nicely.' She looked at the completed three paintings, the sketches and plans for the rest, her head tilted just slightly to one side. 'She's very pretty! Not based on anyone I know, I hope!'

'No! Yes. Jane, I'm not going to lie to you. I'm going to spend the rest of my life with you and I'm never, never going to lie to you.' I started to cry again.

'Good,' she said, quietly.

'The harlot's based on a whore I saw at da Costa's when I was a boy. It was the first ... um ...'

'Bosom?'

'Oh, Jane!'

We both started laughing. I kissed her awkwardly.

'Your brushwork is getting lighter. You haven't been looking at Mr Watteau, have you?'

I jumped up. 'God, you are *amazing!* You're barely human!'

'Hmm. *Not* the most romantic compliment a lady's ever been given.' She got up to look at the three finished paintings more closely. 'I like the blue of her dress when she arrives. Madonna presumably?'

'I don't know. Yeah, perhaps.'

She looked appraisingly at the first painting. '"The publicans and harlots will go into the kingdom of heaven before you."'

'Matthew?'

'Yes. Matthew 21:31. You haven't seen Duerer as well, have you? *Life of Christ*?'

I shrugged. 'Do you know ... At the moment, I honestly can't ... I am so happy to see you, my head is in a spin. Yes, Felix showed me some Albert Duerer. Dutch, isn't he?'

'German. And he's in here somewhere. You are very gifted, William.'

'Oh, *thank* you! Darling, thank you!'

'Oh, it's true! No idle compliment. I am the daughter of a painter, after all. It runs in my blood. My my, your harlot does get undressed a lot, does she not?'

I shrugged with mock elaboration. 'Well ...'

Jane sighed. 'Harlots have it so much easier in that respect. Still, I'm sure something can be arranged. Once we're married.'

I stared at her in wonder. 'Your father … His daughter and a Spitalfields boy. Hardly a surprise he reacted as he did. I wonder I had the gall to ask.'

'We are of lowly stock ourselves, William. My father was the son of a grocer. You leave my father to me. Unless …? Do you not want to marry me, now that you've had me?'

'Oh, Jane! I shall not dignify that with an answer. Except for this.' I kissed her gently, long, only lip to lip to express the most ineffable love.

Then there was silence between us as I met her steady grey-eyed gaze. I took a deep breath. 'How? How are we to be married?'

'We elope.'

'Yes! Yes, of course!' I hit myself on the forehead, aiming at my dent. 'Stupid clodhopper William, not to think of that! Leave it all to me. With you in my heart I can do anything. Anything on earth.'

'Do you know, I believe that to be true. And now, well, I can't titillate the way your harlot can, but I do recall you have been quite resourceful in the past.'

'Yes. And will be so again.' We kissed, we began our love. 'This is no ordinary love, my Jane. No ordinary love.'

16

MY NEXT VISITOR of note was again presaged by the appearance of the faithful maid, Fanny. By now I could read every nuance, fold and tilt of her pretty face: there was tension in her neck, her nose was narrowing, the line of the lips hard. I was with a customer who wished a salver engraved, but I bid Fanny ask the Lady Judith to come in, just as Fanny opened her mouth to announce her mistress.

Lady Judith was discreetly dressed, even muffled for her mission; the hood of her mantua was up and remained up. I saw out my business with every appearance of calm, harnessing the discussion of lines and money to garner strength to face a woman I respected, admired this side idolatry, loved even, but who had become my enemy – as why else would she have been here?

Finally my customer, a fool with money as so many of them were, departed the scene, satisfied that his wishes would be satisfied. Fanny, as when Jane came, was now outside, flutteringly keeping watch, like a goose outside Rome.

'Lock the door. And bolt it.'

That intelligent, piercing gaze looked through me, seeing everything. I did as she bade, indeed commanded. She was herself, only more so, as if the inner essences of her being were concentrated now, fuelling her for the fight.

'Jane does not know I am here.'

'I would have guessed as much.'

'She does not know that I am aware of your plan.'

I glanced towards the window, where the outline of Fanny the maid was visible at her watch.

'No, not her!' Lady Judith spoke with asperity, just a touch of impatience. 'She is as loyal to Jane as any puppy. I had to threaten her with dismissal to change sides.' She sniffed. 'I reminded her who pays her wages.'

'Sides? There are sides?' I waved her to a chair, but she remained standing. I sat at my workbench, looking diagonally up at her. 'And how do you know of our plan?'

'I know my daughter, William. She is hoarding clothes. And she has stopped talking about you.'

I smiled, feeling myself puffing up.

'No, William!' she banged a fist on my workbench like a man. Astonishing! 'I say I know my daughter but, what is more to the point, I know my husband. William, when I was a young woman I saw a fight between a fox and a lone hound, detached from the pack. Do you know who won?'

I shook my head.

'The fox won. It killed the hound because it had nothing to lose. And because it did not fight fairly. While the dog tried to engage, head to head, nothing was out of bounds to the fox: eyes, testicles, it went for what was soft. And it ripped the dog to pieces.'

'You mean Sir James …? Why do you say nothing to lose?'

She tossed her head, imperious, impatient, just as Jane did sometimes. 'He's finished! He hasn't had a decent commission in years. His enemies have undone him. All he has left is his position and his pride. Especially his pride. You take that, boy, and he'll fight like a fox: eat the soft bits then spit them out.'

'But … Lady Judith, please. I truly love Sir James, after all he's done for me. And I take him as my master, as a painter. I am not his enemy!'

'Oh, you bloody child, William! When you put your shaft in a man's daughter, you put your shaft in the man. And James will shaft you back, believe me. You will not become a painter, William. Never! He'll see to that. You'll be lucky to keep what you have.' She waved a vigorous arm round my tiny workshop. 'Tell me you will abandon this intemperate plan, William. This idea of an elopement.'

'I love your Jane, Lady Judith.'

'Dear God in heaven, do you think I don't know that? Why do you think I'm here? Do nothing, boy! Wait! Sometimes no action is the best action, even though youth finds it so hard. Leave it to me. I will find a way.'

'When?'

'When! There's a real boy's question. Look … I tell you this. James does not have long to live. His health is not robust. When he goes, you will have my blessing. And Jane is yet young. An old head on her shoulders, I grant you, except in matters concerning you. But young. So … Now. Will you wait? Leave it to me?'

Her brilliance, her cleverness, disarmed me. 'Yes.'

130

'Good.'

There was no farewell; she seemed to disappear, not leave, magically through the locked door, though when I tried it it was open. I peered down the clamorous street but there was no sign of her or Fanny. Was the visit a dream?

I had always been able to work on more than one project at a time; indeed, I preferred to do so. So while continuing to paint my story of Moll the harlot, I locked the door again, then started work with vigour on a portrait of Jane.

I was waiting at the corner of Covent Garden Piazza, where the hackneys stopped as they waited for trade. The Thornhill residence was in sight, on a diagonal line across the square, but I could not be seen from the windows there. At least I believed I could not.

It was a clear day, towards the end of the month of March. Also clear were the outlines of buildings and of people as they moved, as if my eyes and mind were working extra hard to keep the scene fresh.

The day was important, so important, but I was aware I had no fear. I also had no doubt of Jane. Yet again I wondered that she was so much younger than me; for she was older, senior, superior in so many ways. I felt lost without her, bereft when she was not there. I wanted her with me all the time.

'Hiding behind the horses?'

'Aaagh!'

I jumped off the ground as shock made the world go black. One of the horses, spooked, neighed, started to rear, was pulled down by a farrier. Lady Judith Thornhill was standing among the hackneys, just behind me, with a basket covered by a chequered cloth, tiny, like a grown-up Little Red Riding Hood.

'Oh, come, William! You'll need more courage than that, if you are to elope with my daughter, further than the corner of the square.'

I was still shocked, my breathing heavy. 'Are you here to stop us?' Even as I spoke I saw, with the familiar lift of the heart, Jane making her way across the Piazza, carrying a small valise.

'No, I'm here to bring you some food. You'll need some for your flight, after the ceremony.'

'What made you change your mind?'

'Nothing. I haven't changed it. But, short of chaining my daughter to the wall in fetters in the wine cellar, I cannot stop her leaving with you. At least not for long. If I stop her today, she will leave with you tomorrow. The choice then becomes whether you and she leave on an empty or a full stomach.'

'Thank you. Thank you, fair lady.'

Lady Judith handed over the surprisingly heavy basket. I felt foolish holding it, but curiosity impelled me to look under the chequered cloth: a haunch of ham, rich with fat; slices of turkey; a hunk of cheese, Cheshire by its pallor; underneath, some apples, I believe; cherries, ripe.

'Thank you.' I was limp with gratitude.

'I did not do it for your thanks.' Lady Judith waited, poised, obviously with no intention of leaving. I saw that Jane had seen her. She busied towards us; I could see that frowning line between her eyebrows even from where I stood. Lady Judith had robbed us of our embrace, kisses I would have plied her with, even in public.

Jane confronted her; she was bigger than her mother, by some way, as well as being considerably bigger than me. 'Are you here to stop us, mama?'

'No, I am here to bring you some food. William has it.' She nodded at the basket.

'Will you tell papa?'

'For what it's worth, no. But he'll know soon enough. I'd make that food last if I were you. I don't know where the next lot will be coming from.'

'Oh, shut your mouth, mama.'

'Oh, you shut yours!' But Lady Judith spoke it mildly, with a faint smile.

She walked over to the leading hackney, reached up and gave the driver some money. For a second, I thought she intended to come with us, my wild eyes meeting Jane's. But as the driver leaped down, reaching to help Jane with the valise and me with Red Riding Hood's basket, my Lady Judith Thornhill walked off without a backward glance, back towards her home.

It was, it remains, the most purely aristocratic, the most purely noble gesture I was ever to witness.

17

THE HACKNEY deposited us at the church of St Mary-le-Bone, opposite the bosky Marybone Gardens, in the parish of Marylebone, a haunt of Macheath in *The Beggar's Opera*. Marylebone was where the gamblers were, gambling dens piled upon each other by the hundred, but I took no gambles this day. My Jane was a racing certainty!

This church, St Mary-le-Bone, was London's leading for secret marriages. The ceremonies were exciting because the building was so near collapse that every ceremony may have been its last; the happy couple, or indeed the deceased or the newly-baptised, mewling baby, might be buried under flaking plaster or tumbling masonry as the edifice finally gave up the ghost and sighed down into the ground.

I had given the Reverend Winter two guineas for his offices to make us man and wife, but as we entered, Jane and I, the reverend, suitably outfitted in white vestments, was still occupied with the customers ahead of us. He was racing towards old age, this reverend, fuelled by wine or gin to judge by the redness of his nose: a pair of eyeglasses risking the hellfire at its tip.

The Reverend Winter's teeth having long ago departed his mouth, his undershot jaw delivered the marriage service with so much spluttering that it appeared to be announced by a water sprite just breaking the surface of a river.

Jane giggled, then simpered, suddenly looking something like her own tender age, just old enough to make this stolen union legal, if truth be told. I held her hand while we embraced the scene, gathering it into us for future memory.

The bizarrely assorted couple before us evidently still had some way to go before words spluttered by the Reverend Winter would unite their beings as one forever. And, oh, how odd they were, this couple:

A callow youth in fashionable, yellow silk frock-coat, frothing with lace at throat and cuff, his pale hauteur powdered on thinly, not to outlast the day: ladies and gentlemen, I give you the groom.

The bride was an ancient crone in a thick ivory-white girl's wedding dress and strange white *chapeau* arrangement dangling off her head, a thin-lipped smile of triumph masking a lack of teeth, and her wrinkled, flat breasts peeping out, like antique water gourds: half empty now but still strapped to the saddle after a long horse ride.

Also, she lacked the full complement of eyes, the poor dear, having only the one. This facilitated the groom's gazing at the crone's pretty maid, as she adjusted the ancient's dress, on her blind side. This damsel-bride was old enough to be the groom's grandmother, but, I would have hazarded, rich.

Jane was fighting down giggles as happiness let her be childlike. She nodded at the full basket of food her mother had provided. And indeed, why not eat as we watched our predecessors in the factory of holy matrimony? So we did.

Jane carved the ham with a knife thoughtfully provided by Lady Thornhill; we stuffed ourselves with that, the turkey and the rest of it. The Reverend Winter cast a glance our way, but the words gurgled on. He appeared to wish us to keep some of the repast for him.

And indeed, perhaps he *was* hungry, for his church was dilapidated enough. An inscription on the wall told us that St Mary-le-Bone was beautified in 1725. It paid tribute to two churchwardens, Sice and Horn, who apparently had patched the place up at that time.

But their noble efforts had been smoked and wrecked by the bandit time. Plaster was falling from the walls and the pulpit was a stained, greasy disgrace, while a web so thick it surely represented the work of a whole team of spiders covered the poor box: which was as well, for I suspected the poor were not welcome here.

Even as we munched – and I could have done with a beer, my Lady Thornhill, eh? – a parish boy in a coat that was more hole than coat, with shoes in similar state, placed a kneeler before the crone-bride, though I feared kneeling may have been a movement too far for the old dear. In fact, it occurred to me that if the Reverend Winter did not speed up a bit, he would have to proceed seamlessly to the funeral service, as the bride looked ready to expire.

I shared this thought with my own bride-to-be, my arm round her waist, whispering in her ear. My lovely Jane laughed so much she was obliged to desist from the consumption of any more ham.

But, finally, it was our turn. The callow groom helped his ancient beloved towards the church door, heading, I imagined, directly to her bank, now that he had complete control of her wealth, rather than to her bed.

We replaced them before the Reverend Winter, who held out his hand for payment, then wiped his mouth on the sleeve of his holy vestment before launching into the marriage ceremony again, from the beginning. We put the basket with what was left of the food at our feet, lowered our heads and let the words from the *Book of Common Prayer* wash over us.

We had just reached the point where I was to say *'I, William Hogarth, take thee, Jane Thornhill, to be my wedded wife, to have and to hold from this day forward, for better for worse,'* and all the rest of it, when there was an almighty commotion behind us. A deep chill ran through me, belly up to head, as I recognised the voice of Sarah Young, the assistant at my sisters' shop, who had performed certain pleasurable services for me at my workshop.

I twisted as I spoke my vows, to see Sarah Young and, worse, her mother doing battle with a woman, evidently a churchwarden, as they tried to gain access to my wedding. And, oh calamity, Sarah Young had a baby at her breast, a mewling, squawking baby. As I spoke on with my holy vows, I was trying desperately to remember exactly what it was that Sarah and I did, in the privacy of my workshop.

Did we do enough to make that baby? My recollection was only of her mouth, like Felix Pellett's, only she used her tongue more and moaned more as she went about her work. Best hurry up with the ceremony!

I started to gabble, *'... for richer, for poorer, in sickness and in health, to love and to cherish, till death us do part, according to God's holy ordinance; and thereto I plight thee my troth.'*

Jane heard the commotion, too; one could hardly have missed it as it echoed round the massy walls and off the ceiling of the damp, decaying, holy dump.

'I, Jane Thornhill, take thee, William Hogarth, to be my wedded husband ...'

She looked at me quizzically, the lovely eyes open rather wider than usual. I shrugged elaborately, trying to mouth the name Sarah Young, but it was difficult to communicate this effectively, while speaking marriage vows. The Reverend Winter seemed oblivious, fortunately continuing to officiate.

My fists clenched as I silently cheered the churchwarden on in her unequal struggle with Sarah, albeit handicapped by the baby, and her mother. But, fortunately, reinforcements were at hand. Like good Prince Rupert at the Battle of Edgehill, a lugubrious parson's clerk, supported by the parish boy in the holey garments, charged to the succour of the fighting woman churchwarden. They joined forces, indeed as Rupert of the Rhine and his fellow royalist Lindsey once did at Edgehill, driving the parliamentarians (here Sarah Young, her mother and her baby) from the field.

After the ceremony, with everybody concerned paid their due, I kissed my bride of minutes. Mercifully the coast was now clear. But ...

'Who was that woman?'

'What woman ...?' But a look from the clever grey eyes was enough. 'Ah! That was Sarah Young. She works for my sisters at their little emporium.'

'How did she know we were to be married here?'

'My sisters must have told her. I told *them*. I told them not to come, but ...'

'And she had her mother with her. And a babe in arms.'

'Did ...? Yes, she did.'

'William?'

'Yes, darling.'

'Why would she bring a babe in arms to a wedding? Unless she believed ... William, does she believe you to be the father of this baby?'

'Who knows what she believes? She is a strange creature. Simple. But strange.'

'Well, has she grounds for this belief? William, have you fornicated with this girl?'

'Jane ... Darling, I honestly can't remember. I've been racking my brains all through the ceremony. She used to come to the shop. She wouldn't go away. Before I met you. Naturally. As far as I recall, we only did ... You know. Mouth stuff.'

'Mouth stuff?'

'At least, I think ...'

'But you're not sure?'

'Not a hundred per cent. No. Sorry.'

'Hmm. Well, she's gone now. But I must confess I'm a bit jealous. If you did give her a child, I suggest you give me one as soon as possible. Even things up.'

'Righty-ho.'

'And, husband, you might also tell me where we're going when we leave this hovel of a church.'

'Uh ... Yes. Jane?'

'What?'

'You are truly the most amazing, astounding woman in the world.'

'That is correct. And don't you ever forget it.'

'I won't. My God, how I love you ...'

And so to Lambeth (yes, where?) by hackney, with the woman I was kissing as we were thrown about in the back, a woman now my bride, my wife, my ... whatever else.

After jolting, kissing and yet more eating, for we were determined to plumb the depths of Mama Thornhill's basket of delicacies, the hackney abruptly stopped. I had no idea where we were. After we had left the church, I gave the driver a scrap of paper with an address on it. That scrap was earlier given to me by my true friend, the one and only Pellett (Frenchy-Felix of that ilk). He said he'd got us a room and that was good enough for me.

The coachman demanded a king's ransom for the ride, for we were further south of the good river Thames than I had been in my life: for all I knew, folk had two heads here. But I paid with aplomb before my bride, even with a shout of 'Keep the change, my good man' – an effect spoiled in the event by me, not giving him enough at the first attempt.

'So where is this place, then?' said Jane, as we stood on a street with a hugger-mugger of houses before some fields. Over her arm curved the basket with the mortal remains of Mama Thornhill's benison, like the After in some Before and After version of Little Red Riding Hood.

I consulted the scrawl of the scrap of paper. How in God's name did the hackney driver read that, Frenchy's foreign loops and whorls? Perhaps he didn't. I didn't know where we were. This could have been York, where my harlot Moll came from, when she came to London, for all I knew. I peered down the street, as a strong wind blew off the fields, rustling Jane's dress. Nothing. Nobody lived here. How could we live here?

Agh! A noise behind me. AND THERE HE WAS.

'Felix, am I pleased to see you!'

'Bill? What, have you no luggage at all?'

'Not at the moment. We'll send for it, or something.'

'*Mon dieu!*'

'Frenchy, meet my bride, my lovely Jane.'

Felix, you know, had a quite delightful smile which created the most interesting craters in his face on both sides. There it was! 'Madam Hogarth. *Enchanté.*' He took her hand, slobbering over it in that disgusting Gallic manner, then he looked her in the eye. 'I knew that the person who took Bill Hogarth to marry would be either the biggest fool or the wisest woman in all Christendom. And now I see you, I know!'

Jane's frank, brave eyes met his. 'Well, which then? Do tell?' It could have been her mother speaking.

Felix laughed. 'The wisest, of course. And now let me show you to your quarters, my lord and my lady.' Felix gave a mock courtly bow, which he was rather good at. As we followed he reeled out a monologue: 'I have given of my best with the preparations for your arrival, but cockroaches are the very devil to shift. Moreover, one rat was so persistent with his company that I ended by ceasing all attempts to kill him, in favour of naming him and making him a companion and pet. He's called William ...'

'Felix ...!'

'He's teasing you, William.' Then she whispered in my ear, 'Where did you find him? He's very amusing. Well made, too.'

I whispered back, 'There, I think you might be disappointed.'

'Why, were you?'

I shot her a sharp glance. *How could she POSSIBLY ...?* But her face was guileless.

The room was in the house of an army widow, a Mrs Pettifer, to whom we were briefly introduced by the unflappable and indeed incorrigible Felix. She was a worn, sad lady for whom the business of being alive, even breathing, which she did with difficulty, appeared too much.

The good courtier then left us in our rooms, departing to make arrangements for the transfer of our belongings, joining forces with the faithful Fanny-the-maid in the Thornhill household for matters affecting Jane. To my amazement, all my painting equipment, together with the unfinished *Harlot* series and the unfinished portrait of Jane, was already here. Felix, you marvel!

We are alone now, Jane and I.

Two rooms: rough floorboards, like in a low tavern, a bed, a table, chairs, a stove. How ordinary the list, but the rooms were transformed by their occupants, acquiring a lustre, a glow, the clearest of colours, the shapeliest curves, the brightest of outlines.

For in that room I painted like a fiend inspired and loved as if every day were my last. Only the evenings had a softer pace, reading aloud to each other by the butter-glow of an oil lamp. It was at this time I read Jonathan Richardson's *Essay on the Theory of Painting*.

138

Or we would take all the parts in plays the faithful Felix had brought us: *The Victim* by Charles Johnson was one such, as performed at the Theatre Royal in Drury Lane. *A Woman's Revenge* was another, penned by one Christopher Bullock and performed at the New Theatre. We would shout out the lines as if drunken groundlings were ready to toss us in the air, if displeased. I often looked up to see the shade of my darling papa looking down on us with his smile. Jane, understanding this, would hold my hand.

Jane made a friend of the widow Pettifer; they went to market, to the shops together. Now and again we would invite the widow to eat our meal with us in the late afternoon, when the light faded and I finished painting. I wanted to stay here forever. But Jane said we must go back, face her father. We argued, then more: quarrelled for the first time ever. It was deeply upsetting to me, less so for Jane. *No, Hogarth, that is unfair and unworthy!*

'We do not have much money,' said Jane, with quiet force. 'And we will have none if we stay here much longer.'

'But …' I wanted to say that I did not wish to leave paradise, but my anger rose in me; it remained unsaid.

'My father's anger is spent, or mostly so.' Jane waved a note from her mother, travelled the well-worn path from Mama Thornhill to Fanny to Felix to here. 'Here, read it.'

'No!' My lip jutted like a thwarted child.

It remained jutted as we loaded our possessions onto a hired cart, helped as ever by Felix, to return to town, to my little studio. When I was not so sulking, I was roaring with anger at imagined slights from people and things. I was difficult. Difficult Hogarth. Poor Jane! Poor Felix! I record this mood with shame.

But back we went, back to my studio, to be told by street gossips that angry Sir James had indeed sent his footmen over to seek me out and chastise me. *I was not afraid! I would face them!* I started strutting like a bantam cock, I could feel myself do it.

'Where are you going?'

She had her outdoor wear on, mantua and bonnet. I feared she was leaving me.

'To see my father.'

'No, I forbid it!'

'Don't be silly. I will bring him round to our view.'

'Ridiculous! How?'

'I will show him your paintings.'

'Are they ... am I ... good enough?'

She turned at the door, all cool grey eyes and poise. 'Oh, yes. You surpassed my father some time ago. I think he will love you for it. He is a fighter, like you, but at base a good man. Like you.'

And with that she disappeared. I shrugged and went on painting. Both the *Harlot* series and the portrait of Jane were close to completion. While I worked, I would forget everything, but the me that would forget everything was now composed of part me, part her. So I felt only a mild annoyance at being interrupted when she returned towing both her parents.

I bowed to Sir James, who was a little stiff but returned the bow. Mama Thornhill kissed me on both cheeks, for all the world like Frenchy-Felix Pellett.

'Show papa your paintings.' My Jane spoke like the mistress of a mansion, born to rule.

I waved at the *Harlot* series, then put the six paintings in order, so the plot unfolded. Sir James gave me a startled glance. He looked smaller than I remembered, and far from well. I remembered mama – Lady Thornhill, as was – telling me that he was not long for this earth.

Sir James was taking in my *Harlot* paintings. 'Lovely colour,' he murmured to himself, taking in the ivory of the harlot's gown, as her breast peeped out over it. He was breathing deeply. Jane and her mother stood in a 'V' shape, the model of female discretion.

He walked to the end of the series. Only painting six was not yet quite finished: the scene of the harlot's demise, unmourned at the age of twenty-three, with even her toddler son playing unconcernedly with a spinning top.

He shook his head, wheezing now, hauling each breath up. 'It is not my way, this modern way, these ignoble subjects, this lack of grandeur. Of standing, even. Oh, I know it is the way of the world,' he waved a hand as if to forestall criticism, 'in painting now – as in the theatre, where we have Messrs Gay and Rich to thank for it. *Beggar's Opera* indeed! But, William Hogarth, you have something. You have quite a lot, if truth be told. Talent to burn.'

'You ... like the paintings, sir? Even if you do not approve?'

'Oh, I approve, all right. I approve of women, though I don't wish to be one.' Sir James wheezed with laughter; we all joined in, politely.

140

'I have a present for you, sir.'

The portrait of Jane was finished. I picked it up by the frame – it was 35 by 27 inches – and I put it on a chair, so Sir James could see it. Jane was pictured seated, turning towards the viewer. Her gaze was steady, eyes serious. The magnificent bosom, which made me go off like a musket in my passion, was rendered discreetly, but done justice to, all the same.

'She is holding a miniature of you, sir.' That had been Jane's idea.

'So I see.' It was working; the old man's eyes were rheumy. He clutched my arm a moment, for support. 'So I see.'

'It is a tribute from us both, sir. A tribute from us both. To you.'

Jane found a chair so the old man might sit. He looked frailer by the moment, yet waved a hand. 'Enough, William. Enough, boy. The battle is won, don't slaughter the prisoners.' He laughed at his own joke; once again we all joined in. And then ... 'I'll help you all I can. That's what you want, isn't it?'

I took a deep breath. 'Yes, sir. If you'd be so kind.'

'Oh, I'll be so kind, all right. And you and Jane need to find yourselves somewhere decent to live. Now that you are a successful society painter. Now that you have arrived. Mr William Hogarth.'

'Yes, sir. Thank you, sir.'

Part III

From the Harlot to the Devil
1732–58

1

'I SHALL POSE you before the grand chimney piece,' said Sir James, speaking without enthusiasm nor even satisfaction, but rather in the manner of a man giving orders for this or that dish at supper.

Jane and I obligingly shuffled into place, touching each other the whole time, giggling and guffawing – the giggling by no means limited to her and the guffawing by no means limited to me. I sported my finest, wearing a gaudy mulberry coloured waistcoat and toting a sword. She was a sea of pale green silk.

'Oh, Billy!' she protested, squeaking as my arm encircled her waist, my hand contriving to encompass more silk than it should. 'Billy, you must stand ahead of me. So.' She adjusted me, more touching. 'For you are my lord and master. My light, my guide, my er ...'

'Jenny, my darling, this was ever true. But you shall stand beside me. For one thing, I can see you better.'

We both collapsed into fresh paroxysms of laughter at that, which involved clasping each other round the neck. A kiss was stolen, if anything taken so willingly can be said to be stolen.

'I shall arrange you in a moment,' squeaked the indignant Sir James. 'And where did all this Jenny and Billy rigmarole come from, pray?'

'Where did it come from, Jenny?' I said, all mock innocent, thumbs in the top of my breeches.

'I don't know, really, Billy.' Thus Jenny. 'From you, I expect. You are the originator, after all.' She gave a theatrical sigh. 'I merely follow meekly on behind. Giving you the occasional smack on the rump for encouragement.'

She suited the action to the word, with much squealing, slapping, mirth and horseplay, as we chased each other in circles.

'Children! Children!' protested Sir James, in exasperation half feigned and half real. 'Where is the pose? Tell me that. Where is the pose?'

'Sorry, father,' said Jenny, trying but failing to re-align her striking, handsome features to seriousness, while still fending off her swain's flaps at her seat.

The tableau may have continued to re-arrange itself like this for some time, had not Lady Thornhill at that moment swept into the room, majestic in puffed clouds of pink, her intelligent eyes alert. She was trailing the glassy-eyed Thornhill son, John, in her wake. This customarily debauched figure was even paler and even more the sole denizen of his own domain than usual. He looked about to gracefully die.

The pair was followed by a scampering, yapping pug dog, who in turn was followed by a footman, running after him, trying to recapture him. The pug flailed its little legs towards me.

I delightedly scooped him up. Oh dog, dog! I love dogs!

'Trump!' I greeted the animal by his name. He ecstatically licked my face.

Trump had been a wedding present from Lady Judith, ostensibly to bride and groom but really solely for me. The shrewd Lady Judith knew me, as ever, better than I knew myself.

'Because he looks so much like you,' she had said to me. 'I've always thought of you as a pug, a pugnacious little pug.'

'And so I am, Lady Judith. So I am.'

I had held the pug pup Trump against my chest, upon his presentation, then kissed him and burst into tears.

'You are a wonderful lady,' I had blubbed at Lady Judith. 'All my life I have wanted such a pet. It was never possible for us. But I played with every mangy cur who would let me, all through my boyhood. Oh, you are exquisite!' This last was addressed to the excited animal, not to Lady Judith, even as the object of this adoration pissed on my jerkin, which worried me not a jot.

'Let him stay!' I so addressed the footman, who was trying to relieve me of the pug. 'You may go.' This, too, to the footman from the newly lordly Master Hogarth. (That is me.)

'Judith!' Sir James shouted his relief. One might almost have said 'bellowed', were the tiny frame of Sir James, with his pointy feet, not too frail for so alarming a noise.

But at any rate, hungry English infantry on the march to Blenheim were not more pleased to see their commanding Corporal John with their supper than Sir James was to see his wife. Even Billy and Jenny paused in our not exactly innocent games to become once again William Hogarth and his new bride Jane; such was the moral force of Lady Thornhill.

'Well, come on then, where do you want me? My precious time is flying. I shall pose, dear husband, but where?'

Under Lady Thornhill's commanding presence the family came to order. In next to no time the group was posed. Thornhill himself stood next to his son. John was in the middle, with me on his other side; the three painters thus forming a shallow 'V' with Sir James at the apex. The two ladies were, rather daringly, at the wings, with Lady Thornhill nearer Sir James, and Jane still contriving to be shoulder to shoulder with her William, touching as much as possible. I wanted the pug at my feet, but it kept scampering off, before circling back.

'A conversation piece, then?' I called out gaily, while Sir James was still in pose.

This gentle tease carried a barb within it. Sir James was generally held to have had his day, to be of the old school, less and less awarded the dull respect his due, while excitement mounted for the coming men, among whom was ... well, me. Not that I encouraged such an attitude, far from it. In company and in the presses I was staunch in my admiring defence of Sir James.

Sir James had at best a country-cousin relationship with humour, but he knew raillery when he heard it. Out of bottomless love for his daughter, he had allowed himself a guarded old man's contentment at her happiness. And so he responded in kind to that halfway house between humour and the truth we know as teasing.

'Conversation piece be damned,' he grunted, sounding obligingly croaky and behind the fashion. 'We shall all be painted looking at proper classical art, and showing due reverence for it, especially my son-in-law, even if I have to plaster his phiz on afterwards.'

We all laughed at that, I the loudest.

'What classical piece shall we be looking at?' asked John, picking up my teasing tone.

'The group will be represented looking at *A Judgement of Paris*. The viewer will reflect on the choices of life made down the ages.'

'Yes, but Paris made the wrong choice, didn't he?' This was John. 'That's the whole point of the picture. He was swayed by lust.'

That evening, at John Thornhill's insistence, he and I went out on the town. John insisted we head for Bob Derry's Cider Cellar as he had developed an obsession for the carnal possession of one Lucy Cooper, who he had once glimpsed from afar and who was said to be available to those paying brief court and making suitable arrangements at that place. She was in that night, as was Nell Robinson, who added to the kudos of any man with a guinea and a half and time for conversation.

After we had both enjoyed the various pleasures, I was mightily amused by two molls spitting perfect streams of gin at each other. I wanted to wager on them, but John was growing bored and insisted, as I knew he would, sooner or later, on a visit to the Rose Tavern in Russell Street, whose golden sign proclaimed the lowest pleasures in London.

Here, ladies well past their best in tally'd clothes, with over-painted faces, did posture dances high on tables while the gentlemen watchers looked up from low stools. That night a posture moll with a glass eye balanced on one foot on a tray and pleasured herself.

Setting off for home, at my insistence, it came on to rain just as we set off across the piazza. John Thornhill, being the most inconstant as well as the laziest fellow I had ever met, suggested we head for St Clement Danes for a lady down on her luck, instead of going home.

'The hackneys are only over there,' said John, waving at them. 'Or maybe Hummums to partake of the pleasures of the good Mrs Gould? That's within walking distance. Eh?'

'Not in the mood anymore,' I slurred. My head was spinning with the drink which, if truth be told, I could take less well than John.

At that moment a couple of tuppeny bunters strolled by, eyeing us.

'They'll do,' said John, piling inconstancy on inconstancy.

'I thought you wanted to ...'

I was to wish, many times, that we had followed one of John's many alternative plans.

The bunter suddenly 'mine', for the other had already taken John's arm, was tall, dressed in a silver gown open at her bony chest, with two girlish ribbons in her thinning hair, which was swept back and streaked with grey.

As I looked, a gust of wind in the rain bore the sodden ribbons briefly aloft, before they fell back again, damp and defeated. The high forehead this revealed was a parody of intelligence, just as her stately demeanour, born of a certain stage of hunger, was a parody of aristocratic grace of bearing and movement. She held a closed fan to her wrinkled, much-pursed lips.

The clock on St Paul's rang out eight o'clock, cutting tinnily into the din on the piazza, causing a pause in the brawl erupting in the doorway of Tom King's.

Chapter 1

With the trace of a smile, I looked up at the figure of Time with his scythe and hourglass above the clock, always a favourite symbol of mine as I was always in such a hurry. And below the clock the warning words *'Sic Transit Gloria Mundi'*.

Behind them a fellow was bawling his wares, Dr Rock's nostrum, reminding me fleetingly of my boyhood selling the nostrum prepared by my mama. Oh, that thought of a nostrum had rung a warning bell in my mind, to ring over the tinny chimes of St Paul's. Was there a second there, as the quartet of buyers and sellers prepared to move off to the tight alleyway behind Tom King's, when I could have pulled away? When I could have said no to the transaction and its anticipated pleasures? Whenever I have thought back to that moment, so many, many times, I simply do not know.

Ahead of us, as we moved off, two women, one young one very old, warmed their hands at a makeshift fire. Behind them a young gallant, no doubt fresh out of Tom King's, gave tongue into the mouth of a bawd somewhat more tooth-some than the bunters awaiting John and me.

Another gentleman, with 'gull' written so clearly on his ageing features it may as well have been a placard held aloft, was attempting to woo another bawd whose comely hesitation was designed to raise her price.

Past them all we went. And behind Tom King's the tuppeny bunters slipped the coins into leather purses they tied into their fobs, then hoisted their skirts for the trade. No need for Dr Condom's so useful invention, not with hags of that vintage, at least that is what I thought at the time. Wrongly, as it so transpired.

2

ENSCONCED in our rooms in Sir James's house, I waved a copy of the *Weekly Register* triumphantly on high at Jane, before lowering it to read to her, although I had already memorised what it said.

'The story you see, Jenny dear, the story of the harlot from my poor aching head.' I stroked the bashed groove on my forehead to illustrate my point. Jane started to speak, but I waved her to silence the better to continue to announce my triumph.

'Here's the core of it. Blah, blah ... "would redound as much to his reputation as the late *Progress of a Harlot* by the ingenious Mr Hogarth." You hear that, Jenny darling? The *ingenious* Mr Hogarth. Ingenious, indeed!'

I puffed myself up, only half self-mocking, and went strutting round the room like a bantam cock, chest thrust out.

'Do you know who wrote the article?'

'Mmm? What? Yes. James Ralph. Know him from Old Slaughter's. He's a good fellow.'

Jane nodded, smiling at me indulgently. 'Yes,' she said thoughtfully, her grey eyes open wide. 'You have a name now. And even more importantly, people know what to expect.'

I stopped strutting. 'Clever Jane,' I murmured.

At this point in my life, aged thirty-five and so far from a young man, I was much exercised by what had changed and what had not. The changes were there for all to behold – the strutting Hogarth, wallowing in the soft down of luxury, surpassing Sir James, a man once held as hero. But what had not changed kept me a small man, in my own eyes, constantly tugged back to being a small boy.

For the whole tribe of printers and booksellers, the whole cannibal tribe who fed off the flesh and talent of painters, were doing to me what they had done to my father. I always believed that my darling pater would have lived years longer without their stripping of his flesh. The likes of Edmund Curll, Overton the print seller, Wyat at The Golden Lion, and Bowles. Only Charles Ackers, to my certain knowledge, had had the grace to die, between my father's time and mine.

I could never remember Bowles' first name – I was ever poor at names, but Bowles was the worst of them. When my *Taste of the Town*, a daring exposure of modern morals, first appeared, it was Bowles who obliged me to sell my original engraving plate to the pirates for a pittance, as there was no place of sale for my works but their shops and they would not deal with me if I didn't.

Long and loud I bemoaned my helplessness to control the sale of prints and engravings of my own works – the fruits of my own talent – until Jane, with her simplicity which was rendered down wisdom, said 'Why not simply assume control, then?'

'But nobody has *ever* ...' I was pacing at the time. I stopped.

Jane laughed. 'When has that ever stopped you?'

This particular seed of Jane's was no sooner in than it sprouted. And the result was that the tale of the harlot and her progress, in six pictures, was to be sold by subscription by William Hogarth alone. No printers, no booksellers. I intended to do it all myself, bruit the thing abroad and collect the money. *Tout seul!*

Purchasers had simply to present themselves at Sir James's well-appointed premises in Covent Garden. On production of half a guinea they received a subscription ticket to the six paintings of the *Harlot's Progress*.

When the engravings of *Harlot* were ready, and copies could be taken from them, purchasers of the subscription ticket would receive their six prints on payment of another half guinea.

But could such an audacious scheme work in practice? Would the cannibal tribe still find a way of pirating the material?

The answer to the second question was that they did. Figures were seen lurking outside Sir James's house, sketch pad at the ready, peeking through the downstairs windows. The *Harlot* was quickly ushered upstairs, while the pirating sketchers were driven off by Sir James's footmen. Then, there was even an attempt to inveigle a copier into Sir James's household, in the guise of a new under-footman.

But would buyers accept this mode of purchase? The worry of it, in addition to whether buyers would come, was the need to find skilled engravers to engrave the paintings, for I knew I could not undertake it myself. I had never really risen from my level as Gamble's ham-fisted apprentice engraver.

Only the French were delicate enough to engrave really well. But for all the French in London, seeking the good life, I had so far failed to find one up to the task. Oh, for Frenchy Pellett or his like, but Frenchy had disappeared, some said back to France.

So I tried Sympson (who was English), and found wanting, then Vandergucht, also found wanting. And others. And others. In the end I had no choice but to put my own stubby hands to work and slowly, laboriously, I did the engraving myself, saving anything up to £100, as I proudly told Sir James.

But the uncertainty over the whole daring and new(ish) project was shown clearly enough by the first mention in the press of prints of the *Harlot* – the announcement of its delay, as my stubby fingers struggled along.

In the *Daily Post*, the *Daily Journal* and the *Craftsman* there was this: '... being disappointed in the assistance he proposed, the artist is obliged to engrave them all himself.' It was a full three months later before another announcement in the *Daily Post* declared the six prints 'ready to be delivered'.

By then, Jane and I had more than an inkling of the likely response. More than a thousand potential buyers had made their way up the stairs to Sir James's elegant vestibule and on into the painter's studio, to part with a guinea in two stages and leave clutching their subscription ticket.

A triumph, then, for the ingenious Mr Hogarth as author of *Harlot*, as engraver, as man of affairs and as avenger of his father against the tribe who had done him down. I wept on Jane's shoulder at my first inkling of what a success *Harlot* was going to be. But I didn't kiss Jane on the mouth, let alone make love to her. The hurt in her face haunted me, at the moment of what should have been my greatest success.

The pain in the balls had come first. This was close enough after my encounter with the tuppeny bunter round the side of Tom King's for me to know she had caused it. Then a couple of red raised spots on my cock – big enough, obvious enough. Then came the dripping of smelly yellow stuff into the expensive Spitalfields silk drawers I now wore. And through them into the front of my breeches. I had to keep my waistcoat or even my dress coat on the whole time, in case the growing discharge between my legs became evident.

Angrily, miserably, I considered wrapping my poor suffering member in linen or even wool. What could be done about the French Pox? Five guineas a time to see a surgeon? They knew no more than apothecaries. And if I went to a quack of their circle, like our neighbour John Misaubin, who I had just portrayed in the *Progress*, treating my harlot for the clap, it would be all over London.

It would get back to Jane. So would a visit to the dispensary in St Martin's Lane, where I would stand a good chance of bumping into an artist friend, or worse, an artist enemy, sauntering into Slaughter's Coffee House nearby. I was annoyed about that, because the dispensary would have been cheap. In a fury, I eventually determined to visit an apothecary, somewhere out of the way.

I consulted Mother Douglas, an expert in such matters. I feared her ribald laughter, even as I spoke, or rather whispered out my anguish. But Mother Douglas had heard of my recent marriage and she was sympathetic. I knew she liked me both for myself and for my consideration to the girls, which was, as she once told me, 'at Jew level for its kindness and heart.' And anyway, she regarded such motherly advice as an extension to the service she provided.

'If you want discretion, Billy, an open hand and a closed mouth, Theosophus Taylor of Clerkenwell is your man.'

'A quack?'

Mother Douglas shook her head, laying her hand fondly down on my shoulder.

'He's an apothecary.'

'A good one?'

'Not particularly, but he'll give you the same mercury as those who've got letters, plus he'll keep his mouth closed and that's the main thing for you, my boy. There's only two sorts what are discrete, Billy Boy: them as is dead and them as don't know nobody. Taylor don't know nobody and he ain't far from being dead, neither.'

'Oh, that's a fine recommendation! What's wrong with him? Did he take his own medicine?'

Mother Douglas let go of my shoulder and shrugged. 'He's likely got the French Pox, like you. Most everybody has these days.' She sighed windily at the ways of the world. 'But I'm not sure if that's what's killing him. Anyway, he's not long for this world. I'd get a fast hansom if I was you.'

I laughed. I truly felt better. Mother Douglas was as unruffled as a mill pond on a sunny summer noon. Such folk calm the fears of others and point out the bright side.

The good Mother turned away. Kindness had its place, but it could only take so long. She had an establishment to run and good money to take from bad boys.

I did indeed set off immediately. This Taylor had his establishment in Woods Close in Clerkenwell, not far, Mother Douglas had informed me, from the Skin Market. Aye, and not that far from the mad house either, I had thought, but I kept the thought to myself.

It was well out of chairing distance, so, swearing at the pain of it, I forked out 1s 6d for a hansom. I cheered up when I made a joke to the driver about arriving before Taylor died.

There was, in any case, no question of sending a note on ahead, thus inviting blackmail. And certainly no question of sending one of Sir James's footmen, as advance party, or even Sarah Young, who would do my bidding, I was sure, until death. So I arrived unannounced and alone at Taylor's insalubrious premises and crisply demanded of the girl-child who presented herself to see Theosophus Taylor, forthwith.

'You a pal of his, good sir?'

I puffed myself up to my full bantam-cock dimensions. 'It is a medical matter.'

The girl trotted off, muttering 'Got the pox, then, have we?' knowing her lithe speed would see her clear of my anger.

A moment passed, then a woman appeared wearing clothes cut from the same cloth as the child's – at least the sleeves of her dress were of the same gold material as the girl-child's skirt, with a red rose pattern. But that was not what first caught my attention.

Past the first days of flowery youth certainly, the woman was still comely. Her hair was jet black, her bosom in the low-necked dress creamy and to my eye all the more attractive for being full like a woman's not high like a girl's. Her right breast had an 'FC' stamp full on its swell: female convict. She had not tried to hide it. My battered member stirred again and stirred hard. I stared at her.

'Come this way please, sir.' The woman affected not to notice my stare. She spoke in a common whine, which only increased my low desire for her. 'We have sent out for Mr Taylor.'

I followed her through the small apothecary's shop to a door behind the counter.

'Is Mr Taylor away, then?' I intended petulance, born of my new found status as the ingenious rising star of artistic London, but such was my desire for her my voice went from deep to hoarse to croaking.

Chapter 2

'Mr Taylor is in conference, sir.' She spoke without looking at me.

I snorted. Conference, indeed! In the dram shop on the corner more like.

'And who are you?'

'Mrs Malloy, sir.'

'Are you now?'

Anger born of lust tensed my torso, heading down. But I followed her into the back room like a good 'un. Whereupon, to my disappointment, she left me without a glance. I came close to calling her back, as her skirts swished on the floorboards, but a shaft of sanity prevailed. I thought of Jane and was flooded with shame. Oh, desire! Sweet poisoned torment.

But the contents of the apothecary's consulting room quickly distracted me, so curious were they. There was a cabinet of curiosities, wherein a skeleton made advances to a flayed figure, which I had learned from the much missed Frenchy Pellett was called an *écorché*. Around the room there were signs that this apothecary had once been a barber – a horn and a shaving dish.

Other weird delights included various human bones – I recognised a femur and a skull with holes in it on the table. There was also a tripod shaped like a gallows, a narwhal's horn, mechanical pulleys, a crocodile with an ostrich's egg attached to its belly, a double-headed hermaphrodite, and the sort of plaster model which sometimes hangs outside an apothecary's shop – a life-size tronie figure with a pill in its moveable jaw.

I stared at the ghastly object. At that moment Theosophus Taylor appeared, reeking of gin. He wiped his worn and greasy sleeve across his mouth before shaking hands.

'A medical matter is it, good sir? A medical matter. Well, sir, that's my purpose. That's my area. Theosophus Taylor, at your service.'

Taylor slumped heavily into the chair near the table with the holed skull on it, leaving me standing.

'You were recommended to me by Mother Douglas.' I hesitated. I considered asking for a discount, based on their joint dealings with the bawdy house owner, but thought better of it.

Taylor registered my hesitation, but misunderstood the reason for it. 'Come, come now, sir. We are all men of the world here ...' He belched.

I thought, 'Not of the same world, I hope,' snobbery arising in me no doubt from my new-found worldly success. Aloud I said, 'A touch of the French Pox, sir. What would you recommend?'

For the first time I noticed Taylor's nose, half eaten away by the affliction we shared, as if in dreadful warning to his patients. The nose was briefly turned sideways as Taylor scratched around on the table, searching, but rather in the manner of a blind man. I noticed the motion and the angles it made. Very interesting!

Finally, hands leading the eyes, he took hold of a small silver box, opened its lid and polished the inside of it with a handkerchief black with grime which he pulled from his fob, holding onto the contents the while, so they did not spill on the floor. This operation complete, he reverently parted with three small, round black pills.

'Mercury?' I asked.

'Indeed, good sir. Mercury.'

'How much?'

'For the pills, two shillings. But you should use salve additionally, on the sores.' He flapped around on the table for a jar of salve and handed it over. 'That's another sixpence.'

I saw myself in my mind's eye, a small boy selling jars of my mother's gripe cure, matching the price to the purchaser. I was fond of the small boy I had once been, that plucky boy. How had he come to this?

Once again, the pox doctor misread me, clearly seeing my expression as one of doubt. 'It is efficacious, sir. Of that I do assure you.'

I marvelled at the language of lines on the face, smiles and the rest of it, and its capacity to send signals and their capacity to be misunderstood. It occurred to me that such signals were more various and subtle than, say, the language of flags on ships or the language of fans, but for that more likely to be received incorrectly, as here.

I resolved to make a note of the thought when I reached the sanctuary of home, as Sir James's place now was.

'I have no doubt of the efficacy,' I said, although I had. They said the French Pox was for life, though you could make it milder.

'In addition, you should visit the bagnios,' the apothecary recommended. His old fashioned wig, stiff with grease and flecked with white powder, came down almost to his elbows. It tilted to one side as he spoke, so he straightened it.

'The bagnios?' I felt my eyes open wide in surprise – the face speaking for itself, so to speak. I understood the doctor to mean some sort of 'hair of the dog that bit you' cure, as stated in Pliny, like giving the collapsed drunk a drink.

For once the ghastly apothecary had read my face aright. 'No, not for a night with Venus, sir. Rather for a night in the baths.'

'In the baths?'

'Sweat, sir. Perspire. The evil humours will leave you through the skin.'

I laughed. 'That is quite the most ridiculous thing I have heard in my entire life.'

The apothecary shrugged, again dislodging the newly straightened greasy wig. He made a sucking noise with his mouth, then swallowed. 'Well, there is something else. Nancy!' This last as a roar towards the door.

The girl-child who had greeted and cheeked me when I first arrived came in so quickly she had surely been at the other side of the door. Her switching skirt reminded me powerfully of the mother, with her sleeves made of the same stuff. But Nancy's demeanour had changed completely. She stood meekly before me, lowered her eyes, raised them a second then lowered them again. Then she bobbed a curtsey, the picture of submission. She reminded me of Sarah Young, such was the degree of surrender. She waited with head down.

'Well?' said the ghastly apothecary, quietly, wiping his sleeve across his half-nose.

I had heard the old story that having carnal knowledge of a girl-child or even, God forbid, a baby, transferred the pox to them. To my horror, I felt stirrings at Nancy's well-trained meekness.

'No!' I waved Nancy away, flapping my arms. 'Not her ...'

Again, perhaps with practice, the apothecary read my meaning all too well. As Nancy trotted from the room, he said 'Mrs Malloy, is it?'

I hesitated. 'Is she your ...?'

'... my wife, good sir?' The apothecary chortled. 'Oh, dear me, no. A widow in great distress, is our good Mrs Malloy. But there is no distress so great it cannot be helped a little. Eh, good sir? Eh?'

'Look, I ...'

'Come back next week, sir, when you've used the medicines I've given you. You'll be better by then, but you'll be needing more to keep it down. When we see you again, we can make some arrangements.'

3

THE COMMISSIONS for the new fashion for conversation pieces were coming in thick and fast; Mr Rich was happy with his four figures, all painted directly onto the canvas with no preliminaries, and told Mr Wood, who eventually became happy with his four figures. Mr Jones wanted five figures plus a child, and outside at that. Mr Cock required no fewer than six.

In *The Cholmondeley Family* the children were shown separated from the adult world by two bold diagonals, a screen and a bookcase. This was the family of Walpole's daughter. I was within touching distance of the most powerful man in the land. I could almost see his shadow.

Labouring away at this task, I took Antonis van Dyck as my ideal. Heroes long dead cannot disappoint, and for all my reputation as a man of the moment, abhorring the aspic of the past, I preferred them.

The mighty Antonis van Dyck I took as master not only for his unsurpassed technique but for his ability to flatter and comment at one and the same time. This is the aspiration of many, reached by very few. But I would have grown a van Dyck beard in my bursting efforts to ape the master, had time allowed between commissions, which happily it did not.

I did have time to frequent Old Slaughter's, though, for I have ever been a sociable fellow with time for friends and companions. Old Slaughter's Coffee House, that was – St Martin's Lane, number seventy-six, when they used the numbers, and hard by Newport Street. I went to Old Slaughter's most days.

Old Thomas Slaughter, who had started the place nearly forty years ago, was still in evidence, though tottery now on his spindly gambs and increasingly in need of a restorative lie down. What I adored, though, was the wood panelling, smoked black into strange shapes by the Dutch clay pipes favoured by my friends, the painters Lambert and Hayman, in particular, and by myself on occasion.

The company of artists was divided on whether to sit at the same table every time we met, a policy favoured by George Lambert, Jack Laguerre and I myself, for I liked to watch the same wood panel as the smoke changed what it suggested. Or whether, as a blow against artistic rigidity and for the sake of variety, we should take a different table each time.

This was the policy favoured by, among others, Francis Hayman, another painter by the name of Thomas Hudson, the engraver Hubert Gravelot and the sculptor Louis-François Roubiliac, who had the shortest journey to Old Slaughter's, as his studio was a few doors down, in St Martin's Lane.

The Frenchmen, Gravelot and Roubiliac, between them healed some of the hurt in my heart at the loss of Frenchy Pellett. I knew myself well enough to know that while the French were, in the abstract sense, the enemy, I needed a flesh and blood Frenchman around me to inspire me and I needed French skills.

I had tried to get Gravelot to engrave the *Harlot* progress, but the scoundrel had asked for too much money. This had hurt me more than I let on, because Gravelot's sinuous 'S' shapes and feather-light engraving style, pouring out of his studio in King Street, impressed me also more than I was prepared to let on – far more.

The other Frenchman, Roubiliac, always seemed to me to be older than myself – though I doubted he really was. His face alone fascinated me: his high-domed forehead, amazing mouth with the fleshy lower lip, that strong Roman nose so sharp you could cut paper with it, and the hungry, hooded eyes that sucked a man in. His smile and the air of wisdom secretly daunted and attracted me in equal measure. I wanted to impress Roubiliac, always.

That day in Old Slaughter's, the conversation started with the gossip of the day, which was typical, and the theme was set by me, which was typical, too. Colonel Charteris had finally been convicted for rape. This was the same Charteris who I had portrayed beyond misidentification in the first picture of the *Harlot's Progress*, lowering in a doorway attended by his pimp, John Gourlay, as the innocent goose of a girl got off the coach.

Now a mezzotint had appeared, showing Charteris in profile with his thumbs tied together at the bar of the Old Bailey, together with much bawdy material about the man. I had got hold of *Some Authentic Memoirs of the Life of Colonel Ch---*. I delighted the company with it, especially Hayman who roared at Charteris's taste for 'buttocks as hard as Cheshire cheeses', having always a particular fondness for the combination of carnal matters and foods.

However, under the levity they all angrily condemned Charteris. The latest, as the gentlemanly Lambert knew it – he was always first – was that Charteris's poor wronged servant, Ann Bond, had set up with a tavern keeper in Bloomsbury.

'But Charteris has only contrived to have this tavern keeper arrested for debt,' said Lambert.

I smashed my fist on the table. 'The foul fiend from hell!' I yelled, loud enough to turn heads at other tables.

Again steered by me – their bantam-cock leader, the smallest man in the group – the conversation turned to another talk of the town. John Gay's sequel to *The Beggar's Opera*, *Polly*, had been printed but, as I said, 'that fat country boy who sits on our Parliament' (I meant Walpole) 'has banned it.'

'I hear the fat country boy has taken his salver up to Norfolk, where he regularly serves his cronies sherry off it,' said Hayman, eyes agleam with mischief.

I stared at him pop-eyed, then roared with laughter. Of all those round the table at Old Slaughter's, perhaps only Hayman could have got away with that jibe. As Hayman knew, I had not only accepted Walpole's commission to engrave a salver with alacrity, but the subject of the engraving, Hercules supporting the sky to help Atlas, flattered the plump First Minister. My critical references to Walpole in paintings and engravings had stopped thereafter, an implicit condition of the commission. You have to be practical, you see?

'Shut your mouth, Francis,' said I, giving him a fond squeeze on the arm and even momentarily resting my head on his shoulder to deny the sting of my words. 'I did the salver before I knew he was going to ban the play, didn't I? What sort of man does that, eh, Frenchy? Bans a play, eh?'

It was Roubiliac who I thus singled out, and by Frenchy Pellett's old nickname too, because he knew Edward Walpole, the Prime Minister's son.

'Or do you think that's all right, Frenchy?' I pursued the new tack, the matter of the salver now forgotten. 'Because you know the family. All right is it, to behave like some autocratic Louis-king and stop people from seeing decent entertainments? Eh? Speak, man, what's got into you?'

'He can't speak until you've stopped, Bill,' said Hayman, mildly.

'All right, I've stopped.' To Roubiliac. 'Work your French tongue loose.'

Roubiliac smiled. 'Of course he shouldn't have banned it. Can anyone lend me some money?'

'Probably,' I said. 'See me afterwards.'

'How's Lavinia?' This from Lambert. 'How has she taken it?'

I had not seen dear, fascinating Lavinia Fenton in a while, as her lover, Charles Paulet, Duke of Bolton, had whisked her away out of London, the better to enjoy her, no doubt. But I had received a letter from her, furious at the banning of *Polly*, in which, of course, she was to star.

'Lavinia has touched despair,' I announced, loudly and portentously. 'But she will rise above it, like a true artist.'

'And what is a true artist?' said Hayman, with a touch of mischief.

'I am,' I said, knowingly rising to the bait. 'I'll show you what you can do with a couple of straight lines. And a bit of thought.'

Some of them knew what was coming now, too, and smiled.

I always brought paper and chalks in a leather bag to these meetings with the artists – so did Hayman and Lambert. I lovingly withdrew a piece of blue paper and unwrapped a black chalk. Smoothing the paper with my forearm on the rough oak of the table, I then bent over it, working close as I had learned to do when engraving at Gamble's.

Hayman, having seen my party-piece many times before, gave one of his huge belly laughs and decided he had gone quite long enough without eating anything. He seized a passing waiter by his right elbow and left shoulder and ordered a plate of thin cut ham and some bread. Meanwhile, he more or less lifted Lambert out of the way, sat himself between the two Frenchmen, Gravelot and Roubiliac, pulled their heads towards him and started whispering in their ears.

I, for my part, closed out the rest of the world while my chalk moved over the paper. I was finished quickly. I looked up, to find Hayman shovelling ham and bread into his mouth.

'A *line*,' said I, didactically, 'is not there to *represent* an *object*, let alone an object the world has grown weary of seeing, down the centuries. A *line* is there to *suggest* an occurrence, an event, something of interest as it may be told, for example in the tales of Fielding or Richardson.'

I peered combatively round the company, shoulders squared to battle opposition. My hand even briefly touched the pommel of my sword, slung diagonally across my legs as I sat. I was met with polite interest from the quiet gentleman Lambert, boredom from Thomas Hudson (who had seen it before), almost satiric keen interest from the two Frenchmen, and more boredom from Jack Laguerre. Hayman was eating.

'What is the story here?'

I pushed my paper at the company. It showed a well-drawn straight line, labelled A, a shorter line off it three quarters of the way up to the left, at about a thirty-three degree angle, labelled B, and a much shorter line off it also to the left with a curl at the end, labelled C.

'Could be anything,' said Lambert. 'It is meant to suggest an event, you say? An occurrence?'

Hayman stopped eating long enough to dig both Frenchmen in the ribs with his elbows simultaneously.

'Line A is surely the perspective line of a door,' said Roubiliac, with heavy mock innocence.

'And B!' cried Gravelot. 'B is the end of a sergeant's pike, who has gone in.'

''Ow do we know it's a sergeant?' said Roubiliac, in a stage whisper.

'*Imbecile*!' shouted Gravelot. 'Line B shows the pike of a sergeant! 'Ow could it be a yeoman or a captain, *c'est* Line B? *Idiot*.'

By now everyone round the table was laughing in his own style, from the gentle smile of Lambert to the heaves of Hudson and the roars of Hayman. I was laughing, too. I may tell you frankly, I have never resented jokes at my own expense.

'And that little line,' said Hayman, finishing it off, 'is a dog's tail. The dog is following the sergeant, isn't he, Bill? Because he's hungry.'

'Shut up, Francis!' But I was still laughing.

'The dog is a pug,' continued Hayman, deadpan. 'And he's just about to piss up the sergeant's pike. Heavens above, it's truly amazing, the narrative Hogarth can coax from just three lines.'

The laughter was now so loud it became a contagion to other tables, who laughed without knowing why they were laughing.

'Mr Francis Hayman,' I announced, shouting, 'will now do *his* party-piece. He will pickle his penis in brine. Or I will do it for him.'

'Sorry, William.' Hayman was mock contrite.

'I shit on your sorrow. The class will come to order. I will now show you something none of you has seen before. Including Hayman.' I lovingly took another piece of paper. 'For we can go further!' I cried. 'The line not only has the power to *suggest*. The line has the power to *deceive*. For art, my children, is deception raised to glory! What is art, Hayman?'

'It is exactly what William Hogarth says it is. Deception raised to … whatever it was.'

I waved for silence. And got it. I drew a few lines on the paper, head down, concentration total. And then …

'What's this? *Qu'est ce que sait, mes enfants?*'

There was new laughter round the table. The drawing showed a mournful fellow, no longer the youngest, with horns coming from his wig.

'A cuckold,' supplied Laguerre, obligingly.

'A cuckold,' I confirmed. 'And who has made him a cuckold?'

With astonishing speed, though I say so myself, I made a few passes with my crayon, and there stood a fat lady next to the man.

'His wife has made him a cuckold,' said Hayman, nodding to himself at the ways of the world.

'And why?' I demanded to know.

To a man they looked to the drawing for the answer. I smothered my glee.

'She's younger than him,' supplied Hayman, the naughty boy turned best pupil.

'Yes, she is,' I said.

''Ee can't get it up,' said Gravelot.

'No!' said Roubiliac, wide-eyed. ''Ee's English and so she 'as taken a lusty French lover who can satisfy 'er.'

The table groaned. Hayman playfully cuffed Roubiliac, who playfully cowered.

'Maybe there is a French dimension to this,' said Lambert, the gentleman. 'Maybe he's got the French Pox.'

I gave a thin-lipped smile. I pride myself on my enjoyment of raillery, always easier, mind you, when it was me doing the railing rather than being the butt of it. Everybody else at the table was roaring.

'Be quiet, boys!' I said. 'I'll give you the answer.'

'What's the answer, Bill?' said Hayman, pretending not to have heard me.

Pausing only to throw a piece of bread at Hayman, I returned to my drawing. Behind the wife, behind the man, I sketched a cow. The cow's horns now appeared to be behind the man's head.

They all roared with laughter.

'So, is he still a cuckold?' asked Thomas Hudson.

'Aye, there's the rub,' said I. 'Because I no longer know. And neither do you. The man might be a cuckold. Or he might just be standing in front of a cow. So our *deception* has created *uncertainty*. And why is uncertainty good art, gentlemen?'

'Because it sells well,' said Hayman.

Everyone laughed, including me. 'No!' quoth the master. (That's me.) 'Because it is interesting. The repetition of an old truth is not interesting. It is stale. The creation of a new truth is more interesting. But the most interesting is the creation of a new uncertainty.'

'Like the point of choice,' said Lambert. 'Events can go either way ...'

'Precisely!' I was delighted.

'And artefacts about to fall ...' supplied Hayman, from my well-worn catechism.

'Ex-act-ly!' rewarded the teacher again. 'Will they fall or will they not? If they fall, what will happen? There's the interest. And there's more!'

'I thought there might be,' said Hayman. 'With Hogarth there is always more.'

'Silence, Francis! The creation of new uncertainties is not *the* truth. It's *my* truth. And now my truth is as good as ...'

'No!' warned Hayman, truly alarmed, thinking he was about to hear 'God's truth'. But I am, if I may say so, far too clever for that.

'... is as good as anybody else's truth.'

4

A SADNESS HAD COME OVER JANE. It left me with a feeling of quiet desperation.

Outwardly all was well. She talked and laughed, she contributed to every aspect of my work – if anything more than before. But there was a sadness in the large grey eyes which pained me: a heaviness in the tread, the occasional sigh, a new seriousness in repose. There was a new weight about her, as if the heaviness of her own heart had become a burden to her.

And all this so soon after the sudden fountains of childlike joy when we were first married. Were happy, bubbly Billy and his Jenny to give way to plain William and Jane so soon? Already making the best of it? Just making the best of second best?

I believed at first I was the only one who had noticed the change in her. But I feared Lady Judith's cutting shrewdness as much as I respected it. Sometimes I thought her ladyship could see through walls. When I was angry with her I thought of her as a witch, and was promptly ashamed of the thought.

And then there was the pert Fanny, Jane's maid. Jane would not be the first lady to make a confidante of her maid. Did Fanny know of my treatment for the French Pox? The suspicion was agony to me. Of course, I did not know for certain that Jane knew.

Sometimes I fancied that pretty Fanny looked at me differently now. Fanny was still damnably attractive to me. Once or twice, when I had asked her to help me dress, I had tried to kiss her. She nimbly evaded me then ignored what had happened. A couple of times I had touched her. Or gripped her wrist and forced her to touch me. Oh, this terrible temptation!

But at least I had been able to resume being a full husband to Jane. The mercury cream had healed the lesions, almost completely. The pills had stopped the discharge. The sweat-baths had proved efficacious, as Theosophus Taylor, the egregious apothecary, had promised.

All I was left with was an ache in my limbs, an ache in my gums, a strange need to dribble, occasional headaches, feelings of weakness, feelings of sudden bleak sadness and a greatly diminished desire to do the deed, which I nevertheless did because I loved Jane beyond reason and wished to make her happy. And give her children.

At least I had managed to resist the charms of Mrs Malloy, at the apothecary's establishment, despite the apothecary making it more than clear that such resistance was not necessary. Theosophus Taylor had unfortunately proved firmer in his insistence on limiting the amount of mercury prescribed.

To this, I had testily responded that the small amounts of medication inevitably increased the frequency of his visits at 3s a time the round trip by hansom. At which the ghastly apothecary had most heartily laughed.

The idea of leaving the Thornhill house came upon me slowly, as if it were an idea for a painting. Jane and I naturally wished to set up our own establishment eventually, not stay with Sir James and Lady Judith forever. But I now clutched at our future in our own establishment as the means of my redemption.

I would buy her not a house but a palace, and in it we would be happy – I did not dare even think the words 'happy *again*' – and all would be well, as my father used to say. Somehow or other in the new place, or so I dreamed, I would be free of the French Pox.

And so I found a palace for her. A place to make up for what I had done to us.

The house in Leicester Fields, number thirty when numbered, was actually a better address even than Sir James's place. Covent Garden was by then – the early 1730s – going downhill fast, with the close proximity of Tom King's and Mother Douglas's establishments helping it on its way.

Leicester Fields, on the other hand, was travelling steeply in the other direction. It gained kudos from the north side being occupied by Leicester House, home of Frederick, Prince of Wales. Proximity to the prince's faction, I hoped, would do me no harm at all in obtaining commissions.

The prince's lease for the elegant two storey house, with windows facing onto the square, was rumoured to be of the order of £6,000. I, of course, could not have afforded anything like that. But Leicester Fields ran to houses for the middling sort.

It was something of a forgotten gem, indeed. For a start, it was among the quietest squares in the capital, traffic noise from Coventry Street being cut off by the houses in the northwest corner. The centre was planted with railed-off trees, adding to the mood of established tranquillity, as well as elegance. And the east side, where I had my property, had houses dating back to the 1670s, giving an atmosphere of settled dignity.

And all that for £275 a year, which I rated a bargain, taking full advantage of the fashion in longer leases – mine was until the mid-1770s – coupled with relatively low ground rents.

I was delighted with the house, itself, too. It was of rough red brick with rubbers: soft brick that was sanded into a curve both over the entrance and over the expansive sash windows, neatly flush to the wall.

It consisted of a basement and four storeys, plain but handsome. The line of its front was cleverly broken by two band courses above the second and fourth storeys. The door boasted flanking pilasters and a cornice hood on carved consoles, the very epitome of elegance.

The house, my new home with my beloved Jane, had but one drawback – it faced east-west. Before we moved in, I had a painting room built, giving me the northern light essential for painting and engraving.

And over the door, tradesman to my fingertips, as I am, I placed my sign offering my wares to the world. It was a bust of the immortal van Dyck, compacted out of cork and then gilded. Here, it boldly proclaimed, here is the new van Dyck. (That's me.) 'Come in!' says the sign. And for all my dizzying social rise, the new van Dyck was still no further than a five minute walk from St Martin's Lane and my dear brother artists at Old Slaughter's. That was very important to me.

The showroom was on the ground floor – the part of the house given over to trade. In this we were only aping the neighbours. Trennier, the fashionable tailor, lived across the way from us, also plying his trade from his house, as did Hans Hysing, another painter. In a sense, so did the magistrate Thomas de Veil, who lived a few doors down and had his watchmen visit him at home.

This ground floor showroom, then, contained a colour cabinet with fifty-four drawers for colours, a printing press, models, as well as every unsold painting in my possession. The entire top floor was also functional, being given over to rooms for the servants, with the kitchen and more servants' quarters in the basement.

But there was still plenty of living space for Billy to show his Jenny when we embarked on the tour of the home, which was to contain our love and where our children were to be born. Although even then, such was my overweening ambition, I had a secret fear the place was too small for them.

Unlocking the series of complex locks I had insisted on, I threw wide the entrance door. The hall and the main staircase were to the right, the parlour and backstairs to the left. I made straight for the second and third floors, towing my smiling Jane by the hand.

White cornices were much in evidence, as were dormer windows and Baroque shell hoods. There were plenty of curves among many of the elements the previous owner, the late Lady Mary Howard, had had removed and which were now restored.

But my past, never far from the surface of my present, had returned to me in force when I planned the interiors. I felt again the numbing, bone-breaking cold of my boyhood: chilling the spirit, freezing the flesh, paralysing the mind. Centuries of civilisation wiped away as the likes of our poor family were reduced to animals with the single primitive need to keep warm.

So I led Jane at something like a trot through the elegant first-floor dining room, diagonally crossing the flower-pattern carpet Lady Judith had donated from the Thornhill establishment, past the walnut furniture Jane had chosen, past an ebony bookcase, a pair of oak pier tables and a pair of Italian armchairs with semi-circular backs, to the centrepiece of the room: the fireplace.

'Look at that!'

'It's beautiful.'

I shot her a sharp look, but she meant it. It *was* beautiful. It was a delicate, curved basket grate with traceried filigree work at the front, as fine as lace. The graceful, small basket for the coal was an elegant shallow, which, she saw instantly, would need frequent refilling. But it was an object of loveliness in itself.

I kissed her gently on the lips before the fireplace. 'Happy?'

'Oh, yes!'

I took her hand, holding it firmly enough, but there was something reverent in the pause before I led her away.

'What's next?'

'Your room.'

'My room?'

'The drawing room.'

The drawing room, naturally, was next to the dining room, so the ladies could withdraw there at ease, as the port, brandy and concomitant piss pots were brought in for the gentlemen at the end of the meal. Jane was preparing a bright reaction for her darling Billy even as she was hauled from the dining room, but the squeal-cum-gasp of her delight, arising all the way from her ample bosom, could not have been created artificially. And her Billy knew that with knowledge deeper than reason.

She pressed both fists to the tip of the line between her breasts I referred to as 'the wondrous valley'.

'Billy, it's …'

'It's yours. It's for you.'

It was the outward reflection of how I saw her: her as embodied in a room. One day, naturally, I would paint her again, although the prospect was more daunting to me now, as no Michelangelo ever approached his Sistine Chapel with more reverence. Meanwhile, this would do.

The dominant colour was rose pink, as deep as it was feminine. The stucco walls were broken by two strips of paper stained by me, myself, with motifs of (the newly fashionable) Chinese exotic birds and pagodas. The theme was echoed in the patterns on the upholstery of the couches and armchairs, which were pink and green. They were pushed against the walls at the moment, as were the Dutch marquetry dining chairs with cabriole legs, a wedding gift from John Thornhill.

Jane went to sit on one, wriggling her bottom on the cushioned seat, which I had coaxed into echoing the main colour combinations and motifs. I followed her, bent over her and kissed her gently on the lips. She leaned one elbow on a tea table, which even had a tea set on it, and kissed me back.

I straightened up, seized a silver tray from a small table and pretended to serve 'milady' tea, in a butler's voice. I had retained the ability to mimic voices from my boyhood and could render Hayman's Devon burr a treat, as well as Sir James's increasingly flutey, high-pitched voice.

Jane laughed at the butler voice and pretended to drink her tea. 'Mama has, in fact, found us a butler, I hope you don't mind.'

'Not at all!' I was sincere. 'What would a Spitalfields boy know of such matters?'

The grey eyes opened wide. 'Well, quite! No, seriously, Billy, mama says we must have an experienced man to lead the servants. His name is Henry Tompion ...'

'Ooooh! His name's more distinguished than mine!'

'Listen! He began service as a footman with Thomas Cuthbert, who apparently lived in this very square, somewhere. Then he ...'

'Look, if Lady Judith ...' I always called her Lady Judith, even to her daughter. 'If Lady Judith says he's suitable, then enough said on the subject. I trust her judgement. I'd trust her with my life.'

'She trusted you with her daughter.'

There was an edge in her voice. I wanted to blurt out that I would never let her down, then recalled I already had. I thought painfully of the passionate love-making we had enjoyed before this curse of the French Pox, and its laboured imitation now.

'I worship you.'

She shook her head, as if there were a wasp in her ear. 'I want a husband, not a votary.'

'About the rest of the servants ...' I said.

She let me change the subject. 'We need another four immediately for a place this size. Ideally a couple more, but they can wait. I want to bring Fanny with me, as my maid.'

'Of course!'

She gave me a sharp look, but let it rest. 'Is there anyone you want?'

I hadn't thought about it, but blurted out 'Sarah Young,' without thinking.

'Are you having her?'

'No!'

'Have you ever had her?'

'No! Yes, but it's over. I don't want to anymore.'

'Does she?'

'No! Yes! Perhaps. Look, I'll find someone else ...'

'Don't bother. She'll do.'

The cool grey eyes never left my face. Years later I worked out that I was less, not more, likely to tup Sarah if she were in my employ. There had been real revulsion in London at what the likes of Charteris had done with Ann Bond and any other women servants. I could not let myself be like that, even if I desired a maid of Jane's. I would even have to forget about Fanny. Jane understood all that earlier and more clearly than I did. Of course.

'And Henry Tompion will need an experienced older man as a footman, especially in the beginning, when we are so lightly staffed.'

'Does he know anybody? Or do you want to advertise?'

'Leave it with me.'

'Yes, of course!'

I spoke with relief. The home, it went without saying, was her realm anyway, but I hardly saw myself interviewing potential servants. I would be more nervous than they. Spitalfields boy!

But then I smiled. 'There is another room I have to show you.'

'The kitchen?' Her eyes were twinkling.

'Forget the kitchen. Another room.'

She waved her face with an imaginary fan. 'The boy will stop at nothing ...'

I led the way up the wide staircase to the second storey.

'It was a dressing room when Lady Mary had the place, but ...' I came to a halt, flapping both arms.

'Why are you laughing?'

'Because you look like a duck, doing that. And also because my Billy Boy makes me happy.'

'Then I'll flap my arms like a duck all day. I'll never put my arms by my sides again. I'll stop flapping only to paint.'

I kissed her with open mouth, squeezing her breast when she responded. She let herself sigh, let me hear her pleasure. She never withheld from me, then or later. She was bountiful and generous and womanly in her love.

She cleared her throat when we finally stopped. 'What was I saying?'

'No, it's what I was saying. This room is for the children. Yes?'

She nodded, very slowly. 'Yes.'

Jane and I were in the newly-completed studio, the pug dog, Trump, contentedly asleep in a corner. I was taken over by a deep fulfilment whenever I felt the northern light of the studio on my skin. Indeed, I was in the habit of pushing my neck out to put my face as near as possible to the light and warmth, as I had seen animals do, including Trump.

I did this, even twisting my torso, pacing the length of the room, while my wife sat still, fixed and demure. We were Hogarth and his wife now, not Billy and Jenny. For Hogarth was working, as indeed was his wife.

Pace, pace, pace. Little paces up and down. 'The next *projectus* must naturally be another "Progress". The whole world is crying out for another.'

'Well, some of it.'

'Indeed, indeed. But my last story was told in six pictures. This one shall be bigger, ever onwards, ever upwards, *ad astrum*.'

'It's *ad astra*, actually. How many? How many pictures?'

Pace, pace, pace. Scuttle. Adjust indoor cap as it slips. 'Not sure. Eight? But I have my theme, Janey. I have my theme.'

Her lovely grey eyes twinkled with fond amusement. She loved this side of my personality, when I was, as she said, like a runaway bucking colt, unsure itself of how high it could jump or even what jumping was, but revelling in the movement.

'Your ...'

'My theme, my theme. It shall be a rake like Sir John Galliard in ... What's it called?'

'You mean *The Accomplish'd Rake*? Mary Davys?'

'Yes. Absolutely. Only my rake will be called Tom Rakewell. Like my harlot, only male. A man with his soul in his face.'

'Out on show where anyone can take it.'

'As open to ravishment as a girl. Like George Barnwell in that drama we saw at Drury Lane.'

'*The London Merchant*? Lillo's drama? "I followed my inclinations and that the best of you does every day. All actions are alike natural to man and beast." You mean that?'

'Yes! Yes, that's it exactly. And I'd have him a follower of fashion, I think. From a higher *stratum* of society than my harlot. But, like the harlot, he shall fall.'

'Shouldn't he rise first? More symmetrical.'

I stopped. Faced her. I clenched my fists, my fighter's fists. 'Yes, indeed. A flying man who shall rise and then fall. How should he rise?'

'How does anybody rise? He becomes rich.'

'Suddenly. Yes, but how? Shares? No, I covered that ground with the *South Sea* engraving, all those years ago. Can't repeat myself.'

She nodded. 'An inheritance?'

'Yes! And he squanders it.'

She nodded again, harder. 'Do you know that work of Bernard Mandeville? *Fable of the Bees?*'

'Never heard of it.'

'Mandeville argues that it is unreasonable and a folly to desire being opulent and at the same time to decry the very vices which are inseparable from the opulence. Shall I find a copy for you?'

'No. No time, no time. But you couldn't ...?'

'What? Mark the relevant passages?'

'No time for that either. Just ...'

'Summarise it for you?'

'Yes. Yes, please. But I like the idea that the gathering of riches is not good in itself. And indeed it may even be the seed of evil. That would make them sit up and take notice.'

She smiled. 'No doubt.'

'Right! Come on! To business! Oh, I have wearied myself with walking.' I straightened the red cap again. 'Picture one.'

'Start with the inheritance?'

'Yes, his father dies. Oh, Janey, I'm sorry! Oh, I'm such a clumsy fool.' I struck that bash-mark on my forehead in mortification.

Sir James, never the most robust of men, had now abandoned his lengthy visits to the family estate in Dorset, unable to cope with the rigours of the journey. He was spending more and more time in bed, with a longer and longer list of ailments, of which gout and a rattle in the chest were the latest.

I was still assisting the great man, latterly on his painting of a House of Commons committee. This had seen me, briefly, in the same room as Walpole himself for the first time – dealings concerning the salver commission having of course been handled by minions. But my concern for Sir James outweighed even that trophy of my rise.

The thought was never spoken, but it was accepted that Sir James was not long for this world. Indeed, he himself had begun manoeuvrings to have his son, John, inherit his title of Serjeant Painter to the King, on his death.

So tears from her good heart were indeed pricking Jane's eyes at the thought of her father dying, but she did not blame her husband for them.

'Don't be silly, William,' she said, dabbing at the tears with a lace handkerchief. 'Your Tom Rakewell must indeed inherit on the death of his father. What next?'

'I shall pay great heed to the text below the pictures this time,' I resolved. 'I wish my praises sung equally as the author of the words and the author of the paintings. For they are gifts which run parallel in me.'

Jane, I was sure, doubted that this was true, but I went on:

'I was a dutiful son, who loved my father with all his heart. Sometimes it is better for an author to have lived the opposite experience to that he is portraying, the better to see it clearly. How's this? "Hast thou a son? In time be wise. He views the world with other eyes."'

'Not bad!' she cried out, genuinely surprised. 'You continually astonish me!'

'Huh!' I waved the balled pommel of my fist in triumph. 'Right now, come on. Come on! Picture one, he inherits his wealth. The last picture he ends in prison.'

'Naturally.'

'No!'

'No?'

'No. Suppose he ends … He may pass through prison, we have eight canvases to fill after all. But suppose he ends … *in Bedlam!*'

'That's good. Bedlam is good. Very dramatic. And what sends …?'

'What sends a man to Bedlam?'

We said it together. 'Gambling!'

I had exhausted myself pacing. I stopped in front of Jane. 'Gambling, yes, itself a sign of madness. Very well. But we have quite a few canvases left. We must show Tom squandering his money.'

'Yes, but show him enjoying it first.'

I pointed at her dramatically. 'Good, good. And … How about a wedding scene? Rather like our own!'

'Rakewell marries for money?'

'Why not?'

'Not the daughter of a leading society painter, I hope? That would strain credulity.'

I laughed. 'You're marvellous. You know that?'

She nodded slowly. 'Mmm.'

'Oh, I can't keep all this in my head.'

I seized a piece of drawing paper and a crayon, pinned them to a board, and sat at the easel, silent, gathering my characters into myself. Then I drew eight rectangles, four above and four below. Then below each rectangle small frames for the rhyming text, which should offer commentary and guidance.

I began the cartoon for each painting as it occurred to me, out of order, those strongest in my head the first. Bold lines, shapes as ideas. I had entered my own world, forgetting even Jane, until I needed her to prompt me with ideas, or approve my rhymes for the text.

5

A S I WORKED on the paintings for my *Rake's Progress,* bile rose in me anew at the actions of those pirates, swindlers, copiers and cheats who had stolen my work, lowered my reputation by fabricating and spreading inferior copies, and mocked me with their lofty treatment of me as they pursued their grubby schemes.

It was not to happen again! I resolved it as I prepared and stretched canvases and affixed battens. I willed it as I mixed and applied the grounds then layered on glazes. I knew it as I dabbed on highlights, rendering the faces of people I knew before creating any strange phizes.

IT WAS NOT TO HAPPEN AGAIN!

And I knew very well, clear as northern light, how to stop it – by the law. For I had something of the lawyer in me, like my father before me. But unlike my father before me I always sought a mentor, a hero, a guiding light; though at the time I was not always aware of it.

For there was a sense in which poor, blundering Richard Hogarth was a prouder man than me. More dignified. I, the small son, the genius, forever had someone to take me by the hand and some would say met my doom when I did not, but that was many years hence.

Now, approaching the crest of my fame, I sought out a lawyer to wield the law for me. And I sought him not among strangers at the Inns of Court, but from the tables of my repose, from among my many acquaintances. As I say, I have ever been a social man. The man's name was William Huggins.

William Huggins was the son of John Huggins, who I had first met when he demanded £1 6s 8d garnish for my father's fetters. The very same John Huggins who was arraigned before the House of Commons, or at least a committee of it, for his foul cruelty to helpless prisoners, like my father.

But nonetheless I had painted his portrait, an individual oval of John Huggins in historical garb then fashionable. For the thing was, the going rate for a head and shoulders was £8, and John Huggins was ready to up that to eight guineas.

This was especially tempting to me as I strove to reach £1,500 a year, striving all the harder once I had exceeded it.

And now the morally good, billiard ball head of *William* Huggins, with its comic stuck-on features, sat opposite me at the Bedford Arms and advised me as to the creation of new laws.

'Very little in life is new,' opined William Huggins, bent carrot nose dibbing, both eyebrows arched. 'Everything is based on something else.' A lawyer's point, that.

'That doesn't mean you have to copy it, though, does it?' said I, testily.

The mild, slow thinking Huggins looked surprised.

'Er ... no,' he said, judiciously.

We were both drinking thre'pence-a-pot porter. I wanted to bring Huggins to the point, as I feared I would be paying, as it was I who had issued the invitation to this alehouse for advice. Sure enough, two more tankards of the dark stuff were banged down on the table, unordered, with the waiter away before I could draw breath to protest.

Huggins drained the old tankard, then thoughtfully sipped at the new. 'In your case, what you need is 8 *Anne* cap 19.'

'I do?'

'Most certainly.'

'What is it? Where do I get one?' I took a huge slug of porter, tilting my throat back.

Huggins smiled, extending the lipless slit of his mouth. 'It's an Act of 1709. An Act vesting the copyright of printed books in the authors or purchasers of copies for twenty-one years.'

'Wonderful. Does it work?'

'Oh, indeed. Indeed it does. The pirates must forfeit all the offending books with a fine of 5s a sheet, half going to the Crown and half to the author.'

'And for engravings?'

'That is what you presently require, William. Not an extension, I think. That would be too complicated. A new law.'

'How do I get one of those?'

Huggins drank judiciously, consideredly, the dark liquid making a faint glugging sound as it went down. 'First of all,' Higgins paused to smile, 'get as much support as you can.'

'A petition?'

'Write a pamphlet.'

I was pleased. Writing to me was a concomitant of painting, another form of authorship. I fancied myself a dab hand at it, despite some pedantic criticism of my orthography. And syntax. And logic.

'Good. Then what?'

Huggins shrugged. 'Simply get a champion to present it to the House of Commons. They'll send it to committee. A bit of to-ing and fro-ing, no doubt. Then ...'

'Then?'

'Then you get a law.'

'Who, exactly, do I present it to?'

'As many men of influence as possible. Within the Commons, obviously.'

'What do you think the chances are?'

'Personal opinion? Quite good, actually. The printers are terribly unpopular. And the extension of the Act from Queen Anne's time that you are proposing appears quite logical to me.'

I threw myself into work on the pamphlet later the same day. I entitled it *The Case of Designers, Engravers, Etchers, etc., Stated In a Letter to a Member of Parliament*. I wrote as I have always written, hunched over, furiously forcing the pen to move at something like the speed of my thoughts, making obliterating crossings out, writing over, under and through previous words, blotching, scratching, speaking the words as I wrote, writing the sounds I spoke.

The result, according to Jane, was passionate, but well-nigh unreadable by anyone but me, and difficult to comprehend even by those who could make out the occasional chain of thought. William Huggins visited our home at Leicester Fields. He and Jane helped to shape the pamphlet to a document worth presenting to potential supporters.

And that is how matters stood when Sir James Thornhill died.

Servants at our home in Leicester Fields as well as the Thornhill establishment at Covent Garden were dressed in mourning suits. The funeral was held on a chill April evening, with the family making their farewells after the service as Sir James stared waxily up at us from his open coffin.

I spoke the longest to the dead Sir James, thanking him for his guidance and friendship. Lady Judith, dressed in dowager black, rocked silently to and fro before the bier. Son John said filial words of gratitude on his own behalf and that of his sister, Jane. The mourners returned to the Covent Garden house for drinks and biscuits.

In truth, I was in some turmoil at the passing of this benefactor who was also my father-in-law. But still, in honesty, I acknowledged to myself with sadness that Sir James's passing was good for my career, because the association with a style now perceived as old-fashioned was beginning to harm me. Nevertheless, I would have given anything to have him back.

My main concern in the spring and summer months after Sir James died was my beloved Jane. Jane wept copiously, long and frequently, her shoulders and her full bosom heaving. I had never before seen her give way like this to something beyond herself: to have no remedy, to be so elemental. I had had no real idea of Jane's view of her father in his lifetime, but realised that that was not the matter here. The matter was of loss, of grief, of pain: as if an organ in one's own body had died.

At this time I was absorbed in the *Rake* series, but I resolved to help and comfort Jane, whatever the loss in time. And while naturally sad at her grief, I was almost joyful at this opportunity to bring her comfort and prove my love, despite all my faults.

So I held her, I did. I held her tightly to me, for hour after hour on occasion, while she sobbed her grief. There was something animal-like in it, in her howls and cries and in her refusal to actually speak of her lost father. It was not, I understood, what the dead father had done; it was not about his actions, but about him as a being, an entity that no longer was.

On occasion, Lady Judith joined us, while Jane wept. She was much shrunken and reduced. Once or twice even John came. I gave comfort to them all, as best I could. I knew that what I was doing came from the best of me, and I was glad. Because I needed the best of myself like a salve for what I had done and even for what I had become, with success. That is how I thought of it, then, this comforting of my wife, with those tears: as being like a balm, like applying mercury to the cesspit wounds of sin.

But all the while I continued the fight for an Engraver's Act, as Jane insisted on it. I continued to paint for five hours a day, mainly bringing the rake's journey to life. Jane insisted on that, too.

Mind you, I was never happier than when I was fighting (painting, to me,

being a form of fighting), and the early stages of the battle for justice for
engravers were particularly congenial to me, carried out, as they were, at Old
Slaughter's in St Martin's Lane.

When I had a cause, be it, as it often was, a slight to myself or the cruelty of
man to beast, or man to child, or some other enemy, that cause dominated my
discourse to the near exclusion of all else. So the denizens of Old Slaughter's –
the mild sculptor Roubiliac, the painter Hudson, gentleman George Lambert,
big bluff Hayman, Laguerre, Gravelot and the rest – well knew what to expect
when they saw a swaggering little figure, just one and a half times the size of his
sword, come sauntering in singing the Lillabullero to himself.

Over porter and thinly sliced beef, all talk of whoring stopped. All talk of the
price of a tube of paint and a bit of canvas, the paucity of commissions, especially
for poor Roubiliac and his terracotta work.

And what replaced all that, as soon as I sat down, was full-steam pressure
from their most prominent man, for that I certainly was by then, to sign what
bluff Hayman referred to as 'that bloody petition': namely *The Case of Designers, Engravers, Etchers, etc., Stated In a Letter to a Member of Parliament.*

Hayman, satirically, tried to get the waiters to sign it. Gentleman George
Lambert gave quiet steadfast support. Roubiliac signed, then tried to hide from
the group that the last meal he had eaten was two days ago. Only, between all
the roaring, I spotted it and quietly ordered mutton pies for him – many times.

The artists – painters and sculptors – had to sign first. Then, stage two as I
thought of it, the campaign to get the Whigs and Tories behind it. Finish stage
one before starting stage two. Step by step.

But eventually came the time for the Parliament men.

The core of my connections in Parliament came from my days painting the
Select Committee inquiry into gaols. It had been Sir Archibald Grant of
Monymusk, a close friend of Sir James, close enough to attend the funeral, who
had smoothed my way into the inquiry and the all-important commission to
paint the deliberations.

So it was to Sir Archibald Grant that I turned first in the matter of putting an
Engraver's Bill before Parliament. To my great pleasure, Sir Archibald agreed to
see me by return, at his London house in Hanover Street.

The greeting was warm; indeed, I was ushered into the tasteful green
wallpapered drawing room by the lady of the house herself, Grant's second wife,

Anne. She, I noted with a half-smile, was considerably younger than Sir Archibald, who was my age, give or take a year.

The graceful sweep of Sir Archibald's brown frock-coat and the low bow reminded me of my painting of the Select Committee. Sir Archibald had been posed standing, not elevated at all, with his dandyish manner shown by one hand being tucked inside his waistcoat and a pointing of his left buckled shoe.

Tea was served along with a gooseberry tart which I, mindful of my need of favour from Sir Archibald, fulsomely praised. The pamphlet, *The Case of Designers, Engravers, Etchers, etc., Stated In a Letter to a Member of Parliament*, was waved aside with a swan-neck gesture of his arm by the host, but Sir Archibald indicated that I should outline its contents to him.

Now, when I am master of my matter I can sing like a bird. I outlined the many ways in which booksellers and printers could cheat the poor artists, then proceeded to a clear account of remedy, based heavily on what I had learned from William Huggins, especially concerning the Act from Queen Anne's time protecting writers.

'What do you think my chances are?' I concluded bluntly, all Pug Hogarth now, the ingenious Mr Hogarth having been left behind in the studio.

Sir Archibald shut his eyes, shrewd, calculating. 'The connection to the other Act is gud,' he said judiciously, in his light voice with its strong Scots accent. 'They like laws that build on other laws.'

'Good.' It came out as a pug bark. I could feel my forehead scar flushing pink. 'Thank you. Will you …?'

'Oh, I'll certainly support you, ma'sen. No doubt of that. And I'll give you letters to some people. Let me see. Pulteney, Pelham, Wyndham …'

This was beyond my wildest dreams. 'Yonge?' I suggested pretty much at random, pushing the act of kindness to the point of destruction, as ever.

Graceful swan arm wave. 'Hmm. Mebbe.'

'And what's happened to Oglethorpe? I can't find him. I even went round to his house. It was boarded up.'

I adored James Oglethorpe, sometime chairman of the Gaols Committee of the House of Commons. He had approached the work of prison reform like an avenging angel. A firm friend of Oglethorpe's, James Castell, had died of smallpox while in the Fleet. And, indeed, Oglethorpe had once been imprisoned there himself, for killing a man in a brawl. To my amazement, he spoke of this frequently while he was being painted.

'Oglethorpe? Oh, aye. He's in the New World.'

'America?'

'Aye. Georgia, I believe.'

'What's that?'

'A new colony. But he should be back any day. I'd try him again soon.'

Sir Archibald stood, signalling that my time was over.

I could feel myself flushing again, annoyed with myself for having stayed too long.

Sir Archibald rang a pretty silver bell for a footman, asked for his secretary and instructed letters of support written there and then. He started to usher me out.

'Could I just …? Before I go, I couldn't just have a look at the painting, could I?'

'I'm running a wee bit late for an appointment, Mr Hogarth.'

'Just quickly!'

'Aye!'

Visibly annoyed, Sir Archibald led me through to a small parlour, where my painting hung above an archway, higher than I would have wished. I stared at it. I was still happy with my Oglethorpe, but wished I had made the prisoner look less well.

Sir Archibald left for his appointment, leaving me standing in his parlour, lost in contemplation of my work, feeling pleasure at the best of my achievement and rage at its faults and weaknesses.

The letters of introduction from Sir Archibald arrived the next day. At Jane's insistence I wrote a gracious reply, thanking him for his help. I then arranged appointments with all the influential parliamentarians – Pulteney, Pelham, Wyndham – all of whom promised support, while visiting Oglethorpe's shut up house every day.

It was in Golden Square, within walking distance of Leicester Fields. I soon found myself going there twice, three times a day. My feeble attempts to hide this from Jane were uncovered, like a housemaid pulling back a bed sheet.

As ever when an idea took me over, engrossing my mind, courting madness, she let me see that she was concerned but did not directly try to stop me, even when time was lost from painting the *Rake* series. And eventually I got what I wanted, as I so often did, thus making my previous obsession seem more reasonable.

James Edward Oglethorpe returned to England.

Oglethorpe greeted me warmly in the vestibule of his house. With an informality typical of a certain type of military man, he dismissed his footmen, and led the way himself along mazy corridors to a small panelled study. There he donned a red indoor cap, lit a cheap clay pipe and sprawled at his desk, waving me to an armchair opposite.

I regarded him quizzically, head to one side, just as my pug dog Trump did. The cause of my quizzical look was a sudden realisation that the soldier in Oglethorpe – he had been in the Peninsular War as a young man – was entirely missing from my portrayal in the Gaols Committee painting.

And more. Worse! Oglethorpe was a Tory, a Jacobite sympathiser to boot. Could all that have been shown in a painting? And a conversation piece at that, not a portrait. van Dyck could have done it. Oh, I was wretched!

What had happened? I saw what had happened. Without knowing it, I had rejected elements of Oglethorpe I disliked. I had invented a new Oglethorpe who did not exist. I had told lies. Even on the surface level there were lies. As Oglethorpe was speaking, I noted the curve of his big nose, the jut of his chin. Zounds, the man was almost Mr Punch! The real Oglethorpe, that is, not my milky version.

I resolved then and there to tell the truth in future, to find the real man and show him, not to create my own version – someone I liked. That, in its way, was as wrong as merely copying the sitter as he sat still as a statue, as if he were a still life: like fruit, flowers, a gallipot or a broken earthen pan.

Meanwhile, I was continuing my talk with James Oglethorpe. Although only recently returned from Georgia, Oglethorpe was already aware of everything cooking in the bubbling cauldron of London events. He not only knew of my pamphlet to gain support for an Engraver's Copyright Act, he had read Grant's copy.

'Of course I'll support you,' Oglethorpe was saying. 'The book trade is run by scoundrels and idle incompetents. Always was, probably always will be. But we'll fire a few shots at them, eh, Hogarth? Bit of enfilade, eh? Show me where to sign.'

At that moment the doorbell rang, a high tinkle from the vestibule. Oglethorpe uncoiled himself and jumped up, hanging on to his indoor hat as it slipped.

'Ah, I can guess who that is. Old friend from our new colony south of the Savannah. You know about our work there, Hogarth?'

'No.'

Oglethorpe was moving lithely to the door. He called over his shoulder. 'Oh, you should. The poor will be given another chance, a fresh start. And people hounded for their beliefs. French Protestants and the like.'

'I …' I was aware that Oglethorpe had not yet signed, but he was gone.

He was back shortly, though, chattering nineteen to the dozen with one of the few men I had ever seen who was as short as myself. The voluble little fellow wore a gold-faced red coat of some bastard form that was at most only partly wool, a pair of workaday, grubby yellow gloves and, remarkably, no wig at all. His fine, long grey hair fell nearly to his shoulders.

He stopped talking as he saw me. 'Thomas Coram,' he introduced himself, before Oglethorpe, who had his mouth open to do just that, had a chance to. 'And who might you be, sir?' A blunt chin jutted at me.

I liked him on sight. 'I am William Hogarth, sir.'

'The ingenious Mr Hogarth? The painter? Modern moral whatsits?'

I was gratified. 'Subjects. Indeed, sir. Modern moral subjects. That is me.'

'Mr Coram is a sea captain,' Oglethorpe managed to get out, as he sat down again.

But Coram took over, glaring at me. 'Where do you stand on Walpole, sir? Come! You must be for or against.' He spoke as if countering hours of prevarication on my part.

'I have had no dealings with the man, sir,' fibbed I, carefully. And then, seeing the sea captain's face cloud black, 'He has set himself against actors, playwrights and their plays. I love the theatre, sir. So I think badly of him for that.'

As I spoke, I was calculating that Coram was unlikely to have heard of my commission to engrave a silver salver for Walpole, let alone of my subsequent softening towards him in polemic. Yet something about my fellow little man's directness and blazing, painful honesty made me ashamed of the calculation even as I made it.

'Walpole has been chary of supporting our south Savannah project,' explained Oglethorpe with a smile.

'Chary of ...?' Coram was rigid with indignation. I realised that, like many people with little or no sense of humour, the sea captain was not open to teasing. 'Chary of ...? The great tub of lard has been no help whatsoever. And what we are doing is worthwhile, good work!' Again the little man spoke as if rebutting fierce counter-argument.

While he had been speaking, Oglethorpe had signed my petition to Parliament and silently passed it to me. My business completed, I could have left, but a powerful attraction to the compact force of nature that was Coram kept me there.

'I am a trader, sir, in wood among other goods, not only a sea captain.' Again Coram spoke as if countering powerful slanderous contra-assertions. 'And in my trade and on my travels I have seen enough evil in the world to want to combat it.'

'Indeed, sir,' I said, mildly.

'Yes. Indeed sir, indeed sir. Anybody can say that. So what evils have you seen, sir? What evils would you combat?'

A picture came to my mind, as it usually did before I ventured into argument. It was from my boyhood in East Spitalfields. I had come across two ragamuffins who had captured a poor street cur, tilted it upside down and were ramming an arrow up its anus. I had run at them, yelling, causing enough distraction for the poor dog to struggle free. I had then had to run for my own life as the ghastly urchins turned on me.

Another picture: late at night a link boy laughing, giving light so two of his companions could better burn out the eyes of a hen they had captured.

My eyes filled with tears at the pictures. 'The evil I would combat, sir, perhaps above all others, is our treatment of God's dumb creatures who are mainly helpless before us and who so often are shamelessly abused.' I realised my voice was shaking as I spoke. One more picture appeared before me, my beloved pug Trump who I would have died to protect, or at least so I felt at that moment.

To my amazement, Thomas Coram gripped my forearm with amazing power. 'Your feelings do you great credit, sir. Great credit. And they embolden me to tell you of the evil that burns at my heart and which, indeed, I shall combat.'

'And that is, sir?'

'Why, the greatest evil of them all,' cried the sea captain. 'The death of babies on the streets of our city. Our shameful neglect of our own young.'

To the delighted amusement of Oglethorpe, we two small men were still chattering, clutching at each other's arms, when we left his establishment, apparently oblivious to all around us. It was like love. Perhaps it *was* love.

'I was living in Rotherhithe and walking into the city,' Coram was saying, as we strode out into the rain. 'Day after day, at dawn and dusk, I saw the corpses of abandoned babies by the road.'

'I've seen them, of course ... when I was a boy.'

'Let's go and see it now. Come on!'

'What? Rotherhithe?'

'No, too far. We'll take a hackney to St Giles.'

'But ... Do we need to *see* it?'

'What, you a painter and you ask me that? Yes, we need to see it, William. We need to see it every day. And so do the likes of Walpole. And so does the king. And so ...'

'Yes, all right. We can get a hackney at the corner.'

We took a hackney as far as St Giles' churchyard. I hesitated as we got out, but Captain Coram paid readily enough, even though we had cleared the first mile, so it was 1s 6d. The good captain not only paid, from a healthily plump leather purse, he also gave the driver a thumping 3d for a drink, which, as I pointed out, would be enough in this area to have him thoroughly fuddled on gin within minutes.

For St Giles, as everybody knows, consists entirely of hovels, run down churches and gin palaces, populated by whores, watchmen, sailors and drunks. Nothing but idleness, poverty, misery and ruin. 'Drunk for a penny, Dead drunk for twopence, Clean straw for nothing,' as the first sign they saw announced.

And through this hellscape strutted we two small men, me with my sword, Coram with his coat flapping, looking for dead babies.

'Not a one!' shouted the sea captain as we made our way at a trot down Broad St Giles, left into Dyot Street, right into the narrow Phoenix Street, along to Castle Street, then to Hart Street. Coram's indignation at being thwarted was the equal even of my own.

'I know there are usually many dead babies on the edges of such streets.' I sought to console him, even as I ran out of breath at the pace he was setting.

'We should have gone to Rotherhithe,' riposted the angry Coram. 'I tell you, day after day, at dawn and at dusk, I have seen dead babies in the streets.'

'A sad part of London life,' I said, still seeking to placate.

In this I clearly failed. The sea captain stopped dead in his tracks and turned to face me. We were nose to nose, neither nose much more than five feet off the ground. 'A sad part ... Sir, I believed I had made it clear that my purpose is to end this savage situation. Not to mouth platitudes about how sad it is.'

'But how can you ...?'

'A sanctuary for foundlings, sir. Such as they have in other countries.'

I felt he could not mean the New World, even though he was just returned from Georgia. No doubt France again, ahead again. No wonder we were always at war with them. I thought it politic to say nothing. But I believed instantly and passionately in his cause.

Finally, with me out of breath but the leather-lunged sea captain still in full stride, we came upon a spot with the elegant spire of St George's in the distance. Below this finger of elegance all was degraded squalor: pawnbrokers, gin shops and not a house in tolerable condition. The most palatial establishment was that of the undertaker.

I saw a housewife pawning her cooking pot for gin, a workman handing over the tools of his trade. Over there, a man gnawed at one end of a bone while a dog gnawed the other. Another man, no doubt bankrupt, was trying to hang himself from a beam. And as we looked on, amazement turning to horror, finally a dead baby.

A woman sat atop a flight of stone steps opposite Kilman, the distillers of gin. Garbed only in a ragged shift and a strip of cotton headband, with angry open sores on her bare legs, she had long lost the blessing of youth, but was nonetheless suckling a baby, both full breasts being exposed to the gaze of the populace for the purpose.

Then, before our horrified gaze, the woman appeared to sink into a gin-sodden trance, a ghastly, leering smile lifting her features. As we two small men started forwards to prevent the inevitable, the baby tumbled from the breast, falling, flailing over a wooden railing to smash head-first on the stone paving of a courtyard some ten feet down, its poor, wretched head splitting open like a ripe melon, bits of brain spattering a foot high up the brick wall.

Of the two of us, I was clearly the more shaken. Coram shook his head ruefully.

'You see?' he said belligerently, as if the death of the baby proved some point in argument, which perhaps it had. And then, abruptly, 'I must go.'

'What? Because of … what we have witnessed?'

Coram allowed himself a tight smile – he had thin lips, I noticed. 'No, no. Eunice will be waiting for me.' His face, I noted with fascination, was transformed at the mention of this name – Eunice. It softened, dough-like, the features returning to babyhood, eyes widening and rounding.

'Your wife?'

'Yes, indeed. We met in Georgia. My good fortune!'

He stopped but he wanted to talk about her; that was very evident. He wanted her there, with us, even more than she already was. Coram's face was flushing now, his changing features making a progress every bit as vivid as one of my famous stories in paint.

And at that second, I understood, with lifelong realisation, that what Coram felt in his soul about his Eunice I felt about Jane and I always would. The realisation shook me profoundly with its depth. It was coloured with fear that I might not be worthy and chill regret that I had already lapsed, feeling indeed the mercury weakness in my bones.

But feeling and contemplation, two sides of the same coin with a character such as mine, were brought to a sudden end by the sea captain fleeing from me, calling a 'Farewell', over his shoulder. A chair had just deposited its gentleman client, already unsteady even before his descent into the Hades of St Giles. Coram gave a bellowed hail to the two chairmen and installed himself in the seat just vacated by the unsteady well-born. With a lift and a wave he was off, out of my sight.

6

IT WAS UNDERSTOOD, the very next time the two of us met, as we both knew we would, that I would support Coram's cause of a home for the abandoned babies of London. And this I did with a full heart. Coram, as I expected, indeed took for granted, was equally warm in his support for my cause, the Act of Parliament to protect engravers from the depredations of pirates.

Support for my pamphlet and my petition had been overwhelming, but there was one sad exception. I had had a falling-out with the big, bluff West Country painter, Francis Hayman. Such fallings-out were nothing unusual, for my spleen rose in me as often as food went down the other way, and when the spleen reached my mouth I tended to lose control of my tongue. Also Hayman was sensitive to slights, both real and imagined. His fragile dignity was hard-won and cherished: hard on the outside, soft within.

On this occasion, the artist crew at Old Slaughter's had been discussing the setting up of an academy to teach art and show paintings. I was loud in my insistence that there must be no copying in the teaching, no slavish imitation of dead Roman limbs. Nobody supported me, except the French sculptor, Roubiliac, to whom I was increasingly close. Hayman led the opposition, arguing for a more formal, dignified academy.

But real trouble at Old Slaughter's only arose when Hayman started discussing my painting. In the middle of a paean of praise, broken only to devour a Cornish pasty, the Devon man remarked that my painting had no single light source, unlike, say, Rembrandt. I maintain that Hayman said my work had no focus, all its detail being equal, but Hayman always denied he ever said that.

Considerable quantities of porter fuelled the misunderstandings piling against each other, the muddy and confused argument, melding it into a feud. I was wounded and I called Hayman 'a boy' – I always hated other artists being younger than me – and a 'scene painter': this latter being undeniable as Hayman had indeed painted stage scenery at Goodman's Fields and Drury Lane.

The heated row ended with Hayman refusing to sign my petition to Parliament to protect engravers, something which hardly concerned Hayman anyway, as he did no engravings.

Meanwhile, there was the problem of who was to engrave the *Rake* story. Engravers, as the whole world knew, were French, just as singers were Italian and beef was English. So, with a light heart and a song on my lips, I went to see Roubiliac.

Roubiliac was not at Old Slaughter's, so there was only one other place where he would be: in his studio at St Peter's Court, off St Martin's Lane, working.

Roubiliac was much-mocked for his dedication to his work, for it made him absent-minded. He had often broken off conversation with a guest at his studio in the middle of a sentence, or even in the middle of a word, because an idea for a line in his sculpture had appeared in his mind, obscuring the real world. Roubiliac would then instantly and wordlessly go to work, not noticing when the abandoned guest left his garret of a studio.

The other aspect of Roubiliac's character that provoked much laughter among the Old Slaughter group was his thicket of a French accent. Hayman led the way in imitating this hideous monster of sound but, for all my lifelong facility at imitation, I never joined in because, as I admitted only to Jane, my view of Roubiliac bordered on awe. Roubiliac was the only man I ever met who was, without the slightest question or demur, a genius.

But a genius who was, at this moment, intensely cold, indeed shivering as a knife-edge wind blew in his miserable studio, billowing his thin shirt. There was no sign of his wife, Celeste. Roubiliac had opened the door to me himself, showed me up the stairs to the studio and now sat shivering alone. Alone, not in the literal sense but in the sense that having nobody near him was Roubiliac's natural state, just as being surrounded by clubbable types was mine.

Roubiliac gave one final large shiver, as if attempting to banish all the smaller ones. The sculptor, I knew, was from some hot part of France – Lyon was it? – so felt the cold winters in England keenly. He was new to them, too, having only of late arrived in London after disappointment, so they say, in some competition or other in his native France, which he had, unaccountably to me, failed to win.

'My father was a *marchand*,' Roubiliac had said apologetically once, with that shrug which all Frenchmen are surely taught at school. The sculptor meant he was not used to hunger and cold.

Roubiliac shivered and smiled his thin-lipped smile as I stopped breathless before an amazing work of a reclining female figure, her clothes disarranged, with a man standing over her.

'My God!' I groaned out my admiration. And then, 'Does it have a title?'

'*Gentleman Surprising a Lady on a Couch*. You like?'

'Oh, I like, Roubiliac. My, how I like. A lady with her clothes disarranged. You are my long-lost brother, my friend.'

As I turned back to him I noticed a form in Roubiliac's narrow truckle bed, the only place in the minute icebox where a man could be off his feet. There was stiff black hair at the top of a filthy horse blanket which covered the form.

'There's someone in your bed, Roubiliac.'

Roubiliac started as if poked in the ribs. 'Is there? Oh … yes.'

'Well, go and wake them, man. I can't discuss my business while a person lies there, in front of me.'

'No? Oh, all right.'

Roubiliac strode the two paces to the bed, being all the movement the garret allowed. He pulled back the threadbare horse blanket, revealing the corpse of a black woman. There was a moment's silence in the room.

'Roubiliac, there is dead black woman in your bed.'

'How did that happen?' Roubiliac scratched his head.

'Roubiliac, if you don't know how it happened I fear it may be destined to remain a mystery. Have you seen her before?'

'Yes, of course. I … Her name is Marie-Rose or Rose Marie or something.' Roubiliac waved his arms in a manner no Englishman would be seen dead doing. 'She fucks for money,' Roubiliac added, helpfully.

'That is as may be!' I said evenly. 'The question is, you French poltroon, how did she die?'

Roubiliac unleashed the shrug. 'How do I know? She was alive when we fucked.'

'Glad to hear it. Anyway, Roubiliac, I'm somewhat pressed for time.'

This was a bit much, I realised, as it was I who had disturbed the lugubrious sculptor at his work, but Roubiliac merely smiled his creased-cheek smile.

'I need you to recommend an engraver. This is for eight paintings of my latest Progress. It will take London by storm. I could do it myself, of course, but I simply haven't the time. Commissions for phizes are rolling in. I'm much sought after. Anyway, who's the best man?'

Roubiliac released the shrug. 'Gravelot.'

'No!' I could feel my forehead scar colouring as I recalled Hubert Gravelot's arrogance at the Old Slaughter table: his effortless assumption that he could arrive as an interloper and be the best engraver in London, as of right.

'I know Gravelot is the best,' I said, softly. 'But I won't work with him. I humble myself for no man. Not anymore.' I turned sideways so I could no longer see the corpse of the black whore, which was disturbing my line of thought. 'Give me another name. Another bloody Frenchman if you must.'

'Louis-Gerard Scotin,' Roubiliac said. 'The best for you. Maybe better than Gravelot for you. Not so many curly-wurlies. Straighter lines. More English. Manly.' Roubiliac beat his breast satirically. 'Better English accent too. Even better than me.'

This was rendered as 'Eevern bettair zan mee.' Roubiliac made his already terrible accent even worse to amuse.

I roared with laughter. 'Where is he?'

'He sleeps on floors. French floors mainly. But you can find him at the inn opposite the French church. You know? It has a sign with the head of John the Baptist.' Roubiliac grimaced. 'Horrible. *Ils sont des barbares, les anglais.*'

I grinned. '*Oui, je sais.*'

I went over to the corpse of the black whore, turning my back on Roubiliac long enough to get at my leather purse to withdraw a guinea coin. I put the coin by the corpse's shoulder, then drew the wretched blanket back up over her.

'Will you come back?' Roubiliac said. 'I want to do a sculpture of you. Your head. Your fine head.'

'I would be honoured,' I replied. 'I shall commission it.'

And I would pay top rate for it, to help Roubiliac.

The Engraving Copyright Act, based on the pamphlet I had written, was now being steered through Parliament by the estimable James Edward Oglethorpe. I wanted to be clad in its protection before *Rake*, my most important work to date, was launched on the world.

But no sooner was it launched than it fell to ground. It quickly became evident that *Rake* was not attracting nearly as many subscribers as *Harlot* had done. Also, the machinations of my old enemies, the booksellers and printers, were not, as I had hoped, consigned to the past.

The Engraver's Copyright Act, already being called Hogarth's Act, was now the law of England, having just passed through Parliament. The day I realised that this triumph had turned to ashes has long been engraved on my mind. I was sitting in the drawing room, bewailing the low numbers of subscription-buyers to my long-suffering Jane.

'Where are the people?' I was lamenting for the tenth or eleventh time. 'Where is my public?'

I peered out of the window over Leicester Fields at ghostly queues of people, a thronging crowd of imagined subscribers who were not there. That very day, a disreputable looking fellow in a greasy black frock-coat was caught at the window by our new footman, George Wells. This fellow was peering in, sketching the engravings in order to copy them back at the printer's shop, and undercut my price.

I myself caught the next knave, right outside the house, finished sketch of the third part of the rake's story in his hand. I set about the fellow, screaming imprecations, but the villain tore himself away.

Fellow artists Lambert and Hudson showed me vastly inferior pirate prints they had bought, some from virtually outside my own house. One printer, Giles King of Drury Lane, was even advertising copies engraved by permission of the artist when they were no such thing.

I wept and keened loud and long on the shoulder of my beloved. The wailing refrain of 'Where are they?' echoed round every room of the once so sought after house, now made wretched by the failure at a summit once undreamed of. Many years later, I asked myself if I once noticed how wretched Jane herself was at this time, let alone asked myself what the cause of *her* sadness could be. The answer was plain enough – no!

There were whispers that the rake's story was too far outside the usual course of events. Too unusual. Profligates, it was held, were not usually denizens of the madhouse. In the newspapers I was beginning to be mentioned merely as the ingenious author of small conversation pieces.

The prints of *A Rake's Progress* were priced at double that of *Harlot*: two guineas. Even so, the enterprise made a fraction of what *Harlot* had made, hardly a quarter. I was going backwards, no progress here. And I feared, in the depths of the night when the shadows of the rich are no different from the shadows of the poor, that I was progressing backwards all the way to Spitalfields and the debtors' prison I had come from.

Rake exceeded *Harlot* in one respect only. William Beckford, a prominent Tory, bought the six paintings of *A Harlot's Progress* for fourteen guineas each, but paid twenty-two guineas each for the eight paintings of *Rake*. Some years later, Beckford's most peculiar dwelling, Fonthill by name, a monstrosity in Wiltshire, burnt to the ground.

I received word that, to the accompaniment of a clockwork organ set off by the blaze, all the paintings of the *Harlot's Progress* and all those of the *Rake* were burnt to ash.

Sic transit gloria mundi. We and our works are fleeting. Progress is strictly temporary.

7

I HAD KNOWN Jonathan Tyers for more than ten years. I was always drawn to his ugly, florid face, with its puffy burgundy cheeks, his high forehead; all of which, taken together, made him look like an intelligent, breathless pig.

I have always preferred ugly men, both as subjects of phiz-mongery and as companions. I have painted many squat, powerful, ugly men: Lord Simon Lovat, Bishop Hoadly, and the best of them, Dr Arnold of Ashby Lodge, looking like the criminal Lovat gone to the good. All were portraits of shoulder-driven energy and power, eschewing beauty. I was burstingly proud of them. And that, too, is how I saw myself, at this time, with youth a distant memory, old age not quite a certainty and not quite a fear.

Strangely, perhaps, I never painted Jonathan Tyers, though Hayman did – Tyers and his family in a Hayman-adequate conversation piece.

Like me, Hayman had known Tyers since 1732, when Tyers had opened up the old Spring Gardens, then cleaned it up both physically and morally in an attempt to persuade polite society it could be seen there. The gentlemen could stroll through the manicured paths between hedgerows and neatly pollarded trees, no longer for the old Spring Gardens whores, but for the music at the newly-built bandstands. And they could bring their ladies with them.

At this early time I had been teeming with ideas for Tyers – a shilling at the gate payment for entry to the gardens, instead of a subscription: that was my idea. It was me who had contacted the blind Justice of the Peace, John Fielding, brother of my friend, the novelist Henry, and persuaded him to hire out his watchmen to patrol the gardens, keeping them safe (well, *safer*) from cut-purses, footpads and the like.

But now, with Spring Gardens, renamed Vauxhall Gardens, established as London's premier pleasure park, I had another brilliant (if I may say so) idea for friend Jonathan. Art. Art in the gardens. English art, not foreign art, for the time had come for English art.

I had arranged for Tyers to join us at a table at Old Slaughter's, to commission art for Vauxhall Gardens. He was to begin, I had insisted, with my idea of a major sculpture commission for Roubiliac. But, to my irritation, Roubiliac was not among those present. Why were people not where I wished them to be? My irritation deepened to annoyance. I hoped Roubiliac had not been delayed by the discovery of another dead black whore in his bed.

But, lo, just as Tyers got started, addressing a group consisting of Lambert, Laguerre, Hudson, Hayman, Gravelot and myself, Roubiliac appeared, the familiar genial half-smile playing about his lips.

'Sorry I'm late,' he croaked out in his husky French accent. 'I had to watch something dry.'

This provoked smiles and even some laughter, as did almost everything he said, whether it was meant to be funny or not: something which was a source of pleasant bewilderment to Roubiliac himself.

'I was just about to propose,' Tyers said in his sonorous manner, 'a sculpture of one of my collaborators in the Vauxhall Gardens, Mr George Frideric Handel, to be placed in a grand niche in the gardens. I have in mind payment in the sum of £300. Mr Roubiliac, your name ...'

Such was the popularity of the gentle, unworldly, absent-minded Frenchman that a cheer ran round the table, led by the bass of Hayman and my own treble. Roubiliac unaffectedly started to cry, which, I noted with interest, changed his features far less than the lachrymose activity did with most people.

Roubiliac seized Tyers' hand and kissed it, provoking groans around the table and mock-vomiting from me.

'I take it that is an acceptance of my commission, then?' Tyers spoke with the faintest of quarter-smiles.

'Oui, monsieur. Merci, mille fois. Je ...'

'No bloody foreign languages at our table, Roubiliac, you Frenchie!' I roared. 'Speak the king's bloody English here. You foreigner.'

'You mean the king's German?' said Hayman, deadpan.

The entire table, very much including me, collapsed in ribald mirth, only Hayman maintaining enough composure to order more porter and sliced beef all round as the waiter hove into view. Hayman and I were still not on speaking terms, but that didn't stop me laughing at his jokes in company.

Tyers was plied with food and drink and only allowed to clear his mouth for speech because the assembled artists sensed more benison was on the way. As indeed it was.

Avoiding my eye, Tyers put forward my idea of decorating the supper boxes at Vauxhall Gardens with works by English artists. The idea was pounced on as it went up, like a hungry lion bringing down a leaping gazelle. Hayman was loudest in his support, very closely followed by Thomas Hudson, with me discretely bringing up the rear, so to speak.

'I shall do you an engravure of your gardens, *m'seur*,' Hubert Gravelot said from on high, speaking rather in the manner of a diplomat conceding small ground.

'Why, thank you, sir,' said Tyers, with great gravity. 'And who are you, exactly?'

For the second time the table exploded with laughter. Gravelot, perhaps not surprisingly, did not join in. 'The engravure will happen, *M'sieur* Tyers,' he said. 'That I promise you.'

And it did, of course. Too many wavy lines for my taste. 'Makes the bloody place look like it's an open-air brothel in France,' as I put it, at the time. But that was a small price to pay for commissions for myself, Hayman and the pearl of artists, Roubiliac, all from one carefully planned lunchtime visit to Old Slaughter's.

A grateful Jonathan Tyers gave me a handsome gold medal *perpetuam beneficii memoriam*, showing his own portrait on the obverse, giving entry into the gardens for life not only to myself, but also to a coach full of, namely six, companions who may accompany me on any visit. And as a season ticket to the gardens would set you back £1 9s, that medal was well worth having.

With my sisters established as milliners and my mother free from a life of toil on behalf of her children, I had purchased for the three of them a little dwelling on the north side of Cranbourn Alley, in St Anne's Parish. My sister Anne, in the way of these things, cared for our homebound mother. I never saw mama again, until her tragic death, but I made sure that she and my sisters wanted for nothing, both as head of the family and as a loving and dutiful son and brother.

One hot June day, the new second footman, the Irish lad Charles Mahon, burst red-faced into my studio as I was struggling with the engravings for *Rake*. He was wearing his day clothes; none of my servants were given livery, I loathed the pomp and the expense in equal measure.

'Master Hogarth, sir. You are enjoined to come with all speed ...' The youth fell to coughing.

I looked up from my work, my annoyance at such an unprecedented interruption melting at young Mahon's obvious sincerity and distress.

'Whoa there, boy!' I said, as if to a horse. 'What's all this?'

'Word has been sent from the streets around your mother's place. It's ablaze, sir. There is a fire.'

'What? My mother's rooms …?'

'The whole area, sir. Shall I tell Mistress Jane as well?'

'No, come with me.'

The boy ran ahead, for all the world as if I had never been round the corner to my mother's place before. But then, this was not so far from the truth. The boy naturally was far nimbler and fleeter, as I had grown portly by now. Still in my indoor cap, he left me puffing in his wake and cursing my aching knees. We could see the fire in the sky as soon as we drew abreast of Leicester House.

The further half of Cranbourn Alley, including the place I had bought for my family, was ablaze, the fire continuing towards St Martin's Lane. The street was thronged, as ever at a time of fire, with people watching, thieves going into the burning houses, and pickpockets and cut-purses trying to take what they could.

In the distance, apparently bobbing in the smoke and the dancing throng, to my intense relief I caught a glimpse of my sisters, clinging together. With young Charles Mahon heedlessly shouting 'Make way there,' and even using his elbows on the crowd, a path of sorts was cleared for me, which closed behind me as if I were Moses parting the Red Sea.

My senses were all the keener for my fear; I heard every word around me, every colour assailed me brightly, the acrid smell of the smoke covered my clothes, seeming to rise up to me from inside my own body. I heard a voice close, echoing, say 'It started in that brandy shop in Cecil Court.'

Even as I fought my way through to my sisters, suffused with fear for my mother, an image came to me of the two-penny gin shops I had passed in St Giles that day with Captain Coram. It was etched on my mind, much as it was to be when I etched it with a burin and called it *Gin Lane*, and then did a companion piece called *Beer Street*.

'You are safe!' I shouted, close to tears, as I made to seize both my sisters, as they were practically borne off their feet in the melee.

Anne, the younger, was crying. The elder, Mary, desperately pale, was peering at their home as yellow and red flame licked its timbers, and smoke plumed and billowed into the sky.

'Is she in there?'

Mary nodded. 'We were at the shop. She ... She was at home.'

The boy Charles tore at his jerkin. 'Let me try, sir. I'll effect a rescue, if I can.'

I seized him by the shoulders, even in this desperate chaos repressing a smile at the youth's brogue, together with a tear at his goodness. 'To lose you, too, would hardly aid my mother, Charles. But, thank you.'

The youth miserably re-tied his jerkin. And then, 'Look, sir, the soldiery.'

Troops had indeed been called out to the fire. They were conspicuous in their red coats, already barging people out of the way, trying to tackle the thieves and organising a chain to pass buckets, leading back in the St Martin's Lane direction where there was presumably a pump.

Next to me, a portly man, a gentleman by his garb, was appointing himself the resident expert on the scene. 'The soldiery, indeed,' he said, responding to what Charles Mahon had said, though naturally addressing me, as a gentleman, and ignoring the boy and the women.

'The Prince of Wales himself is in attendance,' said my informant, 'at the head of his Foot Guards. I am reliably informed that Lord James Cavendish and Sir Thomas Hobby are also among those present.'

I glared at him. I was minded to say I did not care if the Archangel Gabriel was among those present, so long as they saved my mother. But instead I turned to the young footman.

'Charles, please escort my sisters to Leicester Fields where they can be cared for. I shall join the bucket-chain to fight this fire.'

'Please, sir. Please let me fight the fire with you. Sir, look!' The boy pointed through the crowd at Henry Tompion, the butler, and George Wells, our footman, making their way to them. The boy's blue eyes were bright with tears. 'Sir, we'd all go down for you. We'd go into the pit of hell itself for you, sir!'

I almost forgot my mother in my startled amazement. I regarded myself as a fair master to my servants. I was the only person I knew who forbade his servants to take vails in front of visiting guests, not wishing them to fawn for money. But against that I paid them all, the two housemaids, the cook and the men servants, £9 a year, far more than anybody else in Leicester Fields. And they were paid on time, too, regular as Sunday, without fail.

Nevertheless, I truly had no idea of their strength of feeling for me. Indeed, even as I thought this old Henry Tompion, who would not see forty again, also volunteered for certain death to attempt a rescue of my mother.

I clasped the good old servant by the shoulders. 'We shall join the chain, Henry. We shall all join the chain. Mary, please …'

Mary nodded. 'Anne and I will go to Leicester Fields, William. You and the men do what you can.'

The snaggle-toothed footman, George Wells, had already inserted himself between two Foot Guards, passing a water bucket from hand to hand. Henry Tompion, Charles Mahon and I joined him, all in a line, master and man. I never forgot that, never forgot their love for me.

As I worked, swinging a bucket with characteristic energy, despite my now tubby frame, I noticed a figure from the past, John Huggins, sometime Warden of the Fleet. I had last seen Huggins when I painted him, but the picture seared on my mind was of Huggins demanding money of my mother, that garnish of £1 6s 8d for removal of my father's fetters. And now, on what was no doubt to be my mother's last day on earth, here was Huggins again, like an evil carrion crow.

He looked much older, as he was entitled to. An old man now, with strands of white hair and pointy nose, not far from death. As I swayed in rhythm with the chain passing the bucket, I said 'What on earth is he doing?' out loud.

He was giving out money, Huggins was. Of course, he was trying to bribe the watchers to form an *ad hoc* watch against the thieves, who were now more emboldened than ever to go into the houses. I remembered that one of Huggins' many houses was in St Martin's Lane.

I stopped watching him, the better to swing buckets of water, until eventually I was taken away, exhausted, aching, coughing from the smoke, back to Leicester Fields, half-carried by my devoted servants.

I was ever the citizen under the law, even though the law had used my father so harshly, so I attended the arraignment of one Mrs Kelloway, an Irishwoman accused of starting the fire deliberately. The arraignment was held at the Old Bailey before my neighbour and fellow mason, the magistrate De Veil. Only one person had died in the conflagration, my poor old mama passed away from the smoke and from fear.

Mrs Kelloway was committed to Newgate. Mama found her final rest in the churchyard of St Anne's, Soho. After the service, I began a portrait of her, working from memory. I also arranged for fire insurance from the Sun Insurance Company, insuring our valuables for the sum of £500. The cover was extended to my sisters.

Jane remained my beloved; I did not doubt that for a second. But her dissatisfaction with our lives, or perhaps with me, increasingly solidified to anger. She was growing plumper, she was getting fractious, she was developing a plate-throwing, screaming temper. Once, just once, I called her a shrew, then fell to my knees weeping and said I was sorry.

But there was the rub, that falling to my knees. I could still do it, but the rising up again was no simple matter. I realised I was becoming more than portly – fleshily plump. My knees ached, my back ached from hours of upright painting, my gums ached (and bled), I vomited on occasion for no discernible reason. I was a prey to rashes, blotches, swelling in the groin and under the armpits, fever.

None of this, of course, was Jane's fault, far from it. But in my public dealings I shut it all away, like locking a skeleton in a cupboard, only to find it breaking loose when I was at home. My weaknesses, corporeal and spiritual, made me impatient with her weaknesses and whatever ailed her. My dealings with her were no longer skilful and no longer always happy. We were distant; we were apart.

As a last-gasp remedy I essayed another portrait of Jane, half-size, 35 by 27 inches, but seated like a queen. She chose an ivory silk dress fringed with lace, with a bow at the breast and matching bonnet. She wore a tight string of pearls at her neck. Her gaze at the viewer was to be steady, dignified, unsmiling.

But from the beginning the sittings went wrong. I know I always demanded much of my portrait sitters, maintaining position for hours, sometimes accommodating my changes of mind and mood until the exasperated sitter felt that he or she was to match the portrait, not the other way round. With Jane, however, it was more than that. The sittings, which I hoped would let us recover our once total ease in each other's company, were making her edgy and petulant.

'William, you seem to think a sizeable house with six servants runs itself.'

'Please, dearest …' At that moment I was attacking the portrait like a fencer on the forward dart. 'Please do not move or look angry, just for a moment.'

'Angry? Angry? You expect me to sit here like a bolt of cloth on a shelf. Then you ask your cronies to dinner and expect food to appear as if by magic. If I do not instruct cook within the hour, she will have no idea what to buy at market for supper today.'

I looked at her, then. I looked at her as a painter and I looked at her as a man. Her full breasts still excited me, even though I increasingly took what pleasure

I was capable of elsewhere, sometimes even imagining some Catherine Street whore was her. Her face was not beautiful, apart from her grey eyes, but her handsome calm was imposing. And I still loved her. I loved my distant wife like few men in London loved theirs.

So why was the portrait as barren as a mule? It was like a work by the current arbiter of taste, the idiot Joshua Reynolds. Or even the boy Rams-ay, the Scotty. Even Hayman-adequate could have done better. Silk, yes. Lace, yes. Very nice. Face, yes. It was a human face, it even had a mood that the viewer could leadenly name. But it said absolutely nothing. It *was* absolutely nothing, except a pile of cloth with a woman in it. It was art without art, representation without mind, let alone soul.

All that was vivid in my life, at this time, were my dreams. The prison nightmares, which had never entirely left me, came back in force every night. The nightmares featured Sir James and me in prison together, as we had been when we both drew doomed Sarah Malcolm.

Incredible though it came to seem to me in later life, I found out precisely what was wrong with Jane only much later. I found out through a painting, one of my own paintings.

8

I HAD KNOWN Daniel Graham for many years, initially because I purchased painting materials – that is to say, paints, ground, turpentine and the like – from Graham's apothecary shop in Pall Mall. Later, as Graham became more successful, becoming apothecary to the Chelsea Hospital, our social circles overlapped.

Neither Daniel nor I could remember exactly when the idea started that I should paint his children, but we talked about it for years before it came to pass. Then, in the way of these matters, aspiration suddenly and rapidly turned to a plan which turned to arrangements.

I have always loved painting children. I feel an affinity for them, based on their energy and truth. I understand their perceptions, because I still remember vividly the various ages and stages of my own childhood. I had inherited this affinity with children from my beloved father, and therefore I cherished it.

Daniel Graham had four children: Henrietta, the oldest; the seven-year-old Anna Maria; Richard, the chubby-faced little boy; and the baby, Thomas. At this point, I was interested in larger paintings, the larger the better, large as life. This one ended up some 64 by 62 inches.

With this painting, I wanted to take on my self-appointed master, van Dyck, especially his *Five Eldest Children of Charles I*. That is why you could see many elements of Dutch still-life in the work, like the curtains and the silver bowl of fruit.

The children were posed at the luxurious and charming Graham residence on the north side of Pall Mall, with the help of Daniel's second wife, the delightful Mary Crisp. They were posed in the hall, so I could copy the Dutch-style tiling. But after that, all the props were added in my studio, except little Richard's *serinette*, which he really was clutching when he was posed, and which therefore gave me the idea for the bird in the cage and the cat about to pounce on it.

At any rate, the nearly-finished portrait of *The Graham Children* was in my studio when Jane saw it. Jane was in black, like a dowager, a style she had adopted some months ago, when our estrangement had become more fixed. I had noticed, meant to ask her about it, but somehow the time was never right. And forcing the matter may naturally have made the chasm between us even deeper.

And then Fanny, Jane's faithful maid, had tried to talk to me, two or three times, about Jane. But somehow I had always been on my way out, or on my way in, or about to paint, or about to visit my masonic lodge, but at any rate too busy to listen. And so I didn't. Perhaps I did not wish to. I do not know. I just do not know.

'What's that?' Jane said, pointing at the picture. She looked odd in black, with her face whey white.

I did not even know what she was doing in the studio at this time. She did not usually come in when I was painting, unless I was painting her.

'It's the children of Daniel Graham and Mary,' I said.

'Look!' Jane touched the image of baby Thomas, still tacky. 'That's what we should have had, one like that. A little boy.'

'Don't touch! And anyway, nobody's got him now.' I was in pain – teeth, guts, my right leg. I knew I was speaking tetchily but was powerless to stop. 'He's dead. Little Thomas died. The Grahams wanted him left in the picture. As a memorial.'

Jane screamed. She beat me on the chest and shoulders with her fists. I felt the force through my thin linen smock. 'Jane! Jane, have you lost your senses? What ails you, woman?'

'Where are my children?' she howled, in a strange low hoot. 'You promised me children. We had a nursery. The servants live in it; it mocks me. You don't care. You're my husband. Give me children, you bastard.' Jane lifted up her skirts with a handful of her petticoats. 'Give me children now.'

'Jane! Jane, my darling. You are overwrought. You ...'

'Do you know what they say about me? The same as they say about any woman who does not give birth for her husband. They say she is cursed. They say she must have sinned. And that is correct, isn't it, my Billy? That is right. I let you have your way with me in my parents' own house before we were married and now I must pay for it. I must pay for your damnable lusts, you dirty boy. The lusts you now void over half of London. I ... I ...' She banged herself in the chest with her fist. 'I am the one who must pay.'

I approached her. I tried to touch her shoulder, tenderly. 'Jane ... Jane, I ...'

'Don't come near me. Don't come near me again. I hate you for what you have done to us.'

And with that she ran out of the room, running to Fanny who had heard the altercation and had come for her. It was the glance that Fanny shot me as she took Jane from the room that lanced me even more than Jane's words had done. It was a glance of bitter disappointment.

9

EVERY TIME I entered Roubiliac's coffin of a studio off St Martin's Lane it seemed to have become smaller, colder, darker and dirtier. This time, I checked the Frenchman's bed for dead whores on entry, thankfully finding none. I was then engulfed in a passionate, foreign embrace, smelling of sweat, semen and fish.

A party of the St Martin's artists were due at Vauxhall Gardens that evening. I had included Jane among the company, hoping to bring her back to her once cheerful ways. The occasion was the unveiling of Roubiliac's statue of Handel, the commission which had my hidden hand in it. But the sculptor had insisted on seeing me privately first.

This, I surmised, was to present the bust of me I had sat for. The role of sitter had not come easily to me. Ever a creature of extremes, as I am aware, I had begun by presenting myself as the world's best sitter; I sat silent and immobile while Roubiliac worked, until the sculptor complained that this rigidity was changing my features.

Never content with mediocrity, considering it the absolute monopoly of Hayman-adequate, I then became the world's worst sitter: jumping about; relieving myself every ten minutes into the sculptor's already brimming piss pot, with the excuse of a nervous disposition; talking nineteen to the dozen, then insisting on seeing the work in progress.

Roubiliac coped with both my aspects as sitter with his customary charming equanimity, interesting lips widening a little, those lines in his cheeks deepening a little, eyes a-gleam and a-dance with amusement.

That was the look on his face now. So I surmised not only that the bust of myself was about to be presented but that Roubiliac knew in his soul, his heart and his viscera that it was good. For artists know, so I believe, in ways beyond mind, when they are fulfilling their destinies in art. And when they are not. I winced as I thought of my portrait of Jane.

'What's the matter?' Roubiliac's face was all falling lines of concern.

'Nothing. Why?'

'Why are you making a funny face?'

'Was I? I was thinking about something.'

'It was bad, wasn't it? It was a terrible face.'

I laughed. 'Yes, it's bad, all right.' I might have lost Jane. What could be worse?

Without another word, Roubiliac took the pace and a half to the end of his bed, then picked up the bust, covered in a piece of dirty coal-sacking. He pulled the sacking away, presenting the bust to me, as if handing a bunch of flowers to a mistress.

'*Voila!*'

I arched my aching back, the better to view it, then laughed and cried at the same time. It was sculpted of warm pink terracotta, which in Roubiliac's hands was as foldable as paper. It was better than I had dared dream. It was better than I knew was possible. It moved. It seemed to breathe. It seemed to think.

I looked for my forehead-bash, the Finger of God, the sign of the storm upon me, and found it. In my indoor painter's cap, Roubiliac had returned me to the handsome Hogarth of my own first self-portrait, not the Pug Hogarth of the second one. Flattering the sitter is never a bad idea. Geniuses do it too; look at van Dyck. There were no arms, there was fancy stuff at collar and tunic fastening.

But somehow, because of the dynamics of the work, the tension between neck, shoulders and the head as it was turned to the right shoulder, *the head appeared to be about to move.* I stood there, as Roubiliac showed his own bust to me and waited for my own head to move to look myself in the eye. And then it did. I swear to you, it did. By all that was holy, IT MOVED.

'Roubiliac ... You do me great honour.'

'It's good?' The Frenchman was smiling.

'No, no, Roubiliac. It's not good. It's beyond good. It's beyond the judgement of the mind. Oh, you clever little Frenchman. You utter bloody genius.'

I launched myself at the sculptor, embraced him, my head coming up to the Frenchman's collarbone.

Then I gave a huge sigh. 'I must go. I must prepare for your unveiling this evening. Your Handel statue.'

'No!'

'No?'

'Don't go, William, please. I don't want to be alone.'

'All right. Come with me. Stay with me all the time until the unveiling. I'll look after you. Is that what you want?'

Roubiliac nodded. Then, very faintly, 'Yes. Please.'

'Very well.' I looked round the room. The sculptor was wiping his hands on his smock and breeches. 'Roubiliac, do you actually possess a shirt?'

We took the wherry across to Vauxhall Stairs, all six of us, making maximum use of my free-entry medal from Jonathan Tyers. There was myself and Jane; the *de facto* guest of honour, Roubiliac, who had been persuaded into a shirt; Francis Hayman, the big Devon painter, currently at uneasy truce with me, still eating even on a choppy crossing of the Thames; Hubert Gravelot, the French engraver, looking mildly bored; and gentleman George Lambert, as elegant and gracious as ever.

The crossing, I noted happily, was doing Jane good. There was pink tingeing her cheeks and she laughed, tossing back her head as the wherry pitched and tossed on the waves. She had been persuaded to abandon the black clothes she had affected for months, now wearing worsted stockings, a yellow bonnet, and a becoming green cloak over a new sack-back gown of pink and yellow chiné French silk. She glanced at me now and again, making me realise that this gesture of hers, once a habit, had stopped some years ago.

Jonathan Tyers met us at the entrance, sternly supervising the waived payment of a shilling each, tut-tutting as I presented my medal to the gatekeeper, as if such evidence of my high status were superfluous. As Tyers ushered us all through, waving his arms like an admiral flagging a message to a ship of the line, he spoke softly to Roubiliac.

'Your statue of Master Handel is in place, sir. I think you will be happy at its positioning. It can be viewed to advantage. Certainly we at Vauxhall are most happy with it.'

The Frenchman's sallow complexion flushed as pretty a pink as his terracotta statues at the compliment. Tyers led the way through a vista of woodland, a contrived plantation sculptured into submission from its wild state by criss-crossing, man-made paths at sharp angles. It was all too tidy for me. I prefer nature to reflect life, in as much as both are an untidy struggle.

'You see those lights?' I demanded of his audience, waving at the oil lamps, presently unlit. 'They are illuminations. The word is from *lucere* to shine. The gardens are indeed most magical and fairy-like when the lights are burning. Tyers, when will the lights be lit?'

The first fingers of dusk were indeed touching the gardens as I spoke. The unveiling time had been chosen to maximise the size of crowds, yet still leave enough light for Roubiliac's statue to be viewed to advantage.

'The lights are being lit as we speak, William,' said Tyers, as we all strolled along down a central pathway. He nodded at a lamplighter with his tapers ahead of us, one of many, as quickly became evident.

I led the way past artfully created groves, from where came the faint sounds of a fiddle and a Jew's harp. We came across a Chinese temple where visitors were dining in supper boxes, regaled by an orchestra playing *Dido and Aeneas* out of tune.

Tyers then overtook me, leading us past a Turkish tent held aloft by Doric and Ionic columns, and by now lit by no fewer than five massive chandeliers. Then on through a series of arches to an artificial waterfall, which clearly afforded Tyers much pleasure and pride.

We diverted to see the art on display at the supper boxes. Indeed, the art was not only on display but tacitly on sale, though prices would be brazenly added only later. All this was my idea. Who else?

And very pleased with the result I was, too. My *Four Times of the Day* was displayed to advantage. The paintings had already been sold to one Baker for over £40, and a set of the four plates in their first state for more than £6. Jane had praised the series, too. What more could a man want?

Well, actually there was something more, and this early evening time at Vauxhall Gardens duly provided it: Hayman-adequate pictures, clumps of them, hung side by side with the Hogarths. The implicit comparison was cruel to Hayman. There was no doubt of the inferiority of works by the big Devon man to those of the great, small Pug Hogarth, the illuminator (not satirist, please, I have never liked the term) of our times.

There was a Hayman-adequate called *May Day*, showing three female figures stiffly cavorting in front of a young fellow with something strange on his head, while an old man with apparently no legs played the fiddle supported by a crutch.

Country Dancers Round a Maypole showed more of Hayman-adequate's stiff figures dancing round a maypole, despite the apparent rheumatic condition affect-ing nearly everyone he painted upright. I found myself grinning with delight and failing to hide my joy or the source of it from Hayman. Our brief cessation of hostilities was at an end, as I was to discover to my cost some years later.

We made our way to the Great Grove, where the statue was to be unveiled.

Roubiliac followed close after me, drawing level with me and touching my arm all the time. He kept looking at me, almost pleadingly.

When we reached the Great Grove a crowd was gathered in the rotunda, round a life-size statue with white cloth draped over it. Tyers ran up the stairs, placing himself in front of the statue before addressing the throng.

'Ladies and gentlemen, thank you for your patience. This is a great day for Vauxhall Gardens, one of the greatest since the old Spring Gardens opened some seventy-seven years ago. Since then the gardens have been a home to many sorts of pleasure ...' That was received with a knowing laugh. 'But never before have we played host to such great art. And I am delighted to say that the creator of this art is here with us today. Ladies and gentlemen, a welcome Frenchman in our midst. Mr Louis-François Roubiliac.'

There was a decent round of applause for Roubiliac, with me smacking my hands together vigorously and Jane smiling at the sculptor as she decorously clapped. Roubiliac had told Tyers he did not want to make a speech, but now looked terrified in case the owner of the gardens had forgotten. Again, he kept looking at me, and touching my arm.

But without further preamble, Tyers gave the cloth over Roubiliac's statue of Handel a vigorous yank, and there, carved from a single block of marble, was the work for all to see.

And what a work of wonder it was. As ever with great art, I took in the whole before any of the parts. It was like being thrown in the air. George Frideric Handel, who I knew well enough, was embodied in marble before me, sitting with one leg crossed over the other so his body formed an 'S' curve of utterly moving beauty. The pose was audacity of the highest order, the execution a triumph.

No dead copying this, such as I had so often inveighed against, as artists aped other artists down the centuries. No Hayman-adequate meeting of lazy expectation. This was new. This showed viewers something they didn't know they knew. Gone the stiffness plaguing the art of the day, gone the rigidity, gone even the formality.

I glanced at Jane as tears streamed down my cheeks. Then I glanced at Roubiliac, who was also crying. Then a step forwards, almost stumbling. I clumsily knelt at the feet of the statue, oblivious to the crowd cheering and braying. I reverently kissed the plinth.

'Oh, Roubiliac! Roubiliac, this is sublime!'

10

THE TOPSY TURVY DAY was my idea; it was a day when the master and mistress of the house became servants and the servants were the masters, or at least were waited upon in the manner of masters.

Jane had liked the idea from the beginning. She regarded it as a sort of running jape or jest, as did Fanny the maid when she was told. Over the decades, mistress and maid had become like equal friends, with Fanny spending hours chatting to Jane so spontaneously that she hardly realised she was talking. Her work had limited itself to dressing Jane, helping supervise the shopping and running the household when Jane was away or indisposed.

The two women had even grown to resemble one another, Fanny taking on more than a little of Jane's stout build. The once pert face was now pouched with flesh, the flush at the cheeks crossed with thin red lines. They finished each other's sentences as they chatted, reducing nature's barriers between them to the point where, in my view, a Topsy Turvy Day would show little difference in their manner with each other.

Of the two other female servants, the housemaid, Sarah Young, had the most to gain from the brief break from work of a Topsy Turvy Day, as her health was so poor that some of the more cruel establishments would long ago have had the butler show her the door.

The consumption never really left her. She had overcome the smallpox, however, after we sent her to the Pancras hospital. Poor Sarah Young had also taken to her bed, over the years, with bouts of thrush, dropsy and, especially in the winter, bronchitis.

The cook, one Mrs Parsons, was a healthier specimen than Sarah, indeed it would be hard to find anyone in the whole of London who was not, but of all the Leicester Fields household she was the least enthusiastic about Topsy Turvy Day.

'Meaning no disrespect, madam,' as she bobbed a curtsey to illustrate the point, 'but I don't want nobody among my utensils, not even you, as owns them, I suppose. I shall never be able to find a thing afterwards.'

Jane laughed and swore by all the culinary gods to put everything back just as she had found it.

So much, then, for the three women. Of the three men servants, the boy second footman, Charles Mahon, was the most pleased by the coming day. Jane had hired Charles Mahon, I had nothing to do with it. The boy's father had just died; he would like as not have starved, or been driven to thieving, and the rest of his family with him. At odd moments Jane had taught him to read, then to write. She had arranged for Henry Tompion to teach him his figures, with a view to one day helping with the household accounts. The boy worshipped Jane.

The day appointed for Topsy Turvy Day was a bright clear Monday. I had no idea that the servants got up at two in the morning, to start the washing and cleaning chores, but was relieved to discover that this applied to the maids only, whose place Jane would be taking. The butler and footmen arose somewhat later.

So while I slumbered, Jane laced herself into her stays, indignantly refusing help from Sarah Young and Fanny, and sleepily began on Sarah's first task of the day, the polishing of all the household's door locks with an oily rag and rottenstone.

This accomplished, Jane flushed red and expected praise, but as Fanny and Sarah warmed to their roles, she received none. A bellows was thrust into her hand by a newly-fierce Fanny, with which Jane was set to blowing the dust off the stucco work and all the paintings, most of them by her father and the Old Slaughter artists – my own stayed in the studio until they were sold. This was a task she rather enjoyed, resolving to ask Sarah if she may undertake it now and again on days that were not topsy turvy.

Sarah sneaked off to empty the chamber pots, utterly unable to let Jane, who she unashamedly loved, undertake the task. Meanwhile, Jane was distracted by Fanny showing her how to polish all the wooden floors with a long-handled hard brush and herbs.

Jane was delighted at her success at this task, neither Sarah nor Fanny telling her that the hard part had not yet been started. The floors required another sweeping when the herbs had dried and another hard polishing until they shone like mahogany. The servants intended to do all that later.

The indulgent Sarah and Fanny then let Jane trundle a mop over the kitchen floor, clean some of the windows from the inside only, and fumigate the drawing room with brimstone against the bugs which infested it. Jane was eager to do more, but Fanny gently pointed out that it was now past the mid-morning hour at which breakfast was normally served.

By now, the footmen, the butler and the maids were up and about, as was I.

'Well, Henry,' I said to the butler, 'what is the first task of the day? Eh? Let me be the humblest footman. Young Charles, here,' I indicated the grinning Charles Mahon, 'what is my first task?'

'To attend to the wishes and needs of callers and guests, sir.'

'But we haven't got any callers and guests. It's too early.'

'Yes, sir.'

This exchange took place in the drawing room. Meanwhile, Jane was helping Mrs Parsons with breakfast, the cook having flatly refused to let the mistress do it alone.

There was an *escabeche*, some of which had been cunningly kept back by Mrs Parsons from yesterday's dinner; Mrs Parsons, like every cook in London, was adept at planning ahead. Even the choice of *escabeche*, not so much because it was fish but because it was served cold, had been made for dinner with the following day's topsy turvy breakfast in mind.

As Mrs Parsons well knew, I would have cried havoc at merely fish being on offer at breakfast, so there had to be some leftover cuts of prime purple beef for me, too. Jane was allowed to make the morning chocolate.

After that, Topsy Turvy Day came to a halt for a while until I received a caller, in my role of footman. It was the playwright Henry Fielding: former sow-gelder, former hackney writer, one of the tallest men in London and certainly, in my view, the one with the biggest nose London had ever seen, bar none. Certainly, as a painter, I delighted in exaggerating the already enormous proboscis in my drawings of the scribe, until the imposing organ resembled the prow of a Roman galleon.

Fielding entirely failed to notice my temporary role as footman, assuming that I opened the door myself because I happened to be passing in the hall. Thereafter, we walked off together, both delightedly aware of the contrast between the smallest artist in London moving in the shadow of the tallest. (As well as the one with the biggest nose.)

We – playwright and painter – talked in the drawing room, the subject of Topsy Turvy Day being well received by Fielding, who had recently married his maid. We talked delightedly and lubriciously about sex with servants until the appearance of the footman, George Wells, reminded me that I had forgotten about Topsy Turvy Day.

I immediately leaped up, seized Wells, forced the alarmed footman into the armchair I had just vacated and commanded him to continue his discussion about sex with servants with the large-nosed playwright. I myself, meanwhile, fetched two bottles of North Country Pale Ale, with which I hoped to refresh the footman and the playwright.

On returning with the drinks, I realised that the demands of Topsy Turvy Day required me to depart, beerless, after the 'master' had been served, so missing all Fielding's best stories about tupping Mary Daniel, the housemaid now the present Mrs Fielding.

A wave of irritation spread through me. I felt it rising quickly to my familiar hot anger. George Wells spotted it immediately; all the servants could read my face far better than I could read theirs, avid student of physiognomy though I was. The footman leaped up with a quick-thinking 'I'm away to the studio to paint a portrait.'

To roars of laughter from Fielding, the servant fled the drawing room, allowing me to resume my conversation over beer, which naturally tasted all the sweeter for being thwarted in the drinking of it for a few seconds.

Topsy Turvy Day reached its apotheosis at the main meal of the day, in the late afternoon. As we had planned and discussed, Jane and I served all the servants a splendid repast, as the six of them sat at the dining room table.

As all the food was, as ever, set out in side dishes on the long dresser in the dining room, strictly speaking, no service was required at all, but this made the master and mistress's solicitous enquiries as to exactly what the servants required all the more poignant.

Fanny, not averse to tucking in on a huge scale, nevertheless required Jane to eat with her.

'This is all well and good madam, I mean Jane, but I shan't enjoy a mouthful if you're not eating.'

Jane saw the sense in this and ate from the chafing dishes with a knife and spoon, while standing up. Previously starving in the sight of plenty, I gratefully did the same, helping myself to wine and beer, too.

As eating, or indeed any endeavour in company, was impossible for me without singing, I led the assembled company in a rendition of *The Ode on Saint Cecilia's Day*.

Chapter 10

At this point, Sarah Young started to cry, and the faithful Fanny, digging her in the ribs in protest, was not far from tears herself.

Mrs Parsons began a strange hissing at Henry Tompion, while raising both hands as if enjoining him to take off from his seat in flight. The good butler flushed red from emotion and beef. And then the youngest of all the company, the boy Charles Mahon, rose a little unsteadily.

'Mr Hogarth, sir. Mrs Hogarth, madam. Mr Tompion has a few words he would like to say to you both.'

The young footman resumed his seat. Henry Tompion rose ponderously, his short upper lip, as ever, failing to cover his top teeth.

'Master, madam. On behalf ... The servants have asked me to say that we never ... There is no better master and madam in all London. In all England. We wish you every joy. Sir. Madam. And we wish you to sit and join us at this meal.'

As Henry Tompion sat heavily, the round-faced, white-foreheaded Mrs Parsons led a round of clapping. I began to cry. I remembered Richard, my father. I remembered the hungry dinners of my youth in Spitalfields. I wanted to feed not only our servants but all the many brave and beautiful folk who deserved it.

Fanny stood, tenderly embraced Jane and kissed her on the cheek. She led her mistress to a place next to her and sat her down like a child. Half-protesting, I was placed at the head of the table.

'Thank you,' I said, still crying.

'Three cheers for Mr and Mrs Hogarth,' called out Charles Mahon. 'Hip, hip ...'

'Hooray!'

'Hip, hip!'

'Hooray!'

'Hip, hip!'

'Hooray!'

A few days after Topsy Turvy Day, I painted the servants. I knew I would never sell it, there would be no buyers and in any case I did not wish any. So, free from the constraints of trade, I could do what I liked.

The faces of six servants, hardly even a Dutch-style tondo, really just the heads, but in those heads six lives and all they contained, forever. In the middle, as befitted his age and status, good Henry Tompion. Kindly, the man was. A little *distrait*. Hair to his shoulders. Forehead wide. That short upper lip failing to cover his teeth forever.

Flanking and ahead of him, on his right, the faithful Fanny, who would have quietly and uncomplainingly laid down her life for my Jane, because that was how things were. She would have counted herself fortunate in the opportunity. Fanny was shown in her white bonnet. Serious. Ready for the next task.

Also in her white bonnet, on the other side of Henry Tompion, we saw Sarah Young, rendered just a little prettier than she was. Wide lustrous eyes. She still loved me, I was her only love. And I loved her, too, in my way. At least, I was greatly fond of her.

Behind Fanny, the cook, Mrs Parsons. Of all of them, she was the one whose gaze might boldly look out to meet the viewer's. But it didn't. I decided against it. None of them met the viewer's gaze, even though Fanny and Sarah were facing squarely forwards. It indicated humility. It showed a life of service, a life for others, willingly given because they met kindness in return.

The two figures at the back were young Charles Mahon, at the top of the painting, and the oldest of them, the footman George Wells. The boy had learned wariness on a still unformed face. His hair was cut short at the front but reached down over his ears at the sides and to his collar at the back, giving him a hint of freedom in his aspect. The pursed lips hinted at a sensuality to come.

And over it all, to the right, the biggest head, old George Wells, bleached bland by life, worn like a poor man's sole calico shirt, but still a decent man: still quietly holding to standards part given by his Presbyterian principles, part learned, part coming from wherever good comes from, which no man knows but all give thanks for.

Ironically, the only touch of dash, in the subdued yellows and browns of the servants' garb, was a quick froth of impasto white at old George's throat, at the knot of his scarf. And do you know why that was there? Because the composition needed it. Not everything has a reason. Some things just are, because the picture requires it.

11

WE DECIDED to buy a villa in the country. The summer of 1749 was an unremitting blaze of heat, burning every blade of grass brown, shrivelling all but the hardiest of trees. I am a quintessential Englishman and that means I detest excess in the weather, heat as much as cold.

Yet another reason for this partial escape from the London which had cosseted, coddled and shaped me all my life, was the beginning of a decline in my health, most especially the running sore on my leg, which now refused to stop bleeding, let alone heal, and was oblivious to mercury, leeches and all other medication to close it up.

Chiswick it was then, a villa in Chiswick, in addition to, not instead of, the house at Leicester Fields. The last house in the village, rented for £10 the year. It lay just a few miles upriver from London by wherry, Chiswick did: a toehold in the countryside, yet not far from the malting houses.

Our Chiswick place was surrounded by a high brick wall. Entry was across a small triangular garden with a mulberry tree at its centre and an orchard behind it, then into a portico with two great lead urns, and in through a doorway much less grand than the one at Leicester Fields. And two storeys only, this little brick-built place, not four as at Leicester Fields. In, up a narrow curving staircase, left to the dining room for the guests, right to Mrs Parsons' domain, the kitchen, scullery and pantry. Then the bedrooms and a delightful small, wood-panelled parlour with inset cupboards and views across the fields.

Sarah Young and Fanny shared one tiny part of the roof space, Mrs Parsons another, and Henry Tompion, George Wells and Charles Mahon a third. In other words, they had much less space than they had in London, on the rare occasions that they all attended at Chiswick together. But most of the time, naturally, either the butler, Henry Tompion, or the first footman, George Wells, held the fort at Leicester Fields, while Sarah Young's increasingly poor health limited her to just two visits to Chiswick.

We had been in Chiswick a year when, one day when I was painting and Jane supervising preparations for luncheon, the house shook, the fields shook, the earth shook: objects and ornaments fell, my easel tilted and tumbled, closely followed by an increasingly portly, stiff and ailing painter. (I refer here to myself!)

An earthquake it was, such a strange, exotic thing to be visited along the Thames. But we survived the shake and the tumble. Our new summer cottage survived. And our world with it.

12

IT WAS MY POLICY to visit the eight masonic lodges dotted around London from time to time, to maintain contacts in high places.

It was at one of these lodges, the Piccadilly, near St James's church by Garlick Hill, that I again encountered Captain Coram. It had been some four years since our last meeting, at the home of the Punch-like figure of James Oglethorpe.

I did not expect Thomas Coram to remember our subsequent rather strange trip to St Giles, finding throughout my life that my memory of encounters was always greater than those who had experienced the encounters with me. But I had met my match with the diminutive sea captain, who remembered not only the cost of the hansom fare but also the tip he had coughed up, on that occasion.

'Three pennies in coin of the realm for the *legem pone*!' boomed the sea captain, as we sat side by side at a masonic Grand Festival.

I winced as I registered this need to display knowledge, whether of the Latin tongue, of literature or of philosophy, so common in those unschooled and to which I was by no means a stranger myself. Not for the first or last time, I saw myself mirrored in the compact form of the choleric pink sea captain.

'But worth every penny for a most enjoyable meeting with yourself, sir!' the little captain boomed on, still reminiscing about our trip to St Giles, pink turning to red over most of his face, both from bonhomie and wine.

I sensed a new joy in Coram, and a new bounding confidence coming from it. I was happy enough to prompt the news which would surely soon burst the bulging breast of the sea captain if it was not released.

'And how is it with you, sir ...?'

Coram's great news, as I hoped, was the fruition of his plans and dreams. After a full score of years and more, as Coram put it, our good German ruler, George II, had put his signature to the charter for a Foundling Hospital during one of his visits to this island when there was nothing pressing to detain him in Hanover.

And as the roar of masonic celebration continued unabated around us, presided over by the Grand Master no less, Robert, Lord Raymond, Coram roared his delight into my ear as both of us continued to drink, eat and talk.

'Patience and the mulberry leaf becomes a silk gown,' bellowed the sea captain. Adding for good measure, '"Beware the fury of a patient man," as our good poet, the estimable John Dryden once wrote.'

Coram's narrow lips, the top one especially thin, were stretched in a permanent smile at his success. He spoke through this smile; he drank and ate through it. Only a churl would have begrudged him his smile for so good a cause after so long a time. And my delight at his success was fuelled by a total belief in his cause, a belief in the rescue of those poor children who were born in the depths, as I was.

I clapped the sea captain on the back, out of appreciation of his virtue and tenacity, and in fellow feeling at the club of small battling men, who had taught themselves what they needed to know and wanted the world to sit up and thank them.

Many years later, as my life draws to a close, I asked myself, as I embarked on my portrait of Thomas Coram, if I knew then that it was to be my masterpiece? The answer, I believe, was yes. I knew it before I started. I knew it would be the best work I would ever do. Yes, I did.

I took on something of Jane, her certainty, as the portrait of Coram proceeded. After so many years of matrimony I had in any case become much of her, willingly so, and she some, though less, of me. But in this case the process was helped on its way by Jane's fondness for Coram, a man so much like her husband, and by her passionate belief in what Coram was doing.

The pattern of the daily sittings at the studio in Leicester Fields was this: especially during the preliminaries, I let Thomas Coram talk until he relaxed into himself, offering the real man, not the stiff being he imagined was required for a portrait.

So while I stretched the canvas, covered it in size to stop the oil seeping into it, then primed it in grey – something I always insisted on doing myself, by the way, I never bought ready-primed canvas – Coram would be chattering away about how he first met Eunice Waite when she chose him for her dance partner at a gathering in Boston.

Another layer of size, another layer of ground, fast right to left with stiff-elbowed, whole-arm strokes. And all the while Coram shifted in the throne-like chair I had seated him in, his little legs not quite reaching the floor, and talked on and on.

Then I arranged the colours on my palette, as my belly tensed, much as it had done when I was in my twenties. I had a system for the arrangement of colours. Of course I had a system!

It was of my own devising, but based on Rubens' three-colour theory (the primacy of the primaries, red, yellow and blue). The tints would be bright, separate and distinct, not blended together, so there would be blocks of colour, even though this was far from fashionable.

Coram, meanwhile, would be expounding on how the charter, when he finally had it, did not overcome certain weaknesses in the Poor Law, so there was yet more work to be done.

And while I lovingly prepared my brushes – the stiff ones of hog's hair, the delicate ones of sable and squirrel – and made sure my maulstick, with its leather knob, was clean of splashes of paint, Coram would be explaining that the governors of the Foundling Hospital could now purchase land not exceeding £4,000.

And by the way would I like to become a governor? I said yes immediately because it would please Jane, but also because of my passion for his work.

So by the time I had prepared the old-fashioned linseed and the walnut and poppy oil, the sea captain was showing all the layers of self that such a man had accrued, by turns hard and soft, by turns warm and shrewd.

And by the time I stood before a canvas that was twice the size of the one I had used to paint my wife and my mother, ready with the restricted palette recommended by Rubens, the sitter, too, was ready: his soul as happily naked as a baby to my sight.

Then I began. I began slowly, as van Dyck had done, not fast like the moderns, like Kneller and Highmore. First, put in blocks of dead colours, working in patches directly onto the canvas, hardly glancing at the most rudimentary of cartoon preparatory sketches, which did little more than establish proportions.

Beneath the certainty in my mind there was controlled excitement now. I was in touch with and working from the deepest and best part of myself. I was aware of that in the same way you are aware that your kitchen cold store contains cheese. There is no need to keep opening the door to check.

And while putting in this background, before approaching the summit of the all-important soul, as outlined in the face, I not only allowed Thomas Coram to continue talking, I encouraged it, I prompted it.

'What will happen to the foundling children …?' I was speaking absently, mixing flesh pinks, sweetening them while still wet. 'What will happen to them after? Have you thought of that?'

'*Thought* of it!'

'Mmm.'

'What do you mean, sir? *Thought* of it. I've *thought* of little else.'

'And?'

'The boys will go to the navy, sir. A life at sea, such as I led myself. "All the rivers run into the sea, yet the sea is not full."'

'And the girls?'

'Why, into service, sir. We will make housemaids of them. Cooks. They will lead useful lives.'

I gave a small smile. You will lift them to useful lives, I thought to myself, and I will lift you to a king. As I painted, I was aware of the effect my creation would have when it was finished, but I did not paint to achieve that effect. I knew better than that. For to have done so would have ruined the painting. I painted the life of Thomas Coram and let Coram, not the painting, challenge the world and all that had gone before.

So, the noble seated pose, tubby stomach bursting out of his waistcoat and red coat opened wide. The royal charter prominent, but the globe carelessly at his feet and one tiny, buckled foot almost kicking the black hat that represented his Hatter's Company associations.

And the crowning glory, in every sense, the hair; Coram's pure white hair tumbled down to his shoulders, reaching the gold-facing on the red sea coat, like a purification of a despot's wig. His smile, lips slightly apart, for all its goodwill dared the viewer to trifle with him or to see him as anything less than regal.

I, Hogarth, Spitalfields boy, had taken another parvenu upstart, of similar diminutive stature, sat him on his throne and fashioned a king from the stuff of a citizen. And in doing so I had made a king of myself.

Resolved to do everything I could to help Coram, I had written to Charles Paulet, 3rd Duke of Bolton, present lover of Lavinia Fenton. With spelling and grammar improved by Jane, I requested he become a governor of the Foundling Hospital.

The reply, when it came, was from Lavinia. In characteristically forthright tones, Lavinia had demanded my appearance at the Boltons' London home to paint her portrait again. Charles becoming a governor of the Foundling Hospital, so said Lavinia, could be discussed then.

Charles Paulet had a mansion in St James's Square, on the Pall Mall side, facing the Earl of St Albans' place. I was much less easily impressed by this address in late middle-age than the callow youth Hogarth would have been, but I was reluctantly won over by the scale of the Bolton pile, even though it was (as I well knew) merely hired on a short winter lease. The place looked like a long, thin castle, abutted on either side by terraced housing.

Hanging from the square-faced towers was the Bolton escutcheon, in three or four places. As my hansom departed, I clutched my artist's materials in the wind, looking up at one of the Bolton crests with the boyhood eye trained by Stout Gamble. Three swords pointing down, that was none too difficult to execute. But the crest, a falcon with its wings displayed, would have been the very devil.

Shaking my head in rueful sympathy at those charged with the execution of the Bolton arms, I rang the bell, to be admitted by a footman in silk livery of a bilious shade of yellow. This flunky carried my artist's burdens for me. I was led to a parlour with flashy mouldings bumping out the ceiling like a child's cheek sucking a bonbon.

An over-ornate, no doubt French, armchair was indicated to me by the flunky, into which I gratefully sank like a lumbering galleon holed beneath the waterline, while my easel and so forth was balanced against the wall. The sitting relieved the lesion on my leg somewhat, and to a lesser extent the pain in my right big toe, although if anything it made the pain in my lower back even worse: a pain shared, for what it was worth, with nearly every artist in the St Martin's Academy.

And there I waited. I know I am an impatient man, but the wait seemed to me an eternity. I glanced up at the paintings; there was one of a Bolton ancestor which I judged even worse than my own recent hack commission of a finger-pointing Daniel Lock, undertaken solely because he was a governor of the Foundling Hospital. There was a Gaspard Poussin (Nicolas's brother-in-law), and there was a landscape which appeared to be a Lorraine copy.

I thankfully shut my eyes. I occupied myself by imagining a young Lavinia naked, a sight I had never seen in fact and flesh. Finally, the real Lavinia Fenton appeared, still not the Duchess of Bolton *de jure*, as the duke's wife, mad Lady Anne Vaughan, still lived and lived well, though not here.

The *de facto* duchess rolled towards me like a siege tower of old being towed into place. A long, platform-like arm was extended. I struggled from the blandishments of the French armchair, wincing as the lesion in my leg protested with a sharp pain. I pictured Lavinia this time as a child at Fenton's Coffee House, then as the portrait I had painted of her in her hovel near the Cowpats soap factory. Could I even equal the freshness of that work now?

'Master Hogarth! You may kiss my hand.'

I made to do so before a squawk of glee just preceded a remarkably hard punch on my arm (fortunately the left, not my painting arm).

'Ouch!'

'I'll give you "ouch" my darlin'! Oh, Billy Boy, that was priceless. Ready to kiss my 'and, you was. Wish I'd offered you me arse now. You'd sure as 'ell 'ave kissed that.'

'Time was, Lavinia …'

'Oy! No lip from you, now, or I'll hhhave the fffooootman throooow you owwwt.' This last was in Lavinia's parody of a fop accent, before breaking into cackles of laughter.

'Lavinia! You haven't changed. Not a jot. Not an iota.'

'Yeah! Apart from being twice the bleedin' size and me looks half gone.' I naturally began the obligatory denial, but Lavinia cut it short. 'Yeah, yeah! Sing a new song, Billy. I got eyes. I also got a present for you.' A sharp look must have come over my face, as Lavinia broke out laughing again. 'Oh, you don't change, Billy Boy. Both eyes on the main chance, that's our Will-ey-um.'

I shrugged modestly. 'Er … what …?'

'I only got you a commission!'

I groaned inwardly. Martin Folkes, also a governor of the Founding Hospital, wanted a portrait. There was this present painting of Lavinia. There were portraits of Lord Viscount Boyne, Pine the engraver, John Palmer of Ecton. Time was when I was scratching and begging for work … Now, all I wanted to do was complete the real work, my apotheosis, the portrait of Thomas Coram. The rest of it could go hang.

'A commission!' I said, attempting to convey delight. 'Good-O. Who?'

'Garrick. The great actor. You know him, don't you?'

'Yup. And his wife.'

''Ee wants doing as Richard II.'

'Would that be Richard III?'

'No, 'ee thought you'd charge more for that.' Lavinia cackled at her own joke. 'It might be. You contact him and find out which bleedin' Richard he wants. Personally, I couldn't give a tinker's fart.'

'Thank you.'

'I've got you £200 to do it.'

'Whaaat!'

She laughed. 'Don't say I ain't good to you, Billy Boy.'

Tears came to my eyes. Nobody got £200 for a portrait. Not Reynolds, not Ramsay, not van Loo. Nobody. It would be a record in England.

'Thank you, Lavinia.'

'Oh, you're very welcome.'

I laughed. 'You've always been a duchess to me.'

'Oh, shut up! You'll have me blubbin' in a minute!'

'So … how's life as the Duchess of Bolton? In a manner of speaking, of course.'

As I spoke, I feared the worst. The duke's passion was gambling of all sorts, from hazard, faro and basset to huge bets on bear and cock fights and (a favourite, this) women fighting in their shifts. Alongside the gambling, whoring with large numbers of women in every room of the house and drinking vast amounts of brandy accounted for the rest of his time.

As if she could read my mind, Lavinia answered 'Charlie ain't the problem. What to do all bleedin' day is the problem. Billy, I am bored, bored, bored. Sometimes the days go so slowly I could shoot meself, just for something to do.'

This interested me, as I had never experienced a moment's boredom in my life, unless the engraving of heraldic beasts for Stout Gamble counted as boredom, but really it was more tedium, as I was doing something: working, in fact, quite hard.

'Well, I'll try to entertain you, shall I? As I paint you? And then …'

'Yeah, yeah, Billy Boy. I'll get my Charlie to be a governor of your Foundling Hospital, never fear. A deal's a deal. I ain't changed that much. But first …' Lavinia rang for a footman. 'Let's 'ave a little drink, shall we? And I don't mean coffee. They're calling it Dutch courage these days, you 'eard that one?'

I laughed. 'No!'

At that moment, Charles Paulet put his head round the door. His dissolute, jowly face with its hooded eyes was the picture of misery. I recognised the syphilis on him instantly, mournfully registering as I did so that my own was getting worse again. The duke glanced at Lavinia and me, and without a word disappeared again. Lavinia shrugged heavily at me, for a second looking almost as miserable as her 'husband'.

13

ABLUSTERY WEDNESDAY evening towards the end of March, with a spiteful wind whipping across Lamb's Conduit Field, saw the opening of the Foundling Hospital, after more than twenty years' work by Thomas Coram. The hospital stood in Lamb's Field, by the Bloomsbury and St George the Martyr burial grounds.

A makeshift orchestra shivered their way through an anthem especially composed for the hospital by George Frideric Handel, *Blessed Are They That Consider The Poor*. Handel himself was not present, but a selection of the blessed, a knot of governors, stood ready to welcome the first children.

Prominent among the governors was the designer of the hospital, Theodore Jacobsen; the Duke of Richmond; Martin Folkes, a vice-president; Daniel Lock, who had the decency to look very much like my hack portrait of him; and Dr Nesbitt, who was to inspect the babies when they arrived.

There was also the distinguished painter William Hogarth and his wife Jane. For by now I was not only a governor, not only a supporter who had found other governors, like the Duke of Bolton, but I had also designed uniforms for the older children, at no charge, designed the hospital's letterhead, ditto, and donated the masterpiece of my life, the portrait of Coram, *gratis* to the hospital.

I had contacted my old patron, the now elderly Anthony (Moses) da Costa, who had given generously. As for our own contribution, in our passion for Coram's life's work, Jane and I had outdone each other in an unintentionally comic auction, deciding how much to give. We had finally bid each other up the maximum Jane knew we could realise in cash, £120.

We looked at each other now, proud, tense, perhaps a little happier with each other, straining for a glimpse of the first children, but also concerned. I said it out loud to Jane.

'Where is he?' I said, still expecting her to know, expecting her to know everything.

Because the one man absent from the knot of governors, medical men and porters outside the imposing hospital gates was the place's only begetter,

Thomas Coram. But before she could give the tense, edgy answer forming at her lips, we both saw a one-horse phaeton trotting out of Great Ormond Street into Red Lyon Street, then coming straight towards us at a brisk trot.

Coram alighted with his sailor's grace and balance, in the opulent red sailor's coat I had painted, but looking white in the face and tense. As the phaeton turned and trotted off, he made straight for Jane and me, ignoring the influential Richmond, who had his mouth open to greet him, ignoring Lord Abercorn, Daniel Lock, Martin Folkes and all the other luminaries. Pleased though I was to see him, I feared for the sea captain's rough and ready ways among the other governors, now phalanxed round him.

'Thomas!' I shouted over to him, 'Your moment, my friend. Your triumph after ...' I ground to a halt at the tense lines in my friend's face, betokening anything but triumph.

'Yes,' said Coram, absently. '"Ask and it will be given to you; seek and you will find; knock and the door will be opened to you."' The over-rehearsed quotation from Luke was murmured into his chest. His eyes were down on his muddy boots and his soul appeared to be down there with them.

'Eunice ...?' Jane asked.

By now Jane had met Coram's wife, Eunice, several times. They had become as close as their husbands were. Funnily enough, like their husbands, they were a match physically, too, sharing the same full, heavy-breasted build. But unlike the robust Jane, Eunice's health was poor. At their last meeting she had been coughing, struggling to breathe towards the end of the evening.

Coram shook his head. 'In bed. She ...'

I kept an arm round my friend's shoulders. 'Nothing to be done now, Thomas,' I said, softly. 'Look, here come the first of our children.'

I had spoken, in truth, only to distract Thomas, who, to this practiced friend's eye, looked in a very bad way indeed. But just as I spoke I saw a trickle then a stream of mothers with babies, with toddlers, with older boys and girls making their way along a little pathway called Powis Wells, then cutting across Lamb's Conduit Field, for all the world as if the wide beaten way of Red Lyon Street, leading straight to the hospital gates, were not for the likes of them.

As they approached, the mothers mainly had their heads down. I thought that was from years of being called 'harlot' for having a child with no visible father. With tears in my eyes, I thought of the chance system which had brought them to the hospital, a system bizarrely based on that used for membership to an elite gentlemen's club, White's Club in Chesterfield Street.

The system consisted of the drawing of balls from a bag: draw a white ball and the child was in, a black ball out, while a red ball meant wait until a place became free. Even the white ball, entry, did not guarantee the child life, as poverty and disease were doing their work, even as the mothers took their children towards the hospital, but a black ball meant death, with utter finality.

More mothers appeared, like the flight from Egypt, bustling towards their salvation in their white bonnets, with their dresses mainly shabby, either carrying their children or holding them by the hand. They were coming from all directions now. I glanced at Coram – a little tightness at jaw and lips, a little narrowing at the eyes, but fundamentally composed.

Jane was standing proud and alert, but with tears in her eyes as she searched the faces of the arriving children, especially the older ones. I knew she was looking for the child she would never have, now, and my heart went out to her.

After what seemed hours of chaos, with mothers, children, doctors, nurses, porters and governors mingling and milling, the children designated as the first two for admittance were located. These were baptised on the spot as Thomas and Eunice.

The weeping mothers made sure their former children had their tokens by which they could be recognised again, one day, perhaps, if a mother were able to return and claim her child. The mother of the male child now designated Thomas had a brass uniform button of a Coldstream Guardsman tied round his neck on a bead necklace, as his token. The girl designated Eunice had a silver heart engraved with '*You have my heart, tho we must part.*'

The porter sent the mothers on their way with brusque, though not unkind, insistence. The doctor ushered the new Thomas and Eunice through the gates to the first experience of their new lives, which would be a medical inspection.

And finally, after what seemed hours, the dull, moist look in Jane's eyes became a gleam.

They located the first of the Billys and Jennys. It was difficult to give them any sort of age; undernourishment had made them small. The new Billy's mother was old for such a young child, and drab. The token she had given her child was half a silver shilling from the time of Edward VI.

'Be good,' said the mother, taking new Billy by the shoulder.

'He shall come to play in our garden in Chiswick,' Jane said to her.

'You hear that?' said the mother, shaking the boy slightly. 'You hear that?'

Then the mother turned and left before the porter could shoo her away.

The new Jenny looked a couple of years older than Billy. She was blonde, like her mother, who was surely a bawd, and a handsome one. Her token was a child's silk purse embroidered with the letters 'MD'. Unlike most of them, the token was not affixed to the child in any way, she was clutching it.

The bawd mother shot me a shrewdly practiced look I knew well enough, then glanced at the girl. I shook my head, angry, though there were tears in my eyes as there were in Jane's.

'Madam,' I said, heavily. 'We have a mulberry tree in our garden, where your daughter shall play. We ...'

'... We shall cherish her,' Jane said, interrupting me.

The bawd mother smiled, not above a coquettish glance at me, to take my look away from Jane. Then she turned on her heel and strode away, proudly, this one, straight down the highway of Red Lyon Street.

I made for Daniel Lock, ignoring everyone else and everything else. Again and again, I rehearsed wild thoughts in my mind; yes, in theory Jane was past childbearing age, but not so very far surely and women older than her had given birth, in the past. It had been attested. It *could* happen ...

Daniel Lock was a simple man, for all his intelligence, and more than a touch pompous. He was supposed to be an architect, though nobody seemed able to name a building he had designed or constructed. He saw me, no doubt looking flustered, barging my way through the melee towards him and guessed what I wanted. There had, after all, been so many questions about the new hospital he was starting.

'Master Lock, good sir ...'

'Master Hogarth!'

'Your new hospital ...'

'The Lock Hospital. Indeed. It's for the poor, sir.'

'Yes. Very praiseworthy, no doubt. But the poor suffering from ...'

'Venereal afflictions, sir. Those somewhat bluntly called the French Pox.'

'Master Lock ... Daniel. Please let me attend your hospital. Treat me, sir. Help me. You are my last hope.'

14

THE FIRST foundling Jennys and Billys were brought to the country home in Chiswick to play and to stay. Mrs Parsons delighted in over-feeding them, young Charles Mahon, the second footman, was messianic about introducing them to beer and getting them drunk, and I devised sunshine games for them in Chiswick's beautiful gardens.

Many of the games I conjured up were improving. I would call out a number and the children had to run and touch that number of mulberry trees, so while they scampered in joy they unconsciously learned their numbers. I sprawled in an armchair brought outside for me, easing my aches, and thought of my father, and how he would have clapped hands delightedly at the game, so cleverly devised.

But to my dismay, the visits of the children did not bring the joy to Jane that I had hoped for. However long they came for, however long they stayed for, she wanted them there for longer, especially a Billy and a Jenny she was clearly marking as her favourites.

She took to writing letters to all governors of the Foundling Hospital, at first collectively, then, when this brought only a polite response devoid of meaning, individually. Even I, her husband, received these letters, as a governor. They were left for me, propped up against a teapot or, on a couple of occasions, on my pillow. The tone of these letters was becoming wilder with time. She wanted to keep the children.

Jane and I quarrelled more frequently than at any other time in our marriage. I acknowledged to myself that this was at least in part my fault.

My humour was not improved by the failure of my treatment at the Lock Hospital. The various purges, sweatings, applications of leeches, applications of mercury and more mercury, the swigging down of Dr Prossily's Water, it had all achieved nothing in the alleviation of my sores, my pain and my pox. And Jane was now no longer able to deny to herself what ailed me, so she refused all physical contact with me, even touching, let alone kissing.

Meanwhile, my good friend Thomas Coram was also plagued with woes. His beloved wife, Eunice, sickened unto death and it broke the old man's heart. Then the other governors of the Foundling Hospital, aristocrats to a man except for myself and Coram, conspired to push the bluff old sea captain out, as I had always feared they would.

Thomas Coram's connection to his life's work was severed. The sea captain's savings were dwindling fast. He was living in a couple of rooms in Spur Street, round the corner from our place in Leicester Fields. I visited him often, but I was the only Foundling Hospital governor who did. I used to take bottles of beer round; Coram beat me at chess while we drank them and talked. I watched the old man's sea captain's coat, which I had painted in its prime, get shabbier and shabbier.

Jane visited, too, bringing a variety of foods but usually pies of different sorts, overcoming the proud old man's initial reluctance to accept such help. She also overcame his stubborn refusal to talk about Eunice. In the end, he would accept his food, pack his pipe and relive his happy years with the only human being he had ever felt at one with.

He talked about Eunice with Jane, never with me. And Jane and I never visited him together, not once. Any more than we did anything else together, anymore.

When Coram died, I read the sermon at the chapel in the Foundling Hospital. In death, all the governors accorded him their company, as they had not done in life. Perhaps they knew how widely the occasion would be reported in the newspapers: a full account in the *London Evening Post*, a page in *Read's Weekly Journal*, a mention at least in all the others.

The coffin was met at the gate of the Foundling Hospital, at the top of Red Lyon Street, by the governors and the children. The little ones walked two and two before the coffin, which was immediately preceded by a governor carrying the charter on a crimson velvet cushion. As the pall was carried by the governors, a burial service was sung, accompanied by Dr Boyce on the organ.

And then I spoke: 'Captain Thomas Coram, whose name will never want a monument as long as this hospital shall subsist, was a man eminent in that most eminent virtue, the love of mankind ...'

At the end of it I cried. I cried from the pit of my soul. Jane cried too, for the first time in a long time. And for the first time in a long time, she fell into my arms and allowed me to cradle her there.

15

AT THE NEXT MEETING of the governors of the Foundling Hospital, I saw the Duke of Bolton again. I thought him even sadder than before, when I had seen him with Lavinia. I thought then that no human being could encompass so much misery, and indeed he could not, being shortly before the taking of his own life.

At that same meeting I saw a most strange creature, a fellow governor. He was one of the ugliest human beings I ever beheld, yet exerted a terrible and very sexual fascination.

As he looked at me across the huge meeting table in the court room of the Foundling Hospital, pale reptilian eyes boring into me, a knowing smile making their power even stronger, I felt a terrible need to surrender to this man.

He was, I knew even then, a form of the devil. He was my nemesis, I felt that too, even then. The man reached out, stretched out a hand to me. Almost swooning with helplessness, I took it. I thought it would be clammy but it was dry as parchment.

The man appeared to know the turmoil he was causing in me, to know and to feel no surprise by it. He said we had met before, many years ago. He said his name was John Wilkes.

Part IV

Finis
1757–64

1

I AM AN OLD MAN and I shall paint no more. My work is done, my race is run. My life now is my beloved Jane, my wife. I have always been a faithful husband, never straying, and I bless the decision to follow that path. I wish now only to make her days as light and delightful as possible, together with those Jennys and Billys sent to us by the Foundling Hospital, who we have with us in Chiswick for all too short a time.

To that end I was instrumental, using my influence as a governor, in having Jane appointed an inspector for the hospital. She supervises not only the main hospital at Red Lyon Street, but the more distant hospitals we have now in Ackworth, which has one hundred and thirteen children, and Aylesbury, which has as yet just forty.

This has much changed Jane's life for the better, for she took the death of her mother, the good Lady Judith, hard. The sketches I made of her then, in her bereavement, were a worthy crowning of a life in phiz-mongering, being among the best work I have done.

I must break off these reminiscences to record a development; I had a note from a young man called Richard Grosvenor. *Sir* Richard Grosvenor, I should say, of the landowning family, who own half of London as well as land in the north: Cheshire, I believe.

Sir Richard Grosvenor wanted to look round my showroom. This, no doubt, being largely occasioned by my accession as Serjeant Painter to George II, following the sad passing away of my good and honourable friend and brother-in-law, John Thornhill, who held the post before me.

So I showed Sir Richard Grosvenor my wares, as displayed in the showroom adjacent to my studio. I had left the showroom untouched, I may add, even though I had foresworn painting. I thought of it rather as a collection of mementos, a museum, even. I was showing him round my past life, or so I believed.

And certainly young Sir Richard – the fresh faced youth surely did not have thirty even on the horizon – was gratifying in his appreciation of my work.

'Master Hogarth,' said Sir Richard. 'I would dearly love a painting from you for myself. Of any subject dear to you, naturally. But a comedy for preference. Your *forte*, I believe.'

I formed the words of refusal in my mind, the explanation of my retirement from painting and so forth. But these words remained unsaid.

'Sir Richard, I long ago conceived the idea of a work on the theme of Sigismunda, the daughter of Prince Tancred, mourning over the death of her lover, Guiscardo, who was murdered by her father. I'm sure you are familiar ...'

'Indeed! The Dryden poem.'

'Yes. Dryden had it from Boccacio, I believe. Guiscardo was a page, low-born, at Sigismunda's father's court. The lovers consummate their passion but the king secretly witnesses it and has Guiscardo murdered. He sends his daughter the page's heart in a golden goblet. Sigismunda mixes poison with her tears and Guiscardo's blood, drinks this from the goblet and dies.'

'Hardly the stuff of comedy then?' said Sir Richard, doubtfully.

'No, sir.'

Even as I spoke, I conceived Jane as the model for Sigismunda, or Ghismonda as she is called in the original tale, one my father read to me when I was a boy. It was that memory, and not, as people later said, the huge amount of £405 5s that another *Sigismunda*, by Furini (not Correggio, as people said), had fetched at a recent sale, that decided me on the subject.

Sir Richard's lined frown clearly expressed his doubts from the beginning, but he accepted quickly, no doubt in fear that I should withdraw the offer of a painting completely.

And so began my downfall, as a painter and as a man.

I still refuse to use ready-primed canvases, no matter how old-fashioned this may be considered, so I quickly primed what was to be my new *Sigismunda* canvas with all speed.

I walloped on the grey ground, the size, the second layer of ground with sweeping movements of my poor, aching arm, for all the world as if the wall of Greenwich Hospital was once again my canvas, as it had been when I learned painting at the feet of my long-dead friend and father-in-law, Sir James.

I was impatient, panting, the excitement overcoming the pain in my leg from the lesion, the pain in my gums, my back and all the rest of it.

I knew with great certainty, as soon as I seized my crayon, that this work, this

Sigismunda, was to be my crowning glory. It would be even greater than my immortal *Thomas Coram*, even more memorable, in the annals of art, than my two lost masterpieces of narrative painting, my progresses, *The Rake* and *The Harlot*. I would finally, finally, put even the likes of van Dyck and Albert Duerer in the shade, with this portrait!

I frantically crayoned in the pose that had come to me, direct on the canvas. I bothered less and less with preliminary sketches these days, let alone cartoons or the modelloes of my youth. No time, old man. No time.

A dark background, then: brown like that old warhorse Rembrandt. Sigismunda seated at a table in her shift, showing the tops of her breasts. Oh, yes! Master Hogarth may be old but he's not yet dead! Her right elbow was up on a casket, which would show even more of her breast, while four fingers were bent at the first digit, pressing against her cheek, with her little finger alone extended.

You know why? Because I can paint hands. Many artists cannot. It is hands, then to a lesser extent feet, then to a lesser extent horses, which sort the men, such as me, from the likes of the boy Ramsay and the Gainsborough upstart, who was my pupil for a while at that ridiculous academy. And do you know what sorts the windy charlatans, like Reynolds, from the true artists? Time. Oh, time will show the difference, you mark my words, though I may not live to see it myself.

Anyway, where was I? Old men digress, old men ramble. Oh, yes, in her other hand Sigismunda held the heart of her poor murdered lover, Guiscardo, cupped in a gold chalice. We saw her just before she added the poison to her tears, to drink it from around Guiscardo's heart.

After putting in the background colour, I brought Jane upstairs to pose for Sigismunda. I also had, pinned to the easel with sharp pins, the sketches I made of Jane when her mother died in 1757. I talked to Jane as I worked. She was enthusiastic about this commission. It was bringing us back together, close, as we used to be, and that was balm for my poor old battered heart.

This time I requested for Jane to pose in her shift.

'It's cold!' she said, in a tone which clearly showed her delight in being the object of my gaze so attired.

I adjusted her hand, I adjusted her bare shoulders, I stroked the tops of her breasts: the greatest pleasure known to man on this earth.

'Billy! Has this to do with the portrait, do you think? These caresses.'

'It makes your skin blush, my Jenny darling. It's quite essential.'

Then we fell to kissing and I lowered my breeches but neither of us was able to encompass the descent to the floor, me because of my leg and her for shortness of breath.

Jane seized her dress from the corner, to my sadness putting it on. But happily this was only to be temporary.

'I'll go and find Fanny,' she said. 'We can go to the bedroom, but I'll not have the footmen or Henry seeing us.'

Jane went off to find Fanny, leaving me to haul my breeches back up, a process which took even longer than the lowering. But when Jane came back there was a gleam in her eye.

'Fanny has sent George and Charles out on errands. Henry is busy.' She held out her hand. 'Come along then.'

With our various afflictions, it took us some time to reach the bedroom, which happily we still shared, unlike many couples of my acquaintance. Once there, though, although we shared many delights on the foothills, I was unable quite to conquer the summit. One reason for this was that I kept studying Jane's face to see how it might look if she were holding a goblet with her dead lover's heart in it.

I had sent to my friend, the bloodletter Caesar Hawkins, for a heart. He had provided one which I later found out was from a pig, but also the goblet to contain it. Heart and ornate golden goblet were a perfect match, the heart peeping redly out of the goblet.

Now that I had that and the casket, I could begin work on my evocation of Sigismunda's grief unto death, the expression that would put me out of reach even of van Dyck. I followed Dryden's poem here, not the original of Boccacio. In Dryden, Sigismunda's sorrow, though profound, is nobly borne.

To the pathognomonics – when the heart grieves, the corners of the mouth sink. Jane's lips, then, slightly apart, with the line of grief roughed with the end of the brush at the corner. The full lower lip was straight, pale red. The upper shorter, curved, a gasp cut off, a pout in the face of agony.

Above this, the nose was noble, evidencing suffering nobly borne. The brow, too, noble. And under it, a tear at the corners of viscous grey eyes. This was a *tour de force*, the conveying of this consistency. Nobody else could have done it, *nobody*. There was a fitness in this face because the proportions were perfect.

And the varying of the features from the norm conveyed a beauty. No two faces since the beginning of time have been alike: mine of Sigismunda would surpass them all.

After two hundred days' toiling at the painting, I was so pleased with my *Sigismunda*, so soaringly, floatingly ecstatic, that out of sheer fun, as a *jeu d'esprit* I put the sprite Hogarth in the painting.

On a leg of the ornate scagliola table, on which the casket and the chalice with Guiscardo's heart rested, I had painted a snub-nosed gargoyle who was me in my painting cap. I was just under the rim of the table, looking between Sigismunda's legs. By putting myself there I was telling the world that I was inviolate, impervious; I could do no wrong.

How long did that euphoric mood last? It ended more suddenly than it started, when that which I had dreaded most occurred to me in the dead of night. I began to see possible improvements. I began to see how I could have done it better. Yet again, this need to revise my work had returned to haunt me, as indeed I believe it does all great artists.

That gold cord on the curtain behind Sigismunda. It looked as though she was about to be hanged. It had to go. I frantically poured turpentine, soaked a rag and took it out, immediately restoring the curtain while the canvas was still wet from the turpentine. That, of course, made the colour weaker than it was in the rest of the curtain, so I had to thicken it up and blend it in.

Then, raining down on me like blows from some footpad's cudgel, I saw more and more faults and problems with the *Sigismunda* I had so recently regarded as perfection.

Fundamentally, her aspect was too calm. Yes, she clutched the heart of her dead lover to her bosom, pushing up her full breasts in the process. *Yes*, the expression I had caught so perfectly evoked anguish at the loss of her one true love. But what of her *bearing*? There was too much symmetry, too much order.

Do you know what had happened? I, who had spent my life inveighing against the dead hand of the past, against the mindless copying of what had gone before, had done exactly that, without knowing it. I had imitated the graceful poses of *past* Sigismundas. Perhaps that of van der Werff, perhaps that of Furini? It didn't matter.

The very shape of the table was wrong. van der Werff's was square; I had followed that. It should have been round. The message from Tancred, sent with the heart, hung over the table. So it was the message that leaped out at the viewer. But all that achieved was to take the viewer's gaze away from the heart, which is where the power of the picture lay. So I launched myself at the painting, frantically altering it to break its calm symmetry in as many ways as I could.

I started with Sigismunda's veil, which had to now hang down on one side of her face only, not both. Her hair had to be taken up, making the face less even. That meant redoing a lot of the skin I was so proud of.

I worked on like this for days, weeks. Jane no longer wished to come and sit for me because I had become so irascible, what with the repainting and the various pains from my stomach, this time, and my leg. I implored her for days, before she finally came. I even had the feeling the servants had grown wary of me, such was my wild state.

Once, I awoke bolt upright in the middle of the night, seized by the certainty that my last week's work had been too timid. I had lowered the hairline, angling it to the left to break the symmetry and portray Sigismunda's distress, *but I had not done it by enough!*

I needed to start again and lower the hairline by far more. Jane was sleeping deeply by my side, snoring slightly. Surely we kept candles in the bedroom? But where? I needed to make these alterations now, even by candlelight. I dared not wait until morning in case the picture I had in my head was vanquished by sleep and I could never get it back.

I struggled out of bed, feeling my way in the gloom. No candles. I woke Jane, shaking her as gently as I could by the shoulder.

'Jane! Jane, my dearest. I need candles.'

Jane moaned. 'There are none here, William. For fear of fire. Don't you remember?'

I snorted in the blackness. I had indeed, for a while at least, forgotten my fear of fire. Fire which had cost me my most famous paintings and my mother's life.

'Go to sleep, William,' Jane said. 'I fear you will end your days in Bedlam if you go on like this, just like your Tom Rakewell.'

I felt my way in the stygian darkness all the way up to the top of the house where the servants slept. I felt my way past the door where the women were and opened that to the garret shared by Henry Tompion and the two footmen. Young Charles Mahon stirred as I came in, shaking his head and blearily opening his eyes.

Chapter 1

'Mr Hogarth? Sir?' he whispered into the darkness.

He raised himself on one elbow, on his truckle bed in the corner.

'Charles!' I whispered. 'I need a candle. I need to work.'

'All right, Mr Hogarth.'

Charles rolled to his feet. Even on such an errand as this, in pitch dark in the middle of the night, I could not but admire and envy his young grace. There was a candle on a table by his bed. There was also a book. Young Charles had been reading, in the darkness.

'Will this candle do, sir?'

'I don't see why not.'

We left the bedroom, both of us in nightgowns, whereupon Charles got the candle lit using a couple of flints. He led the way to the studio, warning me of various pitfalls from tables and stairs on the way, for all the world as if this were not my own house.

When we finally reached the studio, I threw off the sheet of linen I kept over *Sigismunda*, suddenly feeling a wave of tiredness, accompanied by a pang of despair at the size of my task and the futility of it all. Charles put the candle down, leaving the room without a word. I hardly noticed him go.

By the light of a single flickering candle, I began to undo the work of weeks on Sigismunda's brow and hairline. Hours later, as dawn broke, I realised I had ruined it. It had been far better the way it was, before I had started.

Finally, I wished to desist from painting and repainting, not so much because I regarded my *Sigismunda* as complete, more because I was weary in body and soul at my labour of Sisyphus. With no forethought whatsoever, entirely on a whim, I sent word to Sir Richard Grosvenor that his commission was ready and he might have it.

As George Wells set off with the letter, I felt a great relief, only for this to be overtaken by a huge foreboding as soon as he was five minutes gone from the house.

For as long as I have been eminent, I have regarded the opinion of patrons with impatience. They are influential fools, no more, no less. Children with money. But in this case I was consumed with worry at young Sir Richard's reaction to my work. For the first time in my life I ceased to eat and drink robustly, pacing the studio for hours in fear of what his view of my *Sigismunda* might be.

By the time he was indeed standing before the painting, ready to give his verdict, I had convinced myself that my worries had been unnecessary, the mere terrors of an old man. A terrible jocularity overcame me as I drew the linen sheet away, exposing *Sigismunda*.

'There you are, young Sir Richard. There's your masterpiece. Never seen anything like it, eh?'

There was a moment's deep silence. Then another. The expression on his rather asinine face, as it waved on that pole of a neck, was neutral, serious.

'There's blood on her fingers,' he said finally.

'Well, of course. She has been handling the heart of her dead lover, Guiscardo.'

'That would have to go.'

'All right, I can take it off.'

'It's not like a Hogarth at all.'

'I don't repeat myself. I break new ground. I ...'

'You've done that all right.'

I put my hands on my hips and glared at him. 'Don't you like it? I have done all I can to it. If you think the sum of four hundred guineas too much for it, just say so. I have a commission from Mr Hoare the banker, also for four hundred guineas. If you wish I could offer him *Sigismunda*.'

Sir Richard shrugged, head wobbling on long neck. 'If he should take a fancy to the *Sigismunda*, I have no sort of objection to your letting him have it.'

And with that Sir Richard left. There was no commission from Hoare the banker. Sir Richard's rejection was the first time in my life that a man had commissioned a work from me and then not taken it. It confirmed in me more than ever my belief that my *Sigismunda* was a masterpiece, but ahead of its time, just as the *David* statue of Michelangelo had been.

The vultures lost no time in gathering.

Sir Joshua Reynolds, theorist of the copying faction, produced a satirical work mocking my *Sigismunda*. He painted the whore Kitty Fisher, through whom half of London had passed, as Cleopatra, but with her chalice a copy of mine: her brow, her bubbies, everything a reference to my work.

The subscription list for an engraving of *Sigismunda* by Basire had to be withdrawn, having failed to attract above forty subscribers. And that after

Ravenet refused to engrave it at all. My *Sigismunda* was being ridiculed in the newspapers.

I intended to retaliate. I intended to set sail, flying my *Sigismunda* like the proudest Union Jack flying from the mast of a ship of the line. I WOULD EXHIBIT. Do you hear me? I would EXHIBIT my *Sigismunda*, as soon as I had finished changing the shape of the table.

The Spring Gardens exhibition: that would be the place. The St Martin's Lane crowd were organising it. All my friends from the once happy time at Old Slaughter's – Lambert, Laguerre, Hudson, Gravelot, even Roubiliac, all those sometime friends from the golden days – were now absorbed in this bloody St Martin's Lane Academy. It's a wonder they found time to paint at all.

Having failed to strangle this academy at birth, I had contented myself for a while with trying to guide it from within. Guide it, that is, away from ranks and positions and professors and suchlike rubbish of the French, towards a more Greek style of academy, namely a confederacy of equals.

I also wanted a place where artists could draw and paint in spontaneity and harmony, in the tradition of Wren and Thornhill, away from foreign influences and above all away from the ideas of Reynolds and his crowd.

I was, naturally enough, losing heavily in all of these areas. The only good news I had in quite a while was that one of my artist opponents had been sentenced to death. One Theodore Gardelle, a Swiss. He slaughtered his landlady in a rather colourful way.

The cart taking Gardelle to his execution passed Leicester Fields (as I still insist on calling it, it isn't bloody SQUARE). I waved him goodbye from an upstairs window, regretting only that Reynolds wasn't in the cart with him.

But I digress, as old men do. The exhibition at Spring Gardens was intended to promote and sell our wares – the paintings of the St Martin's group. It was the first time something like this had been done, I believe. At any rate, the paintings I entered for exhibition were my surviving series of portraits, *An Election Entertainment* and my masterpiece, *Sigismunda*. It would be *Sigismunda*, naturally, which would make them all gasp.

Before *Sigismunda* was exhibited, Jane warned me against portraying her in her shift, with her bubbies pushed up like that.

'I don't know why you have given her so much flesh,' she said, sounding not at all like herself. 'It looks terrible.'

'All right, all right. I'll clothe her,' I said.

So at the last minute, working fast and with some impatience, I rapidly clothed my Sigismunda in the blue of the Madonna. I dashed in a froth of flouncy white sleeves, covering not only her bubbies but her elbows as well. It altered the entire tonal balance of the composition. For some reason it made her face look more petulant too, but I was past caring.

'There,' I said to Jane, or rather shouted, I admit it. 'I've done what you want. Come and look at it.'

But she didn't. She turned her back, then walked off in a huff. I suspected that I had embarrassed her, with my rendition of her (sometime) orbs. A day later, with her still refusing to look at the clothed *Sigismunda*, a quarrel arose between us which involved her throwing a tureen dating from the time of Queen Anne at my head. We did not speak for days, an increasingly frequent occurrence. At one point we communicated by notes carried by the maid, Fanny.

At any rate, when a crew of rude mechanicals turned up to haul *Sigismunda* away to be gawped at, at this exhibition, my broken-hearted heroine was chaste as a bloody nun. Not a pink and white trace of her bubbies to be seen. Irritated beyond measure by then, by the whole damned business, I yelled at the rude mechanicals when they hit *Sigismunda*'s frame against the walls.

To my horror and amazement, two of them yelled back, which would not have happened in my day, I can tell you. They dropped the picture on the floor and refused to touch it again until I apologised. One of them, a great drunken lout, made to put his foot through the painting, so I apologised with some haste.

Word of *Sigismunda*'s reception at the exhibition reached me almost immediately. I did not take it seriously, putting it down to the jealousy and spite of my rivals:

'A maudlin whore tearing off the trinkets that her keeper had given her, to fling at his head.' That was one of the kinder comments my dear friends, especially Hayman-adequate, fell over themselves to bring me.

They criticised me for the painting I had not painted, as well as criticising the one I had painted (a common fate of the artist). They enquired of me *in absentia* why Tancred was not in the painting. Also, why was Guiscardo absent, apart from his heart? I think this may have been the most idiotic criticism ever made in the entire history of art.

And as to what I *had* painted, my *Sigismunda*, it seemed, bore no resemblance to Sigismunda: 'No more like Sigismunda than I to Hercules' ran one of the toothed barbs.

As the number of parodies, mocking criticisms and denigrating quips increased, so my stock and reputation fell. For a while, I took refuge in the notion that these reports were calumnies spread by my enemies. I stationed a man, my faithful footman George Wells, to stand by the painting and tell me what he heard people say. I started to take the picture back to change it to meet their criticisms. I repainted the newly added white sleeves, for example.

But no matter what I did, the stream of ordure continued to pour down on my head. The good George, in his distress, was clearly hiding the worst of the comments from me.

But even what he told me was bad enough.

'Sir ...' said George, close to tears after some days of his dismal task at the exhibition. 'May I ... could I put forward, do you think, a small opinion of my own?'

Even in my anguish, my torment over *Sigismunda*, I almost smiled. 'What is it, George?'

'Sir, it's the heart that is causing ... the most, well, laughter, sir, to be honest.'

I nodded.

'Could you not make it smaller, sir? And keep it further away from her front, sir. I hope I'm not speaking out of turn.'

'No, George, not at all,' I said warmly. Why should he not be right, after all? He was a clever enough lad. Was his opinion to be discounted because cruel circumstance had given him a lowly station in life?

'I can see you are right, George,' I continued. 'Go and get the painting, now. Take Henry with you. I shall make the alterations you suggest.'

When he left, I sat heavily in my chair, before my easel. Ah yes, the heart, the sacred heart, centre of the spirit. The heart had to be reduced in my *Sigismunda*. Why not? It had already been reduced in me. I wept for a while: feeble, self-pitying tears.

As soon as *Sigismunda* returned to me, I worked non-stop like a demon, scratching away at what I had done before, sometimes using the handle of the brush for greater speed in this task of destruction.

Then I added more blue for the dress over what had been the top of the heart, even raising the rim of the cup, though this involved repainting the intricate gold-work. It was one of the longest single sessions of painting I have ever attempted, albeit with frequent short stops to sit down.

At the end of it, the brushwork was showing all over the place. It wasn't smooth and creamy like my *Election* series. Would I ever be able to paint like that again? I didn't know and I didn't care. I had George and Henry restore the still tacky *Sigismunda* to her place at the exhibition.

Then I took to my bed, a prey to cramps and fevers, vomiting and pains. I knew myself to be very far from well.

But it was all to no avail. Barely hiding their glee, a deputation of artists headed by Hayman-adequate, but with Roubiliac, happily, absent, came to see me. They informed me that the St Martin's Lane group was now known as the Society of Artists.

'First I've heard of it,' I said.

Hayman ignored that and suggested I might like to withdraw *Sigismunda* from the exhibition, as it reflected badly on the Society of Artists. It was, as he put it, letting them down.

This was my death sentence, as an artist. My renown was on the way to the gibbet sure as the Swiss Gardelle, who I had seen from the window. If the present reviled my art, the future would never know it. It had all been for naught. For naught. The muses on high now mocked me.

I put a brave face on it while they were there. When they had gone, I took to my bed again, unable to stand, hardly able to partake of food without puking it back up almost instantly. I was subject to dizzying fits, pains in the chest, my leg swelled up.

The day after the visit of my *confreres* I gave them what they required of me and withdrew my *Sigismunda* from the exhibition. The day after *that* I discovered that the first meeting of this new Society of Artists had been chaired by John Wilkes.

2

I HAD FORGOTTEN it at the time, but I first met Wilkes long before he turned up on the board of the Foundling Hospital, long before that day when he looked into the depths of my being.

I first met him at those gatherings of the Medmenham Brotherhood, whose debaucheries I now regard with shame, but honesty compels me to admit that I did not do so at the time.

The Brotherhood, so called, met at Medmenham Abbey, under the auspices of Sir Francis Dashwood, who I knew from the Dilettanti Society. Dashwood used to dress as St Francis of Assisi before expressing mocking devotion to any pagan object, sometimes a pig, or more often in the latter stages of the debauch, to an unclothed woman. To my shame, I painted Dashwood as St Francis, a work I have repeatedly tried to buy back and destroy.

Oh, how my life mocks me! My glorious progress paintings, the *Rake* and the *Harlot*, consumed in flame, but this shameful daub of Dashwood lives on despite my attempts to wipe it from the face of the earth. And I was paid for it in debauchery, too: paid in women. Is the pain I now feel over every inch of my body enough recompense for that?

I sigh, I groan, but nothing assuages the pain. There is nobody I can confide in now, hence the device of these autobiographical notes I am presently writing. But at any rate, to return to the matter in hand, Dashwood, at that time, appeared able to have his way with any woman he saw, or any man come to that, even without the laudanum that flowed like wine at these bacchanalia.

And this ... this terrible facility, this way with him was shared in equal measure by Wilkes. Wilkes used to boast, back then, that after ten minutes of his conversation any woman would forget his ugliness. And it was true. He was stroking my face as he said it, inducing that terrible somnolence which so sapped the will.

That is why, when I saw him that day at the meeting of the Court of Governors of the Foundling Hospital, I shook my head like a wet dog, occasioning some laughter all round, to keep myself from his out of his powers.

But at a later meeting, once again in the ornate surroundings of the court room at the Foundling Hospital, with my *Captain Coram* and my *Moses and Pharoah's Daughter* proudly on display on the wall, I was able to take my revenge. Or so I thought at the time.

This time, I knew he would be there, so I had prepared myself to meet those pale blue eyes, so sure of their power to assert his will and way. In the event, I avoided them, looking steadfastly down at the huge oak table, but that served my purpose. I was able to defy him, indeed to accuse him.

The mood of the meeting was against me from the start, however, as Wilkes had come dressed in gay and fantastical dress: yellow and red quartered motley, like some medieval court jester, occasioning much laughter.

He was also constantly stooping to fondle two dogs he had brought with him, who lay under the table. These he addressed as Dido and Pompey, proceeding to direct much of his discourse at them, his face upside down, to the hilarity of his twenty or so fellow governors, seated round the table, under Bedford's presidency.

Indeed, before we had even got started, he let fly one of his famous quips, later much quoted as an example of his wit. One of our fellow governors, Sir Joseph Eyles, if I recall correctly, was attempting to get Wilkes to account for a balance of £10 due to him from the Aylesbury accounts, as audited by one Walden Hanmer. Eyles, if it was Eyles, was doing this in a conversational manner before the meeting proper had begun. Wilkes resolutely stared ahead of himself, refusing to reply.

Finally Eyles, if it was Eyles – it may have been the Duke of Bolton, my Lavinia's paymaster, making one of his last appearances before he killed himself – at any rate, whoever it was cried out in frustration 'Wilkes, you will either die on the gallows or of the pox.'

To which Wilkes replied, 'That must depend on whether I embrace your lordship's principles or your mistress.'

There was an explosion of laughter round the table.

And it was against this background that I waved to Bedford to give me the word, on the same subject: Wilkes's stewardship of the Foundling Hospital's money.

Parliament had voted £70,000 for the branch hospitals and, although one

Chapter 2

Dancer was nominally Master of the Aylesbury Hospital, Wilkes, as Aylesbury branch treasurer, had complete control of his branch's allocation of those funds.

Now, Jane, as an inspector for the Foundling Hospital, had visited the Aylesbury branch and met Robert Neale, the secretary, who appeared to be one of the few people Wilkes ever dealt with who was not completely in thrall to him.

Neale told Jane that Wilkes was drawing money to pay tradesmen, but then not paying them. Wilkes was even claiming more money than originally was allocated, causing such confusion that the chairman there, Hanmer, produced false minutes of a meeting, which the honest Neale refused to sign.

At the time of Jane's visit to Aylesbury, Wilkes was absent, at which I confess I felt some relief. Jane, however, encouraged Neale to produce a full account, with figures and chapter and verse. This account, in effect accusing Wilkes of embezzlement, was on the table in front of me. Bolton knew about it from Lavinia, in whom I often confided, indeed she was a great solace to me in every way. Of the others round the table, I believe only Martin Folkes was in the know, he being much involved with the daily administration.

I had tried my best, assisted by Jane and indeed by Lavinia, who was surprisingly good with figures, to master my brief, the document from Robert Neale damning Wilkes, but I must admit my earlier aptitude for numbers was deserting me as I grew older. However, I loudly sucked in air, rapped on the table, took a last glance at Neale's report and resolved to do my best.

'Gentlemen!' I said. 'I wish to present a document concerning the financial affairs of the Aylesbury branch.'

As I stood to address the assembled Court of Governors of the Foundling Hospital, aristocracy and gentry to a man now that they had thrown poor dead Thomas Coram out of his own life's work, all memory of the document accusing Wilkes fled from my mind. I was left with a dizziness in my empty head and a pain in the leg.

'Gentlemen, I am informed by Mr Neale of Aylesbury that the money demanded by creditors ... by tradespersons and so on, was not paid, though charged as paid, and many other articles charged as paid by Mr Wilkes appear not to have been paid, and that he knew it when he made up and transcribed the accounts to the hospital at London ...'

There was a buzz of talk round the table, tending to a hostile tone. I scanned the faces around me, reading them, as I have done all my life. But I must say that I had never before encountered a gathering, among whom I would usually be made welcome, in which I could read so much anger against me on the phizes – with some bewilderment, perhaps, lacing it. Bolton showed some sympathy for me, along with Peter Burrell and James Cook, the merchants, but scant others.

Wilkes himself was not at all disquieted. He smiled thinly at me, touched his top lip with his tongue, then bent to scratch the ear of one of his dogs. He stayed folded over like that, in his fancy dress, occasioning more and more mirth.

Finally, bent almost upside down, he muttered into the ear of one of the dogs, 'What's this fellow on about, Dido, eh? He's a strange little fellow, isn't he?'

The dog obligingly growled, occasioning yet more merriment, whereupon Wilkes gave a loud bark, causing the other dog to bark back. The laughter round the table was by now considerable.

I said, 'There is a sum of £445 received by the Aylesbury committee for which they have given no credit in account with the hospital at London.'

There was absolutely no reply to this, so I went on, remembering that Jane had dinned into me that we had a watertight case against Wilkes. I began, indeed, to read out the list of creditors who Wilkes was supposed to have paid, but had not.

'Thomas Roger, £4 13s 8d; James Lee, £36 11s 1d; James Austin £2 16s 2d ...'

This, of course, was tedious in the extreme to hear. Bedford, in the chair, eventually waved a green silk arm, languorously bringing me to a halt.

Wilkes finally made a great show of pulling himself upright, puffing theatrically at his exertion at having been half upside down. He spoke in a high, confident, though bored sounding voice:

'At the hospital in Walton Street, in Aylesbury, we have from the beginning sought the care of the mothers as well as the children. From the beginning, I say. I refer this committee to the minutes of the committee at Aylesbury, chaired by Walden Hanmer, this last January.'

Wilkes stared at me. I sat down rather heavily. Wilkes piped on, 'Are the benefits of this charity to be limited to children exposed and deserted, that are left naked on Salisbury Plain or a dunghill?'

This drew a murmur of agreement, my ramblings about tradesmen's accounts already fading into the background.

And on he went, the devil: 'I maintain that a mother dying from want with her infant at her breast is an exposed and deserted case. Are we living under the dispensations of Christianity and yet we cripple our notions of charity?'

The idea, vaguely, was that the missing money had somehow found its way to the indigent mothers, for which there was not a shred of evidence, in the accounts or anywhere else. Nevertheless, the meeting was clearly with Wilkes. There was silence round the table, all eyes on him, spellbound, or so it seemed, under his hex. Even his two dogs had ceased from growling, barking or snuffling around.

Wilkes continued to look straight at me with those deadly, pale blue eyes. I squirmed in my seat, afraid and excited. When his eyes left mine and rose to a point above my head I was so relieved I would thankfully have abandoned my case and my cause then and there, if, that is, there had been anything left of it.

He had been speaking a while longer before I realised that those deadly eyes were in fact fixated upon my own painting, behind my head.

'Let us learn from Hogarth's picture of Moses and Pharoah's daughter,' he was saying. 'Let us fall back upon ancient times and take a lesson from the heathen maid.'

To my shame, I felt gratitude at his public approbation of my picture. The meeting moved on. I fell silent, no longer listening. I was shaking slightly and felt an urgent desire to piss, long before I summoned the strength to stand and take a piss pot into the corner of the room.

By the time I finished with this, the meeting, too, was finishing. As we all crowded out, Wilkes banged into me with the appearance of an accident. With his dogs behind him, with his hand squeezing my shoulder, he whispered in my ear:

'I am your enemy now, Hogarth. I am your fiend and your nemesis. By the time I am finished with you, little man, there will be nothing left of you.'

And that is exactly what came to pass.

So ... So, how did it start? I become tired easily these days, spending more and more of the day asleep. And naturally I am becoming forgetful. However, I cannot forget that I am becoming forgetful, as Jane insists on reminding me, as a small part of the daily catechism of my faults she insists on treating me to.

So, how did it start? I believe ... My post as Serjeant Painter to the King meant little to me. Oh, I can see Jane's reaction when she reads those words. That lifting of the eyebrows, that pursing of the lower lip.

All right, then, I had drudged my lines and my colours all my life to reach such an accolade, of course I had to defend it. And that meant pleasing the king, which in turn meant pleasing the king's allies, notably the Whig faction led by Bute. This was congenial enough to me in any case, as I opposed the latest war against the French, their policy. Why should we lose the finest of our red-blooded young men merely for the benefit of contractors in the armaments industry?

This view brought me into disputation at many masonic lodges and many clubs, but most notably, for what was later to happen to me, with the toad-eater and supposed poet Charles Churchill, at the Nonsense Club, in Drury Lane.

Arguing with Churchill was like disputing with a building with a cannon at each window. His huge frame towered over you while spits of fire hit you from every angle and height, high and low. At this time, his wife was about to leave him, taking with her, or so it seemed, what little scruple about humanity the toad-eater had left.

Ostensibly, our disputes centred on the Tory William Pitt, his wish to attack the Spanish fleet before Spain allied with France and suchlike matters. But in reality any disagreement with the toad-eater ended up with him trying to destroy you, to burn your flesh until you were no more.

Churchill had lately become deputy editor of *The North Briton*, a journal edited by Wilkes. He had known Wilkes for years, from the time of their debauches together at Medmenham. And so the circle of fire was complete. I had made enemies of the two most dangerous men in London. And my enemies were already allies.

I then compounded my folly by producing the first and last political print of my life, unless you count painting the ridiculous Tory Bubb Dodington in *Chairing the Member*, part of my *Election* series. I only did that because the fat oaf had snubbed me at the inquiry into prison conditions when I was young, and anyway I got away with it.

Where was I? When I digress these days, I always forget where I started from. Oh yes, I did an engraving supporting the Bute faction, opposing Pitt, and so, as some saw it, challenging both Wilkes and Churchill. Entitled *Time*, the engraving had the biggest print run I have ever ordered, four thousand. It sold well.

My *Time* engraving showed the war as a fire consuming many buildings. One building represented France and Spain united, another Germany, and so on. I had Pitt, looking ridiculous on stilts, fanning the fire. I had Britain as a fire engine with the royal crest, putting the fire out, with the king heroically extinguishing the fire, just as his troops had tried to do when my mother was burned to death, and nobody tried to do when my *Harlot* series and my *Rake* series were consumed in flame.

Now ... here's the rub: my *Time* engraving also had three figures who had emerged from Temple Coffee House, directing their fire hoses not at the conflagration but at the noble (but unperturbed) king.

One of the three was Earl Temple, Pitt's brother-in-law. The other two were portrayed as hacks, the lowest of the low of writers – one was Wilkes and the other, portrayed in his surplice, was the Reverend (for he was that as well) Charles Churchill.

The reaction came swiftly enough, in a letter from Wilkes. My *Time* print, he wrote, was 'not only unfriendly in the highest degree but injudicious.' However, not content with threatening me, Wilkes proceeded to lecture me, talking down to me as if I were a child: 'Such a pencil,' that's my pencil, by the way, 'ought to be universal and moral, speak to all ages and to all nations, not to be dipt in the dirt of the faction of a day ...' Blah, blah, blah. Blah, blah, blah.

There was then a pause in events, which I discovered later was because Wilkes was engrossed in his duties guarding French prisoners as a colonel of the Buckinghamshire Militia. Meanwhile the toad-eater was recovering from the pox and destitution; the latter caused by his wife, who enterprisingly took most of his money with her when she left, the former by the many other women who had caused his wife to leave in the first place.

But when the two of them were ready, they unleashed on me the seventeenth issue of *The North Briton*, which was the first time, as many have observed, that an entire issue of a magazine was devoted solely to the destruction of a single human being.

Me.

I first heard of this dreadful magazine, issued on Saturday 25 September 1762, at the Beafsteak Club, one of the many clubs both Wilkes and I were members of, though he mixed more with the molly young men and I with the older members. Naturally, the first I heard was the tocsin laughter. They were not even reading it in the dining room of the club. They knew its barbs and jibes by heart.

'House painter to the court' was one jibe I overheard being whispered behind hands. Then there was my 'insufferable vanity', my 'rancour', 'malevolence', 'envy', 'relentless gall'. On and on it went. I fled the club, made my way home as fast as my aching bones would carry me, and sent George Wells out to purchase a copy of the dread magazine.

I waited in my studio, trying to work on my retouching of the goblet in my *Sigismunda* painting, yet unable to. Finally George appeared, his expressive face pale, contorted with pity and a desire to soothe, which wounded by the very intensity of its will to heal.

'Mr Hogarth, sir ...'

The good George held the magazine close, as if considering withholding it from me. I snatched it from him more forcefully than I had intended. As I did so, I had a rare moment of clarity as to political issues and the affairs of men.

For some time now, Wilkes's self-interested attacks on Bute had caused him to be seen as a champion of liberty. Wilkes cared no more for liberty than I for a stranger's stool, yet these attacks on me would be cloaked in that garb. I was to be destroyed, so it would appear, not from Wilkes's unfathomable evil, but in a just cause. Liberty. Oh, why do we mortals misperceive each other so? Why cannot we properly see?

I sent George away. I tore at the magazine which had been written, designed and printed to destroy me. And there it was. On page one I was accused of copying one of the many prints which had copied me. It was called *John Bull's House Set in Flames* and showed Pitt and Charles Churchill putting out a fire in St James's Palace started by Bute.

I was accused of ridiculing those better than myself: 'What wonder then that some of the most respectable characters of the age become the objects of his ridicule?' And insults, insults. 'Gain and vanity have steered his little bark through life.'

My little bark? Yes, I am a small man, am I not? And never smaller than now. A small man who has always kept pug dogs. Pug Hogarth. Bark, meaning a little ship, and bark, the noise of a dog. How very clever. How very clever, Mr Wilkes. Or was that particular jibe from the pen of the toad-eater, the catamite Churchill?

My breath was coming in retching gasps. And I had not even read the worst of the poison print.

Somehow, I knew it. I knew it before I read it. And there it was, in Wilkes's vile journal. The attack on *Sigismunda*. My *Sigismunda*'s expression was so ridiculous it could only have come from 'his own wife in an agony of passion; but of what passion no connoisseur could guess.'

I vomited on the floor of the studio, spattering my breeches. They were mocking Jane. They were mocking ... they were saying I had shown my Jane in ... I stared at *Sigismunda*. They had destroyed her forever for me.

THEY WERE SAYING I HAD PAINTED JANE COMING. THEY WERE SAYING I HAD PAINTED HER IN OESTRUS, LIKE A RUTTING EWE OR COW. OH, MY GOD!

I took measures, naturally I did. At one wild time I took a hackney to Wilkes's house at St John's Gate, not far from my boyhood home. I was aware of the ridiculous figure I cut as I stood, bent and stooped, on his threshold. No doubt I looked as mad as they said I was, even as I rang his bell. Old, sick, mad man.

The wait was long. My feeble, fluttering heart began to wish there would be no reply. I certainly did not ring again. A languid footman in extravagant purple livery finally opened the door.

'I wish to speak to Mr ... to your master.' There! I could not even bring forth the devil's name.

He looked down at me. I had come in my indoor garb: my red cap, old worn breeches. I may even have had my smock on still. Oh, where was the proud popinjay of my youth, swaggering with his sword?

'Do you have an appointment, sir?'

He wasn't letting me in. Was there to be no end to my shame on this earth? 'No, I am ... I am ... I am the painter ...'

'Mr Wilkes is away, at present, sir. He's in Buckinghamshire.'

Then he shut the door in my face.

Jane, my dear darling Jane, did her best to help me. Of course she did. She held me like a baby when I cried, which, I am afraid to say, I did more and more often. She made me broth when I took to my bed, where I spent something like half of my days.

But they had spoiled even Jane for me, the villains – Wilkes and his toad-eater Churchill. When I looked at Jane I saw their vile, corrupt jibe; I saw Jane as *Sigismunda* in oestrus.

Others, be they visitors or friends or just the people who while away one's days, tried to help. I would admit few, not knowing anymore who came out of kindness and who to mock, laughing behind their hands.

Hayman-adequate? Hudson? David Garrick? Daniel Lock? My God, even Reynolds tried to see me, but I gave orders he not be admitted. There were so many. I lost track of who was who. The pains in my body increased.

Roubiliac came and held my hand, for I have always loved and revered him. Days later I heard he had died. I staggered from my sick bed to his funeral, where not one of my erstwhile friends, the artists, the one-time Old Slaughter group, even spoke to me. I was to be shunned, it seemed.

The people who came to my bedside were the only ones I saw. I did not venture out to the clubs any more, or even to the streets, for fear of the laughter, the mockery, the ridicule.

When my health improved a little, I tried to take small revenge on my tormentors. To my amazement, I found I could still draw. I produced an engraving of Wilkes looking even uglier than nature made him, with the cap of liberty as a dunce's cap on a pole.

And when Churchill wrote a poem about me, I retaliated with an engraving in which I scored out everything in my self-portrait, destroying myself with the burin to show what they had done to me, replacing it with Churchill as a drunken bear, with drooling mouth and drunken eyes. Wilkes was in it, as an ape, and *The North Briton* and …

But in truth I knew Churchill had undone me, finished what Wilkes had started. Jane tried to stop me reading Churchill's *Epistle to William Hogarth*. She forbade the servants to bring it to me. But eventually I left the house, for the first time in months, and purchased a copy. The vendor did not recognise the scrofulous old man who bought the poem as the object of its venom.

Charles Churchill's poem about me was six hundred and thirty-eight lines long. Its stock of gall was darkened by the gonorrhoea which was ravaging him, though to be fair the same ailment was also ravaging me. It was the equivalent in verse to Wilkes's issue of *The North Briton* in prose. I believe them to be, together and separately, the most hate-filled works of letters ever produced by human hand, if indeed the hands which produced them were human and not fiends from hell.

My entire work as an artist was shrunk, mocked, condemned and damned:

Chapter 2

What but rank folly, for thy curse decreed,
Could into satire's barren path mislead.

I was shamed by name, no cover names, however transparent, like Pope's 'Sporus' for my friend John Hervey:

HOGARTH – I take thee, candour, at thy word,
Accept thy proffer'd terms, and will be heard;
Thee I have heard with virulence declaim,
Nothing retained of candour but the name.

And, finally, Charles Churchill – you see I have no longer even the strength to use my insulting name for him – Charles Churchill, I say, demanded my death: a matter in which I fear it will not be long before I can give my enemies their satisfaction.

HOGARTH stand forth – I dare thee to be tried
In that great court, where conscience must preside.

I have taken to my bed, with no particular wish to leave it. My appetite for food, with the whimsicality of appetites, has returned, and I partake regularly of steak and of coddled eggs.

Jane is calm. She is with me all the time. She gives me what happy tidings she can, even telling me that people are saying my *Rake* was not destroyed in flames after all, but was saved. I do not believe it, but do not say so.

'And *Harlot*?'

She shakes her head, sadly, grey eyes on mine.

'I was a great artist, was I not, my Jenny?'

'You were and are that, Billy, my darling.'

Jane accedes with touching willingness to my every wish. Sometimes my thoughts of women and their flesh return, sometimes even causing me to clutch and closet my drooping, withered member, not at all what it once was, in their memory.

I must lay down this pen soon, together with my crayon, my burin, my brushes and my life. Jane tells me constantly that I am a great painter and I believe her. I look at her and suddenly I understand my life. She was my life, all that was good and happy about it. I should have understood that at the time.

I cry out to her, my Jane, as she holds my hand. I sit bolt upright in bed, in my nightgown and cap.

'If there is something else, I will find you!'

She nods, tears in her eyes, but with that same serious calm she had about her when I first set eyes on her.

If there is something else, I will find you, my love. I promise you that.

Author's note

This is a work of fiction, so some real events have been bent to the demands of the narrative: others omitted altogether, others invented.

Naturally, I read the main authorities on Hogarth before writing this novel. These are David Bindman, Austin Dobson, Matthew Craske, Derek Jarrett, John Nicholls, Ronald Paulson, Sean Shesgreen and Jenny Uglow. I also read everything Hogarth himself had written.

As far as the background to this fascinating period is concerned, I read widely, out of interest, and so it is impossible to mention all the books individually here. The only one I would single out is *The A-Z of Georgian London* (Introductory Notes by Ralph Hyde), London Topographical Society Publication No. 126 (1982).

I started this novel out of love for the art of William Hogarth. I finished it with that love enhanced, and a great respect and fondness for the man who produced it.

As I write, the only monument to Hogarth I know of is a small bust diagonally opposite the public toilets in Leicester Square. I hope readers of this novel will join me in hoping that England one day does better by a man who has a strong claim to be its national artist.

Michael Dean, June 2012

MICHAEL DEAN is a graduate, in History, of Worcester College, Oxford, and has a Masters in Applied Linguistics from Edinburgh University. He is the author of a novel, *Thorn*, and *Chomsky: A Beginner's Guide*. He lives in Colchester.